Comments from amazon.com

Number of Reviews: 5   Average Review: 5 stars

From New Jersey, April 15, 1999 ★ ★ ★ ★ ★

The characters in this book are very believable
This book is thoroughly absorbing. It reads well and the characters are 3-dimensional and real. I was sorry the book ended because I cared for the main characters and wanted to know more about their fate. The ending makes you anxious for the next installment.

From New Mexico, April 4, 1999 ★ ★ ★ ★ ★

Two thumbs up!! You must get a second copy to share. The story and characters...simply entrancing! Contrary to other reviewers, I was compelled to put the book down mid-read to linger in Grimble County, Virginia: I didn't want it to ever end! Hoping there is sequel soon from this talented new author.

From Texas, March 26, 1999 ★ ★ ★ ★ ★

Intriguing! Just had to finish it. Characters were so real. Characters were brought to life and story was intriguing. Just had to finish it in one sitting. Historically well researched and enough suspense to hold your attention. I found myself totally engrossed in the story line and hoping for a happy ending!

From   Alabama, January 4, 1999 ★ ★ ★ ★ ★

Characters you care about, exciting, gripping plot

This book kept me on pins and needles to the end. I want to hear more about the characters. Romantic-thriller-mystery all in one.

From Michigan, December 15, 1998 ★ ★ ★ ★ ★

This book keeps you reading. It is a well written fast moving book that holds your interest from the first page to the last.

The Fugitive

at Greyledge

JACK SCHULTZ

Copyright © 1998 by Jack Schultz

ISBN: 0-9664159-0-6

First printing June 1998

Second printing May 1999

Cover design and illustration by Karen Castaldi

Editor: Roberta J. Buland

Printed in the United States of America

Indvidual orders of this book may be obtained by sending a check for $14 to Millstone Publishing; P. O. Box 274; North Windham CT 06256-0274. Please add $3.00 for shipping and $.84 sales tax for Connecticut residents.

Discounts are available for purchase of more than one copy. For details call 1-860-455-9062; fax 1-860-455-0574 or write to the above address.

AUTHOR'S NOTES

Grimble is a small, decadent county in the Shenandoah Valley of Virginia not far from Harrisonburg or Waynsboro. Even though it is imaginary, I look for it whenever I am in the vicinity. I also look for Jude and Charlotte although I know they are not there. They would be older now, but Charlotte would still be beautiful in her own way, and still delight in making Jude blush as she did back in 1955.

Menominee, in the Upper Peninsula of Michigan, is represented here as I remember it from the early 1940s; but, Billy and his wanton mother, as well as the other people from there, are fictitious. My vision of Fort Knox, Kentucky, is what remains from when I took basic training there in the fall of 1953; the incidents and people are all imaginary.

I am grateful to Nancy Jones and William Harbaugh who provided me with valuable background information regarding the region surrounding Grimble Co. Dolly, Sam and Mike Sheflett told me about the operation of the old manganese mines along the western slope of the Blue Ridge Mountains. I regret that I could not include all of the interesting information these people gave me.

I thank my friends in biology at the University of Connecticut who read early drafts of my manuscript and made important suggestions as well as providing continuous encouragement throughout the long process that takes place after an author thinks his book is nearly finished.

I am especially grateful to my wife Mary and my daughter Karen who pointed out things they didn't like in my first draft. They instructed me in particular on how women think and don't think. Always they supported my efforts and helped in many ways. The illustration on the cover was painted by Karen Castaldi; the model for the painting was Nancy Schultz.

And finally I extend my thanks to my patient and talented editor, Roberta Buland, who was tireless in her attempt to give *The Fugitive at Greyledge* a professional structure.

Jack Schultz

To Mary

To Mary

1

As the rider came down the lane closer to him, Jude realized it was a woman. She was wearing formal riding attire: boots, jodhpurs and cutaway black jacket. And, was that red hair peeking out from beneath her black hunt cap? Jude's spirits soared—God, what a class act! Even the horse was into the spirit of the game, sort of strutting his stuff—whatever you call it, raising his knees high and holding his tail aloft in a graceful curve.

Jude had taken a scenic side route off the Appalachian Trail in Virginia so he could look out across the Shenandoah Valley. A bright trickle of water splashing over the rocks had lured him down the slope to where it had grown into a nice little stream complete with waterfalls and pools. Around the next curve, he scolded himself, and that's it—back up the mountain you go; but, at that point, the stream spilled out of the woods and across an open pasture. He could see gently rolling fields and, in the distance, a picturesque mansion perhaps a mile away. When he spotted the rider, he told himself, hey, this is worth it; I wasn't in any hurry to get there anyway.

The horse and rider passed through the gate into the last field and were nearing the stream, a natural end point for her ride. To Jude's surprise, she hit the horse on the rump with her riding crop and picked up speed to leap the brook. Spectacular! What a sight to see this graceful animal and beautiful rider aloft in the air. The return leap, however, was sloppy. Her saddle had loosened and was sliding out from under her. Jude tensed as the horse broke into a gallop and she lost control. She attempted a graceful fall, but the angle of contact was bad. As she tumbled, her protective headgear popped off. She hit a clump of hard ground and lay still.

Jude splashed across the stream, reaching her side just as she was coming to. God, she's lovely, older than I, he thought, not twice as old, though—certainly not old enough to be my mother. And, yes, red hair, not coarse like most red hair; in fact, quite fine. She wore it in a ponytail in back, with bangs in front. A swatch of white hair lay dramatically on her forehead in a perfect triangle.

When her eyes opened and finally registered on him, she jumped to her feet: "What are you doing on my property? You get the hell out of here," but, her eyes went out of focus and she collapsed in a heap.

What now? Just what the hell am I supposed to do with an unconscious woman way out here in a field? Obviously, I cannot simply, *get the hell out of here,* like she said.

The horse, still wearing the saddle on his belly, stood 50 yards away waiting for someone to open the gate so he could resume his dash to the barn. Jude spoke reassuringly as he reached for the bridle; the horse threw up his head and stepped back just out of reach. After two more attempts, Jude lunged for the bridle; but, the horse turned and trotted around in a small circle back to the gate.

Meanwhile, the woman regained consciousness, and rubbing her throbbing head, tried to think about what was happening. A sense of vulnerability swept over her—here she was, far from home, probably unable to walk, with some kind of vagabond or worse trying to capture her horse. When he was not looking, she tried to get to her feet; but, feeling faint and nauseous, she settled back down again. Damn it, she said to herself, somehow I've got to deal with this guy. Who is he anyway—all those Army clothes along with that gaudy sport shirt? Searching the ground, she found a small rock and clenched it in her fist.

Jude quit trying to catch the horse and walked calmly over to his backpack where he rummaged around for his cooking pot and bag of oatmeal. The horse, curious about the pot and its contents, trotted up to meet him halfway and without hesitation plunged his nose into the pot. Jude quietly wrapped his free hand around the bridle and when the horse finished his treat, led him back to the gate and tied him to it.

As Jude returned the pot to his pack, not far from the woman, the woman tried to appear calm. "Will you be cooking your dinner in that pot tonight?"

"Yes, but I may rinse it first."

Attempting to get some reading on his intentions—whether he was going to let her live or not, she asked, "Is it your expectation that I will now mount this animal and gallantly ride him home?"

"Not really, you could have a concussion. If you black out, within a few days these fields will lose their sweet scent of alfalfa. I'll see if I can rig up some kind of travois and get the horse to pull you home."

She studied him without responding. How much of a threat is he? He doesn't seem as menacing now as when I first saw him. Maybe it was his brown beard that frightened me initially. It makes him look a little fierce—and older. I don't suppose he's more than 23. Of course, if he were to shave his beard now, the white skin underneath would look funny against the rest of his tanned face.

Jude took a small axe from his pack and headed back along the brushy stream to cut some poles. The injured woman shifted her position so she could watch, and at the same time, review what he had said so far. Maybe he wasn't planning to harm her. He didn't sound like a local redneck; in fact, he sounded more like a Yankee.

On his way back to the horse, Jude took a blanket and a piece of tent rope from the pack. The horse viewed all this with suspicion. Every time Jude tried to approach, it sidestepped with its rear end so Jude could not pass. Irritated, Jude smacked him on the rump with the flat side of the axe and yelled, "Get over, you horse's ass!" The horse promptly moved out of the way.

While the rider watched, Jude constructed a bed with the blanket and poles. He attached it behind the horse. She struggled with her ambivalence about whether she wanted this stranger to be taking her up to the house where he would discover she was all alone; yet, she was impressed with the thoughtful way he was dealing with her problem. When he led the horse and travois over for her inspection, she said, "You have to be crazy if you think I'm going to allow myself to be dragged, bumping along behind that horse or, as you call him, that *horse's ass*. His formal name, incidentally, is Alfred—and mine is Charlotte Henderson."

"My name is Jude," he responded, then became quiet— dumbfounded over what to do next. "Should I go up to the house and get some help or call an ambulance?"

"Modern ambulances don't have enough clearance to cross the rocky stream between here and the house. The closest ambulance, which is 20 miles from here, is only a year old; I think it's a 1953 Buick. Besides the people who run it would just as soon see me rot in this field, as you so indelicately put it."

"Is there someone at the house who could help you?"

She was still reluctant to reveal to him that she was all alone. Aunt Millie, her elderly housekeeper, would have gone home by now. Charlotte realized she had run out of choices. Besides, if he were planning to rape or kill me, he certainly had had ample time by now. In spite of his rough exterior, he is for the most part quiet and soft-spoken; and, underneath his unkempt beard, probably good looking, all of which means he couldn't pose any real threat to me—could he?

"No," she finally responded to Jude, "there isn't anyone home at this time."

Exasperated, he said, "Ma'am, if you have a lingering vision from some romantic movie out of your past that I'm going to carry you home, forget it. As a hero, I'm far too puny to play that role."

With the pain in her knee and her throbbing head, romantic scenes were far from her mind; yet, now that he brought it up, this young rescuer of hers was far from puny; and, she noticed again that under the trail dust and beard, perhaps not unattractive. Finally, she told him, "Gallant of you to think of it, but I couldn't impose on a stranger to carry me nearly a mile." Charlotte dropped her rock at this point and began to feel more relaxed. "I guess my options have run out: I'll suffer your torture machine, but, don't expect me to be grateful. I'll blame you for every bump; and, all along the way, I'll be scheming to get even." Jude sensed from the sharpness in her words, even though she spoke them playfully, that she was in a lot of pain.

"Ready?"

"No, but if we dillydally any longer, we'll be doing this in the dark, so let's get started."

He lifted her onto the travois, then took the bridle and pulled Alfred forward. The horse moved a few steps and stopped, trying to look back at the contraption he was dragging. Jude jerked the bridle and a few more steps were taken; clearly Alfred was unaccustomed to pulling things. Erratic progress, interrupted by uneasy inquiry, was the ritual all the way to the gate. Charlotte called forward that she was no longer worried about getting home before dark; but, she really hated missing breakfast. This was a lie, of course. She was a night person and rarely saw breakfast; but, at least her mood was improving and she was not suffering all the pain she had anticipated.

Once they passed through the gate, Alfred lost all concern over what he was pulling and headed for the barn. If

Jude had not held firm, Alfred would have had Charlotte home in less than five minutes.

No words passed between Jude and Charlotte as they worked their way up the lane. It seemed to Charlotte that her rescuer was more inclined toward effective action than idle conversation. Still, she was anxious to know more about him—where is he from and where is he going—and why is she beginning to feel comfortable with him? Meanwhile, as Jude studied the fields on either side of the lane, he wondered why this beautiful farm had lapsed into such a state of neglect. After being part of the careful farming practiced by the monks at Gethsemani, the contrast was puzzling. Here was a field of ripe wheat being harvested by wild birds and a flock of chickens, and what could have been a good stand of corn now struggled in equal competition with weeds. It did not seem proper to inquire, but, since this is what flooded his mind, there was little to say.

The problem of crossing the stream broke the silence. It was only a few inches deep at the ford where rocks had been used to build up the crossing, but dragging Charlotte over them on the travois would be bumpy. He tied the impatient Alfred to a bush and went back to consult with the passenger.

"Couldn't you just pick up the dragging end of this contraption and let the horse carry the head end; we could go across like a wheelbarrow?"

"Probably, if we can convince Alfred he's not nearing the finish line at the Kentucky Derby. Maybe if I run ropes from the bridle back to here and tie them around my back, I could lean back against the rope to restrain the horse while

I carry this end of the stretcher."

"Sounds good. Let's try it."

Jude completed his hookup and leaned over to pick up the end of the travois; the horse felt the slack in the rope and took off for the finish line. Jude was caught off balance and jerked on top of Charlotte, who let out a scream. Alfred dragged them both into the stream—not at the shallow crossing but into two feet of water above the ford. The horse stopped on the bank, leaving the piled up pair soaking in the creek. Jude leaped off Charlotte and raced forward to grab the horse's bridle. With a slight forward tug, Alfred completed the stream crossing and proceeded forward to the house. Jude tied the reins to the white picket fence that surrounded the backyard and a large swimming pool. Then he went back to the travois from where Charlotte had been issuing a steady flow of instructions ever since they left the stream. He untied her and carried her through the gate into the backyard.

"I apologize for ignoring you, but, I couldn't hear what you were saying with the horse in between us and you facing the other direction. Now then, what shall I do with you?"

"I wondered why you were so unresponsive; ordinarily I can produce some kind of aggravation in even the mildest personality. It would be wonderful if you could carry me upstairs and place me gently on my bed; but, if we bring all this river glop into the house, Aunt Millie will break my other leg next time she comes to clean. Instead, put me over there on the lounge chair at the edge of the pool."

Jude carefully lowered her like she was a piece of fine crystal and gently straightened her legs on the chair; then he stood back to admire his handiwork. Actually, it was the first opportunity he had to seriously appraise the object of his struggle. He decided again that she was indeed beautiful—he saw a natural beauty that didn't disappear when her face was smudged and her hair was in disarray. He was surprised at how much she appealed to him, in spite of her being almost old enough to be his mother—but not quite, he assured himself—not that it matters. He was interrupted from his evaluation by a request to see if he could pull her boots off without killing her. It was no small struggle, accompanied by ouches and mild profanity. Next, she wanted him to help her remove her wet jodhpurs. She was amused by his reserve, but hastened to assure him that she was wearing panties underneath and that in her crippled condition he was reasonably safe. What a turnaround, she thought—now it's *his* mental comfort I'm worried about.

His beard did not conceal his embarrassment. He was grateful she did not chide him about it; that would have made him blush more. The tapered legs of the jodhpurs made their removal difficult and painful; but, once he had them off, Jude was faced with another problem. Her long, bare legs and thighs made it almost impossible to focus on anything else. When he realized he was gawking, he tried to cover it by talking about her medical condition. "I don't see any bones sticking out of the skin. You have some swelling of the ankle and knee but your boots braced you against the worst of your spill. Shall I try to carry you in now?"

"No, I want to embarrass you further: I want to get out of this stinking shirt. I'll try to spare you as best I can, but you must try to be brave."

Jude blushed again but promised to try.

"On a rack just inside the door you'll find my pool robe."

When he returned, she directed him to, "Hold it up between us while I shed this foul smelling shirt."

Holding the smock forward like a curtain, he fixed his gaze away from her. She slipped out of her blouse and reached for the robe.

"Jude, could you hold it a little closer. I can't quite reach it?"

Without thinking, he looked to see how far he had to move. He found himself looking directly at her body, clad only in panties and bra. Their eyes met; neither broke contact. She was surprised to feel a little tingly over the excitement she saw in this young man's eyes. Perhaps his flattering glance was a little gift in response to the conversation she had with the mirror this morning, wherein she announced, "Charlotte, you aren't getting any younger."

Without breaking eye contact, she pulled the robe over her and asked, "What do you think?"

"Ma'am, I think you're incredibly lovely."

Shit! Why did he have to spoil it by saying "ma'am"?

"Thank you, Jude. I didn't mean to be soliciting compliments; I was referring to whether or not you might be able to get me upstairs now—without the help of Alfred."

"I can try; but, after all you went through, I should at least remove my boots and wet socks."

"I'm sure Aunt Millie would be grateful."

He removed them, then set about dealing with how to pick her up. The robe barely extended to her thighs and was of a flimsy material that confused his senses of modesty and delight. Placing one arm around her shoulders and the other beneath her legs, he was careful not to contact her bare thighs. Jude was not a large man, but neither was he small. At two inches short of six feet, he was slim, reasonably muscular and hardened by the life he led; still, she was heavier than he expected. Although trim, she was solid and pushed him to the limit of his strength.

The kitchen was reasonably up-to-date, considering the age of the house, which Jude judged to be at least 200 years old. After passing through a spacious living room—large enough for a ball—they came to a spiral staircase. Charlotte asked Jude if he would like to rest before they started up. He said he thought he could make it, but he was glad when at the top of the stairs, she directed him to the first room rather than down the long hall. Her bedroom was spacious and looked like it was right out of a Civil War movie, canopy bed and all. The only modern concession was an adjoining bathroom with a tub shower. She directed Jude to stand her up in the tub and to go busy himself nearby until she called. Then, on second thought, she suggested that he too might wish to clean up and could use a bathroom down the hall. After all, she thought to herself, what good would it do for me to bathe only to be handled by a man who smelled of campfires, perspiration and creek slime?

Jude went back outside to where Alfred was reaching over the fence trying to eat a rose bush, untied his pack from the saddle and returned upstairs. He stopped to see if Charlotte was getting on all right before going down the hall. She yelled above the shower noise that she was doing fine.

When he reached his facility and looked in the mirror, he
was aghast at his appearance. No wonder her first instinct
was to order him off her land. He showered, trimmed his
beard, and put on his last clean outfit, all the while wondering why he was taking so much trouble—he would be
back on the trail soon and never see this woman again. When
he returned to Charlotte's room, the shower was no longer
running; he became concerned that he had taken too long. He
called to her from the doorway, but it was not until his
second call that she responded, "Oh, I'm fine, Jude. I filled
the tub with water and sort of slid down in to it. The warm
water worked wonders on my leg and I guess I fell asleep.
Wait a minute 'til I drain the tub and rinse off the soap.
Then I'll be ready for you to retrieve me. In the wall cabinet on your left, you'll see some big bath towels; would you
please hand me one?"

He poked the towel around the end of the shower curtain
where her silhouette appeared. The intimacy of this
bathroom scene was not lost on Jude. He was beginning to get
an erection and quietly cursed, "These damned suntans don't
hold a hard-on down as well as blue jeans." He tried to
make it go away, but it only got worse. He adjusted it upward and hoped she would not notice the conspicuous bulge.

Suddenly, she threw back the curtain and there she was,
with the big blue towel wrapped around her, sitting in the
tub—her eyes at crotch level. "Is that salute in my honor,"
she said, "or have you been thinking about someone else
while you're in my bathroom?" He didn't know what to say.
His face reddened and he tried to apologize but scrambled it
badly.

"I'm flattered, and particularly so, now that you've freshened up and I see what you look like. I wonder, though, will that thing get in the way of your helping me out of the tub? I don't suppose you can even lean over."

Her bath and short snooze had obviously put her in good spirits; but, God, what kind of woman is this who can speak so openly about sex? In reality, though, he was not certain he could lean over and lift her out of the tub without hurting his back. He finally decided to stand barefoot in the tub in front of her and lift her to a standing position on her one good leg. She agreed, and she also smiled as she thought about the way towels have a tendency to fall off no matter how well they are wrapped. Would he die of humiliation if he suddenly found that bulge in his pants pressed against the belly of a completely naked woman who was standing on one leg?

My God, Charlotte, what the hell's the matter with you? You should be the embarrassed one, not Jude. With a head-ache and a painful leg, surely you aren't getting horny over this kid, who's at least 15 years younger than you! Maybe your brain was jarred loose from the fall. Nonsense, I'm not the least aroused by him or the bulge in his pants; I just have a marvelous sense of humor.

Charlotte's fantasy, came to an end when she was abruptly lifted to a vertical position and swooped up across Jude's shoulder like a sack of grain. He dumped her on the bed; then he pulled a chair up to her bedside. In a formal tone, which seemed a little out of place in view of the previous events, he asked if he should call a doctor or at least a neighbor to stay with her for awhile.

Charlotte interpreted his serious tone as an attempt to avert attention from the bulge in his pants—that's probably why he sat down, so it wouldn't show. Jude went on to explain that hitting her head as hard as she had could cause a concussion that may not show up for 24 to 48 hours. "Someone should check in on you every couple of hours during the next day or two," he said.

"I wouldn't trust any of the local doctors and none of the neighbors feel that kindly toward me. Aunt Millie comes on Mondays and Fridays to clean and set me up with something to eat for the days in between, but she's already gone for the weekend. She has an invalid husband that her daughter looks out for on the days she comes here. How about you, Jude, could you stick around or are you on a tight schedule?"

"I'm pretty much traveling at my own pace; but, I feel awkward about this."

"How come?"

"I don't know, guess I haven't had much experience with women, particularly, women like you."

"What do you mean, *women like me*?"

"Oh, I am sorry, I really didn't mean to insult you." He certainly wasn't going to admit to her that she was so absolutely elegant he was ill at ease being with her. "I guess I really don't know what to think about you and probably couldn't explain it without stumbling all over myself. But, you should know that I hold you in very high regard."

"Oh sure," she bantered. "First you get a hard-on over me, then you pick me up like a sack of grain and throw me on the bed. But, to tell the truth, that's more attention than I've had for a long time. Aside from all of this, I wish you'd stay; we can work out how we feel about each other over the weekend."

"OK, I'll consider this a vacation from my vacation."

"Great!" She reached over and squeezed his hand. "So, Jude, what should we do next?"

"First, perhaps we should fit you out in something more comfortable than a damp towel."

Since I'm bedridden, I suppose I should wear something like a nightgown and cover it with a bathrobe. I'm not sure where that stuff is; I don't usually wear anything to bed unless it's cold—try the closet"

After finding the appropriate garments for her, Jude reflected that she had an interesting wardrobe. Not much has been spared when it comes to color, style and flamboyance. While Charlotte dressed Jude took Alfred to the barn.

Jude was surprised at conditions in the barn. Over an extended period, the horse had been moved from stall to stall and back again, allowing the manure and bedding to dry before the next layer was added. Yet, the problem on this farm was not long reaching; a full range of crops had been planted that spring and early summer, and the accumulation of manure was by no means comparable to the Aegean stables. She apparently had not been completely alone with this operation for more than a few months. I suppose she'll discuss it when she's ready, Jude surmised.

When he returned, Charlotte was lying as he had left her. "I'm glad you're back, Jude; I'm getting bored and hungry. Why don't you check the kitchen and see if Aunt Millie has left anything to eat?"

Jude found a pot of soup with vegetables and chunks of beef. He turned the heat on, and, while it warmed, looked for other possibilities. How about that, a bottle of red wine, and some Italian bread. Aunt Millie, you're all right, he thought. He put some of the hearty soup into bowls, found wineglasses, a tray and napkins. At the last minute, he went out near the pool where he picked a white rose that had escaped Alfred's reach. Rummaging through the cupboards, he found a bud vase to add to his festive presentation.

His patient was delighted and amazed that this young vagabond possessed such sensitivity. He put the party tray on a little table next to the bed and poured them each a glass of wine. She raised her goblet and said, "Here's to those pleasant surprises, outrageous acts, and profound thoughts that can only be shared by dear friends."

Jude raised his glass and as he clinked it against hers, he asked, "Are you referring to us when you speak of dear friends?"

"I hope so, but true friends have to undergo the test of time and trauma. Not many people find me to be an easy friend. In general my acquaintances are ill at ease with 'surprises, outrageous acts, and profound thoughts.' So far, you've had only a small exposure to my repertoire; I expect you'll run for the hills when you find out what I'm really like."

"It's hard for me to believe there's anything that frightening about you."

"Could we drink to that, too?" she asked. He smiled, and after clinking glasses again, they ate in silence; both were famished. When their bowls were empty, Jude returned to the kitchen for refills. On the way, he took a detour around to the other side of the stairwell to see what that part of the

house looked like; he found a large study with an entire wall filled with books. The surface of an oversized desk was covered with papers, a typewriter and books—some lying open, others closed and piled on top of each other. This was obviously the center of intensive activity. The desk also had a framed picture on it of Charlotte with a man and a little girl. Who are these other people, and where are they now?

Halfway through her second bowl of soup, Charlotte put the bowl on the table and said, "Jude, that's twice you've saved my life; and, speaking of saving my life, this vigil you're maintaining over me, what symptoms are you look-ing for? Have I passed any tests so far? Do I have any strikes against me?"

He put his empty bowl under hers, and said, "You seem fine."

"So what does that mean, Doctor? Am I healed and ready to go home, or might I still die before I get out of intensive care?"

"Your chances of full recovery—are fairly good, Madam. You've passed several tests so far. The last one being that you ate with a good appetite, which tells me you are not feeling nauseous. You haven't looked at me cross-eyed, so presumably you're focusing all right, and your pupils are both the same size."

"What if they weren't?"

"Why then, I would have to bore a hole in your skull to relieve the pressure."

"You wouldn't!"

"What choice would I have? You won't let me call a

doctor. Besides anthropologists have discovered, from graves of pre-Columbian Indian settlements, that boring holes in skulls was a common practice even then. Some skulls would have three or four holes of different ages, so it apparently isn't a particularly dangerous operation. They must have used it to cure severe headaches. By the way, how's your headache now?"

"It just went away; I'm all better."

"Kidding aside, I need to know if it's better, worse, or whatever. I promise not to drill if you'll tell me the truth."

"It's better but not gone."

"Do you think you'll fasten the chin strap on your cap next time you ride?"

"You don't miss a thing, do you? That strap is a little tight; I haven't fastened it since I escaped from my riding instructor many years ago."

"Shame, shame."

"Jude, you haven't told me why you're concerned about that little bump on my head."

"It's because I'm not sure how big a bump it is. It was enough to knock you unconscious for several minutes; and, after you regained consciousness, you passed out again. The worst part, though, was that initially you were not nice to me, a sure sign you were disoriented and irrational, which might mean your brain was jarred loose from your skull or that there was hemorrhaging."

"Jude, are you trying to be funny or just scare the shit out of me? I'll tell the jokes around here, if it turns out we need any, and we sure don't need any more about my mental instability." She lay there looking up at the ceiling while tears welled up in her eyes.

Jude never knew what to do when women became upset. Apologizing did not seem relevant; and nothing else could be said without seeming to pry into her past affairs, which obviously had more to do with this outburst than anything he had said. The silence seemed like an eternity to Jude. He watched as her eyes filled and finally overflowed, a big tear running down each check. She was lost somewhere in a painful past. Slowly she returned; she looked at him and said, "Please hold me, Jude."

He gathered her up in his arms and quietly hugged her. She pressed her wet cheek against his and allowed herself to feel helpless, a condition she had not submitted to in many years. Finally she said, "OK, Jude, you can bore a hole in my head if you think it's necessary," as she slowly withdrew from the embrace.

"Maybe, instead, we could use an ice bag to bring down the swelling, if any occurs. I wouldn't want to shave a patch out of your lovely hair."

"You like this hair? I hate it, especially that white patch in front."

"You mean you didn't bleach that swatch on your forehead intentionally! I like it. I think it's wonderfully dramatic and it supports an air of defiance in the face of a conventional world. There'll be no shaving or drilling on this head tonight."

"I'm glad of that. It would spoil the evening."

"What about your leg? Is that any better?"

"It still hurts some. I don't imagine I'll be walking on it for a couple of days. There's a pair of crutches in the attic, but the attic is no place to go after dark. It's full of Civil War spooks—some of them don't like Yankees any better now than they did in 1864."

"Why are they in your attic?"

"My grandfather developed this farm before the war. When he was killed in the war, my grandmother was left with two kids and the responsibility of keeping both the Rebs and the Yankees from burning it. She used whatever method was available to her, and she attempted to stay neutral at a time when people believed you were either for them or against them. The local folks still haven't forgiven the Hendersons two generations later."

"That's a long time to carry a grudge."

"I have always thought so, but maybe we should finish the story another time. We should develop a plan for getting us through the night. I leave myself in your hands."

"First of all, let me look at your leg. Although I've agreed not to drill into your skull, I haven't ruled out amputating limbs."

She tossed the sheet back as far as it would go, which was only to her knees. Jude folded it back the rest of the way and began to examine her legs. "Your ankle doesn't seem too bad but your knee is still swollen." He took hold of her feet to straighten her legs and noticed that they were cold. He asked if they were always that way and she said that they usually were. He rubbed them briskly until they felt warmer, then held both feet in his hands and kissed each of them in turn on the inside, just above the arch.

Initially, she felt called upon to admonish him for his presumptive behavior, but she felt a small tingle in a secret place where none had been awakened for a long time. She settled for asking if he did that to all of his patients.

"Yes . . . but then you're my first patient."

"That's hard to believe in view of your apparent knowledge of medicine and particularly your bedside manner."

"Thank you. My mother was a nurse during the Second World War. She talked a lot about the things she did; she also had some medical books in her closet. My friend Billy and I found them one day; and, after that, whenever she was gone, we got them down to study anatomy. We were particularly interested in the differences between male and female anatomy. Eventually, Mom realized the futility of trying to hide her books and moved them into the living room; she even told us what some of the big words meant."

"Did Billy go on to med school?"

"He died." Jude looked down.

Charlotte waited for him to explain, but when he did not, she broke the awkward silence by asking, "Is your mother still nursing?"

"No." This time Jude shook his head back and forth several times as though that filled out his response.

Charlotte cheerfully asked, "What shall we do next?"

"Since I was up before dawn, maybe I better catch a couple hours sleep before it's time to check your eyes again. Do you mind if I set that clock?"

"No, but where are you planning to sleep? You can use the bedroom down the hall if you wish."

"Unless you object, I'll sleep on the rug," he said, pointing to a thick wool rug, not far from her bed. "If I'm down the hall and you have a problem, I might not hear you."

"It's OK with me, but I think you're making more of this than necessary."

"Um, you're probably right; but, it's too dark for me to find a campsite now and I might end up in the poison ivy. It's safe enough here, isn't it?"

"I think so, but the local folks might express doubt."

"I'd like to hear about these people sometime; all of this sounds ominous."

"It's a pretty ugly story: I don't talk about it easily— maybe after we know each other better. That would be at about the same time you feel comfortable telling me what happened to Billy."

Jude's commitment was to stay for a day or two, until the danger of a concussion passed. It seemed doubtful to him that either of them would be opening their souls in such a short time. *Does she have a longer range plan for me?* Too tired to pursue that, he just smiled and set the clock for 2:00 a.m., then borrowed a pillow and the extra blanket from her bed. After turning out the lights, he said, "Good night, Charlotte," and was asleep within minutes, barely hearing her response.

Charlotte lay awake. Her head hurt a little, and her knee a whole lot, but mostly she was reflecting back on her adventure of that day. It was the first time she admitted to herself that a lot of the unhappiness she had been experiencing was from being lonely; also, she missed having someone around who cared about her. Oh, sure, a couple of her colleagues at the university were interested in her, but it was obvious what they were after. One of them was a man of considerable charm and little substance, who also had a wife and three children. The other was single; but, he was an intellectual nerd, whose concept of foreplay, no doubt, would be a spirited discussion of the causes and effects of the Crimean War.

Charlotte started an argument with herself. You aren't just thinking about relief from loneliness.

Oh? What else am I thinking about?

What you're thinking about is how nice it would be if, instead of sleeping on the floor over there, Jude were snuggled up next to you in bed.

Charlotte, you shouldn't be taking it too seriously when he said you were lovely in your panties and bra. And just now, when he kissed the inside of your feet, he was only being polite and a little corny; he surely isn't interested in a woman so much older than himself.

No? How about that bulge in his pants when we were in the bathroom?

He's been on the trail for awhile; probably any woman would look good to him. If you invited him into your bed, he wouldn't settle for snuggling; and, once he was satisfied he'd be back on the trail in the morning. You can't seriously be thinking about taking him to bed with you?

Of course not.

Charlotte, what do you have in mind?

Well, it would be nice just to have him hang around for awhile for company—and maybe, too, he'd see fit to do something about the way this place is going to seed. Maybe I could hire him as a handyman.

Sure, but how are you going to pay him? You don't have the next mortgage payment yet; besides, it's been nearly a hundred years since this plantation has had slaves.

I know, but it would be nice if I could just call to my slave, over there on the floor, and say, "Jude, time for you to warm your mistress."

Charlotte, when you wake up and this fantasy is splashed with the light of day, you're going to feel awfully foolish.

2

When the alarm went off at 2:00 a.m., Charlotte was startled to find that she was sound asleep—and a little moist. Jude slipped into his pants and lit the lamp at the edge of the room. Charlotte was looking at him when he arrived at her bedside. He squeezed her shoulder gently and asked how she felt. Her headache was pretty well gone, most of the hurt now was in her knee. He reassured her that her eyes were focusing well and the pupils were the same size. "Let's try again at four o'clock." This time they both went to sleep immediately.

Jude awakened to the crowing of a rooster before the alarm went off. He listened to Charlotte's breathing, which sounded normal; now it was his turn to lie awake and consider the recent events in his life. Certainly the last 18 hours had been interesting. But why, really, was he here sleeping on this woman's floor? Face it, Jude, if this had been a man who fell off his horse or even a less attractive woman, you wouldn't have concerned yourself nearly as much. At most, you would've dropped him at the doorstep or next to his telephone and said "good-bye, Joe."

Is this concussion business worth worrying about or are you using it as an excuse to be near her? You're in the process of making an ass of yourself. Your association with women for the last several years has been nearly zilch; you're love-starved. What's it been? A half-dozen conversations with dedicated nuns visiting the monastery and a brief encounter with a short-term guest who saw it as a challenge to seduce you away from becoming a monk. So what about Charlotte? Anyone would tell you she's too old for you; and, it's obvious, as well, that she's a lady of wealth and class—which you aren't. The best you could ever hope for is to worship her from afar; and, if you're at all lucky, have an opportunity to serve her. So, what else does your life hold for you—serve time in prison, serve God in a monastery, or serve this woman on her plantation? The alarm clock jarred him from his reverie. Early morning light flowed softly through the window and across Charlotte's sleeping face. He parted her bangs and kissed her gently on the forehead, so overwhelmed by her that he did not consider the possible outrage this brash act might engender. But, she simply opened her eyes, smiled pleasantly at him and said, "Down boy."

"Are you OK?" he asked. She said she was fine, so after a few more pleasantries he let her drift back to sleep, picked up his pack and tiptoed downstairs. All his instincts told him to just keep going, get back on the trail and continue south. No, not till you do something for that poor horse and find the crutches in the attic so she can at least move around. He fished a pair of jeans and soiled shirt from his pack, put them on and headed for the barn. By now a thin arc of the sun was peeking over the trees in the East, and every bird in the community was trying to be recognized above the general din. While Alfred munched hay, Jude found a manure fork and went to work.

A beautiful day spilled into Charlotte's room, filling her with good cheer. Her headache and general body hurt were gone; even her leg was all right as long as she did not move it too fast. She looked over at Jude's nest; but, it was empty. Worse yet, his pack was gone. "Oh damn. Jude, you didn't leave, did you? I had such marvelous plans for you."

About then she heard the kitchen door close; but she could not tell if he was leaving or returning from outside. It took three calls, each more desperate than the previous, to get a response. Jude was still in the outer entryway to the kitchen, changing out of his barn clothes. He stuck his head in through the kitchen and yelled that he would be up in a minute. By the time he reached her bedroom, she had buried her anxiety under a pile of good cheer.

"Good morning, Charlotte, how you doing?"

"I feel great; if I could walk, I'd be back to normal; but I suspect my knee is still a little weak."

Although she made it to the bathroom by just holding on to his shoulder, when she finished, she was quite willing to be carried downstairs. He placed her in a chair at the kitchen table and set about getting their breakfast. She was anxious to unfold her plan but knew she should wait until his mind was not occupied with breakfast preparation.

Within no time at all, he was serving coffee, eggs and toast—surprisingly well done, she thought. Once they started to sip their coffee, she casually asked, "Jude, are you in a big hurry to get to wherever you're going?"

"I guess not. I'm headed for a monastery in Georgia. Although they expect me sometime, they know I'm walking and not on a rigid schedule. Why do you ask?"

In accordance with her carefully rehearsed plan, she casually answered, "Well, I just thought you might like to hang around for awhile—maybe take a little vacation on an old Virginia farm. You may have noticed a couple cabins north of the barn; they're former slave quarters that we've maintained as sharecropper housing. They aren't occupied at the present time. You're welcome to use one of them for an open-ended stay if you wish. I'm sorry I can't offer you a guest room here in the main house, but the local folks would make too much of it, and Aunt Millie would be scandalized."

Jude's predawn musings flashed through his mind. Of the three choices life offered him, *serving this woman* clearly had more appeal than the other two. How he felt about her was far less complicated with her sitting across from him at the breakfast table than it was in the dark of night. He studied her carefully, still amazed at how much she appealed to him. The nightgown she was wearing and her physical movements, especially as he remembered her on horseback, revealed a well-tuned body. Her hair was fine, like blond hair but it was more red than strawberry blond and she had a light tan; yesterday's exposure to the sun would have inflicted a painful sunburn on most redheads. C'mon, Jude, what the hell does her hair color have to do with anything? The lady asked you a nice polite little ques-

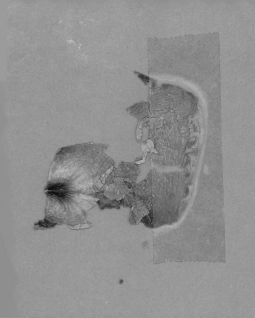

tion, with all kinds of hidden potential. Why don't you give her a nice gracious little answer, like a dumb kid who's planning to become a monk is expected to do?

"It might be fun to hang around for awhile; I'm not important to the people in Georgia. They accepted me as a favor to the people at Gethsemani, not because they desperately need me."

"That would be great, Jude. Although Aunt Millie is here on Mondays and Fridays, I'm gone on Mondays, Wednesdays, and often on Fridays and would feel more comfortable having someone around when we aren't here, or for that matter even when we are here."

"So, would you mind if I did a few little odd jobs around the place when I'm not too busy protecting the perimeters of the property?"

Charlotte smiled, a little embarrassed that her ploy was so transparent, but finally realized that the condition of the place spoke for itself and that she could no longer pretend that her situation was anything short of desperate.

Their casual negotiations were so intense that they barely noticed they had finished their breakfast. Charlotte finally decided to confess: "Jude, if you'll pour us more coffee, I'll attempt a brief *state of the farm* address. I can't give you the unabridged version because it would take all day, and I have work to finish for tomorrow."

While he poured, she collected her thoughts, then started her story.

"When Daddy died ten years ago, he left this farm to my husband and me—or former husband—whatever he is. My mother had died several years earlier; I was their only child. Daddy was reasonably satisfied with John Paul, who came from a respected family on the other side of Grimble County. He felt comfortable leaving both the farm and his *baby* in John Paul's hands. My parents didn't really know me; and, they certainly didn't know him, but then, neither did I know him very well. His method of running the farm consisted of bringing in a series of sharecroppers, who farmed so poorly there was barely enough income to sustain the operation. We had to sell off several parcels of land to keep from losing the whole thing."

"How big was the original farm?"

"Oh, gee, it must have been over 2,000 acres. Now it's down to about 200. Anyway, three years ago John Paul and I split. Since I had never done a serious day's work in my life, I was limited in my capacity to earn a living and pay off the debts we had accumulated. John Paul brought practically nothing into our marriage. Although my parents were still solvent to the end, they left only the farm. I had a brief spell of good fortune after John Paul's departure. A Negro from up North stopped by one day looking for work. I had no capacity for directing a farm hand; and, all I had seen, since my father stopped managing the farm, was the sharecropper's game. So I asked him if we could strike a suitable arrangement along those lines. Lyle was willing; and, since he seemed to be educated and fairly energetic, I was more hopeful than with some of those John Paul had engaged. At that time, I still had sufficient credit to buy seed and keep Lyle in food until we could produce a crop. There was a lot he didn't know about farming; but, he had a friend, named Salvi who advised him from time to time, and he was

"Do you teach, too?"

"At first, the department didn't know what to do with a woman who doesn't take dictation or make coffee; but, finally, they decided I had all the qualifications necessary to teach remedial English, which all of them hate. I could also teach a summer course entitled *How to Write Novels*, provided I could attract enough students to pay my salary. It turns out that wasn't a problem; the class is always over-enrolled. My colleagues assure me it's not because I'm such a great teacher; it's the vicarious thrill students get from associating with the woman who wrote the intimate love scenes in *Plantation of Hope*, my first book. Why do I subject myself to this tripe? I suppose I do it to have at least some human contact. Although most of the faculty are smug, pompous, arrogant, or egocentric, they're still a lot more interesting than the local people. Even students are occasionally refreshing."

Jude listened attentively—almost spellbound—not only at what she was saying but how well she said it: direct, simple and charming. He was also surprised and flattered that anyone of this stature would spend so much time talking to him—even revealing intimate feelings about her life—*as though she cares about me and wants me to understand.* Jude realized even more now that he is not an open person. He had never talked to anyone as freely as Charlotte just had—at least not since Billy's death.

"So that's an abstract of what I do," Charlotte said, "and now I guess I had better do it, or I'll have 18 students hounding me for not returning their papers. If you wouldn't mind going to the attic for the crutches, I would really appreciate it. Go up to the second floor and turn right; the first door on the left opens up on a stairway to history."

Jude was unprepared for what he saw in the attic—several large racks of Civil War uniforms. Although they were covered with sheets, they stuck out here and there so he could see what they were. He tossed back one of the sheets for a better look: uniforms of officers and enlisted men—North and South—hung unsorted, side by side. A few were neat and pressed, but most of them were dirty, wrinkled and worn. Some were tattered and caked with mud or blood. Stacked against the wall were dozens of rifles; and dumped unceremoniously in piles in front of them were swords, pistols and canteens—enough to equip a full-scale battle. No wonder Charlotte thought it risky to come up here at night when the restless spirits who once wore the burden of this equipment were likely to be abroad.

Jude found the crutches in another part of the attic, restricted to family items. Then he hastened back to the kitchen where life was more pleasant.

"What do you think about our attic?" Charlotte asked.

"It'd take some getting used to before I'd be comfortable up there. Are you in the business of renting Civil War uniforms to movie sets?"

"No, they're left over from my grandmother's business during the war. If you're interested, I'll give you a copy of *Plantation of Hope* to read while you're on vacation."

"I'd like to read it. Let me wipe the dust off your wooden legs first. Meanwhile, could you tell me why you speak of this property as a farm, when your book title refers to it as a plantation?"

"This part of Virginia was settled by farmers, who came down from Pennsylvania. Although the farms they developed were similar to other plantations in the South, in that they sometimes comprised several thousand acres, with slaves and all, they were not often called plantations locally. I used the term plantation in my books because most people outside of the Shenandoah Valley are not aware of this subtlety. Besides, plantation has a more romantic connotation than farm."

Charlotte lifted herself from the chair with the crutches and led the way to the study. It was obvious to Jude she had used these crutches before. One whole wall of the study was covered with books. On a shelf near her desk, were a half-dozen copies of books by Charlotte Henderson. She handed him one—hesitated—then said, "Would you like to take a chance on my second book, too, or would you rather wait to see if you can stomach the first one before you sign up for more punishment?"

"I enjoy reading and look forward to doing more now that I'm on vacation"—hoping she would tell him to use her library anytime. But, her thoughts had shifted to the concern that he might take this vacation business seriously and spend his time reading instead of restoring the farm. She handed him the second book; and, after they both made admiring comments about the pile of stuff on her desk, he suggested that he round up his things and head for the slave quarters so she could get to work.

"As much as I enjoy your company, I guess you're right." Then she added, "The first cabin is pretty well-equipped; but, you'll have to go upstairs to the linen closet for sheets and a pillowcase—if you need other things let me know."

As he picked out what he needed from the closet; he became ill at ease about his status. He found her in the study pouring over a student paper. "Excuse me for interrupting, but there are still some loose ends about what we're doing here."

"Like what?"

"Well, for one thing, how do we explain me to Aunt Millie or anyone who drops by?"

"It's rare that visitors drop by unannounced. I'll tell Aunt Millie how you helped me after my spill—but not that you spent the night with me"—she seemed to enjoy saying it that way—"and I'll tell her you're going to stay for awhile and help out around the place. She's loyal and discreet, but don't expect her to warm up to you very fast. If you need things from town, let her know on Monday and she'll put them on my account and bring them out Friday."

"This is very thoughtful of you, Charlotte, but I hope you realize I'm not a qualified sharecropper and would not be able to just pick up where Lyle left off. I would not be able to harvest crops and take them to market. I don't know anything about marketing and I don't know people in the area to deal with."

"Yes, I know Jude, that wasn't my expectation. Just hang around and do what you like to do. Perhaps you could do something for Alfred once in awhile. That, along with having saved my life, certainly justifies throwing in a few groceries and clean sheets to make your stay pleasant. Also Lyle left a wonderful garden, which you should feel free to use, and his chickens are running all over the farm. I couldn't take care of them, so I just turned them loose. They're laying eggs and hatching peeps all over the place. They love that wheat field that didn't get harvested. Feel free to use the eggs, if you can find them; and, eat as many chickens as you like, especially that damn rooster that crows at 3:30 a.m. The pond also has bass and sunfish, and the stream I tried to jump with the horse has trout. There are rabbits, quail, deer—Jude, this is a regular paradise and a much better place to hide out than a monastery."

Jude's face flushed. He felt exposed. It would be ridiculous to concoct a denial or even turn it into a joke. "So, what do you think I am hiding from?".

"I presume you're wanted by the military police for questioning in connection with the deaths of those two soldiers at Fort Knox two years ago."

"Why do you associate me with that?" he parried, trying to regain his wits.

"You said you spent nearly two years at Gethsemani. That takes us back to about the time that thing happened. You don't seem to have an overwhelming interest in religion. Most people who do like to show their enthusiasm for God by spouting religious sayings; instead you show up carrying an Army blanket and an Army pup tent. You're dressed in Army fatigues and Army boots."

"Yes, but I have a Boy Scout jackknife," he joked.

She smiled and added, "You also seem reserved about contact with outsiders. But, actually, I had only a faint suspicion that you were a fugitive; my comment was just a shot in the dark; it was your reaction that told the story."

"I'm sorry you found out before I had a chance to

explain what it was about. I'll put the bedding back, round up my stuff and be on my way. I really have enjoyed knowing you. I hope your knee heals quickly. Good-bye, Charlotte." By the time he finished his little farewell speech, his voice had taken on a slight quiver; he was almost crying. He turned quickly and walked toward the door to hide his emotions.

"Not so fast," she barked. "We had a deal and I expect you to stick to it. I don't have time now to hear about your failed career as a soldier; but, if you're serious about telling this story, I would be willing to listen to it later in the week. Meanwhile, go busy yourself with your fantastic vacation until Wednesday evening, at which time I'm hoping you'll have me over for dinner."

"Yes, ma'am," he beamed in boyish relief and left for his quarters.

Oh God! Charlotte, what are you doing? He probably killed both of those guys. At a minimum you're harboring a fugitive; and, at a maximum, he may do you in and run off with the family fortune. Nonsense, you and John Paul squandered the family fortune years ago. Aunt Millie and Jude are the closest family you have. Her eyes welled with tears. You and Jude need each other and you know full well how infatuated he is with you—probably willing to do whatever you ask of him. One thing you know for sure is that the theory the military police have regarding the Fort Knox murders—that they involved a love triangle among homosexuals—is not true. Jude takes too much pleasure in your sexuality to be queer. Come on now, you have to stop thinking about all that business and get to work on these

damn papers. Now, now, Charlotte, just because your boring life has suddenly become interesting again is no reason
for you to speak disparagingly of . . . of . . . these damn
papers.

Jude tossed his stuff on the bed and looked to see what
his new jail cell was like. It had a full-size bed with a clean
mattress, a rustic table with four mismatched chairs, an
ancient refrigerator, a bureau, a beat-up couch, an easy
chair that was not too beat-up, a small end-table with a
lamp on it and a floor lamp. Hey, these slaves didn't have it
half-bad. The cupboards contained experienced dishes,
assorted cups, plus a few pans and other utensils. A mature
electric stove and a wood stove for heat in the winter
completed the inventory. Now, if Charlotte doesn't call the
cops, life here could be good, certainly better than monastery life.

The pond area was pleasant, secluded by planted ever-
greens and the brush that had taken advantage of several
years of negligence. The stream bed had been scooped out and
a low dam built to add another two feet of depth to the water.
On the upstream end, a sheet of bedrock had been scoured
smooth by torrents of sand and water during the spring
floods.

Since he had seen only the back of Charlotte's house, he
decided to go up and walk around it. The front was a southern
classic like he had seen in Civil War movies, including a
large porch supported by tall pillars. The grass hadn't been
mowed for a long time, and the shrubbery and flower beds
needed attention. On the far side of the house he encountered
a carriage shed that now housed the family automobiles: a

five-year-old station wagon and a red MG roadster, dating back to the time when the fenders were angular instead of curved. The MG was in mint condition; it seemed to be the only thing on the property that had been maintained. He also spotted a riding lawn mower, which came as a great relief in view of the several acres of lawn that needed tending.

In no time he had the mower running, and he started cutting the front lawn. He was a little concerned that the noise might interfere with Charlotte's concentration but decided he would rather have her come out and yell at him than to ignore him the way she was doing. When he finished mowing, he worked in the flower beds for a while, still hoping Charlotte would appear. When she did not, he walked slowly toward the barn to feed Alfred, looking back several times to see if she would call to him. Later, he caught a couple of sunfish to go with his dinner and settled down with Charlotte's book, anxious to find out what had transpired on this farm years ago; and, if possible, to see who Charlotte is.

Jude read quickly; in no time the Civil War was joined in all its fury. The Hendersons had made every effort to stay out of it; but, one by one, the men were drawn in. The character called Zachary, who was modeled after Charlotte's grandfather, was Jude's age when he went to war. His two brothers joined him within four months. All of the other farmers in the region sided with the Confederacy, but the Hendersons were opposed to the break up of the Union; they also saw the evil of slavery, especially as it was practiced on nearby farms, and knew that it had to end sooner or later. The women were left behind in a hostile neighborhood

of southern sympathizers. Most of the able-bodied slaves, with the Henderson's blessings, went North to help the Union.

After a brief training period, Major Zachary bravely led his troops into their first battle. He was killed within five minutes. When Ashley, Charlotte's fictionalized grandmother, learned of his death, she went through three stages of anguish in dealing with it. First she was incapacitated and unwilling to continue living, then she was angry at the waste and stupidity of it all. She wanted personally to declare war on both sides; but, after it became obvious to her that more of the same would accomplish nothing, she decided to declare peace. The Henderson farm would become a war-free zone.

Ashley constructed a sign and posted it out on the road, at the beginning of the driveway to the house, declaring her land to be a place where soldiers from either the North or the South could come to rest before continuing the fight, or withdrawing from the war completely. Rules were set forth to which all must abide: 1) Officers and men from either side may seek asylum. 2) All weapons must be checked in; to be returned upon departure. 3) War ideologies may not be discussed, but guests may exchange experiences or express grief over personal losses. 4) Fighting, drunkenness, abusive language and other ungentlemanly behavior shall be contained.

Jude stopped reading and sat back to reflect. Charlotte's style of writing was compelling and her capacity to tell a story created enough suspense to keep him up well past his usual bedtime. But what the hell, I'm on vacation and what's more it's Saturday night. He had completed the first quarter of the book and could no longer distinguish what was real and what was made up; maybe it was all true. This last thing, though, an escape hatch for war-weary soldiers from both sides, kind of stretched the imagination. There was no way they could coexist for even the brief period it would take to equip them for the trail; yet, he reflected that there was a whole attic full of Grandma's war trophies. Not only was Jude unsure whether Grandma was real, but he also began to harbor some doubt about whether Charlotte was real—but then, if she isn't, where the hell am I? He looked up at the big house, the lights were still on. Perhaps he should go tuck her into bed . . . in your half asleep condition, Jude, you could end up looking like a turkey. At 1:15 a.m., he bumbled off to bed.

The next morning, even though it was Sunday, the cock crowed before dawn. Jude was fully wakened; he struggled to go back to sleep; but, each time he dozed slightly, the cock crowed again. At 5 a.m., he gave up trying and went out to the barn to take care of Alfred. His intuition told him to leave Charlotte alone so she could work on her papers. She'll probably sleep late, no point in even hanging around the house until afternoon.

Jude hiked down through the fields and back to the stream where Charlotte had met her downfall. She was right, the farm was a wonderful place for a vacation or for a fugitive to hide out. It was late morning when he returned to the cabin. As soon as he entered, he knew Charlotte had been there. His pack was not quite as he had left it and her fresh, clean smell was in the air. He checked outside in the soft ground and found the peg prints of her crutches. Initially, he felt badly that he had not been home when she came to visit but then realized that she had come because he was not there. She would have seen him out in the open fields. What did she want? Was she looking for evidence of his past life? It bothered him that she did not trust him, but why should she? It's a wonder she hasn't called the sheriff yet.

Jude decided to work on the flower beds and shrubbery near the house hoping she would see him and come out. Ten minutes later she appeared. She was getting around nicely on the crutches.

"Hi," she called from the porch, "I was just down to your place to see how you are doing, but you were gone. Is it too late to offer you a ham sandwich and a cup of tea?"

"That sounds great."

"Come in and help me assemble them; then we can eat out here."

The teapot had already started to whistle. She told him where things were and he put the lunch together on a tray and carried it out to the porch. How different this genteel scene was from his past life. Charlotte, even with a bum leg, moved with grace; and, her manners flowed with a natural self-assurance he had not experienced before. He felt like a clumsy kid in her presence.

While they were settling into their wicker chairs, Charlotte provided a certain amount of appropriate small talk. Jude quickly worked his way through his sandwich, then asked how she was progressing with her paperwork. She rolled her eyes in exaggerated frustration and explained that the first writing assignment from a new class is always difficult. "I keep hoping the lessons taught to the previous class will carry over into the new class; but, alas, each time you have to start over. Teaching is like rolling a big ball uphill: just as you're about to reach the top, it rolls back down and you have to start over."

"You must be very good at it, though. I read about a quarter of your book last night. It really is compelling and beautifully written."

"Thank you, Jude, but a well-written book doesn't necessarily translate into a good teacher."

"But, I bet you are a good teacher."

"Thanks. With a little encouragement, I can be made to admit that I'm a good teacher. I'm not always so sure, though. Sometimes I feel discouraged when a certain per-centage of every class shows almost no improvement by the end of the course. It's as though their minds are in bondage and I don't have the key that would free them to put their thoughts on paper."

"That's hard to believe. My guess is you're putting too much blame on yourself."

"Oh, it's true. Most of my colleagues believe this category of student has no thoughts for the paper. These professional educators tell me that if a student doesn't think logically, there is no way to get him to write logically. I believe that learning to write helps one to think, but I haven't been at this teaching business long enough to be sure yet."

"Where did you learn to write so well?"

"I started writing when I was quite young. Once my grandmother realized she had become part of history, she was anxious for me to be the repository for her story. Her eyesight wasn't good and everyone else was too busy to pay much attention to her. The notes I took in those early days had a lot of misspellings because many of the words my grandmother used were unfamiliar to me, and my sentence structure was often clumsy; but, the stories themselves were rich and colorful."

"Yes. They really are. I'm anxious to get back to your book."

"Sometimes I wonder if I am a quality writer or just a hacker who served as a conduit for Granny, who was the real writer."

"How can you say that? You're the one that wrote the book."

"My second book, though, was so much less than the first that it would be easy to make that argument. On the other hand, I wrote some decent papers in college, independent of Granny, some of which won praise from people I respect. I think my slump is caused by the nature of my messed-up life."

"What do you mean?"

"Jude, I really don't know why I bare my soul to you like this; I have never told anyone else these inner thoughts."

"It's because you know I care about you."

She reached out and put her hand on his and said, "Thanks, Jude, I really appreciate your saying that. I suppose, on the other hand, the reason you haven't told me much about yourself, is because you don't know how I feel about you?"

"In part, maybe; but, after spending two years with

monks who don't talk, I may be a little out of practice."
This of course was an excuse. Jude knew full well that he
had not had much to say to anyone since Billy's death back in
junior high school. Now that he was learning to accept that,
he still felt more comfortable just listening. "You'll have to
admit, though, that for how little I have said, you know me
far better than I know you. I'm a simple person—easy to
know—whereas, you're pretty complex."

"Jude, you'd like to think you're simple, but you aren't.
A certain amount of that humble monk stuff has rubbed off
on you; but, you haven't fooled me. If you stick around here
for awhile, not only will I find out who you are, but you
will also. One thing I know already, you're not just some
dumb soldier who made a mistake and went AWOL. You're
educated, well-read, and wise beyond your years. I enjoy
your company—unreasonably so—and expect we could
continue this bantering about who likes whom best all
afternoon; but, I've made a resolution not to self-destruct
at the hands of my own indulgence—I have to get back to
work. I'll hand these papers back tomorrow and try to free
myself for dinner tomorrow night. If Aunt Millie isn't too
suspicious of you, she may put something together that we
can share."

"I'd like that."

"Oh, I almost forgot. The 'Honey Dipper' is coming tomorrow, so you might want to make yourself scarce. Mr.
Steinmetz, who owns the company, usually hires people who
function at a fairly low level and it's unlikely that your
presence will arouse any suspicion; but, you can't tell what
an idle comment from one of these guys would generate in

the rumor mill down at the Boar's Nest Tavern."

"What's this Honey Dipper business?"

"Oh, these are the people who come once a year to pump out the septic tank."

Charlotte returned to her torment and Jude went back to the flower beds and hedge trimming. In the late afternoon he fought back an urge to call Charlotte to admire his work; instead, he went off to take care of Alfred. If it were his horse, he decided, he would turn him out to pasture to fend for himself or teach him to do something useful, like pull a wagon or a cultivator. Jude humored himself by rummaging through the barn looking for harnesses. He hung one next to Alfred's stall for him to get used to.

3

Early the next morning a beat-up Model A Ford pulled into the yard, backfired once, then became silent. A small, ancient, black woman, presumably Aunt Millie, emerged from the driver's side and disappeared in the house.

In the kitchen, Charlotte stood with her crutches at the stove pouring her second cup of coffee. "You want a cup of coffee, Aunt Millie?"

"No, I don't drink coffee: make me jitter," she said, as she had a thousand times before. She looked at Charlotte for a long time as if waiting for something to be volunteered, but Charlotte just returned her gaze with a noncommittal smile. Finally, Aunt Millie said, "Look like you have a big weekend, Miss Charlotte, all that grass cuttin', hedge trimmin', flower bed diggin got you crippled up, huh?"

"I did have some help," Charlotte confessed.

"You mean, after all that yard work you done, someone come long and broke your leg? Miss Charlotte, you ain't never got shet of that little mean streak you had when you a little girl. You best tell me now what kinda risk you put this place in so's I knows when to start runnin."

Those were not the best words Aunt Millie could have used to draw Charlotte out; but, there was no escape, Charlotte was going to have to reply and be prepared to face the old woman's inevitable cynicism. Charlotte was often surprised at how much power Aunt Millie had over her. She had always held her more accountable than her parents. Finally, Charlotte started to let out the filtered version she had practiced off and on for two days. "You know I started off for a ride on Alfred before you left Friday. On the back 40, the saddle became loose and I fell off; I twisted my knee and hit my head—guess I passed out. A young man, who was hiking on the upper trail, apparently saw the accident and ran down to see if I needed help."

"Ah huh, Ah gits the picture. Turn out you needs help. He git you back to the house, find you crutches in the attic, you told him 'bout the Civil War, he mow the lawn, you fall in love with him and decide you gonna keep him. So where he at now?"

"He's standing right behind you."

Jude had come to the back door just as Aunt Millie had started her tirade. He did not want to interrupt her, so he just quietly slipped in. Aunt Millie whipped around as best her old carcass would allow and confronted a nice looking young man with a broad smile. "Don't nobody teach you knock or you already live here and don't gotta knock?" She turned back to Charlotte before he could answer and said, "He too young for you—hope you ain't marry this un; you barely over last un."

"C'mon, Aunt Millie, he hasn't worked his way up from the slave quarters yet. You know it took you a whole generation to travel that distance." Aunt Millie's mother had been a slave.

"How you call him?" The old lady inquired.

Charlotte responded in an exaggerated southern drawl, "Mostly Ah calls him *boy,* but he also responds to *Jude.*"

"What kind name that? He plannin' come a saint?"

"Aunt Millie, if he survives more than a week of your inquisition, he'll certainly be eligible."

"Inquisition? Every time I gits near the truth 'bout one you little tricks, you try throw me off by using big words you learnt up that Yankee school."

"Why, Aunt Millie, I do declare, that's the first time you ever admitted that I got anything out of that schoolin', but now I've got to get off to that Confederate school up the ridge before the traffic gets too thick."

"You gonna drive that little car yours with a broken leg?"

"I can make it go forward well enough; as long as I don't have to apply the brakes too hard, I'll be OK. That's why I wanted to leave a little early, so I can go more slowly."

"Yah, I bet you'll slow right down to 70. What I spose do with him?" she said, jerking her thumb in Jude's direction.

"He's my guest from up in Yankee Land, who is taking a little vacation in the South. He'll be staying in the slave quarters—not my bedroom as you inferred earlier. I hope you'll find it in your heart to extend to him our best southern hospitality. And, Aunt Millie, if you tell anyone he's here, I'll tell them that the two of you are having an affair, that I'm trying with all my Christian strength to break it off, but that you just won't let go."

"Humph."

"Also, he'll be needing some things from town; just charge the stuff to my account. And, would you mind making a little extra for dinner tonight, just in case I have company?"

"I thought you say he stay'n down the slave quarters."

"Oh, yes, that's certainly true. Well, maybe I'll go down there with it; you know, I learned some pretty trashy ways when I was up in Yankee Land."

"Yah, you sure 'nuff do, but you better git goin' now; you got no more time for lessons from me on how to be a lady." While Charlotte was gathering her things for school, Aunt Millie turned her attention to Jude. "You learnt smilin' well 'nuff, you talk once while, too?"

"A little bit, but not when I'm afraid of getting hurt."

"By God! You a Yankee all right. Sure 'nuff talk like un."

"Yes. I expect I do."

"I ain't figurt all this yet; all I knows is Miss Charlotte ain't got no sense bout men— don't guess this gonna be no different. So let me tell you right now, you gonna bring any more misery on that girl than she had already, I gonna call in the entire Black Baptist army rip you part."

After a long silence, she asked, "Well, ain't you got nothin say 'bout dat?"

"No. . . . I better help Charlotte into the car with her books and papers."

Charlotte dropped into the front seat. Jude caught the

crutches and propped them up on the seat beside her. She looked up at him with concern, "You going to be all right? I didn't hear what she said to you, but I can guess it wasn't real easy to take."

"I'll be fine. I'm going to go hide out now from both Aunt Millie and the Honey Dipper. Be careful, Charlotte; see you tonight."

Jude watched the car's dusty trail up the long drive until it disappeared. Then he went to trim brush around the pond. Soon he heard a truck pull into the yard. Jude peeked through the brush at the dirty yellow tank truck. A large, black man with bibbed coveralls descended from the cab and walked over to the end of the house. He studied the ground for awhile, then put his back against the house and paced off the distance to where he was looking at the ground. About then, Aunt Millie descended upon him and began a tirade that went on for some time. Although Jude could not hear what was said, he could see that the Honey Dipper was not allowed to reply. Finally, Aunt Millie slowed a little, and Mr. Dipper was able to insert his comments, heatedly at first, but gradually they both simmered down and spoke quietly.

Aunt Millie went inside the house, Mr. Dipper took a shovel from the truck and started digging, and Jude went back to cutting brush. It was already becoming warm. Jude stopped to rest and toss grasshoppers to the fish; but, his diversion was interrupted by a tremendous scream and loud swearing. Jude dropped his tools and ran for the house. Mr. Dipper's sounds were now joined by Aunt Millie calling for Jude. When he arrived, the leathery old woman was pacing back and forth, hysterically pleading for him to help Lyle—

apparently Mr. Dipper's real name. He was sitting in a hole in the ground, pulling at his foot and yelling. Jude could not think because of all the noise the two were making. He told Aunt Millie to shut up; but, that had no effect on her. He put his hands on her shoulders, looked directly into her face and calmly said, "Go over and sit on the steps and shut up. If you don't, I'll throw you in the swimming pool." She did as she was told. With the screaming now coming from only one direction, it was possible to focus more clearly on the situation.

Lyle had dug down to the tank, which was covered with a flat metal lid, five feet across. Next to it was a huge rock. Apparently, Lyle's foot had slipped off the lid and become wedged between the tank and the rock. The rock subsequently had moved enough to compress Lyle's foot. Jude could not tell whether the rock was still moving slowly against the foot or just holding it in a viselike grip. Pushing the rock back by hand was out of the question. A hole would have to be dug behind it so it could fall away into the new hole. Lyle was too impatient for that. "Hang on, Lyle, I have to get some tools from the barn."

When Jude reappeared, he had a wooden post, two wood-splitting wedges and an eight-pound maul. Aunt Millie was still sitting on the porch—exhausted. Lyle had reduced his screaming to repetitive moaning sounds. Jude jumped into the hole, placed the wedges between the septic tank and rock on either side of Lyle's foot and began swinging the maul. Lyle's eyes widened with terror as he watched the big hammer circle through the air over Jude's head and fall alternately on the wedges, close—oh, so close to his foot. The edge of the septic tank began to cave in, slightly at first, then prominently. "Whoa," Lyle said, "let me try it," and with a small jerk of his foot, he was free. He stood up on the tank lid with most of his weight on one foot and looked at Jude, as though seeing him for the first time. "I don't know who the hell you are or where you came from; but, I'm surely glad you're here." This was said without a trace of dialect—almost pure Yankee.

"My name is Jude," he responded, sticking out his hand. "I'm a friend of Charlotte's from up North. She's letting me use what she calls the slave quarters as a residence for a little vacation."

The expression of pain in Lyle's face turned to amusement. "How long you been on this vacation, Jude?"

"Just a couple of days." Jude was not sure why he felt a little foolish about this. Clearly, Lyle's no bumpkin, not only did he see through my vacation story, he seems to know more about my situation than I do. Jude thought it might make a little more sense if he added something about his hiking vacation, Charlotte's spill from the horse, and how he was just stopping off to rest for awhile. All this was unusual for Jude, who was accustomed to remaining quiet while others felt obligated to make conversation or explain themselves.

Finally, Lyle said, "Guess you don't know Charlotte very well yet."

"No, that's true. Why do I have the impression that your life goes beyond that of a honey dipper and that you know Charlotte quite well?"

"You're right, septic tanks haven't been a lifetime

career for me. As for Charlotte—yes, I know her some, but I expect Aunt Millie's the only one has any idea what makes her tick; she won't talk about it." The old woman had quietly disappeared into the house after she saw that Lyle was free.

"By the way, that was an interesting trick you did on Aunt Millie. I didn't think she could ever be made to shut up. Looks like she's gone inside; why don't we get me out of this hole and over to the steps where I can take off my shoe and see what's left of my foot?"

Jude climbed out of the hole, extended a hand to Lyle, and eased him to the surface. With Jude supporting one side, Lyle limped over to the steps where he removed his shoe and sock. Jude had expected his foot to be crushed out of shape— broken bones sticking out, torn flesh, blood clots and all. Instead, it was just red and swollen. "Hell, that's not bad at all," Lyle said. "How come it hurts so much? Shit, I'm really embarrassed about all the noise I made."

Jude picked up the shoe and said, "Guess you're lucky you were wearing steel-toed safety shoes. I expect that explains why your foot doesn't look like crushed straw-berries." Meanwhile, Aunt Millie reappeared carrying a tray and two brandy snifters. "I 'spect Miss Charlotte want me give you little pain killer, view what y'all just been through."

"Oh, you sure are an angel of mercy, Aunt Millie," Lyle declared as he lifted a glass from the tray; and, only after he had it secured, said, "If Miss Charlotte knew who was drinking her brandy, I don't think she would be that delighted."

They each sipped and thoughtfully swirled the smooth liquid without speaking. Jude waited for an explanation as to why Charlotte would object specifically to Lyle drinking her brandy while Lyle wondered how much Jude knew about him, and whether he should tell him his side of the story. Jude now remembered that Lyle was the name Charlotte had used when she spoke of her runaway sharecropper. Could this be the same person?

At the height of the silence, Aunt Millie piped up, "I git blame for havin' 'pinions, but I don't know what you tongue-tied people gonna do you don't have someun like me to start up you moufs for you."

"Guess you're right, Aunt Millie," Jude admitted. "Correct me if I'm wrong, Lyle, but I gather you're the former sharecropper. I couldn't hear what was being said when you first arrived; but, I now presume that before you started to dig, you and Aunt Millie were having an argument about your leaving the farm."

"Yes, that's part of it; but, there's also the question of what to tell Miss Charlotte about who dug this hole. You see Aunt Millie doesn't lie easily; but, on the other hand, she wouldn't want to put Charlotte to any unnecessary stress— she treats her like her own delicate child."

"Yes," Jude said, "and speaking of protecting Charlotte, I expect it would be best if you'd keep my visit here a secret. Not that anything exciting is happening between us, but she wouldn't want the boys at the Boar's Nest too have too much fun thinking about it."

Lyle chortled, then explained that the real name of the tavern is The Boar's Head. "It's a hangout for Klan members and other hard-drinking bigots that Charlotte likes to criticize. She started referring to it as the Boar's Nest and it caught on. The patrons aren't happy about it—these are not people one should antagonize just for the fun of it. Some of them think they're Klan members. I don't think they're real Klan members, though—part of any national organization or anything—it's more like they're local hoodlums with sheets for hire."

"Still a scary business, though."

"Yes." After a thoughtful pause, Lyle went on to say, "So, what it amounts to, Jude, is that I'm supposed to keep you a secret and you're supposed to keep me a secret, and Aunt Millie has to keep both of us a secret. But who's gonna take the lid off that tank and suck the shit out of it? My shoe is wrecked and my foot is out of commission."

"I don't know, Lyle, I'm on vacation," Jude looked at the old woman still standing there with the tray.

"Yah, that sound jist like me, soon's I cleans this big old house and cooks dinner, I'm gon do this hole. Meanwhile, be sure you let me know bout any change in plans." With that Aunt Millie went in the house.

"So, how it looks to me, Jude, if you go in there and knock those wedges out, so you can remove the lid, that rock is going to roll against the lid and you still won't be able to remove it. What you have to do is dig a hole behind the rock and let it fall away from the tank into the new hole."

"That's what I was going to do in the first place when your foot was stuck; but, you were beginning to show signs of impatience, so I thought I'd best find a faster way."

"Guess I did rush the job a little. I'll admit I was pretty

scared, especially when Aunt Millie was the only help I had, and she'd got pretty hysterical. That rock's probably sitting in sort of a teetering position or I'd a had more of it against my foot than I did."

"OK, Lyle, I'll dig the hole for the rock to fall into; but, while I'm doing it you have to tell me what the hell's going on around here, including why you left."

"If I tell you that story, you have to promise not to tell Miss Charlotte."

"Does Aunt Millie know?"

"Yes, she's the one that won't let me tell Charlotte. She protects her from everyone she can and even tries to keep her from inflicting wounds on herself. Aunt Millie never had any kids of her own, you know; she practically raised Charlotte from the day she was born—not an easy task."

"How does Charlotte inflict wounds on herself?"

"I expect by now you know that Charlotte's spoiled, headstrong, flamboyant and smart, but she lacks common sense about her own survival. She really ought to find a more generous place to live than Grimble County."

As Jude picked up the shovel and started to dig, Lyle began his story. "After I won World War II, I went back to Saginaw to reclaim my job at the Chevrolet Foundry. By working the second shift I was able to go up to Bay City Junior College. It's only a two-year college, but they have a couple of good English teachers, and also I was able to learn a little math, history and economics. Meanwhile, I met Liz who was a bookkeeper in the office at the foundry. After a few dates, we got to be pretty close, but she always had this thing about going back to Virginia. She missed her family and she felt that, although Negroes in the North have more freedom than here in the South, they're angry and self-destructive. Finally, she went back home and told me if I wanted her, I'd have to move down there. It took me three months to finish up my second year of college, then I went down."

"Is that when you started working for Charlotte?"

"No, not yet. Liz had a low paying job as a bookkeeper at the feed mill, but I couldn't find even a crummy job. She kept telling me that a lot of my trouble was that I talked like an educated Yankee. Nobody's looking to hire trouble, so I began learning the language and local ways. Now, I'm not saying it's as difficult as learning Chinese, but it's not something that comes automatically with the skin color—especially hard is that humble, step'n fetch attitude that's so popular among southern Negroes. I kept having trouble remembering where I'm not allowed to sit or drink. At any rate, Liz got to know some of the farmers and contractors in the grain business; and, through her I met Salvi, one of the local farmers. He suggested I go talk with Miss Charlotte. He said she had been having some problems and that by now she might be ready for help."

"How did you feel about the possibility of working for a white woman?"

"I didn't much like the idea. On top of that, I really didn't know shit about sharecropp'n; but, Salvi said he'd help me—besides, he said Miss Charlotte won't know the difference. Actually, I was pretty honest with her about my lack of farm experience; I guess she was desperate enough to take a chance on me. I'm still grateful to her for putting her trust in me; I wish we hadn't run into this snag."

Jude now braced the post he had brought from the barn against the rock to keep it from falling in on him while he was digging. "So, what happened?"

"Well, the first year went well: we both made some money. Meanwhile, Liz and I were making plans to marry when, in the midst of it all, she turns up pregnant. This caused us to speed up our plans. The only trouble is she never was thrilled about me working for Miss Charlotte and had begged me to quit at the end of the season. Now all of a sudden she wants me to quit immediately."

"How come?"

"Well, to begin with, Liz found out that Miss Charlotte wrote dirty books. She never read any of them, but hearsay is bigger than fact."

"Are they dirty books?" Jude did not want to divulge that he was reading her book.

"She thinks they're historical novels. I've read both of them and that's really what they are. Oh sure, some of the sex parts get down to the details. If that's all you look at, then these are naughty books. That, of course, is what the 'good old boys' have done. I don't suppose many of them have actually read these books. The same's probably true of the church folk, who are ready to run her out of town. The comments Liz has heard from both quarters, though, leave me in a poor position to defend Miss Charlotte. The good old boys enjoy trying to figure out where she learned so much about sex; they don't believe John Paul taught her that much. Next, they started talking about Miss Charlotte's new slave—wondering if she kept him around to practice on. The last straw came when I let it slip that Miss Charlotte swims naked in that big pool of hers. Liz hit the ceiling, convinced she was trying to seduce me and that she'd probably succeed. Claimed I'd end up swinging from that big magnolia tree over there in the front yard."

"Scary thought."

"Yes. But, of course, you know, Miss Charlotte didn't have any designs on my old black ass; that swimming thing was innocent enough. She did it only when I was some distance from the house, which is where I was most of the time; and, she always wore a robe when she wasn't in the water. The only reason I'm telling you this is so you'll be ready to deal with it; and, I hope you'll do so kindly . . . . You probably wonder why I care. I suppose Aunt Millie and I are the only two people around here who appreciate Miss Charlotte enough to overlook some of her kooky ways. She's also one of the few white people in the area that speaks out about racial discrimination. On several occasions she's put her ass on the line for some poor nigger that violated the rules."

"You talk like Charlotte needs to be protected. She was born and raised around here; I'd think she'd know something about survival in this part of Virginia."

"You'd think that," Lyle snorted, "but the fact of the matter is, she hasn't lived around here that much. Her daddy sent her off to a private boarding school in the ninth grade; from there she went north to Yankee school, then to France for a year. Soon after that she married that asshole, John Paul, and was pretty much isolated from the real world."

"Didn't she come home during the summer?"

"Most of the time she did, but I gather she didn't get to know people outside her own class. She has no idea how ignorant and violent some of these local folks are. She thinks when she stands up at a town meeting and criticizes how things are being done that she's dealing with the local debating team. Some excuse her—that it's just part of her having gone bonkers after her daughter died, but others think she needs to be taught a lesson—and they did damn near teach her a lesson after John Paul disappeared."

"What about Charlotte's daughter? She never said anything to me about her."

"No, me either. She doesn't talk about her. All I know is that there was some kind of automobile accident. After that, she and John Paul started having trouble. I wasn't here then, all I know is hearsay."

"What about John Paul? You say he disappeared?"

"Talk is, that after the accident, John Paul started drinking and running around with other women—more than he already was—and I gather that was plenty. They fought right out in public. She'd lay that sharp tongue on him; and, when they got home, he'd beat her up. People said she was going around with bruises or a black eye much of the time; then, suddenly, he disappeared and hasn't been heard from since. Rumor has it she killed him and buried him somewhere here at Greyledge."

"That's hard to believe."

"Yah, I know what you mean, but after my first summer here, guess it must'a been in October, Sheriff Batley showed up with a backhoe and a flock of deputies. They started digging up the place, looking for John Paul's body.

After about three days, one of them discovered a car in the pond. They got a chain on it and pulled it out. It was full of bullet holes—dozens of them."

"Holy shit! How did she explain that?"

"Well, they took Miss Charlotte downtown and grilled her all afternoon and until 4:00 a.m. They wouldn't let her call a lawyer, didn't feed her; and, they gave her only one sip of water. They were convinced she'd hired an out-of-town hit man, who had riddled John Paul and his car with a machine gun, pushed the car into the pond and buried the body out in a field. When they brought her home the next morning, it was just turning light. They dropped her out on the road, at the end of the drive, and made her walk all the way to the house. She still had enough spunk to call them every foul name she could think of. I could hear her all the way to the barn."

"That must be a quarter of a mile, isn't it?"

"At least. I met her part way and walked back with her. They had ripped a couple buttons off her blouse so they could get a better view. I'm surprised the bastards didn't take turns with her, that's about the quality of law enforcement around here. Through the whole thing, all she told them was that John Paul had shot the holes in the car and that he had left her. If they want to know more, they should go ask his mother."

"Did they?"

"No, but the sheriff and his boys came back several times to hassle her. They even did some more digging. Eventually they got tired of the game, loaded up their backhoe and pulled out. They left the bullet-riddled car sitting next to the pond. It was upsetting to Miss Charlotte, so I dragged it off with the tractor and buried it."

Jude finished the hole and climbed out. He knocked the supporting post away with the maul and the rock fell back into its new position with a hollow *thunk*. Lyle applauded, then told Jude how to remove the lid, start the pump and suck out the tank. When that was done and the lid was replaced, Jude shoved the soil back with the front loader of the tractor.

"OK, Jude that's good, you ready for our next project?"

"Frankly, Lyle, I'm kinda tired. Could I rest first?"

"Oh, sure, take your time, this is a long-range project," Lyle chuckled, "two or three days down the road. What I'm thinking about is those crops out there and how Miss Charlotte and I are losing money every day they sit there. This man Salvi, I told you about, is a pretty good guy. He's got a combine. He could go in there and thrash out that grain and get it off to market with no muss nor fuss. We pay Salvi in grain, Miss Charlotte gets a check for her agreed part; and I get a check for my part. I will not have set foot on the farm, so neither Liz nor Miss Charlotte need get upset. I suppose whatever you get out of it will depend on Miss Charlotte."

"I gather Charlotte could use a little cash about now," Jude offered.

"Hell, yes, if she doesn't come up with some dough by late August, the bank is going to foreclose. At this point her only choice is to sell off another chunk of land or get an advance on a new book. It'd be too bad if she sold another piece; it would reduce the size of Greyledge below what's reasonable for a functional farm; land prices are so low now those bastards at the bank would see it as a good time to try to steal the whole farm. I'm not sure Miss Charlotte is financially savvy enough to prevent it. Whether she's got a new book in the works, I couldn't tell you."

"It surprises me, you know so much about Charlotte's affairs—and other things in town, being a newcomer."

"I've got a couple of good sources. Just about everything in town gets discussed out there on the loading dock where Liz works. The windows are wide open all summer; most of the sellers and buyers are white folk who wouldn't expect a nigger office girl could follow their enlightened conversation, so they talk about anything they please."

"And what's Salvi's source?"

"Salvi? Now, he's another matter. He's got enough money so the big boys kinda forget what color he is. He was a medical corpsman during the war and later worked in a field hospital. When it was over, the Army had all kinds of hospital supplies and equipment they didn't want to haul back to the States. Salvi sold a lot of it to the French at a good profit—100 percent in fact. When he got out of the Army, he bought some farm equipment and went into custom farming. He was one of the first to own a combine around here. He has a lot of dealings with Milo Hogg, the bank manager. Hogg's got a big mouth about other people's business, including Miss Charlotte's. He told Salvi he'd like to get his hands on Greyledge—said he wouldn't mind getting his hands on Miss Charlotte either, but laughingly said, fooling with that woman might be risky."

"Because Charlotte might call in her out-of-town gang

to riddle him with bullets?"

"Probably. Salvi thinks Hogg isn't any more sure about that story than the sheriff."

"Well, Lyle, back to your proposition. If Salvi comes, I suppose Charlotte would just assume I arranged it."

"Then again, Jude, she might want to know how you knew who to contact; she might ask a lot of questions. When that lady gets pissed, she doesn't get over it just for money. I hope we don't end up with two more bullet-riddled bodies buried out behind the barn?"

"Nice collection: a husband, one honey dipper and a white slave. You really don't believe she had John Paul killed, do you?"

"No, I think if Miss Charlotte wanted him dead, she wouldn't of hired it out."

Jude could not tell if Lyle was joking or if he really thought Charlotte killed John Paul.

"Let's take the risk," Jude said, treating it as a joke, but still wondering.

"OK, I'll call Salvi tonight; I expect he'll bring his nephew to help him. If you don't want them to see you, you better get scarce about Wednesday. What you do about the corn is up to you; it's going to take a lot of hoeing to save it. When it's ready you'll have to pick and husk it. I'd be satisfied with just a little pocket change for planting it. If you can save it, I'll have Salvi pick it up. Meanwhile, Jude, I've got to see if I can drive that truck."

Jude looked down at Lyle's injured foot, now red and quite swollen. Small wonder the man had a tendency to wince from time to time as they talked. "I suppose, if you can't drive, Aunt Millie will have to take you home."

"Sheeeit, Jude, if you ever saw her operate that rattle-trap you'd know I'd rather wait 'til Charlotte came home and shot me."

As it turned out, Lyle was able to move around pretty well by walking on his heel and directing his injured toes upward. He pulled himself up into the truck without any help and tried the peddles. "OK, Jude, I think I can make her go." He started it up and hollered down to Jude, "It's been fun—I hope you enjoy the rest of your vacation as much as you enjoyed today." Jude waved as the truck jerked down the drive, then tossed his tools in the bucket of the tractor and drove back to the barn.

By the time Jude completed his list of supplies for Aunt Millie, he felt rested enough to deal with her. He knocked on the kitchen door and went in without waiting for her response. She turned away from what she was doing at the sink and said, "Oh, it's you. Look like you and Lyle finally finish dat mess. Guess it good you here when Lyle git stuck. Good, too, you happen long when Miss Charlotte fall off the horse. Ah can't decide you bring trouble or angels send you. Since you name after a saint, though, I startin take hope."

Jude was glad she had warmed up a little but was irritated over what she and others thought his name rep-resented. He was not about to waste any time telling her how he came by it, though, and just said, "I have the list of stuff I need from the store."

"Can't you see my hands is all wet, jist read it to me."

"There are 15 items, can you remember all that?"

"Ah don't, we try 'gin Monday."

After he read his list, she took a paper shopping bag

from the cupboard and began to fill it with spices, soap, matches and other odds and ends.

Jude said, "Whoa, don't give me all your stuff; you'll need it."

"Won't be long, Miss Charlotte gonnna trick you into cooking for her. Ah's gonna git all fresh spices, make sure mine tastes better'n yours. The grass seed, can of gas, and other stuff Ah gonna bring Friday."

"If your cooking tastes as good as what I'm now smelling, you don't need to worry about whose cooking is going to taste best." He took the bag and headed for the door, "Thanks for the stuff." She waved at him like it was nothing.

Late afternoon, Jude went down to the pond, where he lathered himself all over and plunged into the cool water. When he came out, he dried himself and lay naked on the smooth rocks. The late afternoon sun was still warm, and a slight breeze kept the insects away from his exposed body. He speculated that this piece of outcropping is why this farm is called Greyledge. He closed his eyes and wondered about Charlotte's child, the car in the pond and John Paul's disappearance. She couldn't have killed him—Lyle must have been joking.

4

Jude was awakened by a loud bang and a rattling sound. He did not realize he had dozed off until Aunt Millie started her car to go home. Is Charlotte back? If she comes looking for me, ... He scrambled into his clothes. No evidence of her up at the mansion, yet. He walked slowly toward the house, hoping to see her little car coming down the driveway; when he didn't, he went up and sat on the porch to wait. It was a long time before he saw her car stop up at the main road, apparently at the mailbox. Then she turned into the drive and sped toward the house. Jude barely had time to get to the carriage house before she pulled in. He was opening the car door for her before she had the engine shut off. "Oh Jude," she cried, reaching up to him from where she sat, "save me from this cruel world."

He lifted her from the car and held her close. She melted into him like a child seeking comfort; but after a few seconds he could feel her stiffen slightly and knew this precious moment had come to an end. "Could you grab my crutches, Jude? Also that bundle on the seat?" As they made their way into the house, she was far less jaunty than when she had left in the morning. She dropped into the large leather chair in the study; then acting as though she was too far gone to speak, she gestured toward a cabinet and weakly uttered, "Scotch, Jude, Scotch, look in that cabinet; that's where the liquor rests when it's not being abused." Inside, Jude found a store of hard liquor, including the brandy he and Lyle had shared earlier in the day. As he drew the bottle from the cabinet, she asked if she could have it over ice, and suggested he join her.

"You wouldn't by chance have a beer?"

"I think there are a couple left in the back of the re-frigerator; help yourself."

Soon he was back, one drink clinking cheerfully and the other still in the bottle. "Oh God, Jude, you have saved my life again." She raised her glass and said, "Here's to the miracles you perform." He grinned and, not knowing what to say, raised his bottle high in response and joined her in the first sip.

"Jude, you wouldn't believe those damn students today. Usually, when I return their first papers with red pencil marks all over them, they just sulk; but this bunch cried and shrieked like babies. They even started to get personal. One whispered that he wished I had broken my other leg as well. Later, to top it off, I had lunch with several colleagues and related some of this crap to them. The head of my department, who's a very tense twit, said, 'After all Charlotte, these summer courses are 100 percent tuition supported. If you offend the students, we may lose enrollment and not be able to offer the courses next summer.' I told him, in my most solicitous voice, which to my surprise is said to be sarcastic, 'No kidding, Karl, if I had only known, I would have given them all As.' He really hates that kind of exchange, especially in front of his brown-nosing department members. My afternoon class wasn't quite as bad; but, by then my knee was on fire, so I finished rather out of sorts. Could I have another Scotch, or would you think I'm a bad girl?"

"I like bad girls."

"Come on, Jude, I bet you've never known a bad girl; on the other hand, just in case you are a lecher disguised as a nice young man, give me only half."

Jude felt she needed to relax, so he was generous. He was also hoping she might loosen up enough to talk about some of the mysteries associated with her. When he returned with her drink, she said, "That's yours," pointing to the package she had asked him to carry in from the car.

"Christmas in July?"

"Maybe it's a bomb, open it carefully."

Inside was an assortment of clothing and a pair of work shoes. "Gee, Charlotte this is real nice. Does this mean you want me to stay for awhile?"

"Naw, it's just that when you leave, I don't want you to reflect badly on Greyledge. . . . So, now you know the real reason I was down at the cabin snooping in your stuff Sunday. I was checking your sizes."

As he tried on the work shoes, he laughed at himself for thinking she was trying to find out about his personal life. "I feel badly that, on top of your difficult day, you did all this shopping for me."

"It was the best part of the day—the clerks were even nice to me. What I hope now is that tomorrow you'll make a nice hot fire and burn your Army clothes, including your boots, and even that pup tent. The reason I'm so sensitive about this stuff is the sheriff is convinced that I murdered my husband. He comes snooping around from time to time. It would be difficult for him to understand why I have cashed in John Paul for an AWOL soldier." Even with the elevating effect of the Scotch, her lower lip quivered a little when she spoke of John Paul and the sheriff. "Come on, Jude, let's eat," she said, with a little bravado in her voice to conceal her upset. "Help me up, and we'll see how Aunt Millie felt about our dining together."

Although the house had a large formal dining room, the kitchen had a cozy dinette area; Charlotte rarely used the dining room. The pot on the stove had been left on "warm." Jude looked in and said, "It looks like some sort of stew."

"Probably, pork and greens," Charlotte volunteered, "not exactly a summer dish but one of my favorites. I hope you're not put off by it."

"I've never had it, but I'm not afraid of it. What do you want to drink?"

"I vote for red wine; but, before you vote, I should warn you it won't make me any more sober. I don't become dangerous when I'm crocked; but, I do become talkative, so if you think I already talk too much, you better vote 'no.' Your vote counts more than mine because the wine is in the basement and you're the one with the legs."

"I like hearing you talk: I vote 'yes.' Is the basement as scary as the attic?"

"I never thought so, but I suppose we each have our own collection of demons we bring with us when we enter strange places. If you become edgy, try singing a cheery tune."

Jude had never seen so much wine in a private home; there must have been over a hundred bottles. He had no knowledge about what would be a good choice, so he just picked one with an interesting looking label.

"That was quick," she said, "but an excellent choice."

Charlotte suggested Jude put the French bread on the table. Then he poured the wine and sat down. Raising his glass, he said, "Here's to a better tomorrow, starting today."

"Oh, yes, I'll drink to that," she said, clinking her glass against his.

They ate enthusiastically, sipping their wine and chatting about trivial matters. Finally, Jude said, "I checked the fields today; some of the grain can still be saved, but we'll have to move fast."

"That's great, Jude, if I can get anything out of it, I'll be elated. I really appreciate your taking the initiative on this."

"You're welcome, Charlotte, but this doesn't mean I'm now your sharecropper—I'm still on vacation."

"That's a relief, I was afraid I might have to share some of the profits with you," she joked. "I thought about calling someone and have been struggling to remember the name of the guy we had last year. I think Lyle called him Salvi, but I don't know whether that was his first or last name, or a nickname."

"I'll check it out and see what we can do."

"That'd be great, Jude. Do you think we'll have a crop next year, too?"

"Hard to say how long a good vacation should be pro-longed. In the event I do start scratching around in the soil, though, one of the things I would want to do is put in a cover crop on that first field back of the barn. For some reason, it has a lot of secondary soil on the surface and it's also all roughed up. Why was that piece treated so badly?"

"Jude, could I have another glass of wine?" They had finished what was on their plates. Jude picked them up and said he really enjoyed Aunt Millie's cooking and was going to have more, "Should I add some to your plate, too?"

"No thanks, Jude, I sit around too much; it would just turn to fat."

He served his plate, poured more wine and waited for her to tell him about the field. Just as he thought she was going to ignore his question, she said, "That's where they think I buried John Paul."

"Your husband? That's where they think you buried your husband?"

Charlotte had become silent. Jude sipped his wine and watched her struggle—somewhere else. She came to with a start not sure how long she had been gone.

"I'm sorry, Jude, for leaving you alone at the dinner table; the question you asked about the field was reasonable enough; it just doesn't have a short answer. It's one of those things I haven't been able to talk about, not even to myself. I'm not sure I can talk about it now, but I'll try. I think it would help. I suppose it seems strange, that I would want to tell you about it. It's hard to believe I've known you for only three days."

Jude didn't say anything. He just watched her and listened—nodding slightly to encourage her. Finally, she said, "The second year I was married to John Paul we had a baby girl. Margaret was beautiful—she brought joy to our lives. If it hadn't been for her, our marriage probably would have ended somewhere in its third year. I blamed John Paul for our miserable marriage—he had so many faults—but now I see a lot of the problem was with me. I didn't love John Paul—probably never did."

"Do you remember why you married him?"

"He was fun—always ready to go wherever I wanted . He was handsome and dressed nicely. When we were out together, I knew women were watching him and envying me; I liked that. And then of course there was his mamma, who didn't want him to marry me. That provided me with the challenge of taking him away from her. John Paul and I had little in common. In retrospect, our lives were pointless."

"You had Margaret."

"Yes, and we both loved Margaret dearly, in our own way; but, I have to admit, she responded better to him than to me. The job of disciplinarian was left to me, while John Paul played the loving, indulgent father. She would some-times ask why I was so mean to her, why I wouldn't let her do things daddy let her do and why I yelled at her so much. They spent a lot of time together, talking about little things and laughing at nothing. They often whispered to each other as though they had special secrets and I was an outsider."

"That must have hurt."

"You couldn't guess how much. Throughout all of this, our marriage continued to deteriorate, but we kept it from Margaret, and from ourselves. He gambled, drank and, on occasion, enjoyed low-class women; but, I don't believe it was so much from his ravenous sexual appetite as it was trying to prove to himself that he had any appetite at all."

"And you couldn't divorce him because of Margaret."

"Yes, but I can't put all of the blame on him. I wasn't very understanding, and I certainly didn't make him feel good about himself. Only recently have I come to realize that a lot of his drinking was to give himself enough courage to tell me how he felt about our marriage. When he was in his cups, he liked to call me a sharp-tongued, selfish, spoiled bitch. Somehow, I thought that because I won all the arguments, I was right all the time and he was wrong. Only recently have I realized that when you win an argument, you don't win anything, you just alienate people. Funny, Jude, I sense that you've known that for a long time. But, even though I have now finally figured that out, I still do it, no matter how hard I try to hold back my mouth, there it is, out there well ahead of my brain."

"You give me too much credit. I just have a touch of shyness that causes me to pause before I speak."

"Jude, you think before you speak. Even a split second can make a difference. Anyway, when Margaret was nine-years-old, we were off on one of our frequent visits to John Paul's parents on the other side of the county. The family car was a four-door Cadillac, left to us by my daddy. At the time, I loved it; but John Paul wanted to get rid of it. It was several years old; and, as with most cars of that period, the back doors were hinged in the back and opened from the front. You know what I mean?"

"Yah, we had an old Ford like that. The doors locked by raising the handle, and they opened by pushing the handle down."

"Yes, that's what this was like, but they had started to make cars with back doors that opened from the rear and locked by pushing down a pin on the window ledge. The newspapers had recently published several articles about children being killed or injured by accidentally unlatching the car door and being pulled out when the wind caught the door. John Paul wanted one of these new cars, but I argued that Margaret was old enough to understand about the car doors. I told him, 'Every time there's something I like, you try to spoil it for me; if you're so worried about it, I'll sit in the back with her.' I had been doing this for about two years."

"Did it bother John Paul to be alone in the front?"

"Yes, he said it looked like I was mad at him. On this particular day, Margaret wanted to ride in the back by herself. She said she was too old to have her mamma sit in the back with her. She promised to be careful about the doors. John Paul let her have her own way, as he usually did. We were running a little late, which was my fault because at the last minute I couldn't find one of Margaret's shoes. John Paul was irritated. He normally drove too fast; but, this time, he was trying to establish a new record. At one point, going around a curve, I found myself holding on to the door handle to keep from being tossed to the left. When I realized what I was doing, I panicked and looked back at

Margaret; she, too, had grabbed the handle. Almost immediately the road curved back the other way and we were both
pressed against the doors. Margaret screamed as the door
flew open, pulling her out into midair and dropping her on
to the highway. She tumbled like a rag doll along the road as
I watched helplessly out the back window. I could hear
someone screaming hysterically; I didn't realize it was me.
By the time John Paul was able to stop the car, we were
well up the road. We ran back to where she was lying, all
broken and bleeding, she looked up at us and said, 'Daddy,
Daddy,' and died."

Throughout her narration, Charlotte sat erect—almost
motionless, her eyes filled with tears. Now the tears overflowed and ran down her cheeks and she began to sob. Jude
wanted to take her in his arms and hold her; but the best he
could do was stand awkwardly beside her with his hand on
her shoulders and draw her against him. She tried to wipe
the tears with the back of her hand. Jude handed her a paper
napkin.

"Thanks, Jude, I think I'm OK now. God, that was hard to
do," she sniffed. "I'm sorry I had to put you through that. I
was hoping to do it with a little more dignity—but at least
its done, I think I'll be able to face it better now. It's funny,
a lot of what I told you, I didn't know until now—you know,
the details of the accident, and even my interaction with
John Paul and Margaret."

"Maybe some pain is hidden from us until we're strong
enough to deal with it."

"You're probably right, Jude. The days that followed—
the funeral and all—were like a foggy dream. I must have

been in some kind of a daze, or maybe I had departed from my senses, as some people have delighted in telling me. I'm not sure when I came out of it, but my first strong feelings were a loathing for John Paul. I blamed him completely for Margaret's death and was unmerciful in making him pay for it. At every opportunity I goaded him for driving too fast that day and for being afraid to arrive at his mamma's a few minutes late. I often called him a mommy's boy."

"What was John Paul really like?"

"John Paul had always been a quiet, sensitive person; but, after Margaret's death, he became sullen and resentful. We never talked about how we felt. What few conversations we had consisted mostly of me attacking him. With Margaret gone, I was free to point out all his deficiencies, especially how useless he had become. Our money was dwindling, but it never entered his mind to find a job. I had a lot to say about that; but, he would never respond—unless, of course, he was drunk. Then he always returned to his main thesis about how I caused Margaret's death by insisting we keep the car. Now that I've regained the details of what happened, I realize it wouldn't have made any difference if I were in the back. The accident happened so fast that unless I were holding her tightly at the time, she would have been drawn out before I could have reacted."

"Charlotte, I'm sure that's true. It's time to stop blaming yourself."

"It's hard not to, though. After the accident, John Paul's drinking increased, and so did the time he spent with low-class women. I asked him to move out of the bedroom, which gave him the excuse he needed to continue his behavior. He had long periods of dark brooding over Margaret's death. On one of these occasions, after he had been sullen and drinking all day, he got into the car and drove it over to the high bank of the pond. I thought he was going to try to drown himself and ran toward the pond yelling for him to stop."

"Weren't you tempted to just let him do it?"

"It crossed my mind while he was sitting there revving up the car. Then, he released the clutch and raced for the pond. He jumped out just before it went over the bank. The car disappeared, leaving only a column of bubbles and a multicolored slick of gasoline and oil. John Paul lay there on the grass for a long time. I kept calling to him across the pond to see if he was hurt; he told me to get my ass back in the house and leave him alone."

"I bet you were glad to have the car out of sight."

"Yes, and you were right earlier; after it was over, I was sorry he wasn't in it. That fall it was dry. The dam at the lower end of the pond had a leak in it; without a good flow of water, the surface level gradually dropped. Slowly the Cadillac came back into view. John Paul was incensed. One day, after it was about two-thirds exposed, he took daddy's deer rifle out in the backyard and started shooting at it."

"The trees weren't there then?"

"They weren't grown-up like they are now. He emptied a whole box of shells and went back in the house for more; he could only find another half-box but he shot those into it, too. Later in the week he bought two more boxes. He used one up and about drove me nuts with that constant bang . . . bang . . . bang, each dramatically spaced two seconds apart. I had a feeling that, in John Paul's mind, each bullet had my name on it. "

"That must have been unnerving."

"It was awful. But, that night it rained hard, filling the pond and submerging the car. I don't think I could have taken much more of it. Although the senseless shooting stopped, the rest of the game intensified. I had gone back to work on my book; the evening and the late night hours were the most productive for me. It was quiet then because John Paul was usually out carousing around until early morning. I tried to be in bed, though, when he came home because it was then that he would try to argue with me and blame me for all of the things that went wrong in our marriage, for Margaret's death, and for being insensitive to him and Margaret. One night he came home earlier than usual—drunk and despondent. He flopped in a chair and sat watching me. I was trying to get the kinks out of something I had written earlier, so I just ignored him.

"After a few minutes he quietly said, 'You think you're better'n, me don't you?'"

"That would have been difficult to respond to since you obviously were."

"Thanks for saying so, but that isn't what popped up in my mind. I stopped typing and tried to think of something to say that wouldn't cause a ruckus. Finally I said, 'No, I never think about who I'm better than; it doesn't make any difference to me.'

"'You always have the answer don't you, Charlotte—whatever it takes to make me feel small, you're right on top of it. You know why I can't raise a hard-on when I'm around you? It's because you don't make me feel like a man with a hard-on anymore.'

"'I guess you had a bad night, huh?'

"'See? That's just what I mean. You didn't ask, 'What can I do to help,' or even say 'You're sorry you make me feel this way'—oh, hell no, you have to infer that I've been cheating on you and even that didn't work out for me. The trouble with our marriage doesn't have to do with who killed Margaret, it has to do with who killed John Paul. All these years you've lorded it over me about your fancy education in northern schools and your sophisticated fucking in Paris, and then you expected me to raise a hard-on at your beck and call. Well, let me tell you, Charlotte, from now on I'm calling the shots, and right now, I want you to get your ass upstairs into the bedroom. I'm reclaiming my rights.'

"I told him, 'John Paul our relationship is too far gone for me to indulge your fantasies. If you can get it up, I'd suggest you go masturbate—and no, I don't want to watch.'"

Charlotte noticed that Jude flinched slightly, and said, "I guess you can see, Jude, that what they say is true. I do have a talent for selecting words most likely to piss people off. John Paul became livid. He walked over to me; and, as I tried to get out of my chair, he hit me on the side the head, knocking me to the floor. While I was lying dazed, face down, he jabbed his toe under my shoulder and rolled me over, then he reached down and ripped my blouse open. He tried to rip my bra off but it held fast. 'Take it off, bitch,' he hollered, 'and, next time I tell you to get ready to fuck, you get ready or I'll kill you. I don't have any other reason to keep you around; it sure wouldn't be for your cooking.'"

"I stood up and told him, 'I'm not going to take any more of your abuse. Pack up your shit and get out.'

"'Oh sure, bitch, always talking like it's YOUR farm! Read the will! Your daddy left the place to both of us. We're as married to this farm as we are to each other. The only way this will be your farm is for me to die—with a divorce, neither of us could afford to buy the other one out. So, as long as we're stuck with each other, from now on, we're going to do it my way.'

"I had never seen him this way before: it was as though all of his brooding hatred boiled over. He came at me again, with his arm back and his fist clinched. I gave him a quick shove that caught him off balance. He fell backwards and landed on his rump near the fireplace. Jude, he was livid. He grabbed a piece of firewood and came at me with an insane look in his eyes yelling, 'Goddamn it, bitch, don't think you've won again. From now on you do as I say or I'll lay your head open.' I told him he knew were he could stick his firewood. His face turned purple with rage. 'OK, bitch, you been asking for this.' He raised the club back and took a hard swing at my head. If he had connected it would've killed me. He was either drunker than I thought or he really had gone nuts. Fortunately, I threw my arm up and ducked. As it was, he scraped the skin off the front edge of my forearm. I was really scared: not only did it hurt like hell, it was clear he really could kill me. He was staggering a little and trying to position himself for another swing. I recovered enough to kick him in the balls. While he was hunched over with pain, I took a shotgun from the gun cabinet. He watched in help-less disbelief as I loaded it, clicked the safety off and aimed it at him.

"'QUIT SHITIN' AROUND, CHARLOTTE, YOU'RE GONNA HURT SOMEBODY.'

"He was hunched over, holding his crotch with one hand and reaching the other one toward me at arm's length, like he was trying to stop traffic.

"'Make no mistake,' I told him, 'your philandering, drunken life is over; I've had enough of your crap and there's no chance you'll ever be any different.'

"I was feeling light-headed and so nauseated I had to keep swallowing or I would have vomited. I wasn't sure whether it was from the physical pain or from the disgust I felt for John Paul. Finally, he dropped his club and began to cry, and make a lot of stupid promises we both knew he'd never keep. I was afraid if I put the gun down, he would kill me."

"You and your shotgun were in control."

"I'm glad John Paul realized that. What he said next was, 'Charlotte, if you want me out of your life, I will disappear. I could do that. You don't have to shoot me.'

"'Sure, John Paul, you could disappear until the next time you get drunk, then you'd be back here again to rape or kill me.' At that point, I realized I wasn't going to shoot him; or, I wouldn't have been talking about it—but he didn't know that.

"'If you kill me, Charlotte, your life will be over, too. Or did you forget what they do to murderers? I know you're smart, Charlotte. You could hide it and say I went away. But, you won't own a damn thing, not even that stupid little car of yours, because everything is in joint ownership and I'd just be missing.'"

"Was he right?"

"Yes. My head had started to clear now so what he was saying was soaking in. He had thought about this more than I had, apparently in one of his sober moments.

"Maybe he had thought about killing you at some time earlier."

"God, that hadn't occurred to me. I bet you're right. But then, of all the things to happen, there was a short knock on the door and his mother waltzed into the house, calling, 'You hoo, you hoo.' She had been at a church function over in Charlottesville. Knowing we were usually up at that hour, she decided to stay overnight with us. It took her awhile to stop babbling and focus on what was happening. When she saw me standing there in my tattered shirt, with a bloody arm and a shotgun pointed at her sobbing son, the best she could manage was, 'My word.' John Paul got up and started to move toward her. I raised the gun back to my shoulder and shook my head in a menacing manner. He settled back down on the stool by the hearth.

"So far, neither of us had said anything to his mother. Finally, I told her, 'This is a bad time for you to drop by, Theda; I was about to shoot your drunken, whoremonger son.' She must have been in shock. She just stood there with her mouth open, as though she were about to speak, but nothing came out.

"I really didn't know what to do; but, at least I was holding their attention, so I hung on to the gun. I told her, 'I'm sorry you've blundered in on this ugly little family drama, Theda; now you are going to have to watch me kill your son.'"

"Theda finally found her speech, 'Why ever would you kill John Paul, Charlotte?'

"'Because if I don't kill him, he'll kill me. You should have seen him tonight. He just tried to beat my brains out with that club of wood.'

"'Why don't you just divorce him?'

"I said, 'I really don't think a sheet of paper makes any difference to a mindless drunk.'"

"How did she react to that?"

"Jude, you wouldn't believe it. Theda calmly pulled out a chair and sat down at the table. It seemed pointless to continue the gun waving, so I sat down, too. After we were settled, Theda said, 'Charlotte, I can understand how you feel about John Paul after what he did to you tonight; but, you don't want to kill him. Earl and I are aware of John Paul's drinking problems. In fact, we've had to bail him out of several things you probably don't even know about. We've thought the best solution might be an institution where he could get some help. Our lawyer told us that having someone committed isn't easy; but, if John Paul would sign himself in to a place like Pine Crest, they're equipped to deal with cases like this. John Paul, of course, refuses to go. We couldn't convince him that it was just a matter of time until he killed someone with his drunk driving or violent behavior.' She turned to John Paul and asked, 'How do you feel about it now, John Paul, now that you've nearly killed Charlotte or she you?'

"'I can stop drinking. I don't need to go to any damn institution.'

"'Haven't you said that before?'

"'I suppose so, but this time I mean it. I'll be fine, you'll see.'

"Theda got up from the table and said, 'If you decide to kill him, Charlotte, don't expect to get away with it.' She looked at John Paul, sitting on his stool, said 'good-bye' and headed for the door. He began to plead with her in a most sickening way. Jude, I felt more like shooting him then than at any time since Theda arrived. Finally, he agreed to treatment."

"That Theda is one tough lady."

"She sure is. And next, the tough lady says to me, 'Charlotte? You willing to let John Paul go home with me?'

"'I don't know, maybe—but whether or not the cure takes, I want a divorce; and, I want this farm in my name, as well as all the things in it, except for John Paul's personal belongings. I'll put his stuff in a box and put it on the porch tomorrow afternoon.'"

"Charlotte, you were pretty resilient to bounce back from such an emotional event and be able to negotiate like that."

"Gee, I guess I was—now that you mention it. Anyway, Theda said, 'I would agree to that in an instant, but I expect Earl will want to poke his nose in. Without the benefit of tonight's disgusting performance, he might not appreciate our arrangement. His major concern in life is his social and political image. He worries constantly that John Paul's behavior will affect his position in the legislature or spoil his chances of going to Washington. He would be pleased if John Paul would take the cure, but wouldn't want it known that his son is confined to an institution. The divorce and property arrangement he probably would go along with as long as they aren't made public. If we hush John Paul off to Pine Crest, you'll need to keep quiet about all this. So, what I'm saying, Charlotte, is that John Paul goes on an extended trip; and, you don't know where he is. If that trip ends favorably, when he returns, you can get a quiet divorce and keep the farm. If you become impatient and make public noises, you'll end up with your little red roadster and your lingerie—Earl wouldn't fit into either of them.'

"Earl is a large man?"

"Not tall but round.

"Then Theda went on to tell me,'Charlotte, you know John Paul wasn't this way when you married him. He was a handsome young man with a bright future—that's why you married him. Whether you ever loved him or not, I don't know; but, I do know you're the one that drove him to drink and to other women. I'll never forgive you for what you did to my son.'

"Before I could respond, she continued, 'Aside from all that Charlotte, do we have a deal?'

"'Yes. He can have three minutes to throw some of his things in a suitcase; the rest will be on the porch tomorrow afternoon.'"

"Is that the scar?" Jude asked, pointing to a small white streak on her forearm.

"Yes. It healed fairly well; the psychological mess has been harder to repair."

"You seem fine now, but I'm sure you went through a lot of pain. That was two years ago? Where's John Paul now?"

"It's closer to three years; he's still at Pine Crest,

incognito."

"The cure didn't work?"

"Worse than not work. His loving mama set him up with an allowance so he could live comfortably in his new home. Later she discovered he had the janitor buying booze for him. John Paul and the night nurse were having private parties. He shared his booze with her and she shared her body with him—and her syphilis. Apparently she contracted it while she was a nurse in the Pacific during World War II."

"How do you know? Have you been in contact with his mother?"

"No. I'd never call Theda. I went out to Pine Crest a few times to check on his progress. He looked terrible—gaunt, unkempt and demoralized. He didn't know when he would be released and didn't seem to care. After trying to communicate with him for some time, I left. About a year later, Theda called me to say that a quiet, out-of-court settlement now provides free room and board for John Paul. Earl had one of his lawyer friends talk to them about their negligence in allowing John Paul to contract syphilis from one of their nurses and their failure to diagnose it before it caused irreversible damage. They screen all patients for venereal diseases when they enter the hospital, so it didn't occur to them to treat him for syphilis. I visited him six months ago; his condition wasn't improved. So, Jude, I guess that's the state of my marriage."

"I'm really sorry you've had all of this disappointment and pain to live with."

"Thanks, Jude. But, you know, what continues to bother

me more than anything? It's my failure as a mother—that Margaret preferred John Paul over me, even at the end— when she was dying. I try not to think about it; but, since John Paul left, old conversations with Margaret and John Paul replay in my mind. I think I understand better now what bothered them. Most of it had to do with them feeling that I had to have everything my own way."

"Was John Paul so surly before all the trouble began?"

"You mean before he fell into the hands of the wicked bitch?"

"Charlotte, I would never say nor think that. I can't imagine you in that role."

"Don't be fooled, Jude. Theda was probably right; I wasn't good for John Paul . . . but then I'm not sure another woman would have been any better. At one point in our lives, I tried to get inside his shell—tried to understand his hurts and silent brooding. Guess I thought I could help him. It didn't work—he wanted to suffer. He'd pull in things to brood about that most people wouldn't give a passing thought to—trivial comments I made years earlier. When I tried to put these things in perspective for him, it was always, 'Sure, Charlotte, that's what you say now; but, it's not what you thought when you said it,' or 'That isn't the way it happened'—anything to continue his hurt. When I felt my-self slipping down into his depression, I stopped trying."

Neither of them had touched their second glass of wine. Charlotte stared thoughtfully at hers without seeing it and said, "Jude, I'm unbelievably exhausted; this has been a full day. Normally, I'm able to do the stairs on these crutches but just for tonight would you mind helping me up to bed?"

"Sure, I'd be happy to." He carried her up to the bedroom, then returned for her crutches.

She opened her eyes when he returned and said, "I'm going to lie here for a minute before I get ready for bed; but, before you go, thanks for listening so patiently. Maybe next time we can do your story?"

"Oh, I don't know. I could give you a few clumsy sentences; but, I don't have the way with words that you do."

"You don't talk much, but what you do say is well-phrased. I'll bet this secret life of yours includes a college education."

"I went for a while, but didn't finish." Jude flushed a little over the attention being focused on his personal life. "I'll go now so you can get some sleep." He wanted to express his feelings for her, but did not know how or if he even had a right to.

Sensing his awkwardness, she took his hand, squeezed it and said, "Good night, Jude." He kissed her on the forehead and turned toward the door. "Jude, you always make these sexual moves on me when I'm too weak to defend myself." As he went down the hall, he thought, what she's passing off as a joke is not that far from the truth, as measured by the pressure against my jeans.

Despite her weariness, Charlotte noticed his hard-on. She found his restrained horniness amusing but was glad it was restrained; she was not ready for a relationship; and, even if she were it would not be right. Leading Jude on would only result in his eventually being hurt; nothing could come of it. On the other hand, she was surprised at her reluctance to dismiss the fantasy from her mind.

I don't even know him. I'm the one with all the conversation. Let's see, what has he told me so far? God, almost nothing—what, two dozen sentences? As she tried to remember them, she fell asleep—fully clothed.

5

Jude spent the morning hoeing corn and watching for Salvi. When it became too hot to work in the field, he opened the big doors at either end of the barn to let a breeze blow through. Although Alfred had become used to the harness hanging on the peg next to his stall, he did not like the way Jude was walking toward him with it. He tried his old trick of sticking his rear end in the way so Jude could not come alongside him; but, suddenly the thing was tossed up over his back and there he was wearing it. Such indignities are not born lightly by a stylish riding horse. Alfred fussed back and forth on his short tether and whinnied in protest over Jude's ignorance about how to treat a first-class animal.

Out in the training ring, they went around the track a couple of times with Jude walking behind Alfred hollering whoa and pulling back on the reins to enforce it, or yelling giddyup and smacking him lightly on the rump with the reins. Gradually, Alfred lost his stubbornness and even reached the point where he was willing to pull objects behind him, like boards and a bundle of brush, with a minimum amount of stopping and looking back.

When Jude returned to his cabin, his eyes fell on the new clothes Charlotte had given him. He was still wearing the Army fatigues he had promised to burn. "Shit, I better get out of this outfit before Charlotte sees it and revokes my slave license." He sorted out a new set of clothing and went to the pond to bathe.

After dinner was cleaned up, Jude settled back in a chair with *Plantation of Hope*. There was little doubt about it; Miss Ashley, apparently based on Charlotte's grandmother, was a rare woman. Today, she would be nominated for the Nobel Peace Prize; but, not back then, especially if her neighbors discovered she was sleeping with the enemy. But, who was the enemy? At one time or another she had bestowed her favors on men from either side. It was not that she was promiscuous; in fact, she was fairly discriminating about the men she took to her bosom. It was just that her discrimination was based more on character than on politics or race.

She ran a tricky business with Confederate and Union troops under the same roof and officers and men intermingling; she had only *Miss Ashley's Laws* for guidance. She was aided somewhat by those accustomed to gentlemanly ways, who *reminded* unthinking individuals that they were guests in Miss Ashley's house and might not wish to offend their hostess. A few had to be asked to leave before their travel arrangements had been completed, and others had to be buried at night out in back. Such disquieting matters were not revealed to Miss Ashley until long after the war when some of her visitors returned to thank her for helping them to continue living. It was fortunate that the burials were not behind the barn or Sheriff Batley might have found some bones as evidence against Charlotte.

What Jude was convinced would be the downfall of Miss Ashley's *Plantation of Hope*—patrols searching the premises for deserters—turned out not to be a problem. Several things helped; one was that Miss Ashley's safe house was not widely known among troops until late in the war. By then, morale was so low that desertion versus dying seemed to be the only alternatives. Another was that rumors of this path to freedom were not likely to be passed on to high ranking zealots who might wish to destroy it, but Miss Ashley still took defensive action. She had a tunnel dug from the basement to a well in back of the house. Although it entered the well above the water level, it was deep enough so the tunnel opening could not be seen from above. The well opening was hidden in shrubbery so anyone emerging from the well would have cover.

Only members of one patrol were aggressive enough to enter the house; they were so apologetic about it that they did not search effectively. Miss Ashley had a way of charming and shaming them, so they were willing to settle for a drink of water and go on their way. As Jude put the book down and prepared for bed he wondered if the tunnel was still intact.

The next morning Jude hoed corn for awhile but most of the day he spent preparing for his dinner guest and training Alfred. At the same time he fretted over what to tell Charlotte about his life—about events so upsetting that two years later he still had to work actively to keep them from his mind. Now, he would have to recall them; and, with the stress of Charlotte focused on him, try to find the words to make her understand.

In the late afternoon when Charlotte returned from her teaching job, she wondered if there would be a meal for her down at the slave quarters. She freshened up and was about to go out the back door, when the front doorbell rang. Now, who could that be? When she opened the door, there stood Jude with a bouquet of zinnias he had picked from Lyle's abandoned garden. "Good evening, Miss Charlotte." He bowed slightly and held the flowers out to her.

"Jude, you are a nut—I love it." As she took the flowers, she looked past him; there in the driveway was Alfred harnessed to the two-wheeled cart she used to ride in when she was a child. "Oh, my God, how did you ever get him to do that?" She threw her arms around Jude and gave him a big hug, which she broke off with a fit of laughter, and then invited him in. She led the way to the kitchen, limping a little but without using crutches. She found a vase for the flowers; and, after arranging them, stood back and commented on them admiringly, "OK, Jude, I guess I'm ready for dinner, but my guess is you didn't have an opportunity to visit your vintner today. It so happens that I know where these people keep their wine; it's down those stairs. While I get my sweater, see if you can find a bottle you think might go well with your dinner and another one to flavor the story of your life after dinner."

"I was kinda hoping you'd forget about the story of my life and we could just have a good time."

"Well, we're gonna do that, too. There must have been some things in your life we could laugh about. Heck, after a bottle of wine, even my story lightens up."

As Jude went down to the wine cellar, he realized that Charlotte was in much better spirits than before. Confronted with the wine, he again had no idea what to select; he finally decided to pick a red one and a white one. He intended to maneuver her into choosing the one to open first so he would not have to reveal his ignorance. When he presented his choices, she said, "You have such excellent taste in wine, Jude, those are two of my favorites." He smiled, pleased with himself, but then, how could he miss? The whole wine cellar was stocked with her favorites; she had selected them all.

Other than having to look back at the carriage a couple of times, Alfred conducted himself admirably well. Jude drove the carriage in through the big barn doors, said, "Whoa, boy," and the buggy ride was over.

While Jude put the horse away, Charlotte expressed amazement at how clean and organized the barn had become in such a short time. "Are you happy with your new life, Alfred?

"This isn't a new life for him, it's just an expansion of his old life; he'll still be privileged to carry Miss Charlotte down the lane and through the fields."

"Oh, no he won't, this poor body has been jarred and broken too often to play that game anymore."

As they walked slowly toward his cabin, accommodating her limp, Jude told her, "I'm sorry to hear that; I so enjoy seeing you ride. It's like watching a lovely ballerina on stage."

"Jude, where do you get that kind of blarney? Do you have some Irish in your background?"

"No, my father was English and my mother Latvian, so there's no room for blarney I just know a quality act when I see it."

When they entered the cabin, it was clear to Charlotte that serious preparation had gone into her visit. Pieces of chicken were marinating in a bowl, a salad was in another bowl, and little potatoes were washed and standing ready for some kind of treatment. "Did you bring a corkscrew?" he asked, placing the bottles on the table.

Pulling one from her purse, she handed it to Jude, "Like your Boy Scout knife, I'm never without it."

Jude put the opener on the table and went to the cupboard for water glasses. "Wait, Jude, I almost forgot, I brought you a present." And out of her purse came two thin, long-stemmed goblets wrapped in tissue paper. "Why don't we christen these tonight?" She went to the sink, rinsed and dried them, and handed them to Jude."

"These are beautiful, Charlotte; but, they do sort of remove my dinner from the rustic class."

She could not be sure whether he was offended by this redefinition of his dinner or whether he was pleased. However, she could not drink wine from a water glass anymore than she could drink it from the bottle. As for Jude, he was not sure how he felt about it. At first he was a little irritated; but he finally admitted he would probably let Charlotte do anything she wanted to. He would wind up liking it, so why even consider such a small issue?

"Bring the bottle and glasses and I'll grab the rest of these things. We have to do some outdoor stuff to our dinner now," he said. A small fire not far from the cabin had been burning for hours and had turned to hot coals. Charlotte picked up the white wine and bottle opener, and Jude's problem of which of the wines was appropriate for his dinner was solved.

Jude had found a grill that apparently had once been the shelf of a refrigerator. He placed it over the fire and laid the strips of chicken on it, along with the little potatoes, and pieces of zucchini squash, dipped in corn oil and sprinkled with garlic and herbs. "Now, Charlotte, it's time to pour, while the fire works its magic on our dinner." He took the bottle from her and motioned for her to sit down. The furniture consisted of a log, flattened slightly on the upper surface. Side by side, they sipped their wine and watched the hot coals sizzle and brown their dinner.

The wind had died leaving the surface of the pond like a mirror. Occasionally a fish would poke his nose up through it to suck in an insect, leaving a series of concentric rings to mark the target area.

They were both quiet, absorbed in the beauty of the evening. Finally, Charlotte broke the spell, "I told you this was a wonderful place for a vacation, but I didn't realize you would be able to improve on it so. You've accomplished so much in such a short time—all unbelievable. Jude, this is the first time I have had any sense of well-being since Margaret died; I can honestly say that tonight I'm happy. Who said slavery was so bad? Jude, are you a happy slave?"

He was startled by her question. Although he amused himself with the thought that he was a slave on this plantation, he was surprised to hear Charlotte verbalize it. "Not many slaves get to serve in such a vacation atmosphere, and none have ever had such a beautiful mistress. How could I not be happy!"

Jude sounded just corny enough to cause her to hit him on the arm and exclaim, "Come on, Jude, you've gone Irish again." He jumped up as if to escape her attack but actually to turn the things on the grill. Dinner was served on a box, turned upside-down for a table. He poured more wine and joined Charlotte on the log. She raised her glass and said, "Here's to the good times! We rarely recognize them until they're passed; but, this is a night to make note of now, and to remember forever."

When they finished eating, Jude said, "OK, let's build up the fire; it's starting to get dark. We'll want good light and a hot fire for what is going to happen next."

"Oh, you have a program planned?"

"A small ceremony." He gathered the dinner materials in the box they had used for a table and headed toward the cabin. When he returned, he emptied his knapsack of Army clothes on the ground; and, as the flames leaped up over the fresh firewood, he picked up a pair of Army fatigues and proclaimed: "This burning symbolizes the end of my heroic life as a defender of freedom; it salutes the emergence of a new and happier life wed to the soil."

Charlotte raised her glass high and shouted, "Hurray! Hurray! Here's to the new master of the earth." They were on the second bottle of wine, and their spirits were elevated enough for them to enjoy this backyard theater. Each piece that was tossed on the fire was accompanied by some commentary like: "There goes my grunt suit, or farewell to my formal attire or, Charlotte, don't miss the sex appeal in these long johns."

When the last piece hit the flames Charlotte held out her hand for Jude to help her to her feet. She gave him a round of applause, then suggested they go in, "The mosquitoes have found me."

Jude's bit of theater came as a great relief to her. She had been nagged by a small concern that at any time he might say, "Thank you, Charlotte, it's been a wonderful vacation, now I'll be moving on." Clearly he planned to stay and do something with the farm.

"Before I go in, though, I believe I should use your outhouse; you don't happen to have a flashlight, do you?"

"Yes, I'll get it." Jude was amused over his apologetic feelings that the outhouse was the best he could offer her. At least there's toilet paper, and she doesn't have to use the Sears and Roebuck catalog that someone installed earlier.

When Charlotte returned to the cabin, she looked around, and as if seeing the place for the first time, was struck by its austerity. This run-down shack, that had been in her backyard all her life, evoked different feelings now that it was occupied by someone she cared about. Charlotte, she mused, you weren't bothered when families of black sharecroppers lived here. After all, your original intent was to use this kid and not care whether he got to enjoy life's luxuries. If you're not careful, a decent caring person is liable to emerge and destroy the selfish, mean bitch image you've preserved for so long. A slave is a slave is a slave. They had no choice—maybe Jude's choices as a fugitive aren't any better. Let's get on with his story, so you can find out if he's safe to have around.

Charlotte went to the sink where Jude had placed a wash basin, soap and towel next to a bucket of well water. When she was through washing, she did not pour the water down the sink for fear it would run out on the floor.

Jude had put their glasses and wine bottle on the table and pulled out a chair for Charlotte, who sat down but then got right up again. "Jude, I don't know how you can stand that overhead light. When I get smashed, my image is reflected best by candle light." She went rummaging through the cupboards until she found a couple of old candles. They mounted one candle in the empty wine bottle, the other they let drip into a saucer and stuck it in the puddle of wax. After they sat down again she smiled and took his hand into both of hers and said, "I really am enjoying this, Jude; I hope it hasn't been too hard on you." She felt guilty about her internal conflicts regarding Jude as a slave or Jude as a friend and wanted to return to her good feelings.

"It wasn't hard on me. I enjoyed putting this together. The hard part will come in telling the story of my life."

"I suppose we could skip that part if you wish and let your first glimpse of life begin with a woman riding a horse down a lane."

"I really wish that had been the moment of my birth—not as a baby, of course—it takes a full-grown hormone system to appreciate that scene." He blushed a little, then asked, "Do you want the full story or the abridged edition?"

"Oh, I'm prepared for the full story. Who knows, it

might be exciting enough for me to steal and publish."

"Then, instead of having just the folks in Grimble County on your case, we'd have the United States Army looking in on us."

"It's hard for me to believe that such a nice young man could make them mad enough to come way out here in the hills looking for you."

"They ought to come out here and give me a medal; but, you know how most people are, they can't tell right from wrong, they're only equipped to respond emotionally."

"That's pretty profound for a man as young as you. In fact, Jude, you may even be approaching cynicism. Tell me about your childhood."

Jude nodded thoughtfully, struggling to select a beginning that would show that he was not always cynical. "I grew up in a real nice town . . . Menominee. It had everything a kid like me might have wanted . . . . It's on a small bay off the northwest coast of Lake Michigan—beautiful yacht basin—full of elegant boats. One of the concrete walls of the yacht basin was set up for swimming: life guards, free swimming lessons, high and low diving boards—the whole works. Not only did the town have Cub Scouts and Boy Scouts, they even had Sea Scouts with their own inboard motor launch. The school was a combined junior and senior high—equipped with everything; even the teachers were pretty good."

"Sounds like Eden."

"Yes, but Billy didn't appreciate it. You remember Billy? I mentioned him the first day we met?"

"Yes. I remember."

"Anyway, the things I liked about Menominee didn't mean much to Billy; it was the human interactions he couldn't cope with. He and his parents had moved next door to us shortly after World War II started. I was in the eighth grade, Billy in the seventh. We didn't see much of each other. It was winter; Billy didn't show up at the public ice rink or on the hill where the other kids skied and rode sleds. Nor did he join us on Friday nights at the Boy's Club to watch war movies and sing patriotic and campfire songs.

"One day, at the beginning of summer vacation, I was trying to learn to swim. There were ladders along the breakwater at 30-foot intervals. I was flirting with the excitement of seeing if I could swim from one ladder to the next in water over my head. All of a sudden this great blob sailed off the dock and landed next to me; half of Lake Michigan went up in the air and came down in a frothy spray. Then, right in front of me, shooting up from the depths and into the air, came this grinning cherub—Billy had been let loose. He paddled easily to the nearest ladder and hoisted his young, walrus-like body on to the dock where he grinned and yelled down, "'C'mon, Jude, let's go off the high dive.' It didn't enter Billy's consciousness that I could barely swim, much less go off the high dive. Without looking back to see if I was with him, he scampered up the 10-foot tower and with no hesitation ran off the end of the board, drawing his knees up and forming another one of his famous cannonballs. This was Billy at his best, uninhibited, confident, and happy—this was the summer Billy."

"That's the kind of reckless abandon I had as a kid."

"It isn't gone."

"For the last several years it was at low ebb but I have a feeling it's still there."

Jude smiled and gave her a reassuring nod, then continued. "We spent the rest of that summer in marvelous exploration. Billy was a fountain of ideas, knowledge and energy. We started a small business fixing bicycles, played Monopoly and chess, and went camping by a small river several miles from home. We fished, swam and cooked over open fires. We talked endlessly about becoming famous explorers in the Arctic or along the Amazon. God, how we laughed—at each other, at our parents at our teachers; we even laughed at Turk."

"Who was Turk?"

"Turk was an older kid—a brute. Billy despised him. It wasn't often that he laughed about him. I'll tell you more about Turk later. First, though, I should tell you about Billy's mother. She was young to have a kid Billy's age. He figured she couldn't have been more than 17 when he was born, maybe younger. On the other hand, his father was old, well above the age he could be drafted.

"I thought it was strange the way Mrs. Krammer used to flirt with me. I was just a kid; I had only started to shave that summer."

"She was probably just testing to see if she could still attract attention. What did you think of her?"

"Even though I now despise her after what happened, back then I thought she was pretty interesting. She had black hair and dark eyes that twinkled with mischief. She also had a nice figure and moved in a sensuous way, not like other mothers. I enjoyed watching her."

Charlotte's eyes twinkled, "Sure, just a nice horny little neighbor boy."

"I suppose I was, but I barely knew what sex was about."

"Did you know Billy's dad?"

"Not well. Billy didn't think Calvin was his real father. He claimed Calvin married his mother after she was pregnant—some kind of Christian act to earn him a ticket to heaven. The man apparently went to church quite a lot and held strong moral opinions about how to live. Billy said that some of his relatives enjoyed pointing out to him how much he looked like his Uncle Fred. He thought it was funny to be the love child of an incestuous relationship between a brother and sister."

"He's lucky he wasn't born with extra fingers and toes."

"Yes, that's one of the things we joked about. Summer ended too soon, especially for Billy, who couldn't come to grips with going back to school. Once it started, we saw little of each other. We didn't have any classes together, except for gym, where two grades were combined. Occasionally I saw him on weekends; but Billy was a drag, the spark was gone and in its place was a perpetual sour ass."

"Even in gym class?"

"Especially in gym class. That's where it became clear there were two Billys: a summer Billy and a winter Billy. The other kids, and even the gym teacher, picked on him, mostly because he was overweight—Billy always made matters worse by his hostile response."

"Did he get in a lot of fights?"

"No. Profanity was his specialty—the uglier the better. The war was entering its second year; it permeated everything; physical education was consumed by it. The gym teacher—the kids called him General Krumholtz—had been in the service for awhile and had learned some soldier-like behavior he insisted on sharing with us."

"That really hard-nose stuff like they show in the movies?"

"Yes. That's what it was like. At the beginning of each period, we were assembled into platoons for inspection. Krumholtz had four student lieutenants, each of whom commanded a platoon. These lieutenants were the high school's star athletes: Holtz, Turcott, Schmartkin and Grymkowsky. They walked up and down the ranks with Krumholtz carrying clipboards, recording the merits and demerits of their troops, based on how clean and well-pressed their gym uniforms were or the condition of their fingernails, but especially, how neatly one could suck in his belly and stick out his chest."

"Oh, God. I'll bet that was Billy's downfall."

"Yes. Every gym period a certain amount of time was spent by Krumholtz and his lieutenants trying to get Billy to draw in his belly so it wouldn't protrude beyond his chest. Failing to execute this trick resulted in demerits, not only for Billy but for his platoon as well. If Platoon C missed being chosen as the best unit of the day by a few points, it was Billy's fault, so the whole platoon would be on his case."

"Like being low score on a relay team in the Olympics."

"Yes, same situation. With Billy it didn't end after

inspection. Next we were required to run the commando course: climb ropes, crawl though tunnels, jump across pits and walk logs."

"I bet that was perfect for tormenting little fat boys."

"I'll say, and the lieutenants added to it by yelling at us and timing our performance. Billy always took a lot of crap. In the competition among squads, his low scores provoked groans and insults."

"It must have been humiliating."

"I'm sure it was, but Billy never mentioned it. Whenever possible, he would sneak out right after roll call. At the last gym period of the year, Krumholtz delivered a farewell speech. As he was rambling on, Billy faded back, slipped under the bleachers and headed for the showers. Shortly after he had his water temperature adjusted, Turk swaggered in. He patted Billy on the ass then shoved him aside and took his shower."

"Nice guy. What did Billy do?"

"He bellowed, 'Come on Turk, that's my shower.'

"'Fuck you, you little fat-ass, that's yours over there.' Turk was right, of course, being a senior and half again as large as Billy. Graduating as a three-letter athlete, Turk was about as big a hero as the school had available—even though, he was a flaming asshole. Billy didn't tell me about the shower incident until several days later; by then, he had turned into the summer Billy. The beach had opened; and, although the water was still cold, he was well insulated. He alternated between paddling about in the water and doing somersaults and cannonballs off the high dive. Billy was fully restored from the agony of school. I stood around shivering in the cool breeze off the water while my lips turned blue."

"Were you able to pick up where the previous summer left off?"

"Pretty much. Our main place of business was on my front porch. Mom worked long hours as a nurse at one of the war plants and dad had been drafted into the Army in early spring; we were left alone—free to discuss any subject we pleased—in its appropriate language. We played a lot of chess. Our games were occasionally interrupted by Turk and Holtz, who cut through the yard and stopped briefly to exhibit their ability to piss people off. First it was, 'Hey, how do you play this game? Hey, why don't you jump that guy?' And before long it was, 'Shit! That's a dumb game. C'mon, Holtz let's go see if Billy's mother has some beer.' Usually she did; it pissed Billy off that she shared it with such assholes."

"His mother must have been desperate for company."

"She probably was. Billy's father had a truck and ran a lunch business for defense plants. He was up early in the morning making sandwiches, then hustled off to hit the lunch periods for the different shifts. He was totally oc-cupied about 16 hours a day. Billy's mother, who pre-ferred that I call her Jane, devoted much of her time to reading *True Romances.* "

"My mother subscribed to that and several like it."

"One day, after the two of them had spent about five minutes on my porch with their dumb talk, Holtz said, 'Shit, this is boring. Let's go over and fuck Billy's mother.' Billy acted like they said the same thing they always said about checking for beer. He yelled after them, 'Yah, why don't you? We don't need any more of your shit around here.' Billy continued his air of bravado throughout the game, but played badly; and, after a half an hour, conceded the game."

"Did you ask Billy if Holtz had upset him?"

"Yes. He just said, 'Hell no, but it pisses me off to go home and find empty beer cans all over the kitchen table, and to know my mother has been drinking with the enemy; whatever shit comes out of their mouths is nothing to me. Besides, in a month or two they'll be off to the Army where I hope they get their asses shot off.'"

"Did he go home then?"

"Not right away. He picked up a *Popular Mechanics* magazine and thumbed through it. After while, he said, 'They've probably finished mom's six-pack by now, guess I'll go home and yell at her like she does at me when I fuck up.'

"He didn't come back that evening—nor the following morning. Finally, I went over and called for him. His mother answered the door; her eyes were swollen and red like she'd been crying: 'Jude, I don't know where Billy is; I thought he was with you.'"

"She didn't say anything about what was upsetting her?"

"No. She just said, 'Maybe he's gone to the beach.' I told her I'd check in the garage and see if his bike's gone. It was there, where he kept it near the door, so he could grab it in a hurry. As I was about to close the door and leave, I saw him—just a shadow in the dim light at the back of the garage—hanging from the rafters. I just stood there frozen as Billy's body turned slowly in the murky light."

"Oh, Jude. That must have been just awful for you."

"I was numb. Jane kept calling from the porch—asking, 'Is his bike gone?' I tried to answer but nothing came out. She could see me standing there in the doorway. Finally, she came down to see what was the matter with me. I just pointed.

"'Oh, my God, no Billy, oh no.' She screamed and ran over to him hugging his legs and crying, 'Oh no, Billy,' over and over."

"Did you go in the garage with her?"

"No, I was frozen, except for the tears that welled up in my eyes—they still do when I reflect back to the age of 14, the day I lost my best friend. All I could think was, Why, Billy? For Christ's sake, why? We could have talked about it—we could have dealt with it."

"Did Billy's mother try to get him down?"

"No, she eventually gained control of herself and became aware of me. She told me to go home, 'There's nothing we can do for Billy; I'll call the police.' I went home and sat alone on the porch. The police came, an ambulance came, and a small crowd gathered while they loaded Billy into the ambulance. The police talked to the people standing there, they talked to Billy's mother; his father came home; they talked to him, then they went away; and, the neighborhood was silent for the rest of the day."

Charlotte's eyes filled with tears that ran down her cheeks. Jude's eyes were moist, but he was trying hard not to let go. It was not until Charlotte took him in her arms and held him close that he let go and broke into convulsive sobs.

"It's as though it just happened. I can still see Billy hanging there in the garage, as I stood there dumbstruck."

It was the first time in all those years that Jude released the pain he was carrying. It was continuously with him, sometimes intense, sometimes underlying, but always there. After awhile, Charlotte kissed him on the forehead, on the check, and then on the mouth—that brought him back to the present. He smiled weakly and asked if she would kiss him every time he cried.

"Probably," she smiled.

"Charlotte, on occasion you've referred to yourself as a bitch; you simply are not a bitch."

"Most people have trouble seeing me in any other role. I suppose one's personality depends on the company they're in. Maybe the *bitch disease* is similar to alcohol addiction. Like a *recovering alcoholic* one can become a *recovering bitch*. I notice that since you arrived, my anxieties and irritations are much reduced. But, don't drop your guard. Even a recovering alcoholic can have a good run and still fall off the wagon.

"So what happened when your mom came home?"

"She got home around dinner time—tired but in good cheer. She gave me a pat on the shoulder, which is as close to a hug as a mother can give a teenage boy, then set about preparing dinner. While she worked she chatted about things that happened at the plant. Suddenly, she stopped talking, looked at me and said, 'What's the matter?' I tried to answer, but nothing came out. 'Jude, what's wrong?'"

"Even if you had your voice back, it would have been hard to answer."

"Yes. I kept trying to tell her but nothing came out. My mind was flooded with the vision of Billy in the garage, turning slowly at the end of the rope. Finally, I got a piece of paper and wrote, 'Billy is dead.'

"'Oh my God! What happened?'

"He hanged himself," I wrote.

"'Why? For God's sake, Jude, tell me what happened.'

"All I could do is shrug and shake my head."

"Did your mother ask if you were the one who found him?" Charlotte said.

"Yes, and when I nodded that I was, she said, 'Jude, you shouldn't worry about not being able to talk. Sometimes that happens when you see something frightening, but your voice will come back.'

"I wasn't concerned about not talking, I didn't want to talk. After a few more questions and more head shaking, she said, 'I guess I better go over to the Krammer's. I don't think much of that woman; but, at a time like this, the Lord would want us to set our pettiness aside.' She didn't stay long. When she returned, she didn't look very satisfied."

"Did she tell you why?"

"'Not really. She just told me what the Krammers said, which I guess wasn't much. Mrs. Krammer kept telling Mom, 'It's all my fault. It's all my fault. We had a terrible argument, he was very upset; it's all my fault.' And Mr. Krammer said, 'Somehow the good Lord will see us through this.' He also told Mom the police wanted to talk to me, but decided to wait until she was home. Mom wanted to know how I felt about talking to the police? I told her, 'I hate cops, but I suppose they have to talk to someone who knows something about it.' Joy spread over her face at the sudden return of my voice. She hugged and kissed me and promised to cook me a wonderful dinner."

"Right there, Jude, the cooking part—that's where I always came up short as a mother."

"You always had Aunt Millie."

"Not the same."

"When the police came, they wanted to know if Mom and I had a chance to talk about what happened. I said, 'no'; Mom said, 'a little.' The two cops looked pleased that Mom had not had an opportunity to coach me. If she had known what was about to come out of my mouth, she would have told me to keep it shut—and rightly so. My comments accomplished nothing; they just added more grief to what the Krammers already had and sent me down a painful path.

"The conversation moved slow and easy, like the cops didn't expect me to know much—what the heck, nobody else did. So—did I start off explaining how unhappy Billy was with school, like the others; and, how kids teased him about being overweight? No, I got right to the point and let them know about Turcott and Holtz."

"Oh, God, Jude, you didn't!"

"Yes, Charlotte, I'm afraid I did even though Mom said,'Jude, you sure you want to talk about this?'"

"I told her, 'If anyone gives a shit about why Billy killed himself, I have to tell them.

"Then, I told the cops, 'It was because of those two assholes.' And I went on to describe the afternoon beer parties and about Turk's last comment, 'Let's go fuck Billy's mother.'

Jude blushed and said, "Sorry, Charlotte, I guess when I talk about this, it's like I'm reliving it, language and all."

Charlotte smiled, unconcerned about his word choice. "I'll bet your audience was spellbound."

"Oh, yes, especially my mother, who didn't know about my rich vocabulary. The cops asked if I thought Billy had caught Turk or Holtz in bed with his mother. I said, 'I don't know. Billy thought that part was all bullshit, that all they did was drink beer with her.'

"Two days later Turk and Holtz stopped me on the street. They shoved me against a building, slugged me a couple of times and demanded to know why I told the cops all that shit. I tried to act like I wasn't scared, 'What the hell should I have told them? You were so proud of your visits with Mrs. Krammer, I thought you wanted the whole world to know you were fucking her.' That wasn't the right answer. Turk let me have the first one in the gut, then they took turns pounding on me. Holtz tried to kick me in the balls; but I turned just enough to avoid a direct hit. They left me slumped against a building with a big bruise on my thigh, one eye closed and a couple of cracked ribs. They promised to catch me later in a less public place to finish the job."

"How did you get home?"

"I limped slowly. It really hurt. About halfway home, a neighbor woman saw me and gave me a lift. She wanted to know if I had been in a fight. I told her 'no, I was a punching bag.'

"When mom came home, she found me curled up on my bed sobbing. Against my wishes she called the cops. A uniformed police officer came, took a few notes, and asked if we wanted to press charges. Mom said 'Yes'; I was less certain. A few days later, the cops told us that, since I suffered no permanent damage, they were viewing this as just a squabble between kids. We should work it out for ourselves.

"Later, I heard that the cops also decided not to do anything about the drinking parties with Mrs. Krammer. If Turk and Holtz were old enough to be drafted, they felt it would be ridiculous to discipline them for drinking beer underage. It would be even sillier to charge Mrs. Krammer with anything in view of the risk the draft board was submitting them to. In the very next drawing, Turk and Holtz went off to war."

"How did you and Mrs. Krammer get along after that?"

"She avoided me at Billy's funeral—and for about a month afterward, but then, one day we met on the street. She was her old self, all smiles and charm. 'Jude, I'm so glad I ran into you like this; but, I must confess I really don't know what possessed you to say those awful things about me and those two boys. I can only believe that it had something to do with the terrible shock you suffered after finding Billy like that. At any rate, the police now know that none of it was true. The entire horrible thing was the result of a little argument Billy and I had over his going back to school in the fall; apparently he had become despondent over it and let it grow out of control. I hope we can still be friends.'

"Sure, if you think that's how Billy would have wanted it. "Charlotte, her smile disappeared in a flash, but then returned just as fast. That was the first time I realized how unstable phony smiles can be."

"Yes, funny isn't it when people do that?"

"I didn't hear the real story about why Billy killed himself until seven years later. Meanwhile, the war rumbled on and I bumbled along with my life. When I returned to school in the fall, I had little interest in social contacts— mostly, I was alone. My mother worked long hours; when she came home, she did household chores, wrote to my dad, and had a nightcap before she went to bed. We didn't have much that would interest each other anyway. She was usually tired from being overworked, and I was usually morose.

"When the letter arrived from the war department that my dad had been killed, we were both already so low that it was hard to believe we could sink any lower, but we did."

Charlotte said, "The downward spiral takes place in a dark and bottomless pit."

"Yes. I was a lot like you said you were when Margaret died. I don't remember much about that time in my life. Dad's body was shipped home and we buried him. My mother's nightcaps increased and she lost her job. We had to sell the house and move to more humble quarters in an apartment. Mom got a part-time job as a school nurse, which provided her with more time to expand her nightcap project."

"Did you try to help her?"

"I got her to go to Alcoholics Anonymous for awhile; but she really didn't want to quit drinking or even live for that matter. She wasn't offensive when she drank, and she managed to stay sober during the day to keep her part-time job.

"We took an apartment in a house that belonged to a Mr. Janik. He had a garden in the back, but was too old to do much with it. He talked me into taking it over. I also fished and hunted quite a bit with the equipment my dad left. In total, I produced about three-fourths of the food the three of us ate—counting Mr Janik."

"You still have a strong tendency to forage off the land."

Jude was pleased she noticed. It was something he took pride in.

"School wasn't a strong force in my life. I was attracted to several girls, but too shy and socially clumsy to do anything about it. Some girls tried to help me with my problem, but I wasn't a good student. This activity did gain the attention of my mother, though, who felt it was time to warn me about the dangers of sex. It was during one of these mother-son sessions that I found out the origin of my peculiar name. It turns out that my mother had become pregnant prior to wedlock; and, after several months, her father had a talk with the man she was dating and explained, 'Under these circumstances it would be *judicious* of you to marry her.' My father and mother were both relieved and amused that the old man reacted so calmly and rationally. His use of the word *judicious* continued to amuse them right up to the time they entered my name on the birth certificate as *Jude*. "

"A more appropriate origin than what Aunt Millie suggested."

"Sainthood? That takes too long."

"My last two years in high school, I picked up enough steam to get into Michigan State. I was surprised at how much I enjoyed living in a dormitory with other young people; I began to feel like a regular person. Probably escaping from what was left of my life in Menominee was the best thing I could do. I had to work pretty hard to survive, though. Some things came easily for me, like English, history and biology; but math, chemistry and physics canceled my good grades. I worked in the dormitory kitchen to supplement my meager resources."

"Is that where you learned to cook so well?"

"No, what little I know comes from cooking over an open fire while camping and also from having to shift for myself during the war years.

"During registration for classes the second year, I met Trudy, who changed my life. She was a first semester freshman, on the verge of tears over her class schedule. As a mature and all wise sophomore, I was able to save her and, henceforth, became her protector."

"Just like us," Charlotte chirped.

"That'll be the day! I might be able to save your life once in awhile; but there's no way I could protect you from getting into trouble. Trudy, on the other hand, needed almost constant protection. She was away from home for the first time and didn't want to be. Her parents had insisted that she go away to school to help her grow up. She was trying to flunk out so she could go home, even though she constantly made noises about how hard she was trying. At the same time she was making plans for us to get married. This idea seemed unreal to me. I had more than two years of school to finish; and, after that, two years of service obligation. As long as I was in school, I was deferred; but, if I stopped going or graduated, I'd be off to Korea."

"Hey, you were like a moth flirting with fire."

"Isn't that the truth! We were both in love for the first time and not dealing with it well. We had built a strong dependency on each other that was self-destructive."

"Mumm," Charlotte said, sipping her wine thoughtfully, "and it was the first time you'd ever been laid."

Even in the flickering light of the candles, Charlotte could see Jude blush; she was delighted she could do that to him with so little effort. After he recovered, he continued. "Sex was probably a driving force in our relationship, at least for me; but, it may have been more of a tool for Trudy, who was using it to achieve what she wanted."

"What was that?"

"Me I guess. Trudy was one of the few people I knew who managed to flunk out of school in one semester; usually it took at least two. We were home for the holidays when her news arrived. She called and tearfully urged me to come to her house for the last half of the holiday break. They lived in Saginaw. I soon discovered that what she really wanted was to talk me into not going back to school—but I did."

"Good for you."

"Yes, except Trudy's letters and phone calls kept me on the hook; I was hitching rides to visit her on weekends instead of studying. Trudy had a job clerking in a clothing store and seemed to like it. After a couple of months, she began to change. Particularly she became less interested in sex. She never had been real interested, but now, after I had traveled all that distance, she simply tolerated it or made some excuse to forgo it completely. I kept inquiring about it until finally she blurted out that she was doing it with her boss and he really knew how to turn her on. She even described the things they did: my embarrassment and disbelief stimulated her into giving me all the vivid details. This was not the same girl I knew at Michigan State."

"So you dumped her?"

"I'm not sure that's how I would describe it. In spite of this, she wanted to go ahead with our wedding plans. Since her boss was married and had a couple of kids, she saw her affair as something that would pass. It was purely physical, she said, but I was her long-term plan. I went back to school in terrible condition. I still loved her and needed her; but, on top of it, I was humiliated that my sexual performance was so uninteresting that she took up with a married man. I couldn't study; I couldn't sleep and was incompetent at my kitchen job. I went back to Saginaw a couple times to try to work things out. Trudy felt there was nothing to work out. 'Look,' she said, 'until you finish that school shit and are ready to settle down so we can start a family, I will continue to fuck Tony and give him whatever else he wants.' Actually, Charlotte, she didn't say, 'Whatever else he wants,' she was more direct about what he liked and used words I have trouble saying in front of you."

"Jude, if you continue to read my books, you'll realize I'm familiar with a lot of the words Trudy might have used and the things she did. She probably wanted you to know how sophisticated she had become compared to you."

"Well, it worked. She made me feel like a nerd. That was the last time I went back. She wrote and called me, and she and her parents even drove down in a family effort to tell me how great it would be once we're family. In the end, I did nothing and simply let life suck me down the drain. I flunk-ed out. Instead of going home to face my humiliation, I got a summer job and shared an apartment with some other losers until my draft notice arrived."

"Weren't you concerned about being sent to Korea?"

"Somehow the prospect of getting my ass shot off wasn't real to me. I guess I was too beat down to care. I certainly didn't hear any ring of patriotism in my ears about going to the defense of my country. The cause was too subtle for me. I just couldn't believe those people posed any threat to us— shit, they didn't even have a navy. What the hell were they going to do, attack us in bamboo sailboats? At any rate, I was off to Fort Knox to learn the art of war."

"Jude, you look exhausted. You get up a lot earlier than I do. Would you like to finish your story another time?"

"I didn't realize I was going to turn myself inside out and show you all my scars. Yes, we better take this up later; the rest of the story will take even longer if I tell it in the same kind of detail."

"Under no circumstances would I want you to tell it in less detail. You're really very good at this once you get started."

6

Jude was finishing his lunch when Charlotte tapped on the door and came in imitating her mother-in-law's, "'You hoo, you hoo.' Am I too late for a sandwich?"

"No. Not at all; sit down; I'll make you one."

With her sandwich and tea and Jude sitting across from her, she smiled impishly and said, "Now."

"Now?"

"Yes. Now," she said, shifting her rear about in the chair with antsy enthusiasm. "I want to hear the rest of your story. You were, 'Off to Fort Knox to learn the art of war.'"

"Charlotte, I've thought about it. You don't want to hear about that."

"Quit waffling, Jude, I cut out of work early hoping to corner you."

"You're going to be sorry you asked." Jude took a sip of tea and swallowed hard as he searched for words, then forced them out of his mouth, stiff and formal from somewhere deep within him.

"Fort Knox, Kentucky. . . . October 17th, 1952. . . . There were 250 of us, still in civilian clothes. They had dumped us out of the buses and arranged us in rows on the company street. Even though it was mid-October, and late in the afternoon, it was still hot; sweat ran down my back and soaked my undershorts. The training cadre: two sergeants and two corporals, stood out in front smoking and passing the time of day while we waited. One of the sergeants, the one doing most of the talking, looked familiar but I couldn't place him. Suddenly, a shiver ran through my sweaty body. I was overwhelmed with this feeling of—of—loathing? Disgust? Fear? I couldn't think—like I had some kind of mental block. I kept asking myself, who the hell is this guy? Did that ever happen to you, Charlotte?"

"Sheriff Batley affects me that way—like I'm about to gag."

"This guy's conversation was pretty amazing—the way he was willing to entertain his three comrades with stories about his ugly personal life—and this in a voice loud enough for all of the recruits to hear. But it was more than his crude talk. I felt like it was something out of my past. The other three spoke with the soft sounds of the South; his words seemed hard, like a Yankee's—like my own. Yes, in fact, this animal could even be from Michigan—from Menominee? My God! It's Turk! I became nauseated as that nightmare settled in around this brute. Turk, yes Turk, still the ugly beast he was eight years ago, except now his body was covered with a layer of fat that ran up his neck and into his face, recessing his eyes and giving him a piglike appearance. He looked even meaner now than he did when I was a scrawny kid in junior high. Now the son-of-a-bitch was a sergeant. I felt weak and helpless as I did back then when the two of them cracked my ribs and tried to kick my balls up into my abdomen. By the talk coming out of this pig-eyed bastard now, I couldn't expect much forgiveness if he recognized me. I felt my only hope would be to blend in at the reception center until I could slip away unnoticed to my regular training company."

"What an optimist you were back then, Jude."

"I'd say it was more like desperation. Anyway, Turk and Sergeant Crump, one of the other cadre, apparently had met somewhere earlier and had recently been reunited at the reception center. Crump asked Turk whether he and his wife were still together. I still remember his response word for word.

"'Yah, we're still together. I know she's fucking other guys; but, she's making a lot of money at it. The only thing that pisses me off is that she doesn't split the take with me. I told her several times to cough it up; but, she always had some excuse, like she bought some new clothes or paid our laundry bill with it or some kinda shit. Last night, after one of her excuses, I looked in her purse and found a whole wad—over $200. I took it and beat the shit out of her for holding out on me. She was going to run home to her mother, or kill me or something, so I threw her on the bed and fucked her. She fought like a wildcat. When I finished, I peeled off a hundred bucks and threw them at her. I told her, I bet you never made that much before on a single hump. She continued to wail and swear at me so I went out and got drunk.'"

"And this is one of the guys that was supposed to train you to be a soldier! Was she home when Turk came back?"

"Charlotte, that's exactly what Crump asked him. Turk said, 'Hell yes, where's she gonna go? Not home to her mama, I'll tell you that. Sheeeit, her old lady's a hell of a lot worse to live with than I am. She's born again. Christ! Her mother wouldn't let Ertha smoke, swear, or whore around at all—ain't much else she's interested in so what the fuck's she gonna do?'"

"I guess you know what I'd do."

"Yes, you'd go for your shotgun, but this bastard wouldn't have backed off the way John Paul did. Anyway, this all got interrupted when a second lieutenant arrived carrying a clipboard. Sergeant Crump called the troops to attention, and the lieutenant welcomed the new recruits to Fort Knox. Then he proceeded to let us know that we were Private E1s and said, 'E1s are the lowest form of life on this earth. They are, in fact, lower than whale shit, and you know where whale shit is? It's at the bottom of the ocean.' This information must have been pretty important since it was conveyed to us several times a day throughout the first couple weeks of basic training."

"Was it supposed to be funny or humiliating?"

"I don't know. We thought it was juvenile. Once the lieutenant completed his dumb little welcome speech, he turned his clipboard over to Sergeant Crump who called, 'Company, attention!' The cadre saluted the lieutenant; and, when he left, Crump told the company to stand at ease. Then, without explanation he started reading a list of names from the clipboard. After calling about 50 of them, he said, "The soldiers whose names I have called are in Platoon A; fall out and fall in over here." He designated a place on the road where they were to stand. When that was accomplished, he returned to calling names again. I was tense, 'cause sooner or later my name would be called; Turk could hardly miss a name like *Bartholomew*. Fortunately, he and the other cadre weren't paying attention to the name calling; and Turk's mouth was fully engaged when *Bartholomew* was called."

"You were lucky this time; but, you wait and see, I bet he's going to spot you yet."

"C'mon, Charlotte, don't get ahead of the story.

"After four platoons were formed, each of the cadre took charge of one and led it to its assigned barrack. Again, fate let me escape; I was assigned to Corporal Vitt's platoon; Turk was in charge of the platoon housed on the other side of the company street.

"Nearly two weeks were spent at the reception center where clothing was issued, eyes examined, shots given and humiliation administered. The third day we got our famous GI haircuts, which left only about one-fourth inch of hair. It was upsetting for some of the guys, but I was relieved. I thought even my mother wouldn't recognize me, much less Turk."

"I'll bet you were cute."

"Cute? I looked like a thug. But, after awhile, I kind of liked it.

"Let me tell you about the barracks. There were hundreds of them; all built during World War II and all the same: two stories high, faded yellow clapboard. Each floor had a row of upper and lower bunks along either side of a center aisle. Metal gym lockers lined the walls, and foot lockers were at the ends of the beds.

"Corporal Vitt was housed in a corner room, carved out of the main floor near the front door. He was a mild-mannered man compared to most of the cadre. Occasionally Vitt stopped to chat with the trainees. He didn't know a whole lot, though, about where we were to go for training. The *Army way* is for people at each level to know only what's necessary to function at that level. No one ever knew what was going to happen next until the order came down from above. Corporal Vitt believed we would be moved to our regular training company in a week or two, at which time we'd be reshuffled. Friends made at the reception center weren't likely to be part of the same training unit. I, of course, was anxious to know if the cadre here would be assigned to training units. Vitt said he was housed here temporarily until a new cycle started at leadership training school, where he had been assigned. He thought the other cadre were also temporary. Sergeants Crump and Turk were recently back from furlough after a tour in Korea."

"What did you do during all that time at the reception center—other than hide from Turk?"

"We scrubbed the walls and floors of the barracks preparing for inspection and guarded road crossings, buildings and other things that couldn't be stolen—and could be guarded without a gun. And we spent a lot of time standing in the company street—waiting."

"And all this time Turk didn't spot you?"

"No, at least I didn't think so. I was always maneuvering to keep my distance—always tense whenever Turk was in view. I was really relieved when one day we were told we had five minutes to get our shit together and get back in formation. Once we were reassembled with our duffle bags, we regrouped by a reading of names and left in the hot sun. An hour later the trucks arrived. As I climbed into the one I was assigned to, Turk walked by and said out of the corner of his mouth, 'Don't think I haven't spotted you, you little prick. This truck is taking you straight to hell.' Turk's mind must have reverted back to Menominee when I was a scrawny juvenile. He didn't see me as the well-built, five-foot-ten man I had become; but then, neither did I at that time."

"See, I told you he'd spot you. What did you say to him?"

"I said, 'Hi, Turk.' He said, 'Sergeant Turcott, asshole.'

"I got in the truck while he stood sneering at me with a satisfied look on his fat face. The truck rumbled and jerked across the base; when it finally stopped, it wasn't clear we had gone anywhere. We were on a company street with four faded yellow buildings, identical to the four at the reception center. I wasn't surprised to see Turk among the cadre. I watched as he scanned the clipboard with the barracks assignments and negotiated with the others for Platoon D."

"Had you made any friends yet to commiserate with?"

"I had talked several times with a guy named Tait from Southern Michigan. When we were dismissed to the barracks, I headed upstairs for the bunk most distant from the cadre room. Tait came along and took the upper bunk. We became pretty good friends, but he did snore. During the wakeful hours, I returned to brooding about Billy's death, trying to figure out why Billy killed himself, and where Turk and Holtz fit into it."

"I don't understand why Turk was still so angry with you after all those years—enough to follow you around for no apparent purpose other than vengeance?"

"Yah, that's one of the things I struggled with, too. It was probably just as well that busy work and the nonsense tasks associated with basic training diverted my mind much of the day. We had to memorize our eight-digit service number, rifle number, the hierarchy of our military units, as well as learn how clothes are hung, beds are made and things are arranged in footlockers—endless trivia. Presumably, the basis for all the ritual and indoctrination is to condition trainees to obey superiors without question. When we were watching World War II movies at the Boy's Club back in Menominee, I had wondered how it was possible to get 10 guys to stay behind and hold off an advancing enemy of thousands while everyone else retreated? Now I knew— obey without question and expect new orders to arrive before your position is overrun. It also helps to be less than 20-years-old and still gullible. The Army's picky rules served another function, though. They enabled the cadre to find something wrong with any recruit of choice at any time. This gave Turk ample opportunity to direct punishment at his main target—Private Bartholomew."

"He was that blatant about tormenting you?"

"Oh sure, it became routine. If I made one misstep in carrying out the *Army method,* Turk would holler, 'All right, Barf, give me 10 push-ups.' Last names were all that were used; Turk found Bartholomew too awkward, so he tried *Barth*; but, it soon turned into *Barf*. Some of the guys started calling me Barf, too, which pleased Turk. Before it got out of hand, though, I told a couple of the more sensible guys that I didn't like it; but, if they felt some allegiance to Turk, to go right ahead. They passed the word along and soon only Turk and a few of the other cadre called me *Barf*."

"The other guys must have liked you."

"Either that or they hated Turk quite a lot. I knew the bastard was watching for me to make a large enough mistake so he could really stick it to me. His opportunity came the day after I had had KP duty. I was usually dragged out the next day. When we were assigned to KP, we started at 4:00 a.m. and had to work until the evening mess was cleaned up at night. During a break from weapons class, I was dozing with my back against a building and my legs stretched out on the sidewalk. I was awakened by a painful kick in the ankle and Turk yelling, 'PULL IN YOUR FEET, ASSHOLE!' When Turk was up the sidewalk, out of earshot, I muttered 'son-of-a-bitch.' Corporal Gormy was just walking by—Gormy, who had always passed himself off as a nice guy, stopped and asked, 'What did you call him, Barf?'

"Nothing."

"'C'mon, Barf, you can tell me.'

"'Naw, that's OK.'

"'C'mon, Barf, what'd you say? I might enjoy it.'

"'I called him a son-of-a-bitch.'

"'HEY, TURK, YOU HEAR WHAT BARF CALLED YOU?'

"Turk was immediately interested and came back to hear the good news. 'So, you called me something, Barf?

Would you like to tell me to my face?'

"'No, I'd just as soon let it go. It just slipped out.'

"'What was it, Barf; it must have been pretty bad, huh?'

"'Yah, it was pretty bad,' Gormy volunteered, 'he called you a son-of-a-bitch.'

"'Oh, yes, that's bad. He could be court-martialed for that; but, since I'm such a nice guy, I'm gonna see if I can't get him off with just company punishment. You think that'd be fair, Corporal Gormy?'

"'Generous, Sergeant, but we have to give some consideration to dumb recruits who don't know any better.'"

"Were you scared, Jude?"

"Yes. I didn't have any idea what they could do. The following morning the first sergeant called me to the front of the company formation and announced, 'Private Jude Bartholomew will receive company punishment. This soldier has taken it upon himself to swear at a non-commissioned officer of the United States Army, a man who has served his country heroically in two wars. Private Bartholomew will report to Sergeant Turcott at 1800 hours for company punishment."

"This isn't looking any better for you. What's 1800 hours?"

"Six p.m. Turk equipped me with a shovel and pickaxe and marched me off to a field where a half-dozen tanks were parked. 'Here now, you fucking asshole, is where you will learn to dig a proper 6 x 6 x 6. It won't be the only one you'll get to dig. In fact, if I can arrange it, you're gonna get buried in the bottom of one of these before I go off to my next assignment.' Turk climbed up on a nearby tank and told me to start digging. With a pint of cheap whiskey and a pack of cigarettes, he leaned back against the turret to enjoy the evening.

"I tried to appear calm about his threat by asking if he knew where he was going next.

"'Motor pool—other side of the post. Don't worry, though, I'll have plenty of time to see to it that you eat at least a yard of my shit before I leave.' He washed this down with a gulp from his bottle like he really relished the thought."

"Finally, Charlotte, I asked him outright, 'Turk, how come you're still so pissed at me after all these years?' I'm not sure I was ready for the answer."

"Why? What did he say?"

"He said, 'Shit, Barf, you fucked me up pretty good back there in Menominee. You know Holtz and me had a slick deal going with Billy's mother. She was buying the beer and giving us anything else we wanted. If you hadn't shot off your mouth, me and Holtz could've gone back to bangin' her after she got through brooding over that fat assed kid of hers. It was your big, shit eatin' mouth that got us drafted early and got Holtz killed in the war. My old man could've pulled some strings to keep me out of the fuckin' Army altogether if he'd had a little more time. So, look what you did to my life, you little prick, I went through two fuckin' wars on account of you.' This sad story called for another couple of swigs from his bottle."

"'You ever feel sorry about what happened to Billy?" I asked him. By now I was working up a pretty good sweat from the digging.

"'Hell, no! The only thing I'm sorry about was that I didn't get to see him do it. That would've been great, you know, that fat little ass turning at the end of a rope.' This heartfelt commentary was worth two more slugs from the pint.

"By now, I thought he might be relaxed enough to tell me what really happened, so I asked him straight out, 'Why did Billy hang himself?'

"Weren't you pushing your luck with that question?"

"I wasn't sure, but he did tell me."

"Really! What did he say?"

"He was talking a little slurred now, but he said, 'Barf, you about had it figured; you just missed the best part is all. Think about it, there we are: me, Holtz and Jane, balls-ass naked on the bed when Billy comes walking in. Holtz has his face buried in Jane's muff and I'm sucking her tits. She's moaning like she's in seventh heaven—Billy just stands there with his mouth open, too shocked to excuse himself. We're all pretty hornied up and about half in the bag from the beer. Holtz and Jane don't know he's there until I ask him if he wants to join us. When Jane hears this, she looks up and just about shits. 'GET OUT OF HERE, BILLY,' she yells and tries to get up; but, I'm holding her down. Billy's just standing there like he's stunned.

"'You know, Barf, I always fancied that fat little ass of his in the showers at school. Now, I'm thinking it'd be great fun to stick my dick up it while his mother watched, so I runs around to the end of the bed and grabs him. He squeals like a young pig—and Jane's screaming for me to let him go. She keeps trying to get up, but Holtz is really into the spirit of the game. He pins her to the bed and rams his dick up her pussy while I pull Billy's pants down and lay him over the foot of the bed. He really yelled when I stuck it in him. Guess he didn't like it. I thought it was great. Sometimes I think I'd rather have a nice fat little boy's ass than a pussy. Hard to say, though. What do you think, Barf?'"

Jude stopped telling his story as though he was too disgusted to respond to Turk. Charlotte was anxious for him to continue, but his intensity and his struggle for words were part of his story. She would not wish to lose any of it. Is Turk one of the two people Jude is accused of killing? she wondered. The paper said one was a sergeant. If Jude killed Turk, will he actually come right out and tell me?

Jude continued. "I was too upset to answer. It was all I could do to keep from taking the shovel to him. As that thought flashed through my mind, I noticed Turk had a pistol holstered on his belt.

"'Huh, what'd you say, Barf, you ever try that fat little ass? Sheeeit! You were probably doing Billy's asshole long before I ever got to it. How 'bout his mother? You do her, too? Christ, that was one hot pussy. Best ass I ever had. I didn't hear you answer me, Barf—shit, you're such a square son-of-a-bitch you're probably still a virgin.'

"I took my anger out on the ground. It was mostly hard-baked clay. Without the pick, I wouldn't have progressed at all; as it was, Turk was agitated over how slow it was going and began to fret about running out of whiskey. By midnight, I still had a couple feet to go. Turk was quite drunk and had dozed off a couple times. His bottle was empty and his cigarettes were gone. He could see I was working hard but that didn't stop him from swearing and accusing me of fucking off. Finally, he ran out of patience and hollered, 'Isn't that fucking hole six feet deep yet?'

"I told him, 'Yes, I think it is, sergeant.'"

"Was it?"

"It was only up to my shoulders; six feet would have been over my head. But he told me 'OK, throw the pick and shovel out.' Then, Turk yelled, 'ATTENTION!' He pulled his Colt .45 from its holster, aimed it at my head, and drew back the hammer. I didn't know whether he was going to shoot me or not, but there wasn't a whole lot I could do about it except run around and around in a six-foot square hole. I was too tired for that; besides I didn't want to give Turk that satisfaction.

"'Well, Barf aren't you going to shit your pants or cry for your mother?'

"My throat was so tight I was afraid I would squeak, so I just stood there at attention. After what seemed like a long time, Turk put his gun back in its holster. 'OK, Barf, you can crawl out now; but, don't think I wouldn't a blowed your fucking head off, except too many people know we're out here. Maybe next time.'

"He tossed his empty bottle and cigarette pack into the hole and said, 'Bury 'em.' I was so weak from the emotional drain that I could barely shovel the loose soil back in the hole. It was after 1:00 a.m. when we returned to the barracks. I don't think I slept at all, but I was startled when we were called at 5:00 a.m. to begin the day. I did make it to breakfast, though."

"On top of the sleep you lost the night before, on KP, I

bet you were really beat."

"You would've laughed to see me. Whenever we weren't in motion I fell asleep—got hollered at a lot."

"For the next week or so, Turk was his usual pain in the ass self; then he was gone. Life became more bearable. We'd learned the routine stuff and the cadre eased up on the insults.

"Most of the guys in the barracks got along well with each other. The occasional fights that broke out were over superficial things and were usually smothered quickly by the others. A certain amount of good-natured teasing went on, but not all of it was humorous. Andre Roskov, the guy across the aisle from me, was often the butt of jokes. He stayed to himself, reading poetry and Shakespeare, brooding and writing long letters home. The Army was no place for a guy like that. He had very sad eyes—a washed-out blue color—milky white skin, and a slender build with round shoulders. His entire bearing exuded helplessness and hopelessness."

"They didn't let him have a gun, did they?"

"Yes, all the recruits were issued rifles, but for Andre that was just another problem. I remember when we fired for record with the M1 rifle, Andre was next to me on the firing line. Everyone was finished except for Andre, whose gun hadn't been making a whole lot of noise. When I looked to see what he was doing, he was timidly preparing to fire. He aimed at the target for a long time while the barrel of his rifle made nervous little circles. As he pulled the trigger, he closed his eyes and let the muzzle of his rifle drop. The bullet hit the ground 10 feet in front of him. He apparently had done this at each of the three firing distances. Finally, his coach handed me his leftover rounds and told me, 'Fire them into this guy's target or we're gonna be here till dark.'

"Guard duty at night with live ammunition was played up as a big event. We were sent to another part of the post to spend the night in the guard's barracks until our watch came up. Every two hours a group of eight was marched off to relieve those completing their watch. My turn came at midnight. We were given cartridges and told to count them, then under watchful eyes, to load.

"Andre was part of this guard detail. It was scary to watch him load a rifle; he was so awkward and so frightened of it that before he had it loaded he had pointed it at everyone in the detail. In the end, I helped him close the bolt for fear he would smash his thumb in the mechanism. At the order to shoulder arms, I wondered if he could bring the rifle to his shoulder and walk with it; but he did, and off we went with the sergeant of the guard singing—'hut, 2, 3, 4; hut, 2, 3, 4.' At every other street corner, one guard was left off with specific instructions as to what was to be protected. We were in the motor pool area, so some of us were guarding trucks, others had fuel storage tanks. I had a couple of blocks of warehouses; Andre was to protect the area next to mine, also a cluster of buildings.

"I walked slowly, checking doors to see if they were locked. The night was pitch-black and a little scary. I didn't feel prepared to shoot anyone, even a communist spy. As I reached the side of my territory adjacent to Andre's area, I was surprised to see a dim light and hear two people arguing. After listening for awhile, I realized that it was my old friend, Turk. He was giving Andre a hard time for not challenging him properly, not holding his rifle correctly, and for still being alive. Turk was in his drunken bully mood. From the way the conversation was going, it was unlikely that he had authorization to be in that area at night. I thought about calling the sergeant of the guard. This is done by calling to the adjacent guard, who relays the call to the next guard and so on up to the barracks where the sergeant of the guard is housed. Shit! I thought, that's all I need is to get Turk into trouble again. So, I decided instead to move a little closer to make sure Andre was all right."

"Did you give any thought to what you would do if he weren't?"

"No. I guess that was my first mistake. Turk was pushing and pulling at Andre's rifle, trying to get him to hold it properly at port arms; and Andre was trying to get Turk to show him a pass to be in that area at night. Turk told him his duty assignment was in this truck repair garage and that he had a piece of equipment that had to be fixed before tomorrow. Turk obviously didn't have a pass and was harassing Andre as an evasive maneuver. More than that, Turk was taking unusual pleasure from the power he was exerting over him and had become sexually aroused. He had gone behind Andre and was showing him how to hold his rifle. Reaching around in front, he was drawing the rifle against Andre's chest, pulling Andre against himself. When he started to make little humping movements, Andre asked him to stop and feebly struggled to free himself. 'C'mon, kid, this is what you really like about the Army, isn't it?

Lots of swinging dicks.'

"'There isn't anything I like about the Army; and, if you don't let me loose, I'm going to report you.'

"'Sheeeit, kid you don't know an opportunity when you see one. Get inside there and I'll show you a good time.' He shoved Andre toward the door; but, when they reached it, Andre held his rifle crossways at chest level so he couldn't be pushed through. 'Don't get smart with me, you little fucker,' Turk yelled and put one arm around Andre's neck, cutting off his air; with the other hand, he jerked the rifle away from him and threw it on the ground. Then he shoved him through the opening and closed the door. Suddenly it was dark and quiet. I ran over and listened at the door. A truck engine was running and there was a whirring sound apparently from a big exhaust fan, but above the noise I could hear Andre wailing for Turk to stop. The door was locked. It was a large sheet metal quonset hut, mostly roof; the only windows were up high on the ends. The best I could find was a split in the seam where a truck apparently had backed into it, producing a one-inch gap that allowed a small beam of light to escape.

"By sitting on the ground I could look in. Turk had Andre over a pile of tires; his pants were down and Turk was raping him. I yelled through the crack for Turk to cut it out and banged on the side of the building, but the truck engine and fan were making so much noise they couldn't hear me even though I could hear them. Before I could do anything, Turk let out a triumphant whoop and it was over. He gave Andre a smart slap on the bare ass and said, 'Hey, that was great kid; we ought to do this more often. Why don't you put in for the motor pool when you finish basic? I could pull some strings and get you assigned here.'

"Andre was sobbing and still lying over the tires. Turk lifted him off by the shoulders and stood him up but he just collapsed to the floor still crying. 'Christ, kid, if you feel so bad about this, why don't you hang yourself? One of my previous corn hole comrades did. Trouble is, though, I didn't get to see him do it. You'd let me watch, though, wouldn't you? Shit, I'd hate to have you run off and do it all alone.' Turk went over to a stool where his jacket was lying and produced a pint bottle. The whiskey was three-fourths gone; but, Turk offered Andre a drink anyway. Andre was too busy weeping to even notice the offer, so Turk finished it off while he stood there considering Andre. Finally he said, "OK, kid that's enough of that goddam wailing, time to go back to guard duty like a good soldier.'

"Andre stopped weeping long enough to tell Turk he was going to report him."

Charlotte tensed up, but since she didn't interrupt, Jude continued.

"'That's a pretty poor fucking idea,' Turk said, 'I like the hanging idea better. Look at the boom on that wrecker, Roskov; wouldn't you like to dangle your ass from that. Shit! Damn! I'll get a rope and help you out. You won't be able to live with this anyway.'

"The wrecker he was talking about was the vehicle that was running. It was a huge truck for towing other trucks and buses. The boom rose from the deck just back of the cab and curved up about six feet, then ran back as a horizontal girder, extending six feet beyond the bed of the truck. By the time Turk located a rope, Andre was crawling up the stack of tires and trying to stand up. 'Hey, you're getting stronger, maybe you'll be able to help me with this little project, or come to think of it, seeing your bare ass is giving me another hard-on. Maybe you'd like to take another ride on the end of my dick before you go aloft.' Andre started to pull up his pants but Turk told him to leave them alone. 'I think it would be really neat to have you turning slowly at the end of the boom with your pants down around your knees. You've got a pretty shriveled-up dick now, but I'll bet it'll turn into a lovely hard-on as soon as that rope tightens around your neck.'"

"That's amazing how you could hear everything, but they couldn't hear you."

"I know, and I yelled as loud as I could. I think they were talking loud to each other to be heard above the noise of the truck and exhaust fan. It made it easier for me to hear them.

"I was sure that threatening to hang Andre was another one of Turk's sick jokes, but I wasn't taking any chances. I ran to the front of the building and found Andre's rifle. If this turned out not to be a joke and I had to shoot Turk to save Andre, I didn't want to do it with my own gun. But, you know Charlotte, this thought didn't run through my mind with any degree of seriousness. It was all kind of make-believe, like when we were kids playing cops and robbers."

Charlotte just nodded, not wanting to interrupt the flow of Jude's words.

"When I returned to my peephole, Turk had already run the cable out and had the big hook lying on the back of the truck where he was tying the rope to it. Andre was leaning against the tires in one of his hopeless, passive postures. When Turk finished, he called Andre to come over. Andre started to pull up his pants again and Turk yelled at him, 'Hey, asshole, I told you to leave your pants down; if you can't walk, I'll come get you.' He tossed Andre over his shoulder and carried him to the wrecker. When Turk put him down, Andre just stood there, apparently in shock, while Turk put the rope around his neck.

"I watched in disbelief as Turk engaged the winch with a lever at the rear of the cab and the drum slowly took up the slack in the rope. For the first time, I seriously considered that Turk might go through with this. I checked Andre's rifle to make sure there was a cartridge in the chamber, then poked the muzzle through the peephole. I took aim at Turk's fat head but then wondered if Andre's rifle was sighted in; he sure as hell couldn't have done it. My only hope was that its previous owner had done a good job and Andre hadn't tampered with the sights. Finally, though, I decided on a body shot, which offered a larger target. I was surprised at how clear I was thinking in spite of how hard my heart pounding. My hands were trembling, too, but with the muzzle of the rifle jammed tightly in the hole, it couldn't waver. I watched along the sightline, expecting Turk to snug the rope up to Andre's neck, then laugh like a fool, and release him; but, he didn't. Andre was slowly being raised; he had taken a hold of the rope to support some of his weight, but the rope was now tight around his neck; only his toes were touching the floor. I squeezed the trigger. The roar echoed around inside the building; Turk was slammed against the truck and slid down to the floor where he twitched a couple of times then lay silent as the blood poured out of his chest.

"The winch didn't stop—Turk had locked the lever in the *on* position. Andre clung desperately to the rope with one hand and pulled at the noose with the other; but, he was losing strength and choking. Slowly, ever so slowly he rose into the air. I aimed at the rope thinking a lucky shot might cut it; but, at that distance the front sight was about 10 times thicker than the rope which was now swinging and jerking all over the place, so I abandoned that. By the time Andre was two feet off the ground, he went limp—so had I. I couldn't move. It seemed like an eternity before Andre reached the top, where the winch stalled. He was left hanging as Turk had wished, turning slowly at the end of the boom with his pants down around his ankles. Once he was completely relaxed, a mushy shit poured out of him and plopped into his pants. Eventually, I gathered enough strength to get up from my sitting position. I held my watch to the light from the slit; only an hour had passed since I took my guard post. I wiped my fingerprints from Andre's rifle and leaned it next to the door at the front of the building. During the remaining hour of guard duty, I walked back and forth in my assigned territory as far from Andre's post as possible, trying to keep from vomiting; finally, I gave in to it."

So Jude did kill Turk. Charlotte had thought it would affect her deeply if she found out that Jude was responsible for one or both of the deaths reported two years earlier at Fort Knox. But it did not, at least not so far; it just lay there in her stomach like something undigestible. "Wasn't there some kind of ruckus after you fired your gun on such a quiet night?" Charlotte calmly inquired.

"No, apparently the sound was contained within the building. At the end of my guard duty, the sergeant of the guard came with the replacements. When Andre didn't show at the designated place, the sergeant called for him repeatedly; then four guards were sent out to scour Andre's territory. One of them discovered lights in the truck garage but said he couldn't see in. They didn't find Andre's rifle; it was probably too dark to see it. The new guard was posted and the rest of us were marched back to the guard barracks.

"We were instructed to go back to bed while the sergeant frantically called around the post looking for someone with a key to the motor pool garage.

"Charlotte, this is a good time to take a break."

"What! You've got to be kidding. You're trying to get out of finishing your story."

"I've got to feed Alfred and the chickens. Then, we ought to take a little walk and consider what we're going to do about dinner."

"Already?" Charlotte was surprised when she looked at her watch. "We take a break only if you promise to settle back into that same chair and finish telling me everything right up to the time you scraped me up out of the pasture."

7

When dinner was over, they settled back at the table with coffee.

"OK, Jude, I'm ready. What happened when they found out what was in the garage?"

Jude was amused at the way Charlotte had rushed him through his chores, cut their walk short and settled for leftovers for dinner. But he was relieved, too, that she was still willing to listen to anything he had to say, knowing now that he had killed another human being. "Guess you didn't want me to finish my coffee, huh? OK. Here goes.

"I lay awake there in the guard hut, not believing it was real. About four o'clock the commotion started, mostly flashing lights from M.P. vehicles and an ambulance, but no sirens. The silence made the horror seem even more eerie.

"As we were being assembled to return to our companies, an M.P. captain and a second lieutenant appeared and announced we'd be detained for awhile—no reference was made regarding Turk and Andre. They divided us into two groups; each officer questioned us one at a time. I tried to remain cool but my voice had a tendency to quaver and my hands to shake. I felt the captain, who was questioning me, was suspicious from the start. I asked if they had found out what happened to Andre; he yelled at me like he was pissed, 'That's what we're trying to do.' Somewhere in the midst of this, breakfast arrived on trays; we ate, then the interrogation resumed. After everyone had been questioned, two of us were told to remain; the rest were taken back to their units. This time both interrogators talked to me. They asked the same questions again, mostly about what I heard in the garage area but this time added some personal things like, 'How well did you know Private Roskov?'

"'Not very well, sir; he was kind of a loner.'

"'Was he homosexual?'

"'I don't know. I never saw him take an interest in anyone in the barracks.'"

"'Were you interested in him?'

"'If you mean sexually, God, no!'

"'Did Private Roskov know Sergeant Turcott?'

"'Yes, Sergeant Turcott was our platoon leader during the first half of basic.'

"'Ah ha! Finally we're getting somewhere,' the captain responded excitedly. 'Send the other guy back to his unit; he doesn't even know Roskov and barely knew Turk.' The two M.P.s then hammered at me with renewed vigor.

"'Did you like Sergeant Turcott?'

"'No, we aren't supposed to like the cadre.'

"'Aside from that, how did you feel about him?'

"'I try to be a good soldier and do as I'm told.'

"'Let me remind you, soldier, you're talking to two

officers of the United States Army and we don't need any smart-ass comments; you're already in enough trouble. Now, answer me straight, without any of your horseshit. Did he like you?'

"'No, sir, he didn't like any of us. Why do you keep asking me about Sergeant Turcott? He hasn't been in our company for three weeks.'

"'Never mind why I'm asking about Sergeant Turcott,' the captain said. 'We'll ask the questions. Did Private Roskov like Sergeant Turcott?'

"'No, Andre didn't like him.'

"'How do you know he didn't like him?'

"'No one liked him. He was a brute and a bully; we were all glad when he was transferred.'

"'Did you ever take a shower with Private Roskov?'

"'Sir, I mean no disrespect; but, did you ever look inside one of those barracks?'

"'Of course. Why?'

"'For 50 men there is one large community shower at the far end of the first floor. You usually shower with more than a dozen guys at a time. If you're suggesting that the shower is a place for sex, no, that isn't what happens there.'

"'I notice you evaded my question. Did you ever take a shower with Private Roskov?'

"'Yes, sir.'

"'Now that wasn't so hard to answer, was it? Did he have a large or a small penis?'"

"How on earth did you answer that, Jude? There was no way you could win."

"I was really stuck for a while. Finally, I told him, 'His dick was all shriveled-up from the saltpeter like everyone else's.'"

"Oh, that's good. You're much better at this inter-rogation game than I was when Sheriff Batley worked me over."

"It didn't matter, though, it still pissed them off. The lieutenant snapped back, 'What'a yah mean?'

"I told him, 'They put it in our food to keep us from having erections. They don't want recruits going AWOL to get them serviced.'

"'Whoever told you that? Your putting me on.'

"'That's the widely circulated rumor, sir, and I believe it. I haven't had a hard-on since I arrived and neither has anyone else I've talked with.'

"'You go around asking guys if they've had a hard-on lately?'

"'Sir, if the hard-on issue is so important, why don't you ask the mess sergeant what he puts in the broth?'"

"Charlotte, that pissed them off again. They were both yelling at me. One of them said, "'All right, soldier, that does it. Get your shit together; you're coming with us.'" I picked up my rifle to go with them and the lieutenant snarled, 'You won't be needing this,' and snatched the rifle away as though I were about to shoot them. After he realized how heavy it was, he checked to see if it was loaded and handed it back.

"'Am I under arrest?'

"'We'll let you know when you're under arrest.'

"'Do I need a lawyer?'

"'When you need a lawyer, we'll let you know. The Army will provide one. Just get in the back of the jeep.'

"On the way to the M.P. barracks, I had to hang on tight to keep from being bounced out, they drove so fast over the bumpy roads. Inside the building, the captain dropped some notes on the desk of a female corporal as they hustled me past her and into a corner room. They sent out for lunch, then continued for another two hours asking the same pointless questions. With virtually no sleep the night before, I felt dull in the head. I suppose their irrelevant questions were an attempt to grind me down and get me to confess? They still hadn't told me why I was being detained—nor said what happened to Andre and Turk. Finally, they asked a series of questions faster than I could possibly answer them, ending with, 'Why did you shoot Sergeant Turcott and Private Roskov?'

"I was befuddled, but not enough to blurt out, 'Andre wasn't shot!' I just sat there, sort of stunned, and finally said, 'Andre and Sergeant Turcott have been shot? Are they OK?'"

"Jude, you really are good at this. I would have fallen into that one."

"My slow reaction time probably saved me.

"The captain said, 'Andre is dead but Sergeant Turcott is in intensive care. We expect him to recover and confirm our suspicions that you shot both of them, so you may as well confess now and save us all a lot of trouble.'

"I knew there was no chance Turk was alive but I had to go along with whatever they told me. 'I hope he recovers quickly so he can clear me—except he's such a sleazy bastard, who knows what he'll say?'

"The lieutenant yelled, "WHAT DO YOU MEAN *SLEAZY*? Sergeant Turcott is a war hero.'

"I blurted, 'Sergeant Turcott is a flaming asshole—a disgrace to the Army.'"

Charlotte covered her face and said, "Oh, my God, Jude. You blew it."

"Yah, I did. The captain pounced on me immediately, 'What the hell do you know about it? You're still wet behind the ears. You ever been in combat? Anyway, you finally played the card we've been waiting for, the motive card— you had the means, motive and opportunity.'

"'How many rounds were missing from my rifle when I checked in after guard duty?'

"The Captain snapped back, 'How the hell should I know? I wasn't there when you checked-in.'"

"It's amazing, you still had the wits about you to ask that question," Charlotte said.

"Dumb luck, I guess. All I was conscious of was how nervous I must appear and how shakey my voice was. Anyway, I said, 'Maybe you could ask the sergeant of the guard? He counted the cartridges when we went out and when we returned. As a matter of fact why don't you sniff the barrel of my rifle to see if it's been fired?'

"'You used Roskov's gun,' the lieutenant said. 'Tell us again how you felt about Sergeant Turcott.'

"'I didn't like him, neither did anyone in his platoon. Lord knows how many people worldwide hated him—but, Andre? Why would anyone kill Andre? He seemed like such a harmless person. By the way did Sergeant Turcott have a permit to be in that area? Maybe Andre thought he had a right to shoot him. They probably took turns shooting each other.'"

"More huffing and puffing?" Charlotte asked.

"Surprisingly not. Instead of blowing smoke, the captain leaned over and whispered confidentially, 'What we believe happened was that this was a love triangle that went sour. You and Private Roskov were lovers but you encountered him being unfaithful with Sergeant Turcott and shot them both.'

"'No kidding, your great American war hero was a homosexual?'"

Charlotte said, "Sounds like you were having fun at that stage of the interrogation."

"Yes. That's how it sounds, but I was too tense and scared to enjoy it. Also, I was working pretty hard to keep from getting rattled when they yelled at me.

"This time, though, the captain calmly replied, 'Tell us about it.'

"'I've told you all I know. I'm sorry I can't help. Do you mind if I go now?'

"'You can go, but we'll be in touch—once we get the prints and lab reports.'

"'Thanks, but do you really want me walking around the post, looking for my barracks, with an M1 in hand? I don't have any idea where my outfit is.'

"'Smart ass right to the end, aren't you?' The captain stuck his head out the door and yelled, 'Corporal Tandy, you can take Private Bartholomew back to his barracks now.'

"A WAC appeared, said 'Yes, sir,' then she turned to me

and said, 'Let's go.'

"'Do you know where to go?'

"'Of course,' she smiled; and, as we went outside, added, 'I'm not exactly a virgin, you know, when it comes to this post.'

"'I didn't even tell you the name of my outfit.'

"'Oh, that. I've been typing reports all day long about you and your terrible behavior.'

"'Aren't you afraid of me?'

"'No, if you killed anyone, and I doubt that you did, you sure didn't do it the way they're trying to put it together. From where I sit in that office, I can hear everything that's said in Captain Stein's office. The walls are thin as toilet paper. They really don't have shit on you. It doesn't matter, though, unless someone comes in and insists on confessing, you're it. They don't have another suspect. Once they concoct a story, they marry it for life. I'm sorry they latched on to you, you seem pretty nice; besides you're no homosexual.'

"'How do you know I'm not a homosexual?'

"'I can tell right off when a guy wants to fuck me . . . the intensity of your message tells me you're not even a little bit queer. Too bad you're still on saltpeter, I could take your mind off your troubles.'

"I looked at her carefully for the first time. She was slender with dark brown hair and eyes that sparkled with amusement. Although she wasn't especially pretty, she was keenly aware of her sexuality and had an appealing manner. Sex, however, was about the last thing on my mind. She pulled into the deserted company street before my foggy mind could come up with a response. As I got out she said, 'See you in a couple days, Jude; try to get some rest, your response time is slow.'"

"What did the guys have to say when you went in the barracks?"

"They were recovering from a grueling field exercise and waiting for dinner. They swarmed around me, wanting to know what happened to Andre.

"I said, 'According to the M.P.s, he and Turk have been shot.'

"'What the fuck was Turk doing there? What took you so long to get back?' Wadell wanted to know.

"They were amazed when I told them I was the prime suspect. They could understand why I would shoot Turk but not Andre.

"'So why do they think you did it?' Tait wanted to know.

"'Mainly because my guard post was next to Andre's and I knew both of them.'

"'That's it? Shit, that won't hold up in court,' Tait offered. 'On the other hand, in a military court, they can do anything they want to and you can't do shit about it.'

"'Yah,' Waddel said. 'You weren't here this morning. The company commander addressed the troops on the Uniform Code of Military Justice. He told us that next week we could talk with the Judge Advocate General and tell him if we have any complaints about how we've been treated in the Army. But, it's all a joke. Soon's the captain was out of earshot, the first sergeant said, 'Oh yes, you go right over there next week and git in that line a wimps and screamers; but, I catch any a yo' motha fucks in that line, you gonna wish you was aborted as a three-month-old womb-bastard.'

"I didn't know much about my legal rights; but, I had a feeling mine were being violated, so I started a journal, recording all my conversations with the M.P.s."

"Smart move. I've often wished I'd kept notes on the interrogation Batley put me through."

"You probably should have. It's hard to do, though. I thought for a while I was wasting my time when the M.P.s went a couple days without bothering me. But, just as I was becoming hopeful, Tait came back from the PX with the *Louisville Courier-Journal*. On the front page was an article about two soldiers killed at Fort Knox. No names were being released until next of kin could be notified. The circumstances of the deaths were under investigation. An unofficial source, that did not wish to be named, hinted that a homosexual love triangle was involved and that a suspect in the killings was at hand.

"The next day I was called out of morning formation and sent to the company headquarters. The M.P. jeep was out in front and Corporal Tandy was in the office. She was in good cheer; my plight didn't bother her at all. She said, 'Captain Stein and Lieutenant Cranston have finally thought up some new questions for you. They seem slower to stick it to you than they are in most cases; but then, this is their first murder case and they're probably a little uncertain how to proceed. Don't think that means they aren't still planning to stick it to you, though.'

"'Captain Stein and Lieutenant Cranston, huh? They didn't bother to introduce themselves. So, what do you think I should do about them?'

"'Not much you can do, they'll continue to haul you in

day after day and hammer at you until you confess.'

"'Isn't the Army supposed to provide me with a lawyer?'

"'They will when they arrest you, but it'll be one of their lawyer buddies. Besides they aren't going to arrest you until you make a mistake and give them something.'

"I didn't know how much of what she told me was true. Even though she appeared to be on my side, she still worked for the M.P.s. Her last statement seemed to infer that I was guilty and would soon confess, so I laid on the denial, 'What could I possibly give them that would be incriminating? Christ, I wasn't even near that building.'

"'Oh, hey, you don't have to convince me. I told you right off I didn't think you fit their scenario. I only hope you can get off the hook so we can go out and play.'

"When we went in, one of the clerks told me to have a chair. 'Captain Stein and Lieutenant Cranston will be with you shortly.'

"Corporal Tandy said. 'Good luck in there today, Jude, and remember, I'm rooting for you.' She left. Seconds later, I heard murmuring in the interrogation room. One of the voices was female. Shit, I thought, what the hell did I give her? Before long Tandy returned and with surprise said, 'You still here? Let me see if they're ready for you yet.' She was back in a few seconds to tell me I could go in."

"Jude, you shouldn't have trusted Corporal Tandy."

"Is this what they call female intuition? We'll soon see how good it is.

"My interrogators greeted me with a friendly air. I responded in kind, hoping to express more confidence than I had previously. Captain Stein said cheerfully, 'OK, Private, I think we can wrap this up quickly. We now have all the information we need. We just want to double-check a few facts. I think you know that Sergeant Turcott was shot by someone from outside the building with Private Roskov's rifle and that Private Roskov was hanged. We know that you killed both of them. You and Roskov were lovers; Sergeant Turcott caught you, and you shot him so he wouldn't report you. You hanged Roskov to keep him from telling on you.'

"I just looked at them, shaking my head back and forth. There was a long silence. Finally, Stein said, 'You'll feel better if you get this off your chest.'

"'I don't have anything on my chest.' They didn't appear to have any more evidence against me than before. It was also easier to deal with them now that I was rested and had recovered from the initial trauma of what happened.

"Cranston said, 'I see you're back to being a smart ass again. Well, if you don't have a pain in your chest, we'll see if we can give you one.' With a show of anger, he grabbed my shirt and jerked me up out of my chair. 'LET'S GET THIS SHIT OVER WITH,' he shouted in my face.

"'Do you want me to confess to a crime I didn't commit?'

"'OH, YOU DID IT ALL RIGHT,' again in my face, 'OTHERWISE, HOW WOULD YOU KNOW THEY WERE KILLED IN A BUILDING AND NOT OUTDOORS? WE DIDN'T TELL YOU THAT,' and he slammed me back down in the chair.

"So, what Corporal Tandy had pried out of me, was my comment that, I hadn't been near that building. Charlotte, you score one point for female intuition.

"I knew it. I hope you are more careful of her from now on."

Jude smiled at the way Charlotte was following his story as though it were happening as he spoke.

"I told them, 'I presumed it was in a building since I didn't hear any gunfire. My post was close to Andre's; I would have heard a gun fired outdoors.' Then taking the offensive I added, 'That's an interesting story you tell me, though—lots of information you didn't have last time. I gather Turcott is dead and that he didn't clear me. Are you also saying that he was dead when you found him and that you lied to me?'

"Cranston was red in the face and still huffing and puffing, 'Listen up shit face, you can believe whatever you like; we've got your prints on Roskov's gun, so we know you were at the scene. You shot Sergeant Turcott through a split in the building, then hanged Roskov. You may as well stop the bullshit and save everyone a lot of trouble.'

"Charlotte, I may have missed a fingerprint when I wiped the gun, but more than likely they were lying. At any rate, I told them, 'I helped Andre load his gun before we went to our guard posts. He wasn't handy with weapons.'

"Stein said, 'We can check that bullshit story if we decide to.'

"I couldn't figure out how they were putting this thing together, so I asked Stein, 'Sir, would you please explain something for me?'

"'Why not, if it'll help you remember your part in this?'

"'See if I have this straight. You think Sergeant Turcott

caught me with Andre inside a building, so I grabbed Andre's gun, ran outside and shot Turcott who was inside. Then I went back in and hanged Andre. What was Sergeant Turcott doing in the area? Why did I go outside to shoot Turcott? Why did I hang Andre instead of shoot him?'"

"How did they answer that?"

"They didn't. After a long silence, Captain Stein said in a formal tone, 'Corporal Tandy will take you back to your unit now. You'll be hearing from us.'

"On the way back Corporal Tandy continued to act like she was still my friend. She said, 'Jude, you handled those two just fine. You know, though, they didn't play all their cards today. They found out that you and Turcott are both from Menominee. They called the police there to inquire whether you guys knew each other. The Menominee police are checking their records.'

"When we returned to my company area, the troops were gone. Corporal Tandy stopped at the company office to see where they were and what gear I would need. I got my equipment from the barracks and she drove out to the classroom where they were learning map reading. Along the way she spent her time letting me know what a great time we would have if they hadn't zeroed in on me, 'It's not like they're going to let go, you know. They'll just keep making up stories until they find one that fits. Whatever comes out of Menominee won't matter, they'll find a way to use it against you.'

"'Should I confess to save them the trouble of framing me for a crime I didn't commit?'

"'Whatever happened, if you think they're going to

allow it to reflect badly on a war hero, you have a pretty naive sense of military justice. Once they have your ass nailed to the mast, they'll bring in a lawyer to defend you. He'll tell you they have enough evidence to convict you on two counts of first degree murder and that your best bet is to plead guilty on a lesser charge. You'll get about 10 years at Fort Leavenworth and a dishonorable discharge. After that, you can resume your life.'

"Leavenworth is a military prison?" Charlotte asked.

"I guess so. It was what they often threatened us with. I had a feeling that Corporal Tandy brought it up as part of a message from the boys.

"She pulled up in front of the one-room, wooden shack that was being used for the map reading classroom. A bunch of guys outside, who were taking a break, set off a chorus of cheers and whistles. She smiled and waved to them as she drove off.

"After reporting to the officer in charge, I joined the guys by the class building. One of them said, 'Hey, what I gotta do to get me a chauffeur like that? Shit, man, we had to fuckin' march all the way out here.

"Meanwhile, it was clear I would have to decide soon whether to take my chances with military justice or head for the hills. Neither option looked promising. One guy in my platoon went AWOL three times. The longest it took the M.P.s to find him was one week. Two other recruits were each gone overnight before they were caught. Always, they were picked up hitchhiking on the highway, or waiting at a bus or truck stop. I decided that if I left, I should go overland on foot.

"In the map reading classroom, we were learning to read detailed topographic maps that showed streams, hills, woods, towns, and roads. A large map, hanging on the wall, showed Fort Knox and the adjacent area. I noticed a river, called the Rolling Fork, flowed through the military reservation. Much of its course beyond the post was through forested rural areas.

"Although I didn't hear from the M.P.s for several days, I didn't take that as a sign they were through with me. At every opportunity, I stashed equipment and food that could be carried on the trail."

"Weren't you worried the Menominee police would tell the M.P.s about the squabble you had with Turk when you were kids and decide to lock you up?"

"Yes. That still wouldn't give them much of a case, but Corporal Tandy had me convinced they would produce whatever bullshit they needed.

"We were in formation in the company street when Corporal Tandy pulled up in front of the company office. A minute latter the company clerk delivered a message for 'Private Bartholomew, to report to the company office on the double.'

'Corporal Tandy cheerfully announced, 'Stein and Cranston are pleased with the news from Menominee. They would like to share it with you.'

"'I asked if she had seen it; but she said, 'I can't tell you about it; they want to have the pleasure of dropping it on you.'

"They lost no time in letting me know they had the full scoop on my interactions with Turk in Menominee. My motive for killing Sergeant Turcott, they said, was that I blamed him for Billy Krammer's death. 'You going to deny that?' Cranston asked.

"I told him, 'At that time I believed he was in some way responsible.'

"'You still feel that way?' Stein asked.

"'I don't know. I haven't thought about it for a long time. Does this new motive now replace your old homosexual motive?'

"I suppose that's the end of the comradery?" Charlotte asked.

"Yes, they were back to being pissed off at me. Cranston growled, 'Both motives are still in place.'

"'Uh huh,' I said, 'now all you need is a motive for me to have killed Andre. Did I do that before I ran outside to kill Turk? You did say Turk's body was found inside the building, didn't you?'

"Captain Stein calmly said, 'Why don't you tell us about it?'

"'I'd like to help, sir, but all I know is what you've told me. So far the story makes no sense.'

"Stein said, 'It makes sense to us and it will make sense at the court-martial. The only reason we don't arrest you now is because we want to give you a chance to confess. If you do, it'll go easier on you.'

"After a long and awkward silence I asked, 'Can I go back to my unit now? I understand that if I miss too much of basic training I'll have to take it over again.'

"'You can go back now if you'll promise to think about telling us what happened.'

"Corporal Tandy already knew where my unit was,

'You're going to play with the gas masks today,' she announced.

"'I've already had my gas for the day—without a mask.'

"'Yes—guess you know they don't believe the story they're telling you. They want you to say, 'No, that's not the way it happened; Sergeant Turcott fucked Private Roskov in the ass and hanged him, so I shot him.' When they got your records from Menominee, they also got Turcott's from Germany and Korea. He has a history of arrests for rape and even murder, but no convictions. The charges were dropped before he was court-martialed. The evidence was always a little thin, and he apparently had some sort of politically powerful angel that watched over him. Stein and Cranston don't want to bring charges against a dead war hero if they can't make them stick. Unless you give them a good case, they're going to charge you with both murders. By telling it like it really happened, you're stuck with only one murder. Do you know Turk's angel?'

"'He had an uncle who was assistant secretary of something or other in Washington. I suppose he helped Turk to stay out of jail. But what's happened, Corporal Tandy? I thought we were friends. I thought you were on my side— now you're talking like you think I killed Turk. Are you trying to worm a confession out of me?'

"'We're friends, Jude, and you can call me Patty, that is, when there aren't any officers around. Would you like to take a little ride? Maybe we could find a quiet place to park and talk about our friendship.'

Charlotte broke eye contact with Jude and started to rearrange the salt and pepper shakers.

Jude wondered what was bothering her. Surely she isn't upset over the interest Corporal Tandy was showing in me. If she is, she sure isn't going to like what I have to say next.

"So, I agreed to go for a ride with her, hoping to develop a sense of how the post was laid out. The place was huge; it went on for miles. I was hoping I could get her to drive near the river so I would have a better idea of where to go if I took off in the night. Instead of driving around, she headed directly for a secluded trail, where she parked in a wooded area and immediately became romantic. I went along with it for awhile; she was able to override my diet of saltpeter— either that, or it wasn't true that they were adding it to the food. Then somewhere in the midst of passion, it all fizzled. We just sort of stopped and both said at the same time, 'What's the matter?' We laughed, but then sat waiting for the other one to answer the question.

"Finally, I said, 'My problem is that I have a lot on my mind; I can drive it off for short periods, but it's almost constantly with me.'

"'Maybe if we talk about it, it will help to resolve it.'

"'What will resolve it is for your people to recognize my innocence and leave me alone.'

"'Then you wouldn't see me anymore.'

"'Yes, and that's too bad, because I do like you; but, making love with you would be like fraternizing with the enemy.'

"'How could you ever see me as the enemy? I just type for those bastards.'

"'Yes, but maybe you better take me to class and get back to the M.P. house so you don't get into trouble for being away too long.'

"'Does this mean you no longer enjoy my company?'

"'Oh, I enjoy your company, but you're wasting your time if you think you can get me to tell you that I killed those guys.'

"'What it amounts to Jude, is that they know you were involved and intend to send you to Leavenworth, even if they have to fill in some of the blanks with made-up evidence. They were going to take you into custody today, but I asked them to let me try one more time to get you to talk about it. I tell you this as a friend, because it will go easier on you if you confess and explain the circumstances.'"

"Bitch," Charlotte said, adding the sugar bowl to the salt and pepper shakers.

"Hmm. So then the bitch said, 'Maybe you had a good reason for killing Turcott.'

"'First of all they're wrong—I didn't have anything to do with it; if I did, I sure wouldn't place my fate in the hands of people willing to make up evidence. To me, military justice looks like a piece of shit. By the way, were you hoping to make sergeant over this?"

Charlotte stopped rearranging things on the table and returned her attention to Jude, hoping he didn't notice how bothered she was by Corporal Tandy.

"'Fuck you!' Tandy yelled at me. She started the jeep and tore down the trail at breakneck speed.

"After a quarter of a mile, we came to a river. There it was! We had gone directly to the place I needed to find. Now, I thought, if I can only figure out where we are in relation to the barracks, I'll have it made. At the stream's edge,

Corporal Tandy whipped the vehicle around and headed back
up the trail. In the meantime, I began to worry that she
would report her failure to the boys; and, they would come
immediately to take me into custody. By the time we reached
the main road, she had cooled down enough to resume
conversation.

"'I'm sorry I got mad, Jude. Maybe you came too close to
the truth. I might have hoped subconsciously that a confession from you would help my promotion. I'll take you back
to your company and tell Captain Stein you insist on your
innocence. They'll probably be along to pick you up within
the hour.'

"I struggled for a way to delay them until I could make a
run for it. 'Do they think they have something on me?' I
asked, 'Something I don't know about?'

"Did they?" Charlotte asked, anxious to return to the
conversation now that she no longer had to worry about Jude
being seduced by Corporal Tandy.

"She said, 'Not that I know of. What was most convinc-
ing to them was your nervousness, sour breath, and lack of
eye contact when they first questioned you.'

"'On that they're going to charge me with murder?'

"Tandy assured me, 'They railroaded a guy a couple
months ago for stealing another G.I.'s money out of his
locker. I couldn't see that they had any real evidence, but
they got him anyway.'

"'What if I knew something that might help them solve
this case? Would they let go of me, or are their minds made
up?'

"Corporal Tandy was immediately interested, 'Jude, if

you know something, why haven't you brought it up?'

"'Because I'm afraid they might twist it around and use it against me,' I told her. 'I've been holding out until I have a lawyer to advise me. They said a lawyer would be appointed after they arrest me; but, since they're only questioning me now, I don't need a lawyer—guess that's military justice.'

"'It's not always easy to tell military justice from the Stein and Cranston method. Is there anything I can do to help? Maybe if you tell me about it, together we can work out a way to handle it."

"I told her, 'I appreciate your offer, but it involves something that could backfire. I have to think about it.'"

"Did she take the bait?"

"Yes, she said, 'Jude, if I can get them to hold off until tomorrow, you could consider it overnight. We could talk about it in the morning when I pick you up.'

"I told her 'OK,' and while she drove me to my unit, I looked for landmarks to guide me back to the river.

"That evening I wrote a letter to my company commander, Captain Oris, telling him that my leaving wasn't an admission of guilt; but, that I felt I was being railroaded for the two murders and couldn't get a fair trial. I completed my diary, leaving out Corporal Tandy's attempt to seduce me, and asked Tait to give the diary and letter to Captain Oris in the morning. I also told Tait what was in the letter and some of what was in the diary, so when the M.P.s questioned him, he would have something to entertain them with. Shortly after *lights out*, I slipped quietly from the barracks and out of Army life.

"This is a good place to quit, Charlotte. You're probably tired of listening to me. Besides you found out what you wanted to know—that I killed Turk—that I am guilty of at least one of those murders." He sat silently, his eyes on Charlotte's arrangement of the salt and pepper shakers, then said in a dejected tone, "You can do whatever you want to with that information—even call the cops if you think you should."

8

Charlotte went to the sink and ladled two glasses of water from the bucket. She was not sure why Jude had become maudlin and uncertain of her. When she returned with the water, Jude was still looking down at the table. "Jude, the only reason I would call the cops is if you don't finish your story tonight."

Jude looked up. Charlotte was smiling. Her enthusiasm and support were still there. The stone he had worn on his back ever since his arrival at Greyledge was gone. He picked up his story where he left off. "I had more trouble finding the trail in the dark than I expected to. It was already light when I reached the stream, but it had a nice path running along it through a wooded area. I was able to travel a good distance before I came to a clearing where some kind of Army field operation was in progress. I crawled into a thicket and settled down to wait for dark. To while away my time, I removed my shoulder patches and insignias and buried them under a log; then I hid most of my money and my identification papers in the lining of my jacket.

"By midafternoon the field operation ended. I was about to cross the field and resume my escape when a jeep with two M.P.s in it swept around the circumference of the field, stopping several times to scan the woods before moving on. I couldn't tell if they were looking for me; but, if they were serious about finding me, they could easily track me in the soft ground along the stream—might even get some dogs on my trail. Until now I'd assumed they wouldn't be looking for me anywhere but on the roadways and in the bus, train and plane terminals.

"As soon as it became dusk, I set off across the open area and continued to move as quickly as I could; but, after falling over a log, I slowed down. On top of that, I had developed a cold that made it difficult to breathe."

"It must have been late November. Wasn't the weather pretty brisk by then?"

"Yes, after dark it turned cold, but carrying the heavy pack kept me warm. By the time I reached the boundary of the reservation, dawn was breaking and I was dripping with perspiration. A road crossing with a bridge lay ahead. Just in case they were tracking me with dogs, I walked up to the road, then backtracked to the river to make it look like I had caught a ride. Then I stepped into the cold water and headed upstream. It was only six inches deep along the edge; but the bottom was slippery clay, so travel was slow. It didn't matter, though, with both banks of the stream heavily wooded, I felt safe traveling during the day and was relieved to be off the reservation.

"I had hiked for four hours and was beginning to feel the weight of my backpack. To make matters worse, a cold rain had been falling most of the morning and I was soaked, not to mention the fact that my feet had been in the cold river ever since I cleared the reservation. Early afternoon I reached a place where both banks of the stream were open. I found a thicket and crawled into it to wait until dark. The only protection I had from the weather was half of a pup tent. The Army's plan was that you were to pair up with another soldier for the other half and button them together to form a tent. I tied the corners of the shelter half to some saplings to form a lean-to and changed into dry clothes. I didn't sleep much. At dusk I was still cold and shaking; my bones ached and my chest was full. I stuffed down some tasteless K rations and headed up the trail. The opening turned out to be a highway. I remembered from the map that the river crossed the highway at several points. In what was left of the fading light, I selected a path across some open fields to where I could pick up the river again before dawn.

"I tried to keep moving but felt worse all the time. The rain had stopped and my clothes were dry, but I couldn't stop shaking. I knew I had a fever but this was no place to stop. The course I'd picked was toward a single light in the distance, but more lights popped up—then, there weren't any lights at all. The sky was overcast, without stars; it was totally black. I walked into a fence, climbed over it, and found myself standing in the middle of a road. I followed it for awhile; but, eventually, my hazy mind told me that, if a car came along, there I'd be wandering in the road at night, dressed like a soldier. I climbed another fence, and I remember that my body was weak and ached at every joint— and that's all I remembered.

"What are you doing Charlotte?"

"Putting water on for tea."

"You cold?"

"Yes, aren't you?"

"Yes, but not as cold as I was that night. Anyway, the next morning I woke up in a cow pasture with a warm sun shining on me."

"Was your fever gone?"

"No, I was pretty sick. I was lying on my side against my pack, still strapped to it. Two hooded figures were looking down at me. Not the Grim Reaper, he always wears black; one of these wore white, the other brown. I tried to get up. They watched me struggle for a moment; then without saying anything, lifted me to my feet. The white one pointed toward a slight rise in the land and the three of us headed toward it. My feet trudged along, but most of my body weight was supported by my silent companions. When we reached the crest of the hill, I could see a large, walled fortress—but, it had a steeple with a cross on it. Finally, my dull mind registered that I had blundered on to the grounds of a monastery. These guys are monks!

"We went inside to an office where another monk was sitting at a desk. When he looked up, the white-cloaked monk made some hand signals, gesturing toward me and toward the field. The man at the desk, also white-cloaked, startled me when he suddenly said, 'Hello, I'm Frater Jacob. I'm the guest master at the Abbey of Our Lady of Gethsemani. I understand that you are not well and collapsed out on the south pasture. Would you like to have me notify someone to come for you?'

"I told him, 'I can't think of anyone to call.'

"'Since you're dressed like a soldier, perhaps you're affiliated with Fort Knox. Shall I notify them that you are here?'

"'No, I'm not affiliated with Fort Knox,' I said, glad that I had removed the 3rd Armored Division patch from my shoulder.

"'If you were to request it, I could sign you in as a guest. This would give you a little time to rest before you continue your journey.'

"I told him, 'I would like to rest a while if I could.'

"'We would be happy to have you with us. Could I please have your name for the record?'

"'When I told him, 'My name is Jude,' the two monks that brought me in smiled and nodded slightly.

"The guest master asked, 'Do you wish to add to this, or do you feel that in a monastery Jude is all the name one needs?'

"'I feel awfully foolish about this, but I'm not able to come up with anything more. I have a fever and I'm afraid my brain is a little confused at this time. Would it be possible for me to report back to you later after my mind clears?'"

Charlotte asked, "Had you really forgotten your last name?"

"No, but I was afraid he might see it in the newspaper. I didn't know whether they would turn me in. He seemed satisfied, though, and just said, 'Sure, meanwhile, we will call you *Jude*; I like it so much better than John Doe. Fraters Basil and Edward will help you to the guest quarters.'

"My two rescuers helped me remove my boots and outer clothes, and I fell asleep on top of the bed in my long underwear. I remember that people entered the room from time to time and did things for me, but I was too weak to respond. One may have been a doctor. Slowly, and it was probably after several days, the world returned enough for me to realize that one of the monks had been spoon-feeding me. It was a great relief when I was able to feed myself and soon afterward, join the other guests in the dining room, library and chapel."

"I guess you'll be well enough to drink your tea then," Charlotte said as she set it down.

Jude grinned, took a sip and continued, "My hosts, I discovered, were Trappist monks who had chosen a life of silence. The guest master and the abbot, who ran the place, could talk; but the others spoke only under special circumstances, like teaching or an occasional communication with the outside world.

"Once I was reasonably well recovered, I asked the guest master if I could participate in some of the work activities. They cut wood to heat the place, raised cattle and hogs, and made cheese and fruitcakes. Frater Jacob introduced me to the abbot so I could talk with him about it. I had seen Frater Paul during the services but had never talked with him. He was a large man with a calm, peaceful appearance like many of the other monks. The brothers and the atmosphere at Gethsemani gave me a sense of peace. I wondered if I could stay for awhile to sort out my mind. I couldn't tell if my brain was even functioning right. With none of us talking, I could have been a little looney. Mostly, though, it seemed like a good place to hide out until the M.P.s got tired of looking for me.

"The abbot led off by saying, 'Frater Jacob informs me that you're feeling stronger and would like to participate in some of the activities associated with the abbey. I'm pleased you have made such a rapid recovery after being so ill. I presume you're aware most visitors come to Gethsemani for brief rests from the outside world and to gain spiritual strength. Your entry was less intentional, but perhaps God had his purpose for placing you on our doorstep. I won't ask you about the circumstances that brought you here. The important thing is that you derive spiritual benefit from your association with us. Continued spiritual growth should be the sole basis for determining how long you stay—unless, of course, for whatever reason, you decide to leave. If you would like to work at some of the farming activities, I can arrange that; and, after a couple of months, perhaps we could have another chat to see how you feel about your association with us.'

"'I do have some spiritual matters to sort out; the abbey seems like an ideal place to do it.'"

"You stayed nearly two years at Gethsemani?" Charlotte asked.

"Yes, and all that time I struggled in silence over what I had done, repeatedly reminding myself, Turk was a human being—not an animal—don't tell yourself you just killed an animal. I kept asking myself the same circular questions, over and over. What if I had killed him sooner? I could have saved Andre, a more worthwhile person. Who are you to decide who should live and who should die? Even if I had shot Turk before he started the winch, how would I feel about never knowing whether he really would have killed Andre or not? Rerunning the alternatives and self-accusations was an endless process; it never made me feel better."

"You did the same thing I was doing over Margaret's death. It's funny how we torture ourselves with painful questions that have no answers."

"Yes, that's what I was doing. My only relief came from the hard work of farming and the religious ritual, particularly the chanting. But, always present was the concern that the abbey was not far from Fort Knox, and that I would be recognized. It came to a head one evening when I helped a woman in the parking lot who was struggling with her luggage. She introduced herself as Nancy Oris, and explained that she had come for a four-day retreat. Charlotte, I almost blurted out, "Captain Oris's wife?" In the course of the conversation, she commented that her husband was not able to drop her off as he had on her previous visits, because he was off on a training mission. Now wouldn't that have been dandy, if I had encountered him in the parking lot? I had to move on— but where? When I considered the problems associated with trying to develop a new identity on the outside, and a life on the run, I decided to stay in the monastery business.

"Our Lady of the Holy Ghost in Georgia seemed far enough from Fort Knox to be safe. I talked with Frater Paul about moving to Georgia and told him I would like to enter as a postulant. I had prepared a flimsy reason for wanting to move; but, Frater Paul didn't ask for one. Sometimes, during our conversations, I felt he knew I was AWOL from the Army but didn't want to place me in the awkward position of having to discuss it with him. He was familiar with the monastery in Georgia and told me, 'It's a good place for you to continue your spiritual development.'

"'I would like to be able to do that. If I can catch a ride from someone leaving the monastery who's headed east, I could pick up the Appalachian Trail and hike on down to Georgia.'

"He wanted to know, 'Is this a penance you are inflicting on yourself for some terrible crime, or are you seeking an opportunity for prolonged contemplation.'

"I told him, 'I like to struggle in the face of adversity.'"

Charlotte said, "Yes. I can see that you do thrive on adversity, but what about the continuation of your spiritual development? Were you serious about that?"

"I was then; but, since coming here, I spend less time silently brooding about the past."

"What do you think about now, Jude?"

Before he could stop himself, he said, "You, Charlotte." Then, realizing what he had said, added, "and the farm." But, it was too late. His face had already become warm—he knew it must be turning red.

Charlotte squeezed his hands gently and said, "What the heck, it's better than brooding. So, then what happened?"

"Three days later I had a backpack filled with food and camping equipment and two new, colored sport shirts to break up the Army colors that had been my usual attire. I said my good-byes and caught a ride on a delivery truck headed east.

"It's taken me a long time to get my life on the trail to

Virginia. I'm surprised at how verbose I am now that I've found my voice. I even left out a lot of stuff that was indirectly related to getting here, particularly about my life as a silent farmer at Gethsemani."

"You're not at all verbose. You are, in fact, a fine storyteller, especially, for one who has spent so much time brooding in silence. I would like to make a reservation to hear about the things you left out, but now I better start my limp back up the hill."

"I suppose if I were a gentleman, I would invite you to spend the night and offer you breakfast in the morning; but, having already confessed what a failure I am as a nighttime host, I'm afraid my offer would have little appeal."

"Jude, my concern is that if you haven't had a woman since your college days, I might not get much sleep—thanks anyway for the offer you almost made."

Together they worked their way up to the big house as the last of the light was drained from the sky. Arrival at the kitchen door was awkward for Jude. Should he try to kiss her good night like he wanted to or would that be too forward? He had decided that slaves do not attempt to kiss the mistress of the plantation, when Charlotte took both of his hands in hers and said, "Jude, I can't begin to tell you how important this day has been for me and what a pleasure it is to have you here." She kissed him on the cheek and went in the house. He watched her progress as lights popped on from one room to the next. Yes, the mistress can kiss the slave and measure out the affection with calculated control. I would have buried myself in her soft glow without restraint.

9

Jude spent the next day down by the stream reading and fishing while Salvi and his nephew harvested the grain. Toward the end of the day, after they pulled out, he headed home for a lonely dinner and a quiet evening. The lights were on at the big house. He kept looking up there, struggling with his longings, but knew Charlotte was working and would not want to be disturbed.

On Friday Aunt Millie's car clattered down the drive in a cloud of dust. Charlotte had already left. Jude gave Aunt Millie a little time to settle in before going up to the house. When she saw him at the back door, she said, "Humph, you still here? Ah thought by now you'da moved in or taken the silver and run."

"I just couldn't leave without seeing you one more time," Jude said, avoiding how he really felt about her hostile attitude.

"Long's you still here, couple bags of stuff in the rumble seat of my car belongs to you. Miss Charlotte added

some stuff to the list. She must think you worth someth'n—
or do she feels sorry for you? She even tol me cook nuff for
you and tell you come eat it, case she don't see you 'fore she
leave."

Jude nodded, then took the bags from the car, pleased
with the dinner invitation but irked by the old woman's
comments. Probably it was only her form of humor, which
Lyle and Charlotte seemed to accept as Aunt Millie's *ways*,
but which came across to Jude as some sort of jealous power
struggle between the inside dog and the outside dog.

In addition to the things Jude told Aunt Millie he needed,
the bags contained work gloves, sunglasses and a straw hat
that Charlotte had added to the order. Does this mean
Charlotte thinks about me when she's not with me? Jude
went down to the barn whistling. He hitched the reluctant
Alfred to an old two-wheeled oxcart and went down to the
fields. Too bad he could not have asked Salvi to leave some
grain for Alfred and the chickens. He used a scythe to
harvest what he could from the corners of the fields where
the machine could not reach. By late afternoon, when he was
nearly finished, he saw the the little red roadster coming
down the dusty driveway. Not long afterwards Aunt Millie
left.

Charlotte went upstairs and flopped on the bed. She had
felt restless all day and at odd moments a little horny. As
she lay, looking up at the canopy, she thought about Jude and
his failed relationship with Trudy. It was apparent that he
needed the coaching of an older woman, like she had been
coached by an older man when she was in France. Although
that affair had left her heartbroken for awhile, she had to

admit it was the most exciting time in her life. And here now was Jude's Trudy, who apparently had been brought to life by an older man.

Charlotte thought about the kind of lessons Jude might profit from; but, when she realized the direction her mind had taken, she told herself—C'mon, kid, you better take a cool dip in the pool. She removed her clothes; and, as she passed before the full length mirror, stopped to look at herself. Her hands slid slowly down her neck, glided caressingly over her breasts and down across her belly. When they reached her crotch one hand continued down her inner thigh but the other one stopped—her ring finger had wandered briefly into a sensitive crevice. "Charlotte!" she scolded out loud and pulled herself away. She grabbed her pool robe and went downstairs.

Standing at the edge of the pool, she could see past the barn and down the lane where the loaded cart with Jude sitting on top of the straw moved slowly toward the barn—a tiny figure in the distance. She removed her robe and nonchalantly tossed it over the lounge chair. Then, standing naked at the edge of the pool, she dived in making almost no splash. When she surfaced, she paddled about for awhile testing her injured leg, then broke into laps. The water streaking over her bare skin made her feel alive and sensuous.

When Jude reached the barn, he could see from his position on top of the load that Charlotte was in the pool swimming laps. He stopped Alfred and watched. How smooth and gracefully she glided through the water, every ounce of energy directed toward forward motion. Was Lyle right?

Did she do this naked? He could not be sure. Afraid she would catch him gawking, he directed the horse into the barn and unhitched him. After he fed and watered him, Jude went to his cabin to clean up.

Meanwhile, Charlotte finished her laps and pulled herself from the pool. She put her robe on and went inside to make herself a gin and tonic. After swimming laps she loved to lie by the pool with a drink and let the energy flow back into her body. As she sipped and relaxed, her thoughts returned to Jude and his girlfriend. She visualized Trudy, the young innocent; Tony, the lecher; and Jude, the injured party. Her thoughts rambled as she half-dozed—mostly flashes of Jude moved across her closed eyelids. Somewhere in the midst of it, she took off her emerald ring and tossed it in the pool. She was awakened by Jude, kissing her on the forehead.

"Hey, I'm glad you could make it—I have a special job for you. I lost my ring while I was swimming. I can see it from here, and I can see its glow when I'm underwater but I can't seem to grab it. Would you mind trying?"

In view of the way she had just been streaking through the pool like a seal, Jude thought this was a remarkable request. "Gee, Charlotte, I'd like to but for all the presents Aunt Millie brought me today, a swimming suit wasn't among them."

"You could leave your shorts on if you're embarrassed by your nakedness; that way I can see if the underwear I bought fits you properly."

"OK, I'll try; but it surprises me that a poor swimmer like me has to come to the rescue of an Olympic class swimmer like yourself."

"What makes you think I can swim, and how could you be so silly as to compare my splashing to someone of Olympic stature? If you can retrieve my ring, I'll tell you about my Olympic status."

Jude took off his outer clothes and jumped in; diving was not his best talent. He was also afraid his shorts would come off. Once in the water, he swam to the spot where they had seen the glitter from above, executed a duck dive, and within seconds had the ring. When he pulled himself up on the side of the pool, his shorts did nearly come off; and, as he stood, he had to jerk them up from where they were slung almost at the hairline.

"Oh, you've got it! That's wonderful, thank you so much." As she held up her finger for him to put it on, it flashed through her mind how thrilled he would be if he knew where that finger was this afternoon. She pulled back her stretched out legs and put her feet down on either side of the lounge and said, "Here, Jude, sit here." With her knees spread, her flimsy robe opened almost to the critical point. This was not lost on Jude, who supposed she must have a swimsuit on or she would not take such a chance on exposing herself. Still, another half inch and he would know if she wore a swimsuit—or if she really is a natural redhead.

When he was seated, he said, "What's this about Olympic status?"

"The reason this pool is so large and rectangular instead of cute and kidney-shaped is because my daddy decided when I was a little girl that I was a good swimmer and should train for the Olympics. The local schools, of course, were not equipped to satisfy such aspirations, so he set about to do this on his own. He wanted me to train and be in a state of readiness; so, when I advanced to the educational level where women's competition was available, I could just float to the top and grab the gold. In telling about it years later, it all sounds kind of silly; but actually I wasn't completely out in left field, or maybe I should say not completely out of the water. At one point, I came to within one person of being selected for the relay team. I was surprised that I came that close because I knew all along I wasn't that good. It was actually a relief not to be selected. Can you imagine what it would be like to have the low score on a relay team that almost won? Daddy was terribly disappointed. He ranted and raved and was going to sue, and he made me feel absolutely rotten. In the end, I'm happy to say, he did nothing. I still enjoy the pool."

"It is nice to have one large enough to swim laps in,"

"But, you never did answer my question, Jude—about comparing my swimming to that of an Olympic swimmer." What she really wanted to know, was whether he had seen her swimming and realized she was naked. Not that she minded, since at that distance only fantasies could be provoked.

"When I came up with the last load of oats, I could see you streaking through the water from my seat on top of the load."

She still was not sure what he saw at that distance; perhaps, he was not sure either. To change the subject she held her hand up and explained, "This ring was given to me by my grandmother, who acquired it as a gift from a Yankee major with whom she had shared some tender interludes."

"Does the stone feel warm?"

"Yes, see," and she pressed it playfully against his bare chest. "By the way, Jude, don't think I haven't noticed that you're playing peekaboo with my pussy." She was aware of it from the time he sat down; and had, in fact, opened her legs just a little more to make sure she held his attention. Her attention had already become focused from the time he came out of the pool with his thin white boxer shorts, soaking wet. Charlotte continued to feed her reckless mood as his face turned red. While he fumbled for words, she impetuously added, with some amusement, "Perhaps, you'd like to kiss it?"

Now he *really* didn't know what to say, but finally stammered, "I've never done anything like that before . . . I think I'd like to."

She opened her robe a little more, leaving no doubt about swimsuit or hair color. As he leaned toward her, she let the robe fall completely open. Jude's excitement raced to a pitch he had never known before. This was the first time he had ever seen a naked woman. She was so beautiful with her womanly curves and smooth skin that it was hard for him to believe this was happening to him. He had never felt such enthusiasm about Trudy. They had both been so modest that they had always left their clothes on when they had sex and never looked at each other's private parts.

Jude felt a tenderness toward Charlotte, that in spite of his overwhelming passion, he did not lunge for her. Instead he slowly stroked her feet and legs; then, he kissed her tenderly several times on the inner thighs, gradually working his way up to the fluffy red patch between them.

She took his head gently in her hands and held him to her, undulating her pelvis up and down slightly. "Explore, Jude," she urged him, "don't stop now." Jude explored. She drew her feet up to the edge of the lounge to provide a better angle; and, as the game progressed, he lost all inhibition. "That's it, oh yes, yes, right there, oh God, oh, oh, oh." The interval between the *ohs* became shorter and shorter until she broke into a mixture of sounds between sobbing and laughter.

Jude was never certain when Trudy had climaxed; he even thought she might have faked it. Now he was sure she had been faking it. This was the first time he had caused it to happen. Filled with joy and lust he started to move up to lie on her, but she said, "No, Jude, no, that's out." Bewildered, he got off and stood up, his erection sticking straight up out of the pee hole in his shorts.

"What are you going to do about that?" he asked indignantly, pointing at his upright organ. She stood up, swept her gin and tonic from the table and hung the glass on his pole—ice, tonic and all.

"Here, fuck this," she said and ran in the house. The cold liquid quickly caused him to wilt—he recovered from his shock barely in time to catch the glass as it fell toward the concrete.

Jude was confused. He did not know whether she was angry with him, whether he was angry with her, whether his dinner invitation had been revoked or what to do next. He put his clothes on slowly, hoping she would come back and restore their relationship. He walked back to his cabin, evaluating his feelings as he ambled along. Once his frustration subsided, he decided he was not angry and began to see the humorous side of it. But, what kind of woman is this? Does she feel anything for me at all, or, is this just some kind of a game in which she makes up the rules as we go along? He relived again in his mind what she had done to him, visualizing every detail; finally, he said, "God, I love that woman! But I have to accept the fact that I'll never have an ounce of control over our relationship. If I really want her—which, of course I do—it will be on her terms."

Cheated out of dinner, he ate some leftovers and settled down to read and wait for Charlotte's next move. He kept one eye on the lights at the big house. They were arranged in a trajectory from the kitchen to Charlotte's bedroom and remained that way for hours. Finally, her bedroom light and the hall light went off, and the light in the study went on. Jude read while he hoped Charlotte would come to heal the rift, but she did not and he eventually fell asleep in his chair. When he awakened, it was 3:00 a.m.; the light in Charlotte's study was still on. Perhaps she saw his light and was waiting for him to take the first step. Shit on that, it's one thing to be a slave, its quite another to crawl. He smacked *Plantation of Hope* down on the table, turned out the light and went to sleep. The next morning he and Alfred resumed their efforts to harvest what they could of the grain, but Jude's heart was not in it.

Early afternoon Jude watched from the field as the red roadster left and returned several hours later. He still wondered what he was supposed to do about Charlotte. The answer was always *nothing*. When he returned to his cabin, a package was on the porch. His gloom lifted immediately.

Whatever it is—I don't give a rip—at least she's still interested in my case!

Inside a paper bag was a six-pack of beer, a pack of condoms and two envelopes: one addressed to Judd, marked #1, and the other to Jude, #2. Now, Judd or Jude, whoever you are, do not leap to any optimistic conclusions about the rubbers. This is an unusual woman you're dealing with: in all likelihood, the message is, *if you plan to stick your dick in this beer or in someone's gin and tonic, wear one of these so you don't get wet.* That self-admonition had no effect, he was still so excited he could hardly open the envelopes.

Since the first letter, started with "Dear Judd," Jude was immediately suspicious about the author and looked to see who signed it. Sure enough, it was from Miss Ashley, the main character in *Plantation of Hope.*

Dear Judd,

Being aware that Negroes can't read, I nonetheless write this with the thought that one day it may no longer be against the law to teach our slaves reading and writing: Or if the South loses this terrible war, you will then be able to pursue your education as a free man and learn on your own. I hope you will save this letter until then. I would like for you to be able to read for yourself how much I appreciate the unlimited service you have provided on this plantation. I suppose I could tell you personally how I feel about yesterday afternoon, but I find it easier to write about my feelings and sensations than to talk about them. By writing this, I hope it will help me to sort out what happened and whether or not I should feel ashamed; and, if so, of the several things I should be ashamed about, how much guilt should I assign to each? This is not an easy question. In the face of the exaggerated displays of morality seen in society today, I cannot judge right from wrong based on the professed values of others. In a careful examination of my own feelings, I find that I feel no shame; all I can honestly acknowledge is the sheer ecstasy of what we did yesterday afternoon—I shall always cherish the memory.

I can not apologize enough, though, for hanging my glass of mint julep on your manhood, especially after you so gallantly rescued my ring from the pond. The glass was all I could think of to save us from what would have happened next. Our short-term ecstasy could so easily have turned into long-term misery.

I don't have to tell you that if we were found out, or if I were to have your child, how this sanctimonious community would react, and the baby would have no better chance. I wish I could promise never to thrust my intimacy on you again; but, in all honesty, I cannot take that vow. All I can do is promise to avoid situations where repetition of the act is possible; but, now that I know the unbridled joy you are capable of releasing in me, even that promise seems insincere. God help us! Your grateful mistress, Miss Ashley.

Jude pondered the letter as he laid it on the six-pack and picked up the second letter. I guess that was some sort of an apology to me, but why from a hundred years ago? . . . Oh, God! That woman is about to offer our passionate love scene—my humiliating experience—to the entire nation in one of her novels. What the hell will this next letter do to poor Jude?

Dear Jude,

Ashley's letter to Judd was to a man she knew full-well could read. Granny had secretly taught some of the young household staff to read as she was learning, and they passed it on to others who were interested. It was standard patter around the plantation to speak of the inability of the slaves to read and write since it was illegal.

I presume you have guessed what I hope to do with that letter—if you don't object. First, though, I owe you a more direct explanation and apology than Ashley provides. The basis for my bad behavior yesterday stems from the rebirth of my long suppressed sexuality—and that's your fault. All day long, even in school, I thought about you—becoming increasingly aroused. I tried to squelch it, but it followed me home. I undressed to take a cool dip in the pool; but, when I saw my naked image in the mirror you were with me.

I didn't lose my ring in the pool; I threw it in for no other reason than to have you retrieve it. I don't know why. Neither of the two possible reasons are particularly honorable. You can take your pick; but, of two bad choices, I hope you select the one that in your eyes makes my behavior sufficiently acceptable for our relationship to survive. Did I toss my ring in the water for the fun of getting you to *fetch* it for me? Or was I just hoping to see you naked? Both reasons are possible since they do not preclude each other. I hope you will understand that beyond the *ring toss,*

I had no other plan. The rest of it just happened, spontane-
ously and irresponsibly on my part. Much of what Ashley
felt and conveyed to Judd applies here, just substitute my
marital status and our age difference for the racial barrier
that that couple faced.

I sincerely apologize for my insulting treatment of your
aroused manhood; it deserved better. I hope Ashley adequately explained my dilemma about fear of pregnancy. As
for the dinner I reneged on, if you're not too insulted, I hope
you will join me tonight. I have the courage to suggest that,
having seen that you are still here today, working the farm.
At one point, as I was lying on my bed last night trying to
account for my bad behavior, I considered that you could be
angry enough to end your vacation. If you do come tonight,
though, don't do so under the illusion that I'm cured: I'm
just sorry is all. My irrational behavior is probably in-
curable. Signed: Charlotte, Loving Mistress of Greyledge.

Jude put the beer in his refrigerator, took out a clean
outfit and went to the pond to bathe. The slab of smooth grey
rock took on new life as he thought about Ashley and Judd
enjoying each other there.

When he arrived at the mansion he knocked and went in.
A note on the kitchen table told him to start his beer and she
would join him in the study. Or he could help himself to the
liquor cabinet or wine, if he preferred. This time he found a
glass for his beer, surmising that drinking from a bottle
might be a little crude in a house like this. When Charlotte
joined him in the study, he was admiring the gun cabinet.

When he saw her, his heart skipped a beat. She wore a

full-length dress, which was dark green and hugged her body closely almost to her ankles. It was held together in front with hidden buttons arranged so one could fasten or leave unfastened as many as one wished, at the top or bottom. Charlotte used that flexibility to full advantage. All of this was supported on high heeled shoes and set off with gold earrings and a pearl necklace. Jude was glad he had changed into clean jeans. "Charlotte," he said, "you are absolutely elegant. If this is all for my benefit, you couldn't have a more appreciative audience."

"Jude, I'm so pleased you like it; I bought the dress today, just for you—green, you know, to fuel that Irish blarney in you—I see it's working."

"Oh, it's working all right, but not on Irish blarney."

"Jude, I noticed you were looking at the guns, do you like shooting?"

"Yes, I really do. Just for fun and for hunting, though, not for competition. Those trophies with your name on them suggest you have quite a serious interest in shooting. Were you really the the junior skeet shooting champion of the Shenandoah Valley?"

"Yes, but the competition was limited; when I moved up to the state level, I quickly realized I was out of my league. My local wins weren't good for male egos, though, and just added another layer of resentment on Greyledge. A lot of the guys around here are really good with squirrel guns. I wouldn't go up against them in that category; but becoming good at skeet shooting is expensive because of the high cost of shotgun shells, clay birds and range fees. Not many folks around here can afford to put enough into it to become good.

This is probably another honor my daddy bought me. If you think you would have some use for these guns, feel free to borrow them. I expect that if you're a hunter you'll start getting antsy in a month or two."

She sat down in a comfortable chair and crossed her legs. Half of the skirt of her dress she draped over one knee, the other half fell off to the side, liberally exposing one thigh. All of this appeared casual and innocent, but it did not escape Jude's attention. He held up his beer and asked if she would join him. "Thanks, Jude, I'd rather have Scotch. Would you mind pouring for me? I have to grab something from the kitchen." As she got up, her dress and body flowed in sensuous unison, raising Jude's level of excitement another notch.

The ice was already in a bucket on the liquor cabinet. He poured the Scotch and called out to the kitchen to see if she wanted water with it. "No thanks," she said, smiling. She had already returned to the room and was standing next to him with a platter of crackers, cheeses and vegetable sticks.

"Oh, wow!" he exclaimed, "And you teased me about my mighty preparations."

"This is nothing, Jude, wait 'till you see what else I have planned."

"Why does that sounds ominous? Charlotte, should I be frightened?

"Maybe a little; but, since you survived Friday's ordeal, I believe you're stronger now. That exchange we had by the pool was really exquisite, up to the time I *dropped the ball*—no—wrong cliche: until I *dashed cold water on it*." Jude blushed a little and could not imagine ever being able to come right out in the open and talk about something like that. "I guess I haven't had any real sexual interest for so long, it kind of caught me by surprise. You really are a very sensuous man, you know."

"I guess I really didn't know that. You certainly have a way of getting me all worked up. I suppose I shouldn't say this; but when I'm around you, I can hardly keep my hands off you. And, after the other day—you know, by the pool—whenever I close my eyes, I see you there."

"Naked?" she asked. He was already blushing—she did not need to add that. He also had developed a bulge in his pants that assured her that the poolside adventure was not just a thing that happened; she had not lost her appeal—even to a younger man. She was beginning to feel tingly and wished he would not be quite so shy. Why doesn't he come over here and touch me?—even kiss me? How about fondle you? Do you want that, too, Charlotte? she asked herself as she felt her panties becoming moist.

They sipped at their drinks while their hunger for each other mounted; but the distance between their chairs was too great for Jude to overcome. Finally, Charlotte went over to Jude, took him by the hand and silently led him up the stairs.

Charlotte had already closed the large velvet drapes and laid the tiebacks over the headboard of the canopy bed. The room was quite dark with the drapes drawn and was illuminated only by a small lamp in a corner. The bed had been striped of all covers except for the bottom sheet. Jude looked around, not knowing what to make of this or what to do next. Charlotte went over and kissed him, rubbing the full length of her body against him; then she drew back and said, "Jude, I'd like to have you take all your clothes off and lie on your back on the bed."

"Really?" he asked in astonishment. His erection, held down by his jeans, would have been happy to be released to an upright position; but he was not quite courageous enough to strip naked and go flop on Charlotte's bed with his pole sticking straight up in the air.

"C'mon, Jude, you were anxious enough yesterday to make love to me."

Slowly he removed his clothes, embarrassed about his hard-on. Finally, all that was left were his shorts, which poorly concealed the bulge. At this point he asked if it would be all right to leave them on for awhile.

"I suppose you could for awhile, but eventually they have to go."

In his shorts, he lay on the bed as instructed, but asked Charlotte if her plan called for her to remain fully clad.

"Why, Jude, is my new dress losing its spell?" She walked over and kissed him full on the mouth, prolonged and sensuously. As she lay across him, the palms of her hands ran up the side of his chest, through his armpits, and along his arms, straightening them upward as her massaging hands traveled. By the time he became aware of what was happening, she had slipped a noose over each wrist and had him tied to the bedposts with the tiebacks. While he was trying to figure out why he was letting her do this, she tied his ankles to the lower bed posts.

"Hey, c'mon Charlotte," he laughed trying to be good-natured about it, but still a little uncertain, as he realized she had him helplessly bound.

"There, I've got you; I can do anything to you I please. You're mine." She stood back to admire her work; and, at the same time, Jude had a chance to admire her, standing there with a mischievous grin, still tantalizing in her revealing gown. He guessed maybe he didn't mind being her captive. Neither did the bulge in his shorts mind, he noted. Just as that thought crossed his mind, it entered hers as well.

She took a pair of scissors from the drawer of the night table and said, "We've got to do something about that problem, gesturing toward his shorts."

He panicked. No, Charlotte, he thought, for Christ's sake get away from my dick with those scissors. Oh, God, she really is crazy. . . . No, she wouldn't do that. Shit, she's just fooling around. I could make an and awful ass of myself by becoming hysterical. C'mon now, Jude, keep calm, he told himself. So, he lay straight and stiff while she made a cut along the outer seam on each side of his shorts leaving them held together by only a hinge of cloth at the crotch. She folded the front down and pulled the bottom out from under him. Now he was completely naked as she had requested in the first place.

She put the scissors away and came back to Jude who asked, "Wouldn't it have worked as well just to pull them down?

"Heck no, Jude, with your ankles tied, I wouldn't have been able to get them off; but, what happened to your beautiful hard-on? Oh, my God, Jude! You thought I was going to cut it off. I wouldn't do that," and she went down, cupped it in her hands, and kissed it. "Won't it come back?" she asked with concern and disappointment. "Shall I untie you? You aren't still scared, are you?"

"No, I'm not scared; I don't think I ever was," he lied, "just distracted."

"Well, then, let's get on with the fun," she said, resuming her cheerful tone. She stood up, where Jude could see her clearly, and slowly undid the buttons on her dress. Starting at the top, she worked her way down to the last one. It fell open, revealing a bra and scant panties. She let the dress slip off her shoulders and tossed it over a chair. She removed her bra and, noting that Jude was returning to life, placed one cup of the satiny bra over his semierect organ and stroked it up and down until it was fully restored. Without shame she removed her panties and stood before him, enjoying his renewed passion. She moved her hands all over his tanned, muscular body, kissing him here and there and trailing the tip of her tongue over places he had never realized would be arousing.

"Now, Jude, what did you do with the small package I gave you?"

"It's in the right front pocket of my pants, ma'am."

She fished it out, and laid the pack of condoms on the night table. Then sat on his stomach and leaning forward rubbed her moisture all over his stomach and chest. Then she let him taste her. When they were both wild with excitement, she installed the condom, mounted him and rode him like she was on horseback. It was not long before she started her "Oh, oh, oh-series," and Jude was right with her. When it was over, she collapsed and lay full length on him, still holding him tightly inside her. She freed his wrists. He was completely relaxed. As he stroked her hair and face, he became fully aware that he had just experienced the greatest joy of his life.

When she recovered her strength, she untied his ankles, spread a sheet over him and climbed in beside him. Jude kissed her gently and held her close. She snuggled and purred.

Jude said, "I love you, Charlotte." He could feel her stiffen.

"You don't love me, Jude. You are not permitted to love me; and I don't love you. We have a mutually beneficial arrangement; and we have just satisfied a longstanding physical need. It was splendid, but we can't do this anymore. I've paid you back for my bad behavior yesterday and now we're even. Do you understand, Jude, we are not in love?"

Reluctantly, he said what he was supposed to say. "Yes, Charlotte, I understand what you're saying, and I suppose you have your reasons—probably because you are the mistress of the plantation and I am the slave. But, one thing you need to remember, I've got two rubbers left." He hopped out of bed, slipped on his pants, and pocketing the two condoms said, "C'mon Charlotte, let's eat."

"You're not taking me seriously," she called after him. To herself, she said, I guess I'm glad. I don't mind having an uppity slave. She slipped on a pair of shorts and a blouse, and joined him in the kitchen.

Nothing was on the stove, but in the refrigerator there was a large sirloin steak. Charlotte took the steak out of the refrigerator and said with exasperation, "Whatever is on that woman's mind? She knows I don't have the least idea what to do with this."

"Maybe she expects you to have some help with it," he said. Then he teasingly suggested, "Aunt Millie probably expects me to look after you when she's not around."

"You mean you know what to do with this hunk of raw meat? Gee, I suppose you do." As Jude took over the dinner preparation, she was disappointed to see his attention shift from her to the steak.

What is there about this man that I need his full attention? She watched his confident movements as he put things together—already he seemed to know her kitchen better than she did. But, is Jude looking after me? How do I feel about that—is that really what's happening? Well, for one thing, he certainly isn't as helpless as the other men in my life. It's amazing that Jude, with his modest and a gentle manner, has killed a man. So . . . he was trying to save another man's life. The miraculous part is that he managed to hold himself together enough to escape. Charlotte, this isn't a man you can push around. You could manipulate Daddy. He had money and power; but when it came to his little girl, he was soft. John Paul was just plain weak. Whatever would you do if you had a man you couldn't dominate? Do you know what you want? You've always been fiercely independent—yes, right up to the point you land in deep shit, then you're pretty happy to have someone like Jude come along and fish you out. No, not just someone like Jude, but Jude himself. The fact is, you like having him around. He seems to like being here, but he really doesn't know you. Once he does, will he disappear in the night like he did from the Army? At that instant, Jude put something on the table and as he did, he looked at her and smiled. His eyes met hers and lingered a moment—just long enough for her to wonder if they were saying *I love you.* She felt a rush of warmth to her cheeks and thought, my God, Charlotte, you're feeling like a schoolgirl. You told him he wasn't to fall in love with you and that you don't love him. Now you've got electrical pricklies over your body from what he might be saying with his eyes. You better stop this daydreaming and set the table.

She went through the motions of helping him, but her mind was not on it. In the midst of her fumbling with the dishes, Charlotte asked, "How come you didn't tell Captain Oris about Corporal Tandy's attempt to seduce you?"

"I don't know—guess I was embarrassed about having gone along with her lovemaking."

"Did you like her?"

"Yeah, I guess."

"Do you still think about her?"

"Once in awhile."

"You sorry you didn't get to have her?" With the table half set, Charlotte just sat down, bothered at the thought of Jude and Corporal Tandy together.

"Charlotte, of all the things I told you the other night, why have you focused so strongly on this?"

"I suppose you think I care how many woman you've been with?"

When he looked at her, she was just staring down at her hands folded in her lap. Not knowing what kind of mood she was in, he was afraid to answer, so instead, asked if Aunt Millie might have bought some Italian bread.

She opened a cupboard door and said, "Yes, there's a loaf

in here. How did you know?"

"She thinks we're living like a married couple. She would want to provide us with proper meals instead of the hit or miss diet you've been on for the last several years," he teased.

"Married couple! If she knew what we just did, she'd throw a fit. She's got that old time religion and makes no allowance for sinners. . . ." Charlotte interrupted what she was saying and began pointing at the stove. Jude turned to find that the steak was going up in flames—a near disaster; but, as it turned out, it was only a little more blackened and overdone than he had hoped. He told her if it were not for her culinary skills, all would have been lost. "Yes, that's the truth, Jude; but, if you're setting me up to cook next time, forget it; this flash of gourmet cooking was about it."

As they started to eat, Jude said, "So, tell me, Charlotte, who was it that tied me to the bed and served me with such wild delight? Was it Ashley or Charlotte?"

"Does it matter?"

"Yes . . . at least I thought it did . . . but, maybe it doesn't. I'm still trying to sort it out. I suppose, in view of your proclamation banning any real love between us, it doesn't matter. At the time, much of my joy was from the intimacy I thought I was sharing with you; but, if this all took place nearly a hundred years ago and with another woman, the remembrance loses some of its sweetness."

"How do you feel about yesterday afternoon? Did you mind sharing that experience with the previous century? Perhaps, if I use the current version in my fourth novel, it will be shared with this century; and, maybe even carry over into the next century. Since these are historical novels," she teased, "we could be fucking our way through history."

Jude smiled at her joke, but felt jolted by her verbiage. Up until now, he had always viewed her as the epitome of gentility. Even though he suspected she chose some words purposely to shock him, knowing that didn't alter his vulnerability. They left the subject unresolved and chatted about the farm, including Salvi's visit.

"How much do you think the grain will bring?" Charlotte asked.

"It's hard to tell how much the birds have harvested, and I don't have any idea about the price of grain." Jude really did not want her to have any estimate that would allow her to recognize that half was removed for Lyle's share.

As dinner drew to a close, Charlotte brought the subject back to their intimacy, needing to be reassured that Jude really did enjoy her in spite of their age difference.

"That was the most exciting experience of my life; but, now that I'm beginning to sort it out, something's missing."

"What's missing, Jude? I thought for a simple country girl, I had planned a fairly imaginative program."

"Oh, you did that all right, but what was missing, I believe, is illustrated best in the letter from Ashley to Judd. She made no attempt to understand how Judd felt about her. Was he some kind of prey organism for Miss Ashley to feed off at will? Maybe she thought she was doing him a favor. Did he worship her so much that he was happy to serve her in any way he could? Or did he resent the power she held over him? Maybe he resented his own willingness to be treated in such a humiliating manner. At first he may have felt honored to be the chosen one, but repeated abuse of her privilege, with no hope for gratification on his part, could have been a tough assignment."

"That's interesting; keep going."

"What white folk don unnerstan is dat us niggers has feel'ns too and dat some a dem feel'ns has to do with how us feels about da mistress and how she do bout us. Some us love da mistress and be happy just to lick her if'n she say, but some us niggers hanker fer tender feelins."

Charlotte laughed at Jude's attempt at southern black dialect and told him that he might want to organize a union among the slaves on the plantation. He could negotiate the amount of licking time one had to deliver in order to receive one unit of stroking time. It was all in good humor, but Jude began to suspect that the tenderness he craved could not be won by negotiations.

Then she said, "All kidding aside, Jude, I think you're onto something. You remember when you were nursing me back to health, after my riding mishap, I told you that my third book was in trouble, and that one of the criticisms was that my sexual interludes had lost their spark? Well, I have a feeling that, since you entered my life, that problem may be resolved. The letters I wrote to you were an attempt to apologize and to explain my way back into your life; but they were also, as I'm sure you've guessed, an attempt to capture on paper some of the excitement of the event. Now, though, you've opened the door on a side of life I haven't adequately explored in writing."

"What's that?"

"Isn't it just like the mistress of a plantation to use her slaves as she sees fit with no consideration for the feelings or psychological effect it has on them! Jude, I may be able to do something now to retrieve my crippled book, but you'll have to help me; you have to give me the slave's perspective." Charlotte interrupted their conversation to gather some writing materials. "There Jude, jot down some of this stuff when you think about it."

"I'd be happy to try; but I couldn't imagine I'd have a whole lot to offer. Also, I don't want to spend all my time with Ashley—once in awhile I'd like to spend time with Charlotte. Sometimes I don't know who you are; and, worse than that, Charlotte, I don't think you always know who you are."

Charlotte went over to where Jude was sitting and hugged him. "Jude, it's sweet of you to worry about me like this, but I'm not sure it makes any difference who I think I am. If it makes a difference to you, though, let me assure you that right now you're with Charlotte; and she really appreciates having someone who cares who she is." She was holding his head against her chest and gently moving back and forth. Jude was enjoying the softness of her breasts without a bra; they moved about with such a bouncy freedom. In her haste to put on her blouse before she came downstairs, she missed a button; occasionally he caught a glimpse of a bare nipple. With very little movement, he opened the gap enough with his nose to reach the nipple with the tip of his tongue. When she felt what was happening, she drew him closer and held on to the . . . moment? No, it was longer than a moment. She unbuttoned another button and told herself, just a little longer; then he has to quit and go home. He tried to give some attention to the other nipple, too; but she had to open the rest of the buttons before he could get at it. Before long they were back in her bedroom. This was not as tempestuous and urgent as the earlier encounter; it was slow and tender. Charlotte traced his hardened muscles with her fingertips and kissed him in all the sensitive places. At the same time, Jude, now with his hands free, was able to lovingly caress the soft and exciting curves of her body. This would all be so perfect, he thought, if only she loved me like I love her. His feelings overflowed as he entered her. When it was over, she reached up to the nightstand and handed him a couple of tissues. He wrapped the condom and tossed it under the bed, making a mental note to retrieve it before he left. She lay across his chest, kissed him and said, "That's two; you better save the next one for a rainy day."

"Charlotte, do you expect me to wear it on rainy days so I don't get my thing wet? When we start spending rainy days together, one of these won't be enough. Maybe you should buy a 12-pack next time."

"Damn you, Jude, you still don't understand that we are not going to do this regularly. Besides, do you have any idea how hard it is for a woman to buy these? I had to drive over to a little town on the other side of the valley, where no one is likely to know me, and find a drugstore where a female was clerking. She chuckled, "There was this shy little moon-eyed girl at the counter, who didn't look at me all the while the transaction was taking place. I think she was as relieved as I was when it was over."

"Why did it have to be a female clerk? Couldn't a male pharmacist have handled it?"

"Maybe, but it would be my luck to run into one with a warped mind like yours, who would say, 'lady, don't you think you ought to take the 12-pack? You wouldn't want your stinginess to spoil your evening.'" They chuckled and whispered to each other a little longer; then they fell asleep.

At some time in the night she went to the closet for a blanket and shut off the small light. She also opened the drapes and looked out at the world that had become a better place to live in than it was two weeks ago. When he awakened, she was sound asleep. He found a piece of paper and wrote: I love you, Miss Charlotte; but us slaves has to be in the fields early, if we gonna have a corn harvest—you better be gitt'n ready for the next rainy day.—Love, Jude

10

On Monday Jude had to face Aunt Millie again. He had be-come dependent on her deliveries, a fact he regretted but not enough to cut certain staples from his diet; particularly milk and bread, as well as little presents that Charlotte thought to include. He had put it off until midafternoon.

As usual she acted surprised that he was still there, but it was done with a smile. She did, however, accuse him of taking something. She did not say what, but seemed willing to forgive him, "Miss Charlotte happy this morning—she not like that for years."

Oh my God! I forgot the condom under Charlotte's bed. He felt the red color creep up his neck, across his face and into his hair.

"Now don't you fret none, Mr. Jude. When Miss Charlotte happy, we's all happy. I jes hope she don't git hurt."

He thanked her—somewhat awkwardly—for the things she had picked up for him and returned to his cabin. Along the way he mused over his advancement in rank to *Mr. Jude*. This slave business is unpredictable, but a lot more gratifying than the monk or prison business.

The rest of the afternoon he worked in the field. When he came back, he found a note on his door from Charlotte asking if she could come over for dinner that night. She realized it was late notice but she wanted to tell him something. Don't struggle with anything fancy, she said.

He watched through the screen as she came down the path, a bottle of wine under one arm and a six-pack of beer under the other. She knocked and entered before he could tell her to come in. She put the things on the table, and excitedly said, "Jude, you did it! You saved the farm!" She hugged him and pulled from her pocket the check from the grain elevator. This will cover the mortgage for a whole year and buy the seeds and fertilizer for next year. You can't imagine how close I was to losing it all."

"That's really great, Charlotte! I'll get some glasses and we'll toast our good fortune."

Even though Jude knew about the mortgage from Lyle, all through dinner he was bothered that Charlotte had never talked with him about it. While he served coffee, he asked, "How were you able to hide your concern from me that you were on the verge of losing the farm? It would've stuck out all over me like giant hives."

"Are you bothered that I didn't tell you, Jude? You shouldn't be; after all we've only known each other for a couple weeks; and, during that time, we've been too busy baring our souls and bodies for boring mortgage talk."

"Charlotte, were you keeping this from me because you

didn't want to worry me or because slaves aren't privy to business matters pertaining to the plantation?"

"Oh, I believe the Number One slave is entitled to know about the business of the plantation. I guess I didn't want to set you to worrying about the possibility of losing your new home before you were even settled."

"Should I keep things from you, Charlotte, things I think might upset you?"

"No, I'd resent it. Aunt Millie does that to me all the time; she thinks she's protecting me from the evil world like daddy did when I was a little girl. She doesn't tell me things she thinks will bother me because she knows I'm liable to throw a temper tantrum. I'm sure I was downright bitchy to her while John Paul and I were having trouble; but, she's tried to protect me all my life. Part of it may also be to protect herself from my moods when I have disappointments . . . ." She stopped talking and studied Jude's face, "What's happening here, Jude, are you setting me up for some kind of confession you're about to make?"

"Yes, but before I make it, I have to lay one more brick in the foundation. I want you to promise not to get mad at me."

"How the hell can I promise that without even knowing what I'm dealing with? Besides slaves don't negotiate with the mistress."

"No, they just keep the secret."

"I could have you whipped for that. No, I wouldn't have it done, I would want to do it myself."

"Charlotte, are you getting horny?"

"Yes, but then I'm always a little horny when I'm

around you."

"Did you pick up that 12-pack yet?"

"No, and I haven't said I would," she grinned defiantly. "Besides I'm having my period. Meanwhile, you better not be pestering Aunt Millie."

"Does this mean we're going steady?"

"Yes, but that doesn't mean you're getting it steady—or at all, particularly if you keep secrets from me."

"I guess you've got me 'cause I really have to get this off my chest. I'll have to hope I'm talking to Charlotte and not Ashley. Frankly, I don't know what to think about that woman."

"You wouldn't know what to think about Charlotte either if you could check the stories about me around town."

Jude tentatively said, "But, I do know some of those stories about you."

"How would you know?"

"From Lyle."

"From Lyle!"

Jude could not tell whether the flash of emotion across her face was from surprise or anger, but it was too late to stop now. Haltingly—apologetically he told Charlotte how he came to know Lyle; and how they had conspired to save the crops and give Lyle his cut. He explained how Lyle's fiancée had forced him to quit Greyledge, fearing that gossip might lead to his swinging from the magnolia tree in the front yard. He assured Charlotte that Aunt Millie is still protecting her, that she was the one who would not let Lyle tell her why he was quitting.

When Jude finished, Charlotte said nothing. Is she going

to blow up and stalk off home? Or tell me to hit the road?—
an order I am prepared to defy. He watched her just sitting
there, occasionally swirling a small amount of wine left in
her glass, but transmitting almost no clue as to what was
going on inside. Once in awhile, he thought he saw a faint
smile at the corners of her mouth; but it was just a flicker.
Finally, he could take the suspense no longer, "Charlotte,
what's happening?" Against the long silence, his voice
seemed too loud and it startled both of them.

She reached out and took his hand, "Thanks, Jude, you
were right. If you had come to me with the proposition of
cutting Lyle in on this, I would have hit the ceiling, killed
the entire deal and probably lost the farm. I was really
angry with Lyle and felt betrayed. I would have been in deep
shit if it hadn't been for you. Lyle would have, too, if you
hadn't saved him from the septic tank hole. How did this
farm ever get along without you?." She found herself flooded with a deep inner warmth that was rapidly dissolving her
protective shell. She struggled to return to a business-like
tone to keep herself from melting into Jude's love.

"Now then," she said, "since we have come to trust each
other, I have something else to tell you—you do trust me,
don't you, at least far enough so you don't worry any more
when I have a pair of scissors in my hand?"

"Yes, but if this message is going to be painful, you
better hold both of my hands."

She squeezed his hands and said, "I hope you won't feel
differently about me when you hear more about the risks
I'm subjecting you to. In addition to the reasons I gave you
earlier, as to why the local folks view Greyledge with such

animosity, a more immediate and potentially more dangerous issue exists."

"Dangerous?"

"Yes. During the Second World War, my father became
involved in manganese mining. Essentially, he was a silent
partner who put up some of the money to start the mine. He
didn't know beans about mining, but the business went well
and he made a lot of money, mainly because it was heavily
subsidized by the government. One day there was a cave-in
at the mine and 14 men were killed. After it happened, the
union claimed the owners had allowed unsafe conditions to
exist that caused the accident."

"How did the accident occur?"

"Most manganese is taken from open pits. Daddy took me
out to see the mine one day. It was an unbelievably large
hole, so big that trucks drove down into it on a road that
wound around the outer wall of the pit going deeper and
deeper until they looked like little ants.

"At one place in the mine, the ore ran deep under the
mountain. They put a shaft down and brought the ore to the
surface in little cars. Some of the men were coal miners
from Pennsylvania who had worked in deep shafts. Daddy
presumed they knew what they were doing. Apparently they
didn't—either that, or conditions were different than they
were accustomed to. Anyway, the shaft collapsed and along
with it some of the wall of the pit also caved in. There was
such a volume of rubble covering the men that they just
called it a grave and left it as it was."

"That must have been very upsetting to your father."

"Daddy was so upset about the accident that he sold his
share of the mine. The families of some of the dead miners

continue to claim they were never adequately compensated for the loss of their loved ones. Daddy despised the money he had made off the business and would gladly have given it to them; but, since he had never been involved in the operation of the business, he didn't have any records and didn't know whether they had been compensated or not. After the company folded, nearly a hundred people were left unemployed. The community had a low educational level, so there wasn't much else for them to take the place of mining. Daddy felt that the best thing he could do for the community would be to build a new school and set up an endowment fund to help support it. The town accepted the money; and, even though they knew my family had supported the North during the Civil War, named the school after Jefferson Davis."

"In the long run, though, weren't they glad to have the school?"

"The families of the miners didn't give a rip about the school; they spent their energy culturing meanness and resentment. When daddy was alive, they were surly but not threatening. They were still afraid of his money and power. They were even somewhat intimidated by John Paul because they thought he could buy them some harm. But as time goes on and it looks like John Paul may not be coming back, they have become more bold and threatening. It's possible even that the bank manager, Milo Hogg, stirs them up, hoping I will be intimidated enough to sell and leave the area".

"Have they ever tried anything?"

"No, they make verbal threats when I go into Grimble, and I've received phone calls that ranged from sexual harassment to threats on my life."

"Did you notify the sheriff's office about the calls?"

"No point in that; some of the calls probably came from there. It's ironic, isn't it?" she continued. "You were giving me a hard time about not confiding in you that the mortgage was coming due, while at the same time I'm risking your life by seducing you into staying here. It's even more ironic that you felt you had to dance all around the barn, so you could save my farm from the bank without upsetting me.

"Jude, now you know the risk you're taking by staying here. If you want to go, you should feel free to do so; but, I hope you'll stay."

Jude stood up and lifted her hands gently as a signal for her to stand. She melted into his arms and he kissed her tenderly and held her reassuringly.

Charlotte whispered, "What if I lied about having a period because I knew that condom was burning a hole in your pocket?"

"Oh, Charlotte, please say you lied," and his kisses became more passionate as he unbuttoned her blouse and began planting them down her neckline.

"If we do this, will you be gone in the morning?"

"No, if I'm being held captive by sex alone, I have to wait a few days to see if you buy the 12-pack."

"Oh, God, please save me. Now it's all turned around. Instead of being the mistress of the plantation with a dutiful slave, I'm a whore turning tricks to save the farm."

All talk ceased as Charlotte allowed Jude to undress her and kiss and stroke every part of her body while she stood naked before him in the dim light of the evening. When their lovemaking was over, they snuggled and dozed briefly in a tender embrace. Jude sensed that Charlotte felt closer to him now than ever before; his love for her brought him a happiness beyond any he had ever imagined. His dreamy thoughts, though, were interrupted by Charlotte's stirring.

"Where you going?" Jude asked. "Why don't you stay all night and I'll make you some breakfast in the morning?"

"Thanks, Jude, but some other time. It's still early and you have given me some interesting ideas I want to get on paper before I lose them. Besides, we're out of rubbers; and, you probably wake up every morning with a hard-on."

"Wait till I dress and I'll walk you home."

"No, that's OK, there's still a little light." She kissed him while he was still lying there naked. She looked at him lovingly and said, "Jude, you're really wonderful. Thanks for being my friend. See you tomorrow."

11

Charlotte went up the path humming a happy tune. She bounded into the kitchen still humming, and there at the table, with a beer in front of her, was Madge. "Charlotte!" the woman screamed in delight, jumped up, and threw her arms around her; and, in a serious gruff voice, asked, "Where the hell's the Scotch? I've been sitting here for nearly an hour trying to drink this stuff and couldn't find anything to wash it down with. When did you start drinking this crap? Or is John Paul back? Christ, I hope he isn't. I'd rather see you shacked up with the devil. Where's the Scotch?"

Madge was a boisterous extrovert, almost always of good cheer. She was dressed smartly, in a way that made her excess weight inconspicuous—even attractive.

"Oh, Madge, I'm so glad to see you. It's been nearly six months this time. What on earth have you been up to? Don't start telling me yet. I'll get the Scotch; I keep it in the liquor cabinet in the study now."

"Wow! Aren't you gitten' fancy," Madge yelled after her. "I always thought it was handy when you kept it in the kitchen."

"Yes, that's why I put it in the study." Charlotte returned shortly with the Scotch and poured them each a drink over ice.

"Well, here's to the good ole days," Madge said, raising her glass high. "May they never get in the way of the good times to come."

"Yes, to the good ole days and good times to come," Charlotte repeated, clinking her glass against Madge's.

"Christ, you look good, Charlotte, who you fucking?"

"Madge! I'm still married."

"Oh, yah, I keep forgetting, but then I've been married three times and could never remember to say 'no' when a promising dick presented itself. But the fact is you have more glow than I've ever seen you with before, including when you came home from your honeymoon. Come on, Charlotte, tell me about him. You know I won't let go until you do."

"Madge, you know I can't be out whoring around; John Paul's mother would just love to catch me in an affair so Earl, with the help of his crooked friend's in the judiciary, could grab the farm."

"Shit, Charlotte, you'd get more out of life if you'd just say *fuck the farm* and walk away. You'd probably live longer, too. Are those assholes down at the Boar's Nest still on your case?"

"Ever since I was born a Henderson. Enough about me, what've you been up to? Are you and Ron still together?"

"Yes, we've worked out some kind of half-assed compromise. You remember how bothered he was that I was on the road so much—even suggested that I might not always be faithful to him? Well, he has a new secretary now; I think they're sexually compatible."

"Have you met her?"

"Several times. She's a young, mousy little thing; but kind of pretty. I think the two of us provide Ron with an interesting contrast; she probably lets him be on top more than I do."

"Does it bother you that he's doing her?"

"Nah. I'm happy for him. And for me. Now he doesn't pester me to find out how many different ways I did it with our store manager in Memphis or what I did to the buyer in Kansas City; instead, we can enjoy our time together."

"I suppose that can work if neither of you has a jealous streak."

"You still writing, Charlotte?"

"I'm revising the book I sent off just before your last visit. The editor came close to incinerating it, but he had poured so much piss on it before he threw it in the fire it wouldn't burn, so he sent it back with strict orders to fix it or find a new publisher."

"Can it be saved?"

"For awhile I was having trouble seeing what was wrong with it. I made changes, but I couldn't tell whether it was getting better or worse. Recently, though, I've been able to see that the book really isn't very good and that my earlier changes have been just another boring way to tell a poor story. I'm really quite excited about it now, even hopeful."

"That's nice. When can I meet him?"

"Damn it, Madge, why do you think a woman can't do creative work unless she's inspired by a man?"

"Charlotte, I don't believe that in your business, and for you in particular, inspiration arises out of the mist. You used up your grandmother's sporting life in your first book and your French experience in the second. I'm sure John Paul didn't recharge your batteries with anything original. So, who is this new guy?"

"Madge, you tell me enough love stories in one visit to fertilize several novels."

"Sure, Charlotte, I'll watch for me in your next book. Meanwhile, if you're not talking, pour me another drink; and I'll tell you about the rag pickers convention in New Orleans last spring."

The next morning they arose long after Jude. Charlotte poured orange juice from a can but Madge insisted on making the coffee, claiming that some jobs are too important to leave to the inexperienced. Charlotte had hoped to wake up before Madge, so she could warn Jude about her visitor in case he wanted to go into hiding. She did, in fact, wake up before Madge but lay there thinking about Jude and some of their conversations and their intimacy. Her hands moved slowly over her naked body as she massaged herself back to life. Maybe her dawdling was a sign she really wanted Madge to meet Jude.

Charlotte was allowed to make toast but was interrupted in the process by an urgent request. "Charlotte do you still have those binoculars you bought when you took that bird-watching course?"

Sounds of someone hammering were coming from outside; Charlotte presumed it was Jude repairing the fence, part of which was visible from the kitchen window. Before answering, she thought OK, kid, brace yourself. "Yes," she replied as calmly as she could, but her heart was pounding. "I still enjoy that wild sport—even put up a bird feeder in the winter. Look in the drawer next to the sink." Without saying anything, Madge took them out and went to the window where she studied the man with the hammer. Then she put the binoculars back and returned to the table where her toast, coffee and orange juice were waiting. She sipped, nibbled and smiled ever so slightly, while the mounting silence raised a wall Charlotte had trouble climbing over. Finally, as casually as possible, considering the tightness in her throat, Charlotte said, "His name is Jude; he was hiking along the run at the back of the farm about two weeks ago and happened to see me fall off the horse. I hit my head and was knocked unconscious. I had sprained my knee, too, and never would have made it back to the house if he hadn't helped me."

"Yes . . . I see."

After another awkward silence, Charlotte blurted, "He brought me back to the house, nursed me back to health and probably saved my life, so I told him he could stay and take a little vacation here if he wanted to and could use one of the slave cabins. He's just a kid, but he's fairly handy and a good worker. He mows the lawn, trims the hedges and plants flowers. He saved the honey dipper, whose foot was caught and being crushed by a rock; he taught Alfred to pull a buggy, and arranged to have the grain harvested, which provided enough money to save the farm from foreclosure by the bank."

"Yes . . . I see . . . young, you say? I don't suppose he's reached puberty yet? . . . Charlotte, you're about the coolest woman I know: confident, poised, the whole works; but, right now you're completely unhinged. Will I get to meet him or does he have to go off and pick cotton this time of day?"

"He's a little shy; but, if you're careful not to spook him, we might be able to sneak up on him so you can get a closer look."

"Thank God, you've recovered. I have no idea how to deal with teenagers in love."

"C'mon, Madge, I'm certainly not in love with this kid. He's only 23. It's your accusations that make me feel self-conscious. Let's go meet him right now and you'll see that he's just a young drifter who's handy at odd jobs."

"Wow! What a relief!"

They walked down to where Jude was hammering. His back was to them so he did not see them coming until they were nearly upon him; he had no opportunity to innocently walk off as though he did not see them.

"Jude," Charlotte called from the short distance, "I'd like to have you meet an old college friend, Madge Eckhardt. Madge this is Jude Bartholomew."

"I'm pleased to meet you, Jude. Charlotte has told me some good things about you; but, I'm really more interested in the bad than the good, so we're starting at ground zero."

He smiled at her unconventional introduction and said, "You better talk with Aunt Millie if you want to know about my dark side. She's got the date marked on the calender when I'm going to steal the silver and run."

Charlotte assured Jude that, "Madge's name is on Aunt Millie's calender, too, marking the day that Madge will be turning Greyledge into a brothel. She claims it would have happened a long time ago except that Madge can't decide which of us should be the madam and which should provide the pleasures."

"Yes, that's a serious problem for me, having had extensive experience in both management and pleasure."

"Madge does have managerial experience," Charlotte explained. "She's district manager for a women's clothing store chain called *Extremes*. She covers the whole Midwest. I know she'll want to tell you herself about the pleasure part of her experience; she likes to do her own bragging about her conquests."

"Yah, Charlotte skips too many important details."

"What I was wondering, Jude, was whether you would be willing to treat Madge, and me, to one of your world famous chicken cookouts."

He looked at his watch and said, "Yes, it's early enough yet to put it together." He turned to Madge and said, "This is pretty rustic fare for a city girl; do you think you're up to it?"

"Sure, I'm an old Camp Fire girl from way back. Besides, the alternative is risking my life on one of Charlotte's chemistry experiments."

Charlotte acted deeply hurt, then said, "That's great, Jude, we'll bring the refreshments and the appetites. In the meantime we better get out of your way. What do you want to do next, Madge, go for a swim, a hike, or somewhere in the car?"

"Let's walk down to the end of the lane. You can show me the exact spot where you would have died if Jude hadn't saved your life. Then, we'll have lunch, rest a bit in the shade, and go skinny-dipping in the pool. Jude, you want to join us in the pool?"

He flushed slightly but recovered enough to say, "I'd love to, but I'm afraid Aunt Millie would find out."

"OK," Madge said, "but you'll regret turning this down for the rest of your life."

"I know, but it's these lost opportunities that feed my fantasies."

Charlotte and Madge walked along the lane chatting casually but Charlotte was only half-attentive to their conversation. What occupied her mind was waiting for Madge to render judgment on Jude. Madge said nothing— teasing Charlotte, forcing her to ask Madge for her opinion so she would have license to ask rude and personal questions about Charlotte's relationship with Jude. When Charlotte could wait no longer, she tried to frame her question as nonchalant as possible, even though she knew Madge would see through her. "So, Madge, what do you think of my handyman?"

"Hmm, yah—thought you'd never ask. So, you're not fucking him, huh? If I were to believe that, all I could ask is, why not? I think he's old enough and he certainly seems more mature than your usual 23-year-old. Piss on John Paul's mother, just don't invite her to watch; and if the manor house catches on fire, either let it burn, or piss on that, too. You deserve a hell of a lot more out of life than what you're getting. To hell with the age difference and to hell with whether it lasts one year or 30 years. If you could see the difference in you since my last visit, you'd just reach out and let it happen. Oh, God, Charlotte, I can just see his brown beard buried in your red pussy."

"So, Madge—you think he might be a pretty good handyman?"

Madge looked at her in disgust and gave her a shove off the lane into the tall grass.

When they reached the last field, Charlotte explained how they met and how Jude saved her life. Madge was in stitches. "Charlotte this has got to be the funniest thing in your life. My admiration for your handyman continues to grow. Too bad he didn't drill some holes in your head; they might have let some of that old shit out and some sunlight in."

Charlotte told her everything except, of course, about their intimacy and how they really felt about each other, which she had not admitted to herself yet. After lunch they lazed around in the study, chatting and dozing to make up for their lost sleep the night before. Once their lunch had settled they went out to the pool. Charlotte modestly remained in her robe until she entered the pool and put it on again as soon as she came out, but Madge made no pretense to cover up. Jude was the only one around who might peek at them and she really kind of liked that thought.

While the women were swimming, Jude prepared the cookout. He started his fire down by the lake and arranged the seating and a makeshift table. He could hear them laughing at the pool and could not help thinking about their naked bodies. The view was mostly blocked by trees; only a few gaps allowed a distant glimpse of the pool area. Jude was discreet enough not to look in that direction, except that every once in awhile he forgot and found himself enjoying the sight of the slender, athletic lady and her stout, jolly friend. He admonished himself for peeking, and he scolded his hard-on for getting in the way of his work.

His preparations were nearly completed when he saw the two of them coming down the path. "Good timing," he shouted.

Charlotte waved a bottle of wine to let him know they heard him. Oh shit, he said to himself, I have only two wineglasses. Well, that's all right, I can drink beer; but, when he set out the two goblets, as if by magic, suddenly there were three. God, I love that woman, he thought; and when Madge was not looking, he squeezed Charlotte's upper arm affectionately.

They gathered the food and drink and took it to the lake where the setting was as Charlotte had hoped it would be. She knew that many of Madge's previous visits were not very pleasant and were duty calls out of an old friendship. Even after one glass of wine Charlotte was feeling it; but, then, they had had a gin and tonic at the pool not too long before they came down. With her second glass of wine she raised it high and said, "Here's to my good and loyal friend, Madge; I'm so happy you have come to visit us." Jude liked her use of the word "us," as though they were a couple. Madge liked it, too, for the same reason; but Charlotte did not notice what she had said. She went on to explain to Jude that Madge was her oldest and best friend and that she had named Margaret after her.

Madge said, "And Margaret and I were good friends, too. You would have loved her, Jude." Then Madge steered the conversation to a safer, happier ground while they devoured the dinner. When it was over she said, "Jude, that was wonderful; you were right, Charlotte. Here's to Jude's world famous chicken." After they drank to the chicken, Madge started to sing a dirty little ditty about a rooster but interrupted it to ask Charlotte if she still had that old guitar she had in college. "No don't tell me: I already know, it's in the attic and we don't go up there after dark; that's all right, I brought my Gibson. It's still in the car; I'm going to get it. Stoke up the fire, Jude; I'll be right back."

"Let me get it for you," Jude said.

"No thanks; actually I'm after the Scotch; I presume you don't know your way around the big house enough to find that," she grinned like that was the best joke of the evening.

While she was gone, Charlotte thanked Jude for putting up with all of this. "I didn't have time to warn you. She arrived last night and spent until the early hours of the morning trying to find out who I'm sleeping with—seeing how much happier I am compared to her previous visits. I fended her off last night; but, when she saw you mending the fence this morning, her vulgar mind focused immediately on you. She's been pestering me for the details all day. Without blatantly lying to her, I have been trying to dodge her direct questions. I don't think we have given her anything yet to work with. I wouldn't mind if she knew what good friends we have become, but she wouldn't quit until she vicariously shared every sensation with us."

"We could let her watch."

"Jude!" she exclaimed, slugging him on the arm. "It's amazing how rapidly your morals have decayed since your arrival. You really do see this as the Plantation of Hope, don't you? And the worst part of it is, Madge would be perfectly willing to watch. What chance is there for a nice girl like me when her two closest friends are so depraved?"

"None, I'm afraid. You better get the 12-pack," Jude responded. "I'm not all bad, though, at least I didn't accept Madge's offer to join you in the pool."

"No, but you did peek through the trees at us."

In spite of his bold talk, she caught him off guard and was rewarded with one of his shy little blushes she so enjoyed.

"It was . . . an accidental glance."

"Sure."

"Did Madge know I saw you?"

"No, she would have been thrilled had she known. Heck, I didn't know until just now—when you took my bait."

"Are you going to tell her? Perhaps I should apologize?"

"Are you crazy? She already sees you as some kind of deprived sex symbol waiting for someone like her to save you from the cold-hearted mistress of this plantation. The only thing that restrains her is her lingering doubt about the chastity of our relationship. We have a fine line to walk; if she becomes completely convinced you're being denied, she'll try to save you. But, if she discovers you're not, she'll pester both of us for the details. Unless, of course, you'd like to try a fat lady—here's your opportunity. A lot of men find it exciting."

"If I ever decided to try one," Jude teased, "she'd be my first choice; but, currently I'm going steady."

She did not know whether to slug him or kiss him; but, since they could now hear Madge walking back down the path, she settled for calling him "a shit" and changed the subject. When Madge arrived at the picnic site, Charlotte was saying, "Madge and I saw feathers and the remains of a chicken when we were on our walk earlier today."

"I was afraid of that; I saw a fox cross the fields on a couple of occasions and had been concerned about the chickens."

Madge said, "Jude, you better borrow one of those cannons, from up at the main fort and see if you can't reason with that renegade." She parked the guitar and, from a shopping bag, took out the Scotch, ice bucket, and three of Charlotte's crystal glasses. "I hope I haven't offended the host by supplying the glassware and all; but, I don't know how well-equipped these slave quarters are for drinking fine Scotch."

"Oh no, Ma'am, Ah takes no offense; usually I drinks from the jug; but, when I has a fine lady come to visit, I offers her the long-handled dipper from the water bucket. It never entered my mind that I should be equipped to entertain two fine ladies at the same time."

"Jude, after that wonderful flow of shit, you need to restore your lost fluids." Madge poured the Scotch liberally over ice and handed it to him.

"Thanks, Madge, I can see that you do have managerial skills. Speaking of which—this company you work for—you say it's called *Extremes*? What are these extremes?"

"Color, material, design and the amount of meat exposed."

"Is this a fairly successful company?" Jude asked.

"Yes, at least in the Midwest. We're continuously expanding. One of the limitations to growth right now is finding good store managers. What I need to do is get you to go back to Chicago with me and enter our store manager training program."

"Well, that's very nice of you to put that kind of trust in me, but I would have to think about this for awhile, and I would have to finish the season here on the farm. Would I be able to bring Charlotte with me?"

"Hey, I've been trying to get Charlotte into the rag business for years, not as a manager, she'd be terrible at that, but as a buyer. She has superb taste in women's clothing—if you haven't noticed. She is one of the few people I know who can walk the fine line between bold color and gaudy. But, she won't come. Seriously, though, I'll give you my card. If you ever decide to run away from the plantation, call me.

"Don't carry my card on you, though. One day those Henderson-hating maggots are going to crawl down out of the hills looking for Charlotte; if you get in the way, it won't bother them to kill you, too. Whoever is cleaning up the mess might find that card on you, and send me the body— on the other hand, it just occurred to me that if you die with a hard-on, it might not be so bad to have the body around for a few days."

When they finished laughing at Madge's macabre little joke, Charlotte said, "Jude tell Madge the story your friend from Tennessee told you about his grandfather who died with a hard-on. Without admitting he was shy about telling it to Madge, he got Charlotte to tell it.

"Madge they had to jack him off three times before they could close the lid on his casket."

Madge cracked up with laughter. When she regained control she said, "Jude, carry the card at all times; just get some of the white lightening that old man was running on to make sure you die right."

"I'll do that. It'll give me comfort to know there can be life after death."

"You know, Jude, I had to work pretty hard to bring Charlotte to the point where she could use words like *hard-on*. I take full credit for expanding her vocabulary enough so she can be understood. When she first arrived at Mount Holyoke, her speech was so limited that about once a week I had to sit her down in a chair and tell her to repeat after me: 'fuck, dick, hard-on, pussy, etc.' Then she'd go home on vacation and we'd lose all we'd gained. Finally, the lessons took; I'm proud to have been part of the education of this famous writer."

"Madge, I owe it all to you."

"You thanked me in the acknowledgements of your books but you didn't say what for. By the way, Jude, I've noticed that you have considerable speech impairment. If Charlotte hasn't straightened you out by my next visit, I'll have to take you in hand." At that she gestured vulgarly to be certain her double meaning did not escape her audience. Then, she picked up her guitar and said, "Well, that's enough dirty talk, time for some dirty singing—back to the rooster." After a couple of verses, Jude and Charlotte were able to join in on the chorus. Next Madge led them through the well-known campfire songs, then some old popular songs that she and Charlotte knew; but, Jude mostly had to just hum along. Finally, Madge declared her fingers to be shredded and put the guitar down.

"So, Charlotte, how is the teaching going?" Madge inquired.

"Oh, God, I have to have another Scotch before I start on that piece of pain." But, when she raised the bottle to the light of the fire to check its contents, it showed empty. "This is terrible. Who do you suppose drank our booze?"

Madge said, "We better head for the fort; if the Indians catch us out here this sober, we're liable to die a painful death."

"You're right, Madge; it's one thing to die out on the prairie, it's another to die in pain."

"I'll escort you back to the fort," Jude said. "If any of the maggots have crawled out of the hills, I'll hold them off with my Boy Scout knife while you two load the cannons."

"You will join us for a nightcap?" Charlotte asked Jude.

"I'd like to, but that damned rooster woke me again this morning. I couldn't get back to sleep, so I'm starting to fade. I wouldn't be able to keep up with you two, and the next thing I know, you'd be making fun of me. Besides, I'd like to pick up one of those cannons Madge spoke of and open negotiations with that fox."

When they reached the house, they all went into the study. Charlotte took Jude to the gun cabinet, as though this was the first time he had been in the room. Madge went through the liquor cabinet looking for something appropriate for a nightcap. Charlotte told Jude to take his pick, and without hesitation he took the .30-06 semi-automatic that John Paul had killed the Cadillac with. She pulled open a drawer and removed a box of cartridges. "I know you'll need only one," she teased, "but if you find out where that rooster spends his days use the rest of the box on him."

Madge found a bottle she was pretty excited about and asked Charlotte if she thought it would be right for the occasion; with her assurance they all headed for the kitchen. Madge started for the glasses but stopped to ask Jude if he was sure he couldn't stay. She promised they would tuck him into bed if he fell asleep. He politely declined, and he felt a slight shyness creep over him, not being quite certain what her offer implied. Charlotte said, "If you feel you really have to go, Jude, I want to thank you for an absolutely wonderful dinner and good time." She very formally took both of his hands in hers and kissed him on the cheek.

Madge looked amused and bounded over, throwing her arms around him; she gave him a hard hug and kissed him full on the mouth. "That was really a great dinner and a great evening; it's been a long time since I had that much fun or such good company."

"I enjoyed it, too; I'm really glad I had a chance to meet you." With that he picked up the rifle and cartridges and headed for home. He was more comfortable now that he was armed. This talk about the unpopularity of Greyledge, and the fixation of the local folks on Charlotte, sounded more serious than he had initially thought.

Madge busied herself fixing their drinks while Charlotte looked for crackers and cheese. They were still feeling enough of their silly good cheer that Charlotte thought they probably did not need a nightcap; but she was not willing to be called a *party pooper.* Just as she thought that, Madge said, "Too bad Jude's a party pooper. We'll just have to muddle on without him. It won't be the same, though; not that he dominates the conversation with party talk. He's just nice to have around."

They sipped at their drinks thoughtfully but quietly. Finally, Charlotte said, "You like having him around, huh?"

"Yes, you?"

"Yes."

"You fucking him?"

"Guess we're back on that, huh?" Charlotte fended, as they both felt the impact of what was now clearly one drink too many—if there had been any previous doubt.

"Charlotte, you didn't answer my question. As your best friend, I'm entitled to know."

"Madge, I'm married; I can't be fucking every drifter that strikes my fancy—or yours."

Very slightly slurred now, Madge said, "Charlotte, what I'm not hearing is *yes* or *no.* Now do not be so crude as to say to me, 'Madge, it is none of your fucking business.'"

"Madge, why do you have to know?"

"Charlotte, I'm not so drunk as to be unaware that you just told me, in the polite form, it's none of your fucking business. But—even though I have always told you all the shameful details of my fucking life, I'm not going to take offense. You have every right to hold this back from me—me your best friend . . . . OK, Charlotte, I'll tell you why I want to know—if you aren't fucking him, I want him."

"You want him! Madge, what on earth would you do with him?"

"Never mind. Can I have him?"

"What for? What would you do if I said *yes*? "

Madge walked over to the window and looked down at the slave quarters. "It's dark over there; he's in bed already."

She returned to the table, took another sip on her almost empty glass and said, "What I will do, if you say I can have him, is go down there; quietly open the door and go over to his bed. I'll take off all my clothes, then I'll slip in beside him and fuck and suck all the juices out of him."

"Madge!" Charlotte cried out, "You wouldn't."

"Charlotte, if you're not fucking him, then, that young man deserves better than what he's getting here on this plantation, 'cause that leaves only Aunt Millie or a gelding horse. I'm gonna tell you flat out—he's beautiful. My crotch has been damp all evening. Now I didn't hear you lay claim to that fine piece of property, or say I couldn't go down there, so I guess I'll be on my way." She pushed back her chair and started to get up.

"Madge," Charlotte stalled, "what if he rejects your kind offer? Won't you be embarrassed?"

"I have never been thrown naked from a man's bed."

Madge might be serious—and just drunk enough to try. Charlotte had seen her do more outrageous things when she was less drunk than she is now. What if she succeeded? How would I feel about that? Her mind was too foggy to bring that into sharp focus; but, she knew she wasn't comfortable with

the thought of Madge lying naked next to . . . to . . . her slave
. . . to Jude.

"Madge, you better have another drink before you go."

"What are you saying then, can I have him? Thanks for
the offer of another drink, but I think I'll decline. I would
not want it to interfere with my performance. Who knows,
he may never have experienced a real woman before; he
might be so taken with it that he'll come back to Chicago
with me. See you in the morning, Charlotte, don't wait up
for me."

"Madge, don't go."

"Don't go? Why not?"

"Please, just don't go."

"He needs me, Charlotte." Madge reached for the door
knob.

"He doesn't need you, Madge."

"What do you mean, he doesn't need me?" she said,
jerking the door open to leave.

"He doesn't need you because I'm fucking him!" she
screamed . . . . "And I love him." She put her head down on
the table, sobbing and laughing at the same time.

Madge closed the door and walked back to hug Charlotte,
rocking her back and forth like a baby saying, "There,
there sweet Charlotte, that wasn't so hard, was it?"

Charlotte raised her head; tears were running down her
face, but she was laughing. "You shit, Madge, you knew all
along."

"Of course I knew. After spending the evening with two
of the lousiest actors I have ever seen, I just had to hear you
say it. You could hardly keep your eyes or hands off each

other."

"When did you first suspect?"

"When you came into the kitchen the night I arrived, you had the glow of a woman who had just been fucked. But it didn't make any sense to me until I saw Jude the next morning. At that point I knew where you had been when I arrived, and it wasn't saying good night to Alfred." She hugged her again and said, "Oh, Charlotte, I'm just so happy for you. Kid, you really deserve this."

"I am happy, Madge, but I'm scared. I'm scared for both of us. This is the first time I admitted, even to myself, that I love him. So don't think I was trying to keep it from you; you got to know about it as soon as I did—even before Jude."

"You haven't told him then?"

"No, I can't let him know. We have to maintain some distance so no one finds out about it, especially John Paul's mother."

"Is that why you keep him down in the slave quarters instead of up there under the canopy?" and she pointed up to Charlotte's bedroom.

"Yes, at least most of the time. He has had his turn under the canopy, though," and she smiled as she remembered the excitement of their first time in bed.

"When did you realize you had the hots for each other?" Madge was suddenly sober and excited to know everything.

"I felt he was hopelessly entangled that first night when he was nursing me back to health—after my fall from the horse. He claims he fell in love with me when he first saw me riding—even before I fell."

"But you, Charlotte, were strong and resisted any early

feelings?"

"Yes, sort of, but I knew I liked him, and thought it would be nice having him around. It was really Ashley who laid the plot to capture him and use him in various ways."

"Yah, anyone who has read *Plantation of Hope* would know that. She's so much more aggressive and horny than Charlotte—immoral and depraved; wouldn't give a shit about John Paul or his mother. I presumed immediately she'd be the one to make the first move."

"Yes, and the second, too," Charlotte responded.

"Does he know he's having it with two different women?"

"Sort of—I don't think he has completely evaluated it yet—but, then, neither have I. Sometimes, in the heat of passion, I lose track. Often it isn't until later when I write it up that I can sort it out. Maybe it's then that I take credit for what is socially acceptable and blame Ashley for the devilish fun I have.

"You know, it's funny, Madge, I know you better than I have ever known anyone else in the world; but, that's been over a period of more than 20 years. I've known Jude for only two weeks and I feel I know him almost as well as I know you."

"That's interesting. He seemed very quiet; I had a feeling that he was internal, and revealed himself to no one."

"You're right, that defines him exactly. I don't know whether it was our desperate loneliness or some trust we saw in each other; but suddenly we were revealing deep personal secrets neither of us believed we would ever tell."

"Was that before or after you consummated your

relationship?"

"Consummated our relationship? Madge, what happened to the "f" word?"

"This is different—sort of holy. I don't think I know about this. As I hear you talk about it, I know you're experiencing something I have never known. Do you have a plan?"

"No, I don't know what to do, except to hang on for dear life. Because of my situation, I can't have him move in with me, which is what I'd like to do. I guess he'll have to stay in the slave quarters, so if he's discovered I can try to pass him off as a hired hand."

"Doesn't he have a plan to do anything with his life; or, does he have such low self-esteem he's willing to be your slave forever? He might be pretty quiet, but behind those grey twinkling eyes lies a pretty good brain. He could do things."

"We haven't looked at tomorrow; we've been too busy living today. I think he hopes to extract something out of the farm, but mostly that seems to be in my best interests more than of any long-term value for him. Maybe that's his way of courting me, since he has no resources to wine and dine me in the usual way. He obviously likes the land."

"And you!"

"Yes, I think he does. Now, though, I'm going to drink a large glass of water to dilute all this poison in my system and go to bed. I hope to get 15 minutes sleep before that damn rooster starts crowing."

The next morning they were assembled in the kitchen just early enough to see Jude headed down the lane with

Alfred and the oxcart.

"Christ! That's rural," Madge commented, "just beautiful." They took turns watching with the binoculars until he was out of range. "If I were you, I'd send Ashley down there to spoil whatever he has planned for today."

"I expect you would want to come along and watch?"

"Yes, I would and I appreciate the invitation; but, I have to be on my way, right after breakfast."

"No! You can't leave so soon; you just got here. You have to stay at least one or two more days."

"I normally would; but, it doesn't seem right for you to bring a friend along, on your honeymoon. If it were just Ashley and me, we could show Jude a helluva good time; but, Charlotte's such a prude, she probably has an attitude problem about threesomes."

"If you leave this morning, you have to promise to come back soon. As a writer, I don't dare suffer a loss of vocabulary, or become any more prudish; I really need you."

"OK, I'll come back soon, after the flames have died back to a bright amber. I could handle that. Or, what the hell! You and Jude come up to Chicago. It'd do you both good to get away from here and see the lights.'

After breakfast Madge assembled her stuff and hauled it down to the car. "I didn't have a chance to say *good-bye* to Jude; give him a big hug and a you-know-what for me." Charlotte was not certain what this *big you-know-what* was supposed to include. Now that Madge had taken to expressing herself so indirectly, she was not as easy to understand. Charlotte was just as well pleased, though, that the interpretation was left up to her—now that they were going steady, as Jude liked to put it.

Once Madge's car had disappeared, Charlotte went inside and sat with her cold coffee and re-ran the events of Madge's whirlwind visit. She certainly had a way of getting things out in the open where they could be examined. Madge had forced her to face things she thought she was not ready to deal with; and, with that in mind, she got into her little red roadster and drove to the pharmacy in that part of Virginia where nobody knew her. Along the way she stopped off at the bank in Grimble to deposit the check from the grain elevator and to make a payment on the mortgage. Milo Hogg saw her come in; and, as soon as she left, casually wandered past the cashier to check her transaction. He did not reveal to the teller his disappointment to discover that she had made a payment on the mortgage and deposited money in her savings and checking accounts. He quietly returned to his desk, disgruntled but assuring himself that Greyledge was going to be his, one way or another.

12

When Charlotte arrived at her secret pharmacy, she was pleased to find the moon-eyed girl alone in the store. Since the condoms were hidden from view, Charlotte had to ask openly for the 12-pack. The moon-eyed girl reached under the counter, dropped the pack in a small bag, and then calculated the tax. While Charlotte was counting out change, the moon-eyed girl said, "Guess you enjoyed the last three I sold you, Miss Henderson." Charlotte was caught completely off guard. She continued to look at the change in her hand while she searched for an answer: she was buying them for her mother? Her son? A student? Finally, the moon-eyed girl reached over and took the proper change from her hand. About then, Charlotte recovered and said, "Yes, you should try it some time."

"My mother says I'm too young." She glanced up at Charlotte and, with a girl-to-girl smile, added, "What does she know?"

As Charlotte was leaving the store she spotted her two novels on the book rack; *Plantation of Hope* had her picture on the back.

She was a little annoyed at first, with her own naivete, to think that she could ever get away with anything, but she was so amused by her new young friend and confidante that brooding about it seemed out of the question. Perhaps Madge was right; I should live my life, even if it costs us the farm. We'd be better off somewhere else anyway.

So, how come it's *we* now who represent the farm? Don't bother to answer that; what we need before we can afford to run away from home is another best-selling novel.

As Charlotte pulled out of the parking place and headed the MG homeward, she vowed to be more discreet about her activities, as well as to ration these balloons more carefully than she had the previous three. They had been intimate for only a week and already two people knew about it. If she had known about Aunt Millie's discovery, she would need to conclude that almost everyone who knew them was aware of it. As she drew closer to home, the image of Madge climbing naked into Jude's bed crossed her mind. This was replaced by the image of Ashley climbing naked into Jude's bed and finally even Charlotte. The latter image was so intoxicating that she went a half-mile past her driveway before she came to and wondered, where the hell am I? When she saw the sign to Hadley's Orchard, she felt pretty foolish and was glad no one saw her turn around and go back. This humiliation was short-lived, though; images of her making love with Jude returned before she reached the driveway from the other side. As she drew closer to the house, she could see Jude and Alfred just starting up the lane. She dashed down to the slave quarters and left him a note saying, "Come up to the house as soon as you can—you can use the shower in my room."

Charlotte met him at the back door. While he took his shoes off, she told him that Madge had to leave but would come back in a month or two. He asked if she had a good time; and, as she led the way upstairs, Charlotte told him, "She really liked you. It was all I could do to keep her from going down to spend the night in the slave quarters."

"She really is a wild card."

"You couldn't imagine the kinds of cards that are in that deck."

It was not until they were in the kitchen, nearly an hour later, that Charlotte told Jude how Madge had wormed it out of her that they were intimate. While he scrambled ham and eggs, Charlotte regaled him with the drunken conversation she and Madge had the night before after he left, playing both parts and overacting just enough to fuel Jude's laughter. She told him everything except her admission to Madge that she loved him.

Jude thought about what Madge had said regarding Charlotte's disposition; truly it had improved from the time he had scraped her up out of the pasture. Since she had lightened up, he felt more at ease with her and less conscious of the differences in their ages and educational levels, as well as differences in their financial and social back-grounds. By the way, Jude, he asked himself, what do you and Charlotte have in common, other than a hunger for each other's body? Before he could sort that out, he took another look at her and decided that was enough.

While they ate, he brought up Madge's unsettling comments about the threats the community had made against Greyledge. Charlotte did not respond, so Jude just continued, "Now, on top of this old problem, you have to worry about keeping me a secret. You know, as the days grow shorter, I won't be going to bed at dusk—5:00 p.m. in December. If you have visitors after dark, they'll see lights in the slave cabin and want to know who lives there."

"So, what's the answer?" Charlotte asked.

"We need some dark shades, boxed in around the edges so there won't be any light leaks. Do you have a recent Sears catalogue? The one in the outhouse isn't up-to-date."

"Yes, after dinner I'll dig it out. There may be other things you want to order, too, now that we have money."

Early one morning, while Jude was working in the barn, he thought how nice it would be to see Charlotte ride again. Several times she had told him emphatically, "No more." Just to see what would happen, he put the sidesaddle on Alfred and led him up to the house where he tethered him in the shade of a tree. Every once in a while Jude checked to see if Charlotte was responding.

Charlotte was not up yet, but it was not long before she came out and scolded Alfred for shitting on the lawn and for all his past crimes. Then she went back inside the house. Jude watched his experiment fail with some amusement. After awhile, he decided it was dry enough to work in the corn; he took his hoe and headed down the lane, leaving Alfred to work it out with the mistress.

Jude had completed a couple rows of corn and was about to start the third when he heard Alfred's clippety-clop. From between rows, he could see the horse and rider coming toward him. She was wearing an 1800s style dress with a long, full skirt, white gloves, and a white, wide brimmed hat. She was a perfect picture of the grandeur of long ago, and Alfred was playing his part well, too. Jude knew immediately it was Ashley who was riding Alfred. Oh Lord, he said to himself—what am I in for now?

"How do, Miss Ashley. Fine day for a ride ma'am."

"Yes, it is, Judd, I thank you for saddling my horse so I could move about and enjoy this fine day."

"May I help you down, Miss Ashley?"

"Yes, I believe you could, if you don't mind."

Jude held the bridle with one hand and took her hand with the other to steady her as she dropped to the ground; then he tied the reins to a nearby bush.

Charlotte said, "The corn looks quite good now. It's easy to see where you've hoed it, that makes a big difference."

"Yes, I believe with the rain we had the other day and then again last night we could get something out of it."

"That's nice, but the truth is I didn't come down here to talk corn."

"What did you come to talk about, Miss Ashley?"

"I didn't come to talk at all. What I want, boy, is for you to get over here on your knees," and with her riding crop pointed to the ground in front of her.

"What'd I do wrong, Miss Ashley?" he said in mock fear as he kneeled before her.

"Nothing, boy, I just wanted to make sure you didn't forget how to pleasure your mistress. And, with that, she raised the skirt of her grand dress and threw it over his head. Although she had a full petticoat on under the dress, enough light shone through for him to see that she was not wearing panties. She pressed him to her and sure enough he had not forgotten how to pleasure his mistress. His tongue caressed all the exciting places and soon she was murmuring, "Oh God, oh, oh"—finally, throwing her head back, she broke into a convulsive sobbing laugh. When it was over, she backed away, freeing her slave from the tent. As he stood up she said quite formally, "That was just fine, Judd. Now if you will help me back on my horse, I'm expecting some ladies for tea later today and must be off." As she rode away, she stopped, and looked back, "Boy, you better go off in the corn and take care of that bulge in you pants. I can't afford to be buying you new trousers all the time because you keep poking holes in them." She smiled sweetly at him and rode off. He watched her for awhile then went off in the corn and did as he was told.

The rest of the afternoon, Jude worked in the field and pondered how he felt about this experience, looking at it from several perspectives, one of which renewed the stress on his trousers. It was that perspective that came most easily to him; but, by the time he reached home and settled in for the evening, he was able to arrange in his mind two distinct points of view: one that gave him pleasure to be able to satisfy the needs of his mistress, as well as pride to be the chosen one, and the other filled with resentment at having been used and to be helpless to do anything about it. He pulled out the pad of paper Charlotte had given him earlier and tried to write down some of his thoughts, but it turned out to be more difficult than he had imagined. He spent several evenings at this. Each time he read what he had written, it sounded juvenile and awkward. There was no way to make it like Charlotte's smooth flowing prose. Even when he wrote in the morning while his mind was fresh, then read it in the evening after it had time to cool down, he was still disappointed. Over these several days, Charlotte was busy with her writing and teaching. During a brief exchange, she had invited herself to dinner. Jude was ill at ease over not having completed what he presumed was a writing assignment. Had Charlotte become too many different people for him to deal with, especially now that she was also his teacher? "Come on Jude," he said out loud, "you're starting to develop an ego just like other people; you're all tensed up over this writing, over being less than perfect in front of Charlotte. You had an easy run up to this point because most of what you do, like farming, saving lives, and bullying a dumb horse around came easy for you. Even your sex education came easy; you only had to be told once, and you caught on right away."

Charlotte arrived at their outdoor dining area with her usual offering of wine; she had also stopped at a bakery in Charlottesville and bought a cake for the occasion. She was excited about it and said she had not felt she could afford the calories for a long time but her scales this morning had said, "Charlotte, today is the day." She whirled around a couple of times so he could see that she had lost two pounds.

"Charlotte, you always look so good to me I'd never be able to detect changes as small as two pounds. Why don't you take your clothes off so I can see where the loss occurred."

"Hmm, sounds like a good idea to me; but it's time for the mosquitoes to start looking for me. I don't want to make it too easy for them. Remind me to do it another time, though, in case I forget. What's for dinner?"

"Trout. With the rain we've had lately, their appetites for worms have made them easy to catch."

"I see you have a wood fire going that ought to be fun; I've never had trout cooked over an open fire before. What can I do to help?"

Charlotte was talkative and in good cheer throughout dinner. Halfway through dessert, she suddenly interrupted what she was saying to ask, "What's the matter, Jude?"

"Nothing. Why?"

"You're not completely with me, hanging on every word I say. I don't expect you to detect that I have lost two pounds; but I do expect you to laugh at everything I say that I think is funny. Did Ashley upset you the other day?"

"No, I enjoyed that little bit of historical theater. Ashley brings out the best of my perversions. What has me stymied, though, is trying to write about it. That's what you wanted isn't it?"

"I didn't realize you would start writing before the end of the farming season; but I'm glad you have. I could use more of your fresh perspective in my dull version of *Charlotte's Third*, or whatever it's called. Did you save any of it, or did you destroy it all in a fit of vengeance?"

"Four or five of my attempts are still alive, but they have no right to be. I'll probably shoot them at dawn."

"Can I see them? Maybe they aren't as bad as you think."

"No, I would be too humiliated."

"Humiliated? Horseshit! How do you think I feel after writing a bestseller, only to have some half-assed editor try to convince me that it's all over, that I'm a one-novel author, who should be looking for a nice shady place to lie down and die. He doesnt even count my second book. Jude, you learn by being humiliated, not from undeserved applause. You have no more reason to suddenly know how to write than you do to be able to play a concert violin your first time in the theater." She gathered an armful of picnic materials and headed for the cabin; then stopped, and grinning back at his stunned expression said, "If you don't show it to me, I'll beat you up so badly you won't be able to lie next to me tonight."

"OK, I know when I've lost, but you have to promise not to laugh."

"I will if I think it's funny."

Once they were settled in the cabin, Jude produced the pad. Four pages were folded over on to the back; the facing page held his most recent effort.

"Does each sheet represent a failed attempt?" she asked, paging through them. "This isn't normal, Jude; most writers feel obligated to punish their disappointments by crumpling the paper and throwing it across the room."

"Each page had a few sentences I thought could be saved."

Charlotte took a pair of glasses from her purse and lapsed into serious concentration. Jude worked on the dishes with mounting anxiety; seeing her so intense was scary—paying such close attention to what he had done. Out of the corner of his eye, he saw her put down the pad and sit thoughtfully, then slowly she started to nod her head up and down as though approving of at least something he had written. "Jude, this isn't as bad as you think; in fact, it's quite hopeful. Initially you had a tendency toward verbosity, but you corrected that on your own in your most recent rewrite. The few clumsy sentences you have can easily be repaired by rearranging them. Do you mind if I use it?"

"I'm really relieved. My struggle had grown into such a monster that I feared our whole relationship depended on my being able to do this."

"I hope you're over that now, and remember that our relationship is based on sex, not on how well you write. If your uncomfortable, though, about having an affair with your writing teacher, you could work on writing projects of your own choice; and I could ask one of my colleagues at school to help you."

"No, it's time for me to grow up. Our relationship could settle comfortably into you doing the intellectual part of our lives and me doing the farming; and when we have physical needs, we meet out in the cornfield. That may be fine with you because you think you have a short life expectancy. I don't buy that, Charlotte. I'm looking for something of longer duration. I think we should grow together, bridging the difference in our educational and social backgrounds. Some day sex and relief from loneliness aren't going to be enough for our relationship. I'm going to have to develop so that I'm interesting to you beyond your present needs. And as for this notion of yours that you are going to have a short life that comes to a violent end, we're going to build our defenses against that danger instead of just accepting it. You're not alone anymore."

"Jude, aside from when you told me about your former

life, this is your longest speech."

"Yes, but this, too, is my life—our lives. Other than the length of the speech, did you notice anything else about it—like what I said?"

"Yes, Jude, I think you might be too mature for me. At a minimum you have overestimated me and you have over-estimated how much education a bachelor's degree actually provides. You've forgotten that I have spent most of my life as a spoiled child and self-indulgent woman, who in concert with an irresponsible husband, squandered my inheritance. Is that the social background that makes you feel less than me? Now, all of a sudden, you have me on a pedestal. It's very flattering and I'm doing my best to live up to the image you've created, but I hope you don't let all this seriousness spoil our fun—it has, in fact, already cut into it." She turned on the lamp by the chair and turned out the overhead. "I hate that glaring light; we have to get something different for over the table." Then she took all her clothes off and climbed into bed.

The next morning they did not hear the cock that crows too early—they did not hear anything until Aunt Millie's car clattered into the yard and backfired. Charlotte said, "Oh shit!" and started to get up, as though she was going to sneak back into the house without being caught; but, Jude pulled her back down and took one nipple in his mouth; and, after flicking his tongue back and forth across it a few times, looked up at her grinning and said, "I make pretty good pancakes too."

She lay back with resignation and said, "I guess if it's all part of the room service—what the heck."

13

Charlotte was annoyed to discover how soon she had to visit her *secret* pharmacy again. She could not blame Jude, though, because she or Ashley always initiated the activity. Madge's accusation that she always had to be in control was not that far off. Jude was good about it, though, and never pressed her, but clearly he would have liked more than she offered.

To Charlotte, however, the more immediate question was: Should I find a new place to shop now that the moon-eyed girl has recognized me, or would that just open another locality where Miss Henderson is known to buy rubbers? With my picture displayed on almost every bookrack in the country, there isn't much chance of me sneaking by unrecognized. It's that damn triangle of white hair on my forehead; I might as well have a big red "A" painted there. I can already hear the exchange: Mrs. Whoever selects a book from the rack, spots my picture, and says to the clerk, "My what a pretty woman," and the clerk responds, "Oh yes, that's Miss Henderson, she buys her condoms here."

I guess it's better not to scatter my purchases all over the countryside, besides the moon-eyed girl and I are getting used to each other.

When Charlotte entered the store, the clerk was sitting on a stool behind the counter. Without looking directly at Charlotte, she took something from under the counter, put it in a small bag and asked, "Will there be anything else, Miss Henderson?"

Charlotte was surprised at the girl's forwardness but relieved that she didn't have to ask for them. She quickly put the correct change on the counter; and as she did, saw that her young friend had been reading *Plantation of Hope*. Charlotte asked if that book was any good.

"Oh, Miss Henderson, I just love it. This is the first book I read since I finished high school a year ago. I had no idea reading could be such fun."

She looked so young, Charlotte was surprised that she was old enough to be a high school graduate. "What did you read in high school that was so bad?"

"A lot of old boring stuff with big words, you know, like *Silas Marner* and *Ivanhoe*. Could I show you something, Miss Henderson?"

"Sure, what is it?"

She took her purse from beneath the counter and opened it for Charlotte to peek inside and see her pack of condoms. She told Charlotte in a confidential whisper, "I didn't know women could carry them, until you started buying them here. It's really a good idea and I'm thankful to you for letting me in on it. I ain't that anxious to spend my life in a shack full of squalling kids. None a the guys around here carry them, they don't care about nothing except sticking their thing in and giving you a squirt with it. If you get pregnant they all just blame each other for it and move on to the next girl."

"Why do you let them do that to you?"

"I don't have no choice; I have to let them do it or they won't go out with me. Besides," she looked down at the floor and blushed, "I really don't mind. Sometimes, though, I wish they'd be a little nicer about it—like the men in your book. These guys I know are always in a big hurry to get it in and get it off. Do people really do it the way you tell about it in your book?"

"Yes, some people find that a lot of the pleasure they get out of sex comes from satisfying their partner. Do you have a regular boyfriend? Perhaps you could tell him how you would like to have him make love to you?"

"I guess you'd sort of call Jimmy Joe a regular boyfriend. He's a little older than me and has a big, old car. I like him, except sometimes he brings Quirk along. I don't like doing it with him. He's kind of rough and a little mean about taking what he wants."

"Why do you do it with Quirk?"

"Wouldn't it look dumb if I let one do it but didn't let the other one?"

Charlotte hesitated. Finally she said, "I don't think it would look nearly as dumb as being pregnant and not knowing which one was the father."

"Wouldn't make no difference; ain't neither one going to stick around to claim no babies."

Charlotte just shrugged and let it go.

"Miss Henderson, would you do me a really big favor?"

"Sure, if I can."

"Would you please autograph my book?" she said holding up her copy.

"I would be happy to; how shall I address you?"

She looked bewildered and said, "Oh, I don't know anything about that, I was just hoping you would write your name on it."

"I meant, what shall I call you?"

"Oh, you mean my name? People call me by different names; most of them I don't like. My real name is Martha."

Charlotte wrote on the inside cover: "Best wishes to Martha. May your successes not all be little ones—Your friend, Charlotte Henderson," and returned it to her.

Martha read it, and beaming proudly, said, "Gee, Miss Henderson, that's real nice. I'm going to show this to everyone who comes in the store."

Charlotte thought, and you'll also tell them Miss Henderson buys her rubbers here.

As if reading her mind, Martha whispered confidentially, "But don't you worry none, Miss Henderson, I won't tell them what it is you come in here for. I'll just let them think it's 'cause we're such good friends. We are friends, like you said, ain't we?"

"Yes, Martha, we are."

Initially, Charlotte thought her affair with Jude would be just an occasional thing; but, clearly the time had come to find a doctor *in some part of Virginia where no one knows her.* With an IUD in place, she had no reason to visit Martha; but, one day, while in the vicinity of the pharmacy, she stopped there.

Martha was happy to see her and said she had wondered if Charlotte had broken up with her boyfriend since she hadn't been in. Charlotte assured her that her life was still good, whereupon Martha burst into tears and confided that hers wasn't. "Miss Henderson, I know I shouldn't be crying on you like this, but ain't no one else who understands things like you do." Under stress Martha's English broke down more than usual.

"Martha, that's what friends are for; what can I do to help?"

"Oh, you can't help me none; my life's down the toilet. It's just I have to talk to someone who ain't gonna holler at me or beat the shit out of me."

"I promise not to do either."

"Well, you know those rubbers I was carrying in my purse? Turns out Jimmy Joe didn't mind using them and we were having a pretty good time. I took your advice and told him I wasn't going to do it with Quirk no more. He seemed to like that, except the very next time I saw him, Quirk was with him. They'd been drinking. I didn't want to get in the car; but they promised to take me right home. It looked like rain, so like a fool, I got in. Right off, Quirk who was driving, headed for the place where they used to do it to me. I kept hollering for them to stop and let me out but they just kept laughing. Guess you know what happened. There wasn't no way of stoppin' them, so I quick-like grabbed a rubber from my purse but they both said they don't like those goddamn things—it's like washing your feet with your socks on. Anyway, now I'm pregnant. I'm gonna lose my job and my mother's gonna throw me out; I ain't figured out yet what to do."

"Mothers have a way of softening their position when a new baby is expected. I'll check back later and see how it works out for you."

"Thanks, Miss Henderson."

The days had grown shorter and the evenings cool; but the warm, sunny days of October were still pleasant enough for a dip in the pond after a day's work. Jude dried himself off and was lying on the warm rocks, soaking up the last of the season's warmth. He relaxed and thought about his life on the farm. Except for a few nagging concerns, he concluded that this was probably the most pleasant time in his life. As he lay there with his eyes closed, his thoughts focused on Charlotte; in no time at all, he had an erection. Even, with the farm to himself, he was self-conscious about his naked-ness and thought about pulling the towel over his privates. Instead, he fell asleep.

A slight scuffling sound awakened him. Charlotte had come home early and had gone looking for him. Jude grabbed for his towel, but it was too late.

She did not even tease him—it was, in fact, a soft and loving Charlotte who said, "I know I don't have a reser-vation but would it be possible for me to stay for dinner and hang around for a while?" Her mind was still on Martha's life and problems.

"Sure," Jude responded, "but you'll have to put up with whatever we can do with our standby emergency ration from the chickens."

"You always manage to turn eggs into a gourmet meal."

Jude slipped into his clothes and they returned to the cabin. "Before I undertake this miracle of the eggs, though, I'd better draw the blinds. I presume you're still concerned about your mother-in-law catching you fraternizing with slaves."

"Yes, at least I should be; but I guess I'm getting careless. God, what if she had caught us down in the cornfield the other day! Hey, I like your shades. Do they keep the light from showing outside?"

"It's probably dark enough now; go out and see if any light shows."

She returned from her inspection and declared them *perfect*.

"I still want to hook up a buzzer, so, if you need help, you can just press a button in the kitchen. I bored a hole in the wall here with this flap over it. I can look through that to see if you're behaving yourself."

"Hah! That'd be the day that I misbehave, but it's probably good to keep an eye out in case Ashley or Madge come around."

"Can you stay overnight? I really love to wake up in the morning and find you beside me."

"I'd probably stay more often if you had better bathroom facilities."

"Yes, I know—that outhouse is an embarrassment to me. I'll have more time to deal with toilets next week after I finish harvesting the corn; maybe then we can afford some plumbing."

"With a shower, too? Bathing in the pond in winter

chaps the skin."

"I think I can arrange it, if you're willing to invest in a hot water heater."

"You know I'm willing to spend any amount on creature comforts."

"No! That surprises me," he teased. "Instead of a shower, I was thinking we might order a washtub large enough for two and heat our water on the stove."

While all this banter was going on, Charlotte was trying to find a way to talk about Martha; she finally decided just to plunge into it. "Jude, you know the moon-eyed girl I told you about at my favorite pharmacy? Well, I was in the vicinity a few days ago; and, on a whim, stopped in to see her." Jude listened attentively as Charlotte told him about Martha's shattered life. When she finished, she silently studied the concern on Jude's face hoping he would suggest they help her.

Jude slowly shook his head as if in disbelief.

"Well, what do you think?" Charlotte asked, disappointed that he didn't offer more.

"I feel badly for her."

"Do you think I should invite her to come here to have her baby?"

"No."

"Just no, without any explanation? Are you returning to the nonverbal style you had when you first came here, or are you just trying to piss me off?"

"Charlotte, I know what you want me to say, but I simply don't agree with you; and, I know that if I tell you why I disagree, you'll get mad at me—I don't handle that well."

"Arguing is part of developing a mature relationship."

"It's the immature part we've been enjoying; I don't want to spoil it."

"If Martha moved into the big house for a few months, it wouldn't interfere with our intimacy if that's what you're worried about. I'd just spend more time here, especially after you upgrade the plumbing." His silence told her he had more concern than just their sexual relationship. "You take it seriously, don't you, that no good deed shall go unpunished? How do you expect we would be harmed by helping her? C'mon, Jude, talk to me."

"I just don't know how much you can help people who keep making the same kinds of mistakes."

"Underneath your pleasant, easygoing facade, you're really a hard-ass, aren't you?"

"Charlotte, inviting Martha here may reduce your guilt feelings over being raised rich; but, it won't have any lasting affect on Martha's life—anymore than your name-calling will win this argument."

"Name-calling isn't as insulting as using my vulnerable feelings against me to win an argument. I really hate it when you do that to me, Jude—you make me feel like a child."

"I have one more point to make, if you're interested."

"I'm not . . . oh, all right; go ahead, sooner or later you'll drop it on me anyway and just make me mad all over again later."

"You're mad?"

"It doesn't show?"

"I thought maybe you were, but I didn't know why."

"Never mind why; just drop you're goddamn bomb."

"Actually, I have two more, I just thought of another one—if Martha is here, before long, her low-life friends will be hanging around."

"OK, so what's the last one?"

"The baby—when Martha and her baby leave to return to whatever shitty life is out there for her, you're going to be heartbroken—or do you plan to keep them both?"

"Jude, I never would have dreamed you could be such a heartless prick." Charlotte got up from her chair and headed for the door.

"You leaving? I thought you were going to stay all night."

"I was, but my nipples just turned cold."

"I could warm them up."

"No thanks. You can sit here alone and think about what you just did to me," and she was gone.

Jude spent the rest of the evening and well into the night trying to figure out what he had said that upset Charlotte so much. Although he developed some suspicions, none of them were sufficient to account for her strong reaction.

Charlotte was still upset when she reached home. She poured herself a glass of Scotch and tried to pinpoint why she was so mad at Jude. The alcohol only made her feel worse and it revealed nothing, so she went to bed.

The next morning she went off to teach, still not sure why she was so upset with Jude—or why she was depressed. Jude spent the morning picking corn. The overcast day added to his gloomy mood, and on top of that, Alfred was not cooperating.

Jude had trained Alfred to respond to giddyup and whoa, so he could keep the cart close enough to toss in the ears as he picked them. Alfred had worked well for the last several days, but now he had a tendency to overshoot when he was told to stop. As Jude's patience grew thinner, Alfred tested him further. By midafternoon, he ranged so far ahead that Jude frequently missed his toss. In anger, Jude stalked over to holler some unkind comments in his face. Alfred took off for the barn at a full trot with only half a load of corn and no driver. Jude dived out of the way just in time to keep from being hit by the wheel of the cart. When he picked himself up from the ground, he had a sore hip and limped all the way back to the barn. Meanwhile, Alfred had plunged into his stall and wedged the cart in the doorway. Jude tried unsuccessfully to get him to back out so he could unhitch him from the cart. Jude finally had to climb on the wheel into the cart, then jump down inside the stall. He tried to do this calmly, but Alfred became spooked, reared up, then pranced back and forth until the cart suddenly popped through the door, just missing Jude a second time.

Charlotte arrived home in time to see Jude enter the barn. She turned the ignition off and let her little red roadster roll silently down the hill to the barn. Usually she wore sneakers for driving, but, she left work in a hurry still wearing her high heels. At first, she thought Jude's predicament was amusing; but, when she she saw the cart lunging at him, she dashed into the stall as though she thought she could hold it back from hitting him.

"Oh, thank God, you're all right," she said running up to him as if she were going to pick him up and carry him to safety.

"Yeah, I think so, guess this is my lucky day. That's the second time Alfred almost got me with that cart. He's been a pain in the ass all day." Jude got up, put his hands on Charlotte's shoulders and said, "We've got to get you out of this stall, though, you're ruining the horseshit."

"What do you mean, I'm ruining the horseshit?"

"Look what your doing. Your impaling them with the heel of your shoe—you're turning the biscuits into donuts." She looked down, and sure enough, there she was clopping around with a horse turd skewered to the heel of her shoe. "You go on out while I detach Alfred from the cart and put him in another stall. If I leave him in here, he'll eat all the corn in the cart. We won't be able to squeeze him or the cart out of the stall in the morning."

"OK, I'll go up to the house and change; come up when you're ready and help me eat Aunt Millie's offering."

"OK."

The dinner conversation was polite but strained; it was frequently punctuated by periods of silence. They had finished eating and were relaxing with their coffee, when Charlotte asked, "You still mad at me, Jude?"

"No, I never was mad at you."

"How come you don't love me as much as you used to?"

"I thought I wasn't allowed to love you."

"You know why that is, though; it's not because I don't want you to, it's because I think it isn't good for you and you could be hurt by it. I guess I'm afraid of assuming the responsibility for any harm that might result from your loving me. I'm being illogical again, aren't I? I need you to love me and I need your help with the farm; I do everything I can think of to keep you here; and, yet, I tell you it's too dangerous for you to stay. Until yesterday, I thought I was even making gains on reducing my bitchiness." Her lower eyelids filled with tears and her voice wavered. After a brief silence, while she gathered her composure, she asked Jude what he thought about after she left last night and during the day today.

"I don't know, Charlotte, since we're OK now, maybe we should just drop it and go back to enjoying each other. I'd hate to think the honeymoon is over, and we have to confront the reality of adjusting to each other."

"Jude, I want to do that. I have never done it before, and it might be worthwhile. I really never faced a mature male-female relationship before—never wanted to—I almost always got my own way, except with John Paul when he was in a bully mood.

"I didn't agree with all the things you said last night; but, I think you showed me how to talk about things rather than to scream foul-mouthed epithets at each other. If my ego hadn't gotten in the way, we could have finished the discussion last night and cozied up nicely in bed. As it is now, we have this tension between us that frightens me. What can I do or say that will bring us back to where we were?"

"I'm OK now, Charlotte, don't worry about it. I was just a little upset about your being mad at me and not knowing why; it will all pass."

"You're holding back on me, Jude. You have to help me retain my status as a recovering bitch. You wouldn't want me to backslide, would you?"

"Not if it meant you might run out on me again in a huff."

"We sure don't want to risk that again, so tell me some of the things you thought about today," Charlotte insisted.

"Mostly, I struggled trying to understand why you stalked off, apparently, just because I disagreed with you. This led me to thinking about our relationship, most of which can't be changed anyway—at least, not now."

"So, the truth comes out: you are dissatisfied with our relationship. See, I didn't know that. What can I do to make it better."

"Talking about this makes it seem larger than it really is; but, I guess if I put it all on the table, next time we have a disagreement you'll know what background my whining sounds are coming from."

Charlotte took his hand to encourage him and told him that she had never heard him whine.

"What happened yesterday," he began, "was the first time I openly disagreed with you. By your reaction, I wondered if I wasn't allowed to disagree with you. Are you always to be the one who decides when we will make love, and will you make all of the other decisions as well? I began to think wouldn't it be nice if we shared an equal partnership. I was envious of John Paul, who blew such a wonderful opportunity. I would have been so pleased if I could have been the one to help you through the loss of Margaret and to encourage you to have another child. I considered that your interest in Martha may have to do with wanting to have a baby around the house, but I still don't think that would have a happy ending. I won't raise additional objection if you want to have her here; I'll even help you pull it off and help you to recover from the consequences if it goes sour. This is dumb I know, but, if you want to have a baby around the house, I'd rather it would be ours." Now it was Jude's turn to develop moisture around the eyes and when Charlotte noticed it, her eyes became moist.

Charlotte stood up and silently led him up to her bedroom. Before they climbed under the canopy she hugged him and said, "If you can beat this IUD and my 40 years of wasted life, we'll have a baby and worry about the consequences later. Remember, though, if my mother-in-law comes walking in the house calling 'yoo hoo, yoo hoo,' don't holler, 'we're up here Theda.'"

"OK, I'll try to keep your former relatives out of this. As for your being 40, a woman in my neighborhood back home had a baby when she was 44 and she wasn't in nearly as good physical condition as you are. What's this IUD thing?"

"Now that's what could slow us up the most," she responded. "It means intrauterine device. It's a little plastic gizzy I had a doctor insert so we wouldn't have to bother with condoms. It prevents a fertilized egg from becoming implanted in the uterus and developing into a baby."

"Guess that kinda finishes any fantasies I might have had about our having a baby, doesn't it?"

"I sure hope so. You know I never was anxious to join you in that reckless scheme: sometimes you forget that I'd still have a lot to lose by having a baby while my husband rots away at Pine Crest."

Salvi came to take the corn to the mill. Jude decided to introduce himself and take a chance that Salvi would not blab it all over town that Charlotte had a man living on the place. He then loaded the corn on to Salvi's truck with the bucket loader. When he finished, Salvi said, "I'm glad Miss Charlotte got someone to keep the farm from falling into ruin. I hope you'll also kinda look out for her."

"I guess you know her."

"Yah. I know her. She don't really know me, though. I see her come into town once in awhile; but I also read about her in the newspaper—'bout how she pisses the white folks off at school board meetings with talk about integrating the schools. The nice people of Grimble are maneuvering every which way to keep the blacks out of their schools. She stands up there all alone and tells them what a bunch of hypocrites they are and how ashamed they ought to be for how little money they put into black education. They know she's right, but they'd like to kill her for saying so. That woman's what I'd call real class."

"I had no idea she was so reckless."

"Lot of us appreciate what she's trying to do, but she's gonna get herself hurt."

"Yah, Lyle expressed concern about her, too," Jude said.

"Well, I gotta get this corn to the mill 'fore it closes. You ever get over on Jerusalem Road, Jude, stop in at my place. I got a jug of some of the smoothest shine you ever did taste."

Jude hollered after the truck, as it pulled away from the barn, "I'll do that, Salvi, first chance I get."

14

Jude spent some time familiarizing himself with the performance of John Paul's rifle. The hunting season had opened, so his gunfire did not draw attention. One day, after shooting at still targets for awhile, he threw a can in the air. His shot from below sent it spinning higher in the air. All of a sudden from somewhere behind him came a BLAM . . . BLAM; the can lurched two more times before its shredded remains hit the ground. Jude whirled around, and there was Charlotte grinning mischievously, with her shotgun in hand. "Hey, you're not bad with that thing," she said, gesturing toward Jude's rifle.

"Thanks, but look what you did to my can."

"That's OK, look what I have." At her feet lay a box of skeet and a trap for hurling them into the air. "Do you think you could hit one of these if I let one loose?"

"Oh, God, it's Humiliate Jude Day . . . OK, have your fun, send one up."

"You better use my shotgun. You'd never hit one of these with a rifle."

"Let me try."

She sent one straight out; Jude aimed at it but let it go without firing. "It went faster than I thought it would; I wasn't quite ready. Could you send another one up but maybe a little higher?"

"OK, here goes."

As the pigeon reached its zenith, Jude blasted it into a dozen pieces.

"Unbelievable! You've done this before."

"No, only cans—they're a lot bigger and slower. This is a whole different game. You want to try it?"

"Lord no! With a rifle I couldn't hit that can if it was sitting on a fence post. This scatter gun is my medicine stick." Charlotte loaded two skeet into the trap and handed the device to Jude. When he released the trigger, they sailed off in diverging paths—BLAM . . . BLAM—both of them blew apart.

"Wow! Can you do that regularly?"

"Yes, mostly I can do that one. The one that gives me trouble is birds coming toward me at an angle."

"I wouldn't say that's any great weakness. I can see why you're not afraid to live out here alone. It must give you confidence to be able to handle a gun like that."

"It does, but I can't imagine what it would be like to shoot somebody."

"Like I did, huh? It's funny, you know, I used to have a real hard time saying that even to myself. Tell me, Charlotte, now that you have had some time to let my story sink in, how do you feel about my having killed someone?"

"It doesn't seem real to me. On the other hand, it must

be a subliminal part of how I view you. I sense that you could deal with anything. Instead of focusing on the fact that you killed a man, I see how you collected your wits in a crisis and escaped. It's all part of your resourcefulness and capacity to survive. Handling a rifle the way you do adds another facet and gives me a sense of security, even though I don't think about your having to use it on another person."

"If that makes you feel good, maybe you would spring for another box of cartridges. I have only three left. I hadn't intended to run this low but I was having too much fun to stop. Oh, I almost forgot to tell you, I got the fox yesterday. He had caught the rooster and was busy trying to subdue him, so I was able to move in close enough for a good shot."

"Did you get the rooster, too?"

"You know, I was about to pop him while he was still stunned from being mauled—I just couldn't do it."

"So now we know the origin of the phrase, chicken-hearted."

"Yeah, guess I am, or I would have shot Alfred on at least two other occasions after you told me to the first time."

"I knew I was safe in telling you to do that. You fell in love with him at the same time you fell in love with me. I could tell by the way you hit him on the rump and called him a horse's ass."

"Yes, I remember, I hit him with the flat side of my axe instead of the cutting edge. By the way, how come you're home so early? You get fired?"

"Not yet—we don't have classes the afternoon before Thanksgiving so the kids can get home."

"Wow, Thanksgiving already. How do you celebrate

Thanksgiving here on the plantation?"

"We used to spend all the holidays at my in-laws. They don't invite me anymore. You think they're mad at me? Now, I spend holidays writing, eating simply, and drinking lightly."

"Pretty wild. Any chance I could tear you away from all that fun to spend a boring day down in the slave quarters where we eat too much and drink to excess?"

"I thought you'd never ask. I'd be delighted to join you, sir."

"Does this mean if I hadn't said anything, we each would have spent the holiday alone?"

"I probably would have—you didn't know it was a holiday. I didn't feel I should raise the issue after you expressed your desire for us to have an equal partnership. Up until now I have been doing all the inviting, whether it was to your place or mine."

"Charlotte, you're putting me on."

"Yes—if you hadn't invited me, I would have invited myself. Far be it from me to let social graces or a personal power struggle between mistress and slave get in the way of a good time. Shall I go buy a turkey?"

"Shouldn't our first Thanksgiving dinner come off the land? With a famous skeet shot like you on the property, we should be able to put something in the pot to go with some squash and potatoes from the garden."

"Jude, are you talking about us shooting some more tin cans or clay pigeons for our dinner?"

"Good as they sound, what I really had in mind was quail. I've seen a couple of big flocks running around in the fields every time I walk down there. They never fly though; they just run ahead of me. How do you ever get them into the air? We didn't have many quail in Michigan."

"They hunt them with dogs; I don't know how to get them to fly without a dog. I presume it's sacrilegious for hunters to shoot them on the ground. For all the skeet shooting I've done, I bet you think it's odd that I've never been hunting. Daddy always acted like hunting was strictly a man's sport. Little girls could shoot skeet. Let's go back to the house and pick up a shotgun for you. If you wouldn't think it unlady-like of me, between the two of us maybe we could bring in the Thanksgiving dinner."

Back at the house, Charlotte took a shell vest and a double-barreled shotgun from the gun cabinet, and handed them to Jude, "I don't know why Daddy liked hauling that extra barrel around with him, but he did. You think you could run this thing?"

"It's possible—we'll have to wait and see."

Down the lane, they turned off into the first stubble field where Jude had previously seen quail. They spaced themselves about 50 feet apart and started down through the field. When they came to the end of it, where a dense thicket grew along the fence row, a flock of quail took off from right between them, startling them both. Jude quickly recovered, singled out a bird and dropped it. Charlotte fired four times, but only one bird fell. As they were picking up the birds, Charlotte seemed disgusted with her performance. "You know, I don't think I did that right. I got all excited and just shot into the flock. I bet you're supposed to track and shoot one bird at a time. Is that why you only fired once?"

"Yes, the bird I picked flew up and over my head; by the time I turned around and dropped him, the rest of the flock was pretty well gone except for one. I drew in on him, but just as I was about to squeeze the trigger, you fired your fourth shot and he fell."

"It was on that last shot that I came to my senses and realized that I wasn't going to kill the whole flock by spraying them with shot. C'mon," she said excitedly, "we've gotta do that again: this pair isn't enough for two growing children."

They walked the rest of the fields without success. Although they saw quail, the birds kept well ahead of them, running along the ground. It was nearly dusk when they entered the last field, where Charlotte had fallen from the horse.

Jude said, "Look, there they go, do you see them?"

"Yes, but they're running ahead again."

"Swing wider," Jude yelled. "That's it, don't let them double back; keep pushing them toward the stream."

Finally two of them realized they were boxed in and took off. Charlotte dropped one and and Jude the other. As soon as they fired, the whole flock took off. Jude missed his second shot and stood there with an empty gun watching Charlotte systematically sort out and drop three in a row. "You are so beautiful," he said, "I can't believe what I just saw you do."

She was delighted with her success and his approval. "So that's our Thanksgiving dinner, Jude? Do you know what to do with these to make them edible?"

"I think so, I've cooked grouse but maybe we ought to

look in a recipe book; maybe quail are different."

"I'll see if I can find one of my mother's. She didn't cook much, but she bought cookbooks once in awhile thinking she might like to try. Aunt Millie doesn't put much stock in recipe books—I expect you know by now she can't read. That excuse of not having her glasses doesn't work well when you know she never owned a pair."

"That was really fun today," Charlotte said, while they were having dinner, "and you know what I enjoyed the most?"

"Killing things?" Jude teased.

"No, I didn't even think about that. If we'd been after deer or rabbits, it might have bothered me, but birds? Naw, I could have shot the rooster. What I really appreciated most is how graciously you accepted my shooting more quail than you; most other men I know would have turned surly. Only a mature, confident man could be as genuinely pleased as you were over my success."

"I really was pleased, but aren't you afraid my ego is so poorly developed that it doesn't bother me to lose? Maybe I don't think I deserve to win."

"You're putting me on, Jude. You like to win. You were pleased enough with yourself when you hit that clay pigeon with one shot from your rifle. You're damn good at what you do and you do a lot of things."

"How come we're talking about this, you worried about me?"

"No . . . well, maybe a little bit. I reflect some on what you said the night we made up after *the Martha argument.* "

"What about?"

"About wishing you had equal rights—like you might be getting tired of being a slave."

"Oh, if you want to worry about me, what I said was that I would like to be an equal partner with you. That goes well beyond sharing in the decision-making about who lives with us and whether we should plant the back 40 into soybeans this spring. What that has to do with is deciding which side of the bed we're going to sleep on, whether that canopy bed is right for us and what we'll name our baby. But don't worry about that, I won't allow my fantasies to intrude on reality. I just thought you might be interested in how lofty my dreams become sometimes."

"What's wrong with my canopy bed?" she yelled in faked indignation to shift the conversation."

"Nothing, I love it. It's a well-tended bed."

"OK, I'm glad that's settled. We'll squabble about which side you get to sleep on tonight after we've planned our Thanksgiving dinner. I found a couple of cookbooks."

The next day it was raining. They decided to risk being caught having Thanksgiving dinner together at the mansion rather than hiding out in the cabin. Theda would be too busy overseeing the preparation of her own dinner to be poking in Charlotte's business. Charlotte built a fire in the fireplace in the study to take the damp chill off the day. "I have always loved this room," Charlotte said. "I grew up in it, that is, as much growing up as occurred in my particular case. Daddy used this desk as his office for the various businesses he was involved in. It never bothered him to have me playing in here, even when he was working on something. As an only child, they let me do almost anything I wanted to as long as it wasn't dangerous."

"Or immoral?" Jude teased.

"I didn't have a problem with that as a little girl: immorality didn't set in until I left home. Even at that, for southern gentry, my daddy . . . and mama were surprisingly liberal in their attitudes about my relationships with boys. They took the position that I was intelligent, had good common sense, and should regulate my own life. They really didn't know me that well; or maybe they did and didn't think there was much they could do about me anyway, except make all of our lives miserable. You can't let a child have her own way most of the time and then, just because she has reached puberty, impose strict regulations. I think that's what drove Madge to extremes."

"Speaking of Madge, I notice that your language has softened. Next time she visits she'll want to take you back into training. I hope this lapse hasn't interfered with the revision of your book."

"No, that's not my excuse. I've just had too much schoolwork this year. Along with the increase in momentum to give more rights to minorities, universities across the country are pretending to extend rights to women as well. They're trying to have a showcase woman on as many committees as they can. All of a sudden, there's a critical shortage of us. Even though I'm not a regular faculty member—what I mean is, I'm not tenured and have to be reappointed each year—they think it counts to have me on committees. It'd be pretty funny if it weren't such a boring waste of time. Universities have an overwhelming love of democracy—no matter how trivial the issue, faculty members are willing to talk it to death. It's the sound of their own oratory that compels them, each attempting to be more erudite than the other—to hell with solving any problems."

"Students don't get to see that side of their professors—well, maybe they do, they just don't recognize professorial ramblings for what they are."

"You recognized the symptoms, you just didn't know what caused the disease. As for my revision, I hope to work on it now during the holiday break, then finish it over Christmas. We have nearly a month before the second semester begins. You want to help?"

"How on earth could I help?"

"Now that you're two different characters in the book, you should make sure I've captured your feelings. I think you could also provide a good assessment of how I handled other parts of the book . . . . You seem reluctant. Do you have big plans that preclude your helping me?"

"No, I'll have time now that the farming season has ended. All I really have to do is take care of Alfred and the chickens and put up enough firewood to stay warm. Oh, I also have to install the plumbing in the cabin, if you still think we can afford it."

"Jude, I'm glad you said *we*—that's equal partner stuff showing through. Before we talk about budget, though, I want you to look at the clock and tell me what time it is."

"Charlotte, it says 12:05, the same as your watch."

"What that means is that we can now have our first holiday drink; and, if we're going to talk about budget, I recommend Scotch."

"OK, I'll try to be grown-up about both the budget and my drink. I'll get some glasses and ice."

Charlotte swirled the amber liquid and ice around a few times and raised her glass, "Here's to the best holiday I've had in many years."

"It certainly is for me, but I would think you'd find it a little dull."

"Oh, not at all. It was really fun putting our own dinner together with food off the farm, then being together all last night—and now this calm, pleasant day—it's really what I needed—I love it. Did you know that sometimes my spring gets wound too tight?"

"Yes, but I wasn't sure you were aware of it."

After they had several sips, Charlotte said, "You ready to face the budget? We're in this together, aren't we?"

"Feast or famine—flush toilet or outhouse."

"So this is how it is, Jude. With what you brought in from farming, my meager salary and the dwindling royalties from my books, I calculate that we can survive for about six months."

"Does that take into account that we ought to give Lyle about a quarter of the corn money?"

"Yes, I already sent it to him, with a note thanking him and telling him that I understand and accept his reason for leaving Greyledge."

"I'm glad you did that, I think Lyle's a good guy. How about fertilizer and seed for next year's crop and the cost of of plumbing?"

"Whoops, maybe we have only five month's of survival money. Anything else we need to worry about?"

"How much do you think Martha is going to cost us?"

Charlotte swirled her drink, and looking down, smiled

slightly, "Jude, you really are a turd. You've known all along I haven't completely abandoned the possibility of helping her. How much would you really care?"

"If you listened to all my reasons for not bringing her here, and still want to do it, all I can do is pull you out and wash you off when it's over."

"Thanks, Jude, for not being too adamant on this issue. I've considered all of the things you said and you're probably right about most of them. I still don't know if she'll need help; or, if she does, whether I'll offer, but at least you let me feel more free to make the decision if the situation arises. I wouldn't expect that this item would add to our budget significantly . . . . Anyway, the bottom line is that either I, or we, have to be sure that this revision is accepted in a timely fashion or we are both in the cesspool. So, will you help?"

"I'll try. My only reservation is that it might be hard on our relationship."

"I bet you're remembering that tirade I released when I told you what my editor said about the manuscript. I promise to control my ego. I really need the help of someone who'll be honest and can provide an outside perspective— just be gentle, please."

"I promise. When do you want me to start?"

"The first three chapters are in that envelope on my desk. You can take them home with you tonight if you're willing."

"That means you don't want me to stay overnight again— huh?"

"Yes, I do, but Aunt Millie will be here tomorrow and

there's always the wicked witch from the West to concern us."

"Have you seen her lately?"

"About a month ago she showed up to have me sign some papers. You were down in the cornfield at the time. She comes every month or two, usually for some contrived reason."

"Well, Charlotte, in total, that was a lot of business we conducted for a holiday. Let's see how our dinner is coming."

It was mid-December by the time Jude finished the plumbing. Along with it he had been occupied bringing in firewood and, in the evenings, working on Charlotte's manuscript. He found the editing business remarkably compelling. The week before the university's Christmas vacation he put the envelope back on her desk and returned to his cabin to wait for her. Charlotte still mooched dinner off him midweek when Aunt Millie's offering was running low. Jude had prepared an elegant dinner.

Charlotte burst into the cabin without knocking, hollering, "You shit, you goddamn shit! You didn't even say whether you liked it or not." The candles burned brightly on the table, the wood stove had made the place warm and cozy, and a bottle he had filched from her wine cellar stood open and ready to pour. "Oh, Jude, does all this mean you like it?"

"I love it," he said with gusto; and, when she flew into his open arms, he picked her up and whirled her around and around.

"Oh, Jude, tell me again—I want to hear it again."

"I love it. I love it. I love you."

"How could you love me? I'm so cruel to you. I keep you confined to this cabin all winter and make you work without pay on this book—for which I will receive all the credit; I can't even list you in the acknowledgements for fear the M.P.s will get you."

"Yes, it's terrible and what's more there's the sexual abuse you inflict on me."

"And tonight you're really going to get it."

"Oh God! Cruel mistress, what now?" he asked melodramatically.

"I can't tell you yet; it might spoil your dinner."

"To take my mind off it, let me give you a tour of the plumbing system." At the kitchen sink, he turned on both faucets and announced, "Here we have hot and cold water; see how it disappears down that hole without running out on the floor."

"Amazing!" she applauded.

Jude led her across a chalk line on the floor, that symbolized bathroom walls. "And, over here we have a shower stall, also with hot and cold water that goes down that hole, never to be seen again. Finally, this stool," he said, pressing the lever, "provides as fine a vortex as ever a mistress would want, making it possible to quickly disappear the truth about certain similarities between mistress and slave."

"Jude, sometimes you come so close to being a turd that I'm frightened to have you stand near one of these vortex makers."

"But are you impressed?"

"I really am—and that shower stall offers all kinds of possibilities for the sexual abuse of slaves."

As Jude poured the wine, Charlotte returned the discussion to her manuscript, "Jude, you couldn't believe how relieved I am that you like my book."

"Why is my opinion so important to you? I don't have enough education to be in the business of evaluating books."

"You're well-read, you have a lot of common sense, you're sensitive, you're right here on the job site—and I did so want you to like it."

"Yes, the last reason is especially important," he joked.

"How would you compare this book to *Plantation of Hope?* "

"That's an excellent book, but this one's better."

"Why?"

"Your character development is better, and the action is more clearly described. I'm anxious to read the rest of it."

"Over Christmas vacation, I'll try to finish it."

All through dinner, Charlotte sparkled with excitement as though her editor had just told her what a wonderful thing she had done. She never tired of having Jude tell her how good her novel was. While he was pouring coffee, she finally tore herself away from manuscript talk long enough to think about Jude—how much he was alone. "Wouldn't it be worth the risk for us to take a little drive sometime— maybe get out and talk to some people?"

"What do you have in mind?"

"Well, I thought we could take the station wagon, which is less conspicuous than the MG, and drive around the valley a little, maybe even stop over and see how Martha is doing."

"I guess it might be nice to get off the farm and see what the surrounding countryside is like. Sometimes I think I get a little funny in the head talking to Alfred so much."

15

It was a beautiful winter day when Charlotte took Jude sightseeing. They started out with a tour of the city of Grimble, which Charlotte introduced as, "*The Cream of the Shenandoah Valley*—what it lacks in size it makes up for in decay."

Next they toured the more prosperous cities of Augusta and Harrisonburg, and they ended up in that part of Virginia where Charlotte thought no one would know her.

Martha was not at the pharmacy. Jude wandered around looking at things on the shelves while Charlotte talked with the pharmacist. When she came back, she told Jude, "Mr. Katz said Martha no longer works here. He gave me her home address, but doesn't think she's living at home. He wouldn't say much about her. I think it troubled him to let her go."

"Do you want to go over to her house and see if her mother knows where she is?" Jude asked.

"Yes, if you don't mind, I'm really kind of worried

about her. Mr. Katz told me where it is—I hope we can find it."

After a couple of wrong turns, they crossed the railroad tracks and ended up at a house on a street of dilapidated houses, obviously constructed by the same builder. Jude stayed in the car while Charlotte went to see what she could find out. She stepped onto the porch with some reservation. The footings were decaying, causing the porch to separate from the house. A knock at the door produced a scurry of activity but no one came to the door. When she knocked a second time, an irritated voice inside yelled, "Lena, what the hell's the matter with you? Go answer the door." A little girl pulled the inner door open and stood behind the screen. She wore a faded dress—wrinkled, soiled and a little too large for her. She stood there without saying anything.

Charlotte asked her if Martha was home.

"Martha don't live here no more."

Charlotte asked if she knew where she was.

"No."

"Would your mother know where she is?"

"I don't know."

"Would you mind asking her?"

"Ma," she called, "some lady wants to know where Martha is."

A harsh voice responded from inside the house. "Tell her she don't live here no more."

"I did."

"So, why is she still here then?"

"I think mama wants you to go away, lady."

Charlotte yanked the screen door open and went in.

Immediately she was hit by the smell of cockroaches and old bacon grease. The living room floor was strewn with comic books. They half covered the carpet, which was worn down to the warp in heavily traveled areas. An exhausted sofa and a couple of mismatched chairs, losing their stuffing, comprised the main furniture. Two teenage boys, one sitting on the sofa and one lying on the floor, were too busy reading comic books to look up. Charlotte worked her way across the floor toward the voice in the adjacent room, trying to avoid stepping on the comic books. The woman with the harsh voice was in the kitchen. She was sitting with her dress hiked halfway up her fat thighs, soaking two remarkably swollen feet in a basin of water. When Charlotte walked in, the woman looked up and snarled, "What the hell do you want?"

"Are you Martha's mother?"

"I don't see how that's any a your goddamn business."

"I'm a friend of Martha; I'm trying to locate her," Charlotte said, struggling to be civil.

"*Locate* her? You that writer lady she keeps talking about—'*My friend Charlotte?*' Shit, I thought she was making up all that crap. You really her friend?"

"Yes, I was told at the drugstore she doesn't work there anymore; I'm concerned about her."

"Well, if you knew what she did you wouldn't be so goddamn concerned about her. The little bitch came into heat, and right off, went out and got herself pregnant—lost her job—I threw her out."

"Yes, I know all that," Charlotte said in a calm voice, still struggling to conceal her rage. "I just want to know where she is."

"I'd be the last to know. She was pissed when she left—so was I. I wouldn't give a rat's ass to know which dung heap she landed on."

"All right, thanks for your time." Charlotte turned toward the door, but stopped and added, "By the way, I hope your fucking feet rot and become infested with maggots." Mama was too stunned to answer. In the living room the teenagers struggled unsuccessfuly to cover up their snickering. When Charlotte reached the front door, one of them, without looking up from his comic book, said in a muffled voice, "She's down at Klute's."

"What's Klute's?" Charlotte asked.

"Klute's Coal Yard. She's livin' with Jimmy Jo, helpin' him guard the coal."

"Could you tell me where it is?"

Without answering and without looking up, he jerked his thumb in an easterly direction. After a period of silence, the lump on the floor quietly said, as he turned the page of his comic book, "Down by the tracks."

Charlotte was relieved to breathe fresh air again.

It amused Jude to see Charlotte's response to the lower end of the cultural scale. She made a fast U-turn, squealing the tires as they sped back toward the tracks. Up the tracks a couple of blocks was a large sprawling coal yard. Near the gate was a small white building, blackened with coal dust. Beyond it was a drive-on scale for weighing coal trucks. Charlotte parked next to the shack. Before they could get out of the car, the moon-eyed girl—body bulging with baby—opened the door of the shack and stepped out into the bright day. Charlotte hopped out of the car and ran over to her and was about to hug her when she saw the smudges of coal dust on her clothes, face and arms. "You look great. How do you feel?" After asking several more questions and receiving no more than a word or two in response, Charlotte became conscious she was carrying most of the conversation. She began to feel awkward—maybe coming here wasn't such a good idea. Charlotte called Jude over and introduced him to Martha as her friend, *Jude*—without further information. Martha said, "Hi" but did not look at him directly any more than she looked at Charlotte directly. The conversation did not flow any better. After about a dozen failed attempts by Charlotte to stimulate some contribution from Martha, Jude thought he might be the inhibiting factor and asked Martha if anyone would mind if he went over and watched them load the trucks. "It's OK," she said.

As he walked off, Martha, without a coat, began to shiver and was forced to invite Charlotte inside. The shack was small for two people to be living in it. Of two tiny rooms, the bedroom was only slightly larger than the double bed. Storage was in boxes under the bed or on nails driven into the wall. The other room functioned as a combination living room and kitchen; an outhouse served the rest of their needs. Everything was covered with coal dust.

"No use wiping it up, it jes' keeps comin' in," Martha explained. The small table had two wooden chairs; Martha shook the dust off a magazine and put it on the seat for Charlotte to sit on. "I suppose you're wonderin' why I'm here with Jimmy Joe after what he and Quirk did to me?"

"I was concerned about you."

"Anyways, I was tryin' to stay away from Jimmy Joe and Quirk? 'bout a month ago, I walked 'round a corner and there was Jimmy Joe. We almost bumped into each other. When he seen I was pregnant, he got real interested in it and wanted to know if it was his. I told him I assumed it was since he went first and I ain't been with anyone else since he and Quirk raped me. 'Aw, com'on, Martha, we didn't rape you; we was all jus' havin' fun.' I didn't see no sense in arguing with him, so I didn't say any more. He wanted to know if he could start seeing me again now that I was carrying his baby. I told him, no, I wasn't about to go back to providing free poontang for him and Quirk. He told me Quirk was living down in Roanoke now. 'Besides,' he said, 'I wouldn't never let that happen again.'"

"Now that I'm carryin' his baby, he said, I'm like a wife and I ought to be livin' with him. Then, he told me about this job here at the coal yard. They pay him a little to help with the coal deliveries; and they let him stay in this house for nothin'—they like having someone here at night to keep people from stealin' coal. I didn't want to live with him. I didn't think he cared shit about the baby—that he was just tired of doin' it in his hand—if you know what I mean." Charlotte nodded, but Martha probably did not see her nod because all this time she was either talking to the salt and pepper shakers on the table or looking out the window.

"I didn't want to piss him off, so I said I'd think about it. Then, a short time later, when Mr. Katz let me go, and my mother threw me out, I had nowhere to go, and ended up movin' in with him. It's been OK. Now that Jimmy Joe's gettin' it regular, and Quirk ain't around, he's easier to deal with."

Charlotte glanced out the window and said, "I see Jude is back and waiting in the car, I better go now; but, I'm relieved to find that you've worked something out."

As she stood up to leave, Martha said, "He looks like he'd be real nice."

Charlotte pretended not to catch the inference and said, "Yes, he is nice; he has run the farm for me since last summer and has done very well with it."

Martha said to herself, I'll bet he did—that's when you started buying rubbers from me. She walked out to the car with Charlotte, hoping to have another look at the rich lady's lover. She even stifled her shyness enough to walk around to Jude's side of the car, look right at him and say, "I'm glad to have made your acquaintance, ya'll come back, now." Then she went to the other side and said, "Thank you, Miss Henderson, for worrying about me; but, I'm all right for now."

Charlotte was quiet as they drove toward home. Jude asked if Martha had opened up more after he left.

"Yes, she talked," Charlotte said but then let the conversation drop.

"Do you think she'll be OK there with Jimmy Joe?"

"She says she will."

After a long silence, Jude said, "Guess you're mad at me, huh?"

"Why do you think I'm mad at you?"

"Because you're not talking to me."

"You're not talking."

"That's not unusual for me, but it is unusual for you not to talk."

"Yes, even when I don't have anything to say."

"That isn't what I meant, Charlotte, and you know it—you *are* angry; and, if we don't get this thing out in the open and talk about it, I'm not going to invite you over for dinner tonight: I can't stand it when you give me this silent treatment."

She didn't respond—they rode on in silence. After a while, she pulled into the parking lot of an Italian restaurant. "Dinner comes with the tour," she said. "After I've had a drink I may talk to you—if you're hungry enough, you'll take the risk. The place is a dump, but it's clean and they have good pasta."

While they waited for Charlotte's double Scotch and Jude's beer, she explained, "A few years ago I was invited to speak at James Madison University. A group of students brought me here for dinner afterward. They said the quality of the food made up for the lack of class."

When their drinks were served, Jude raised his glass toward Charlotte and said, "Thanks for the tour, dinner and talking to me again."

"You're welcome, I'm glad you came with me, it made it easier for me to face what I discovered, even if I did get pissed at you." She appeared thoughtful and not very happy as she sipped her drink.

"You really were mad at me then?"

"Of course I was, you think I'm made of steel that you can treat me the way you do?"

"Treat you how, Charlotte? You know I wouldn't do anything intentionally to upset you."

"No, not intentionally, but the fact is you do."

"What is it I do, Charlotte?" Jude asked, exasperated.

"It isn't what you do; it's that whenever we disagree, in the long run, you always turn out to be right."

"Charlotte, maybe if you gulp that instead of sipping it you will loosen up enough to tell me what the hell you're talking about."

"I am wound up tight, aren't I? OK, Doctor, as you have prescribed," and she took a couple more swallows of her drink. "Ah, that helps. OK, Jude from the beginning—after you left us and went off to roam about in the coal yard, we went into the shack." Charlotte went on to explain what the place was like and how Martha and Jimmy Joe got back together.

Jude said, "So I guess she has it worked out?"

"Not really, she says they get along OK, but she had a bruise on her upper arm that looked like she had been grabbed quite hard. Also, that place they live in isn't big enough to raise rabbits, much less a child. With all the coal dust they're breathing, they'll probably all die prematurely from black lung disease."

"So, do you plan to help her?"

"I did initially. When we set out on this trip, I wanted to get you off the farm and show you what the surrounding area is like. I also wanted you to meet Martha. I had hoped that, if she were in trouble, you would understand my interest in bringing her to Greyledge."

"I don't suppose it's too late, if you still feel strongly about helping her—but what does any of this have to do with your being mad at me?"

Charlotte leaned over the table; and, with an irritated

expression whispered, "It's because you're such an FFC."

"An FFC?"

"A flaming fucking conservative—and what's irritating about it is that you're right. Here I am reared with all the advantages money would buy—prestigious private schools, travel, living abroad, and there you are, raised among the jack pine savages of Upper Michigan, then cloistered in a monastery for two years. Yet, you have a better sense and understanding of people than I do. It just pisses me off for you to be 17 years younger than I and 20 years wiser."

"Charlotte, aside from all this shit you're serving me, what's really bothering you?"

"What's bothering me is that little moon-eyed lech, all the while I was in the cabin, was watching you out the window. She couldn't keep her moon-eyes off you. Then she had the goddamn gall to say to me, 'He looks like he'd be real nice.' She sure wasn't talking about the way you recite poetry in the moonlight. If I brought her out to Greyledge, she'd be after you right up to delivery time."

"Guess you didn't tell her we're going steady, huh?"

"That wouldn't hold her back. She knew as soon as I introduced you what your status is on the farm. I think it just increased her interest in you." She started to add something, but the waiter delivered their order; and, as he was placing it on the table, she turned to order wine. "You did want wine, didn't you, Jude?"

"Yes, now that I'm civilized." This comment was more for himself than it was for Charlotte, hoping to counter the flickering thought he just had about his *status* on the plantation as some kind of farm animal— at stud.

When they had finished dinner, Charlotte handed Jude the keys and asked if he'd like to drive. "Not that I'm crocked, but I'm a little too mellow to be attentive."

"OK, but I don't have a driver's license."

"Just don't ricochet off any police cars."

While he drove, she apologized for her bad mood and for taking it out on him. "When we get home, I hope you'll still be willing to tuck me into bed."

Charlotte did have some social life beyond Jude. Sometimes she wondered if there was any way he might fit into it. In the early stages of their relationship, when he was a fugitive and a slave to be taken advantage of, it was not a problem. Now that her feelings for him had matured, she wanted him to be part of her life. Keeping him down in the slave quarters like she was ashamed of him was beginning to make her feel guilty. Her immediate concern was the Christmas party she often had for the faculty and graduate students from school. She had delayed discussing it with Jude because . . . well, why had she? Was she embarrassed that someone would wonder why she had invited a farm hand to an academic party? Of course, she wouldn't have to tell anyone he was a farm hand, but then what would she introduce him as—her cousin? Madge always made her feel like such a lousy liar that she was sure Christopher Dell would immediately take her aside and ask, "How is he in the sack?" The academic world was sufficiently separated from the world of her in-laws so that even if she replied, "Delightful," it wouldn't present any risk. Of course there were faculty members who would consider her scandalous behavior reason for not renewing her appointment. Dell always supported her at this annual event. He told her later that it was because he liked her legs. Legs, indeed! It was more often her breasts his eyes were focused on. This is the guy the female students call Professor Ding Dong and allege that his favorite sport is standing near the stairs, looking up girls skirts as they go up and down.

She found Jude out in the barn threshing oats with a flail, like he did not know that practice had ended many years ago. He was glad for the interruption. "Jude," she announced, "I'm having a little party tomorrow night for some of the people up at school, would you like to come?"

He gave her one of his winning smiles and said, "Gee ma'am, I ain't sure us niggers should be fraternizing with the gentry."

"Aw com'on, Nig, I'll buy you some shoes and they'll never know the difference."

"It's tempting, Miss Charlotte, but I heard tell folks up at the university read newspapers. If you were able to figure out my infamous past from newspapers you read two years ago, one of them might, too. Besides, how would you explain me to them? Whatever cover story we used, I would blow it the first time someone made a pass at you; and, I don't see how any red-blooded male, after having a couple of drinks, could keep his hands off you."

"Jude, I hope you're not planning to spend the whole evening alone in your cabin, worrying about the possible violation of my virtue?"

"Yes."

"How can I make it up to you?"

"Your imagination regarding my pleasure is always better than my own—surprise me."

Jude helped her prepare for the party. Aunt Millie actually had done most of the work. Jude and Charlotte trimmed a Christmas tree and arranged the food on serving plates. Before it was time for the guests to arrive, Jude took a couple of beers and a plate of goodies back to his cabin. He tried to read, but found it difficult to concentrate. Was it because he was sorry he didn't go to the party, or was he jealous? Shit, Jude, you hate parties—people standing around sipping drinks and making small talk. Oh yeah? What do you know about what those professor types talk about at parties? Maybe they spend their time saying wise things—trying to impress each other. They probably talk about how dumb the students are and what a waste of time it is to try to teach them anything—or worse than that, they might talk about basketball games the university almost won. C'mon, sour-ass, why don't you just go to bed; life will be better in the morning.

After lying awake for several hours, Jude got up to go to the bathroom. He peeked outside—the lights were still on at the mansion, but most of the cars were gone—he could see only one. Maybe others were parked where he couldn't see them. He watched and waited, but the car didn't leave. When he could stand it no longer, he put on his clothes and went up to the house. What'a you doing, asshole! he chastised himself. This is cheap, petty, unmanly, jealous—goddamn you, Jude, go home. But he didn't, he checked the front of the house—there was only one car. He stood around shivering in the shadows while his panic mounted. When he could stand it no longer, he started looking in the windows. He found them in the study; the lingering guest still had a drink in his hand. They were talking, but Jude couldn't tell whether he was trying to convince her to take him to bed or whether she was trying to get him to go home—or, they could still be talking about basketball.

Jude went back to his cabin, disgusted and ashamed of himself. Nonetheless, he turned out the cabin lights and put up the shades; then, he moved the big chair over to the window where he could see the house and car. Face it, Jude, that's a good-looking guy up there trying to win her heart— slightly grey around the temples, very distinguished look- ing, not much older than Charlotte, and probably only a little bit drunk—that's hard to measure when you can't hear the words—Christ, I feel miserable!—what if she does go to bed with him? Should I go over there now and throw the bastard out, and claim what is mine? Horseshit, Jude—what is yours?—you dumb ass—what you really mean is should you go over there and claim what is John Paul's? If nothing was really happening, wouldn't Charlotte love that kind of behavior in front of a colleague!

After an agonizing half-hour, the lights went out downstairs. Jude was frantic, he pulled out his old Army knapsack and started to pack. Oh, God, I love her so much! Why is she doing this to me. Even if she does fool around once in awhile, he argued with himself, I would still have her most of the time—can I really live without her? Can I leave her? And for what? Oh, God, what am I going to do? About ten minutes later the lights went out upstairs—the car was still there. Jude got a blanket and sat in the big chair in the dark. Tears filled his eyes and ran down his cheeks into his beard. He tried to stop, but it only got worse; until he just gave up and sobbed.

When the cabin door quietly opened, he held his breath to listen.

"Jude, you asleep? Can I come in?"

"Yes, come in, Charlotte."

"There's a left-over drunk asleep on the couch in the study. I didn't think he should drive, so I talked him into taking a nap until he sobers up. He won't know where I am, or where the rest of the world is either, until noon tomorrow. I'm looking for a warm bed."

She shined her flashlight at Jude's bed. "Jude, where are you?" The light fell on the partially filled knapsack on the floor, then on Jude in the chair struggling to untangle himself from his blanket. She flicked on a cabin light and went over to help him.

"Jude! What's happening? Have you been crying?"

"Grown men don't cry," but the quaver in his voice gave him away.

"Yes, they do, and that's what you were doing, but whatever for?" She took him into her arms and hugged him swaying back and forth. "What were you upset about?"

"Nothing, I'm OK."

"You didn't think—OH MY GOD, YOU DID!—What else would you have thought! Oh, Jude, I'm so sorry. She kissed him all over his wet face and head and said, "Jude, how could you ever not trust me—we're going steady!"

"I always took that *tongue in cheek* joke seriously," he stammered, "but I had no way of knowing if you did. When I look at the worldly people you come in contact with, then I look at what I have to offer you, all I see is a poor slave hopelessly in love with his mistress."

"Jude, I'm just beginning to learn how to love. I'm not interested in building a collection of lovers. Besides, you have no idea how you compare to those people. You should have come over. If I could have introduced you to those *worldly people*, you wouldn't have been so impressed. Most of them are very knowledgeable about one or two subjects and dismally ignorant of the rest of the world. They think that what they know is the only thing worth knowing and everyone else is dabbling in trivia. Most of them couldn't survive without the protection of the university. They're a novel collection of misfits that together embody a lot of interesting knowledge, but individually their egocentric conversations soon run dry."

"I looked in the window," Jude admitted sheepishly.

"And, what did you see?"

"I didn't go over until only one car remained and I started to panic."

"Really," she said amused. "You came to check out the competition?"

"Maybe I came to see if you were in trouble and needed my help."

"And maybe you came to see if I was fucking him on the couch," she laughed and pushed him back in the chair, then plunked herself on his lap. "What did you think of him?" she said grinning.

"He looked like a well-dressed, handsome man in his early 40s, who was very interested in you—more than just your mind."

"Were you jealous?" she asked coquettishly.

"Painfully."

"That was Professor Christopher Dell; he has a wife and three kids—and has been trying to get into my pants for years."

Charlotte was delighted by Jude's concern. Then, realizing that her fun was at his expense—not the kind of game she should be playing as a *reformed bitch*—said, "Don't worry, Jude, Dell didn't have a chance even before we started *going steady*. His wife left him two weeks ago, took the three kids and went home to her parents. She finally became tired of his philandering. He insisted on telling me how poor she was in bed; and, since he provided her with a good home, how he deserved a little extra pussy on the side. He kept on drinking while he dragged out his tail of woe. By the time he finished, he was too drunk to drive. When I suggested he take a nap on the couch, he tried to pull me down with him. He didn't try very hard, though, it was more like a social grace offered to flatter his hostess."

"I should go over and pummel the bastard and throw him out in the cold."

"Jude, this isn't like you. Come to bed, love, I'll make it all better for you." She dragged him and his blanket over to the bed and after she tucked him in, she turned out the light, took off her clothes and joined him—the crisis was over.

The next morning when Jude looked out the window the car was gone.

16

On Christmas Eve Charlotte was still upstairs dressing when Jude arrived; he slipped her present under the tree beside a large package with his name on it as well as several smaller ones. Then he went to the kitchen to pour her a Scotch and himself a beer. She arrived looking exquisite in a new party dress, hairdo and earrings. "Since you missed the party the other night, I thought we would have our own private party tonight."

"Unbelievable! I never knew that a woman could be so beautiful. You know, it's kinda scary, my first reaction is animal-like: to seize and devour; but, then, it would all be over in about four minutes."

"And what is your second reaction?—This is getting good."

"To worship this goddess with overwhelming awe."

"But, do you think you can retain that hard-on all evening?"

"You are naughty, Charlotte. You always check my

barometer."

"Let's drink our drinks and eat some of the goodies, maybe that'll distract us for awhile. Then, I'd like to have you open your Christmas present—I'm really quite excited about it."

"You got me a Christmas present!" He faked surprise, so she would not know he had already made a visit to the tree. "If we follow your schedule, Charlotte, I'll bet we'll manage to stay up until nine o'clock tonight." Jude raised his glass and said, "Here's to our first Christmas!"

Charlotte clinked her glass against his and added, "And may they let us have many more!"

Jude gave her a wan smile and said, "You never stop thinking about the temporary nature of our relationship, do you."

"I don't think about it all the time; it's just a cynical streak that lights up every once in awhile. Compared to my years with John Paul, what I have now is like being reborn in the Garden of Eden. And, having enjoyed the forbidden fruit, I can't help wondering sometimes when my newfound joy will end."

"That kind of talk, Charlotte, is causing my barometer to fall. Why don't you just settle for being the spoiled, self-indulgent, sex machine that I'm desperately in love with?"

"You're right, Jude, back to the party." When they had sampled a half-dozen cheeses, pickled herring and caviar, and Charlotte had eaten most of the can of black olives, they put the food back in the refrigerator and went to the living room.

Charlotte went to the tree and, as she reached for Jude's

big present, spotted the one he had put there for her. "You got me something!" she exclaimed with childlike excitement. "How on earth did you manage that on slave's wages?—and confined to the plantation?—You made it—you whittled it out of wood." She started to open it but Jude stopped her: "That one is to be opened last."

"You are a spoilsport, Jude."

"You won't think so after you open it. You'll know how much of a sport I really am."

"OK, here, you open this first," and she slid the big box over to him.

She had bought him a chain saw. "Charlotte, that's wonderful, how did you ever know about these?"

"They were using one on campus to cut down a tree near my building. It looked like it was just what you need. I went out and talked to the guy using it, who was more than happy to tell me all about it and where to buy one. This is not a totally unselfish gift, though. You've had to spend nearly half your time this winter hustling firewood with that little bucksaw. I expect to be pushing revised manuscript at you pretty fast over the next couple of weeks and I want to make sure you're available to read it."

"Whatever your motives—it's a wonderful thing you've done. They had a chain saw at the monastery. I always admired how much wood it would process, but I wasn't allowed to use it."

"OK, Jude, let's see what Santa wrapped in these smaller packages." Charlotte had outfitted him with dress shoes, slacks, shirt and sweater.

"Wow, what does all this mean?"

"It means that when WE finish my book we're going out

to celebrate. It also means that you are all done living like a hermit. There are places we can go where no one will ever put you in the context of a wanted man—besides, I don't think they're looking very hard for you anymore—it's been three years now."

"That sounds like an emancipation proclamation."

"That's what it is: you are a slave now only when you're on this plantation—most particularly in my bed."

"What about in my bed?"

"Oh, I suppose it wouldn't hurt for you to have your way with me on occasion. Can I open my present now?"

Jude fished it out from under the tree and handed it to her. She quickly tore off the wrapping without ceremony. The first thing she encountered was a delicate, very feminine pair of panties which she held up to admire, totally astonished; next was a bra equally exquisite; and finally a lovely slip. "Oh, Jude, I just love them—how on earth did you ever pull this off?"

"Well, about the same way you found out about chain saws. There was this woman outside my window taking her clothes off, one stitch at a time and I said to her, 'Say, where could I get some fine tools like that?'"

Charlotte slugged him in the arm and hollered, "Jude, you are such a shit—c'mon, how'd you do it?"

"Wouldn't it spoil the magic for me to tell you?"

"It will spoil it if you don't, because I'm going to start breaking your fingers one at a time until you tell me."

Jude held out his hand and told her, "Start with the outer ones, save my middle finger for last."

Instead, of breaking them, she took his hand and kissed

each finger, "It's Christmas, Jude, I can't achieve full vio-
lence in the presence of all this Noel stuff. If I agree to
demonstrate how these undergarments work, will you tell
me how you bought them?"

"I was hoping you would demonstrate them for me."

"Not until you tell me how you got them—once you see
me in them you'll become incoherent."

"That's no doubt true. OK, you'll find out anyway when
you get your phone bill and discover a couple of calls to
Madge that you didn't make."

"Oh my God, why didn't I think of that—you were in
cahoots with the devil."

"Yes—the she-devil herself. I called her right after
Thanksgiving and explained what I was looking for. She sent
me a couple of catalogs, which I had to sneak out of your
mail before you saw them, then I called her back to discuss
my choices with her—I think she got a vicarious thrill out
of helping me with this. I sent her the cash in an envelope—I
had some old Army money left over."

"I just love these things—and you really picked them
out yourself! You wait here while I try them on."

After what seemed like a long time, Charlotte called.
There she was at the head of the stairs in a model-like pose
wearing only the panties and bra.

She was right, Jude became incoherent. Delighted with
the effect she had on him, she led him off to her bedroom.

True to her word, the manuscript revision and editing
went into high gear. Charlotte started her days at about 11
a.m., but was still going strong after midnight. Sometimes

they got together to eat a hastily prepared meal or something Aunt Millie left them, but mostly they ate sandwiches or leftovers. When Jude's swollen need for affection reached undeniable levels he would crawl into Charlotte's bed before she was awake in the morning and coax her for attention. If she was too slow to wake up, he would threaten to take his love to Miss Ashley—"That fictitious hussy," she'd respond sleepily, "you deserve better than that, hard as you work—WOW! and hard as you are."

The manuscript was in the mail before school started up again, but it was more than a month before she was able to drag Jude off the farm for the long weekend vacation she had promised him. They traveled through southern Virginia and North Carolina sightseeing and buying additional clothing for Jude, as well as for Charlotte. Jude was concerned that they were spending too much money, but Charlotte assured him they were going to make a bundle on the book and continued to spend without restraint. When they returned, they checked the mailbox on the way in. Charlotte was right. There was a response from her editor.

"Whoopee!" she hollered, hugging and kissing Jude. Then she gave him the letter to read.

The editor predicted that *Slaves Can't Read* would outsell *Plantation of Hope* three to one. "We plan to expedite the printing," he said, "and go all-out on the marketing of this book."

In a near manic state of excitement, Charlotte produced her best bottle of Scotch and coaxed Jude into joining her in a ceremonial sip of *firewater,* even though he preferred beer. In the middle of their celebration, Charlotte's joy suddenly turned to tears. Jude took her in his arms, where she clung to him in uncontrolled sobbing. It was some time before she recovered enough to tell him what was the matter.

"Oh, Jude, our life is just too good to last. Something terrible is going to happen—I'm so frightened."

"Charlotte, I thought we had settled this and decided it's all right to be happy."

"I know, I'm sorry about spoiling the party—why am I doing this? Am I going through change of life?"

"Maybe you're pregnant," Jude impishly suggested.

17

Several valleys over from Greyledge, a gravel road follows a stream up a narrow cut into the Blue Ridge. Wherever a bit of flat land has allowed it, scattered pockets of small dwellings have been established—two to five in a cluster. They have a sameness about them—clapboard siding and rusty metal roofs that extend out over porches across the front. The yards have small gardens, sometimes a hogpen, and a mix of disabled and functional vehicles, mostly old pickup trucks. Well-beaten paths to outhouses and wood piles reveal that not all the comforts of city living have infiltrated these mountain communities. The lots are connected to the road by driveways that cross the stream over plank bridges.

At one dwelling, an old Ford pickup was left overnight on the bridge, its left front wheel had broken through the planks. A flock of neighbor kids, had gathered around the truck to argue about how to get it out. On the porch, an immense woman, sunk down in an overstuffed chair, nurses a baby—the exposed breast considerably cleaner than the rest of the woman. A toddler, wearing only an underwear shirt, sits bare bottomed on the porch, playing with his mama's grimy foot as it taps out the beat to a nursery rhyme she is humming to the baby. From time to time she mindlessly brushes flies off the baby as the argument over the truck becomes louder.

"What's all the goddamn racket out there?" a voice boomed from inside the house. "Jesus Christ! Can't a man even git any sleep in his own goddamn house anymore. Where the hell's my breakfast, Jolene?"

"You missed breakfast, Burt. Your lunch is on the stove. All you need to do is warm the pan and add some flour."

"Why the hell didn't you call me?"

"You got in late last night, I thought I'd let you sleep." She liked him best when he was asleep or away.

"Well now, that was mighty fuckin' sweet of you! You know goddamn well Saturday's an important day for me, and you can see fuckin' well my truck is stuck in the bridge.

"Ouch, goddam it, Jolene, now I've gone and burnt ma-self. Git off a yer fat, lazy ass and light this fuckin' stove afor I blow the goddamn place up."

Jolene struggled to raise her bulk out of the sunken chair with the baby still in her arms. When she entered the kitchen, the screen door slammed. Burt, still shaky from the previous night's revelry, dropped the matchbox.

Balancing the baby on one hip, Jolene picked up the matchbox, turned on the stove and lit the burner. The flame was red at first and smelled strongly of kerosene; but, after a little adjustment of the wick, it turned blue and soon the white fat in the pan began to liquify. She added flour and water to make gravy while Burt settled himself at the table. Then Jolene wiped a towel across one of the dishes the kids had used, added four slices of bread and ladled gravy over it. She put the plate and a cup of rewarmed coffee in front of Burt and headed for the door.

Burt never failed to correct Jolene when he was displeased with her speed or performance; usually it was with a slap on the rump or a string of profanities and uncomplimentary remarks.

"Where the hell you goin', ain't cha gonna set here and watch me eat?"

"Watchin' you eat ain't no picture show." She calculated that Burt, with his face now buried in his bread and gravy, would let her get away with that comment.

"Fuckin' bitch, don't know how good you've got it," he muttered to himself. When he finished lunch, he let a prolonged fart reverberate off the chair, then sat back to congratulate himself on how much better he felt. It was during fleeting moments like this that Burt was most satisfied with his life. He looked around the cabin—at least the roof did not leak and the well did not go dry during the drought. These three rooms are enough for us and the eight kids—God, that Jolene is a fertile sow. She still moans about losing those two to cholera, but we'd a had to build on by now if they'd a lived. Someday, when I git steady work, I'll put plasterboard around the walls of the bedrooms. Jolene never lets me fergit it—worries that the kids'll wake up and see me on top of her. Those old blankets she hung up on the 2 X 4s close off our bedroom pretty good. Hell, we get us some more blankets and close the kids room off, too, and she'll have all the privacy she needs. Well, 'nough of this shit, gotta git rollin'. He stood up, stretched his six-foot four-inches of muscle and fat and headed for the bedroom to put on his bibbed coveralls.

As he walked toward the truck, the kids scattered. None of them liked Burt, including his own kids.

Oh, yes, the truck is hung up all right; good thing I was smart enough not to try to back out of that hole last night. Most people woulda reared back and ripped the wheel off or maybe the whole front axle. That still don't leave me anywhere but up the fucking creek, though. Easiest thing would be to get Salvi over here with that truck a his with the boom on it. He could cross Kiel's bridge, drive next door to my yard and hook on to'er from this end. 'Course Salvi ain't gonna want to take his truck over Kiel's puny bridge. Besides, he'd want ten bucks for that one little lift—cash, too. That fuckin' nigger acts like he don't see what color he is. Never could understand why Hogg won't let us hold that uppity bastard to the fire and learn him some manners. But, ain't none a this shit gitten' me inta Grimble and I sure as hell don't want a ride with Reverend Hainus, if'n I kin help it. Maybe I git a big pole; me, Jolene, and the kids could raise that mothafucka right up out a there. 'Cept where in hell I gonna git a big pole soon enough to put me into town on time?

About then a black truck rattled down the road, on five cylinders, puffing black smoke. A sign on the door announced Reverend J. A. Hainus—Hogs, Ice and Coal. Four empty barrels in the back jostled about creating a din and emitting a sour odor. Reverend Hainus collected garbage from grocery stores and restaurants to feed his hogs. He brought his barrels hoping to make a pick up at the Boar's Head after the meeting.

Hainus, a slender man with a mustache, grinned out of the window at Burt and said, "Looks like you might be needing some help, brother."

Burt growled back, "Yah, you think you can pray that fuckin' truck up out of there?"

"I'd be happy to offer some prayer, but I'd be afraid of offending the Lord by asking for quick delivery of a miracle on behalf of a sinner."

"Where you git off callin' me a sinner?" he demanded as he opened the door and dropped his huge body into the seat beside the preacher.

"Why brother, you know I have never seen you nor yours in either of my fine churches. If you opt for hell for yourself that's one thing, but the souls of those youngin's . . . ." The preacher kept looking straight at Burt as though he had no intention of driving off until they came to terms on this issue. Burt was holding his breath waiting for the truck to move and circulate some air through the cab.

Finally, the truck started to move but the preacher was not about to change the subject. "You don't need to worry about gittin' your truck on the road before Sunday. I come right by here with the bus; be happy to stop and pick up your whole family." The reverend had increased the size of his two congregations considerably when he purchased the old school bus and started collecting members of his flock who needed transportation. After one service, those who liked to hear about the goodness of the Lord a second time could ride with him to the other church.

"Well, that's mighty considerate of you, preacher, but I tell my family whatever they need to know about religion." Reverend Hainus kept on smiling.

The Boar's Head Tavern they entered was pre-Civil War style, but it was not likely to be marked as a national treasure to be preserved. It was just a run-down, two-story building. Green curtains covered the lower half of two large, dirty windows in front. Last year's sun-faded circus poster leaned against the curtain. At the bar, a solitary figure ignored a man and woman in one of the booths who were laughing too loud and reaching for each other underneath the table. Pictures of baseball players and calenders of nude women graced the walls and mirror behind the bar. The floor was covered with a dingy linoleum, worn thin and molded to the wide floorboards underneath. Burt and the reverend walked by the bartender, who nodded without smiling. In the back room, Shaflee and Howard were already on their second drink from an open bottle of bourbon. "Where'd that come from?" Burt asked without saying *hello*.

"Where the fuck you think it come from?" Shaflee responded.

"What's that asshole want this time?" Burt inquired.

"How the hell we supposed to know?" Howard asked. "But you can bet your dick he didn't buy that bottle jess 'cause he likes hillbillies. Maybe he thinks we'll make a big deposit in his fuckin' bank."

The bartender brought in three more glasses and left without a word. The four men looked at each other in mock wonder; finally Shaflee said, "Ain't it strange how un-friendly Walt is? You don't suppose he fails to recognize the importance of our work, do you?"

"I don't think Walt has any fuckin' idea what all we do fer this town, or what the Klan does for America," Howard commented. "He's a goddamn Yankee, yah know. Clyde's his uncle, gave Walt this job when he got laid off from the steel mill up North."

"Some nigger's probably got his job now," Shaflee offered as he poured bourbon into two of the empty glasses.

"Who's the extra glass for?" the preacher asked.

"I suppose it's fer Hogg. Yah don't suppose he'd spring fer a bottle without gettin' his snoot in to it, do you?" Shaflee asked.

Sounds of good-natured joshing came from the other side of the curtain that separated the back room from the bar. One of the voices was Walt's, the other was their host, Milo Hogg, who soon came bursting through the curtain with his jovial facade overflowing. He quickly took charge of the bourbon, pouring himself a good measure and freshening the other four glasses.

"Thank you, Mr. Hogg," several of them mumbled.

"My pleasure, boys—always nice to get together with good friends and responsible citizens. Guess everybody's here. We don't need a large group to deal with this particular issue; it's better if not too many people know about it." They gulped from their glasses and soaked up Milo's good will. "OK, now, this is what I think we need to consider. It turns out that Miss Charlotte, out there at Greyledge, has published another one of her filthy books."

As he spoke, he drew from a paper sack a copy of the recent threat to decent society and slapped it on the table to emphasize his disgust. "Any of you had a chance to read this yet?" None of them had, anymore than they had found time to read her other books. Milo was good at book reviews, though, and had already advised them on the unhealthy nature of her earlier books. With this one, he took special pains, reading several passages that described the heroine lovemaking with a black slave. When he finished, he put the book down with a distasteful expression on his blubbery face. Everyone was quiet. Milo sipped from his glass, waiting for the expressions of outrage over this vile nigger lover, right here in their community. Instead, each basked in his own fantasy—engaged in a wondrous experience with Miss Charlotte.

It was always difficult to anger them over the mistress of Greyledge. The whole town, for that matter, was ambivalent about her, even though everyone felt duty bound to hate her for what her family stood for. When Charlotte came to town, men and women alike stopped to stare. She would zoom up to the curb in her little sports car and in a quick, confident manner go about her business. Her bright colors and charming smile always lit up the grungy downtown area. Deep down the women envied her and the men carried a hidden lust for this *terrible* woman. Milo hoped this new book would fuel new hostility toward her. His fear, though, was that it would be profitable enough to save the farm for her. If Milo was going to have that property, Charlotte would have to be driven out of Grimble County.

"So, boys, ever wonder how Miss Charlotte thinks up these dirty little games she writes about? Don't suppose she's got herself a slave out there to practice on, do you?"

"Hard to say," Shaflee offered. "Her place sets back from the road so far you can't see what's goin' on. I seen a white guy cuttin' grass along the driveway but she probably hires him just to come in and do that."

"You boys forgetin' something?" Milo asked. "Two years ago, you remember, she had that uppity nigger from up North out there sharecroppin' and liv'n in one of the slave cabins. I believe his name was Lyle. It takes about two years to put a book together and have it published, doesn't it?"

"Gawd, yah know, it's been so long since I wrote one," Burt said, "I hardly remember what it takes."

Shaflee reached over and paged through Milo's book and said "Sheee-it, Burt, that book's got over 400 pages in it and no pictures; you couldn't read it in two years." Among them, only Reverend Hainus could have read it in two years and, at that, it would be a tight race against time.

"You sayin', Milo, that Charlotte has been fuckin' and suckin' the nigger what's driving the honey truck?" Burt asked in shocked amazement.

"Unless you boys come up with another name, I'd guess he's the one."

"What the hell did he quit fer?" Shaflee wanted to know, "Seems like ideal work to me."

The preacher had not commented yet because he feared he might reveal that even he felt some lust for this sinful woman. Finally, he said, "Lyle probably realized he had sunk so low in God's eyes that he was no longer worthy of anything better than cleaning septic tanks."

"Horseshit, she used him up and threw him away," Burt said.

"What a way to go," Shaflee exclaimed and the rest agreed, except for Hainus, who felt compelled to keep his facade in place.

Milo was disappointed over the way the meeting was going. Instead of driving Charlotte out of the county, it sounded more like they would rather offer her their services. "Well, now, this has all been a lot of fun," Milo said, trying to get things back on track, "but we really ought to look at the serious side of it before that woman destroys the moral fabric of this community."

"Amen." The preacher offered, quick to realize that Milo had stepped into his sphere of expertise. "What did you have in mind, Milo?"

"Well, I was hoping you gentlemen would have some suggestions. Maybe you favor a hangin' from that magnolia tree in front of the mansion or just a whuppin'. Whatever you do ought to be out at Greyledge, though, so Miss Charlotte understands she'd be happier livin' up north. I'm gonna leave now so's you can think about what to do. Meanwhile, I'm gonna give you each $50 to cover expenses. On the way out, I'll talk to Walt about settin' you boys up with a nice dinner and another bottle. You convince Miss Charlotte to move on, I'll add another 50."

"Mighty generous, Mr. Hogg. Any chance you cleared this with the sheriff?" Howard asked.

"We've talked about it in general terms, Sheriff Batley and Deputy Bream would like to go with you. You know

Batley's still pissed at that woman over the smart mouth she gave him when he brought her in to question her about John Paul. He still thinks she had him killed—not that the sheriff gives a damn about John Paul. It's just that she made him look like such a fool in front of his men. Guess ya'll know he's not a forgivin' man."

"He ain't," Shaflee agreed. "Never ferguv Greyledge fer that mine accident that took his brother. Not much he can do to Miss Charlotte's daddy 'bout that, but he's still tryin' to git even by wackin' at Miss Charlotte."

"Well, gotta go, boys. Have a good time." Once he cleared the tavern, he let out a chest full of air as though he had been holding his breath the whole time. "Christ, that place is dismal and those four are about the bottom of the barrel."

The kitchen was next to the meeting room. One of Salvi's four daughters, Rosemarie, was the daytime waitress and cook at the Boar's Head. She was married and had not lived at home for some years, so the regulars did not connect her with Salvi. Unattractive and not particularly friendly, she was essentially ignored, except when an order was filled too slowly.

Rosemarie usually did not pay attention to conversations through the thin wall between the meeting room and the kitchen; but when she heard her daddy's name mentioned, she stopped to listen. She could not wait to hear the whole conversation because the tavern was starting to become busy as the dinner hour approached. Clearly, Lyle and Charlotte were in trouble, and possibly her daddy, too, although she was not sure. She had heard enough, though, to know that Lyle and her daddy should be warned; if they wanted to tell Miss Charlotte, that was up to them. For her part, if the Klan wanted to terrorize a white woman once in awhile, it was nothing to her.

By the time her shift ended, nothing seemed resolved, except it was clear that Lyle and Greyledge were the targets. No more mention was made of Salvi. When the four were gone, Rosemarie left for home as fast as she could walk. By the time she arrived, she was so out of breath she had trouble explaining to her husband, Jefferson, what was happening. Finally, he understood and went to warn Lyle, who could do whatever he wanted to about saving that white woman's ass.

When Shaflee, Howard, Burt and the preacher left the Boar's Head, they took what was left of the bourbon with them. It still was not clear what they were going to do; but, at a minimum, if they were going to have a cross, they would need the materials they kept in Howard's barn.

Howard lived in a large unkempt place that prior to the accident at the mine, had served as a boardinghouse for immigrant miners. Most of them were middle Europeans who had moved south when the Pennsylvania coal mine strikes turned violent in the early 1900s.

The boardinghouse, run by Howard's mother, Verna, provided six to eight men with all their needs. She cashed their checks, gave them a few dollars for beer, and deposited a small amount every payday in their savings accounts; the rest she kept for their room and board. Verna did their laundry, prepared their meals and made the rounds of their rooms to take care of their sexual needs. She was fairly skilled at this, and in spite of five kids and middle age, there remained enough hint of her former good looks so none of the boarders complained about how slowly their bank accounts grew.

Verna's kids were all different, both in looks and in temperament. They had only one thing in common: they were all surly and meanspirited, except for Pamela, who was the youngest. Slightly retarded, she usually missed the subtleties of meanness practiced by the others and had no concept of proper treatment for people like herself. The miners and her two older brothers were sometimes abusive and took sexual advantage of her.

Verna was aware of what was happening, but did nothing to discourage it since it reduced the amount of effort she had to put into servicing the boarders. She tried to shame her sons and Pamela for their sexual activity, but the distinction between what Pamela did with the miners and what she did with her brothers was too complicated for her. Because Pamela was retarded, Verna was able to have her sterilized while she was still quite young.

The father was never included in discussions of boardinghouse etiquette. Like the other miners, he put in 12- to 16-hour days; but he was older than the others and so worn-out by the end of the day that he was pretty much out of touch with his family.

After the accident at the mine, life at the boardinghouse changed. Howard's father and two older brothers were among those left under a mountain of soil and rocks. Two of the boarders were also missing. The four remaining boarders stayed for a couple of months, hoping the mine would reopen. By then, Verna had drained most of the money from their savings accounts. Three of them decided to go back to Pennsylvania; only Stush Weisnesky remained behind. It was no surprise that Carl, one of the departing miners asked Becky, Howard's 15-year-old sister, to go with him. She was the one with the red hair—almost orange. One of the miners that was killed had red hair, which had caused a certain number of rude comments at the dinner table until Verna angrily put a stop to it.

Howard, who was 12 years old when the accident happened, had trouble figuring out how he felt about the loss of his father and brothers. Frequently people tried to help him get through this, but it really did not bother him. They thought his surly nature was a reaction to the tragedy. Howard had always been surly. Previously, people had ignored him so were not aware of his bad disposition. What the hell do I care, he thought, the old man probably wasn't my father anyway. Carl was a more likely candidate and he was still alive and fucking his sister. The fact that his two brothers or half-brothers—whatever they were—had been sealed in the mine, was more of a relief to him than it was pain. They never did nothin' for me, he thought, 'cept slap me around and try to get me to be their ass wiper after they became big deal miners.

Stush Weisnesky joined Verna in the master bedroom the day after the memorial service for the lost miners. He and Verna continued to run the boardinghouse, but it never had enough guests again to make it pay for itself. Stush pimped a little for Verna but that, too, was only modestly successful. When Verna's nest egg began to run low, Stush tried to push Howard and Pamela out. Howard quit school at

15 and got a job as a gas station attendant. Stush took most of what he earned for room and board. A couple of years later Verna developed ovarian cancer. Before she died, she confided in Howard that she had started a bank account years earlier: "There's enough in it to pay my doctor bills and funeral expenses. I recently put your name on it as a joint owner of the account, but don't tell Stush, he'd just take the money and run. I want to leave this life with all my bills paid and with a decent funeral. You're also co-owner of this house, don't let Stush get his hands on it or he'll throw you and Pamela out."

Verna died on Howard's seventeenth birthday. Howard expected Stush to make the funeral arrangements—he got drunk instead. Finally, Howard went to the funeral home to see what should be done about getting her body out of the house. The funeral director showed Howard some caskets and talked about burial plots. Even with the cheapest casket, the most undesirable plot in the cemetery, and no service, there would not be enough left in the bank account to buy a new pickup truck. "What about cremation?" Howard asked. When the funeral director tried to convince him that cremation was barbaric, anti-Christ and contrary to Verna's wishes, Howard realized he was on the right track. About then the funeral director saw the frighteningly, vicious look developing on this kid's face. He accepted the fact that he was not going to make a large profit on this funeral and told him what the cost of cremation would be. The deal was struck and Howard left for the Ford dealership.

Howard arrived home at the same time as the coroner and the hearse. Stush was still too drunk to know what was going on. Several days later Stush faced his hangover and the loss of Verna. He wanted to know when the funeral would be.

"Won't be no funeral; she's being cremated."

Stush exploded in a barrage of profanity and insults.

"That's all I could afford. Didn't see you coming up with any dough, or even helping with the arrangements." Stush went off mumbling and looking for something to help his throbbing head.

For the next two weeks, Pamela would not stop asking, "Where's mamma; when's she coming home?"

With rising anger, Howard kept telling her, "She's dead, she ain't never comin' home."

On top of that, Stush kept telling him, "Take your dim-witted sister and get the hell out of my house." Stush repeatedly searched through Verna's papers looking for the deed. It irritated Howard, but he knew Stush would blow up if he told him whose name Verna had put on the title. Finally exhausted with Stush's tirades, Howard took the title from his drawer, showed it to him and told him to get the hell out.

"Bull . . . shit, that hunk'a paper ain't legal."

"No, well you just haul your ass down to the courthouse and see for yourself, then just keep right on going."

"Makes no difference. Even if she did sign it over to you, I got common-law rights. I'm going to get me an attorney and prove it." He snatched the title and headed for the bedroom.

Howard grabbed him by the arm and yelled, "Give me that, you son-of-a-bitch." Stush turned and drove his fist into Howard's face, knocking him to the floor dazed, then, went to lock the title in the chest at the foot of his bed. When he returned, Howard was picking himself up off the floor. Stush kicked him in the ribs and sent him sprawling, "I catch you in my room, I'll kill you."

Pamela rushed to Howard's aid when she heard them fighting. She helped Howard to his feet and into his bedroom where she wiped at the blood on his face and fussed over him until he chased her away.

Common-law marriages, Howard had heard of, but he did not know what their legal status was; neither did Stush, who could not afford an attorney to find out.

When the letter arrived indicating that Verna's remains could be picked up at the crematorium, Howard asked Stush if he wanted to go with him.

"Don't take two of us to carry her."

Howard put the box of ashes on the coffee table and plopped into a chair. Stush was sitting in the living room smoking and drinking beer. Neither spoke, they just sat and looked at the box. After a long time, Stush asked, "What are you going to do with them?"

"I don't know. You say she's your wife, you decide."

Stush was a little taken back by Howard's offer. "Did you look inside?"

"Yah, the guy opened it to show me there was something in it."

"What's she look like?"

"She's different now. Look for yourself if you want to know. The top comes off easy."

"I thought they came in a vase with a lid on it."

"Urn's extra."

"The box is OK."

When Pamela came into the room, her eyes fell on the box. "What's that?"

"Verna," Howard replied. He had never referred to her as *mama*.

Bewildered, she walked over and lifted the lid and said, "It's full of ashes."

"Yah, Verna's ashes."

"What do you mean?"

When he explained, she screamed at him, "YOU LET THEM BURN MAMA—BURN HER UP LIKE GARBAGE? WHY DIDN'T YOU ASK ME? I HATE YOU. I HATE YOU," over and over again she screamed as she tried to beat him on the head.

Finally, he slapped her across the face and said, "Shut up." She withdrew to a corner of the room where she sat on the floor sobbing and rocking her body back and forth.

When the sobbing subsided, Howard asked if she wanted to help decide what to do with the ashes. She nodded, *yes*, with tears still streaming down her face. They all looked at each other without saying anything until at last Howard said to Pamela in a detached manner, "You want us to bury that box in the garden?"

"Yes, put mama in the garden."

"OK, Stush?"

"OK with me." He got up and started to leave.

Howard asked, "Where you going?"

"Gotta see Clyde about a beer—not that it's any of your goddam business."

"When do you want to bury the box?"

"You can do it anytime you want to."

Pamela said, "Mama would want us to do this together,

like a family."

"Oh yah, that'd be real nice," Stush smirked. "We'll do it later this afternoon, when I git back."

Stush returned on time for dinner—only slightly drunk. Pamela insisted that they bury mama after dinner. When they were through eating, Howard went to the barn for the shovel, then called Stush and Pamela to bring Verna out.

Pamela carried the box; Stush carried a beer. Howard chopped around the perimeter of the grave with the shovel and started digging.

"What the hell you making it so big for?" Stush yelled, "We ain't burying her whole carcass, for Christ's sake. It's just a fucking little box of ashes."

"After it gets deeper, its gotta be big enough to stand in while we dig."

"Don't need to be that goddamn deep."

"It has to be deep enough so the neighbor's fucking dogs don't dig it up."

Stush shrugged and took another sip of his beer while Howard went on digging. After he had dug a couple of feet, he climbed out and handed Stush the shovel. "What the hell is this?" he said, "I ain't doing any of this digging shit."

"We're each gonna do half."

"Bullshit! It's your mother, and you're the one wants to dig to China."

"You're the hotshot, deep shaft miner. Git your ass in the hole and do your share."

Stush stepped into the hole and nearly fell. He dug for a little while but the beer had sapped his strength. In no time at all, he declared the hole deep enough, so Howard had to take over again. Pamela was losing interest and wandered off to catch grasshoppers, which she threw at Howard when he was not looking. Always they took wing before they hit him so she was saved from Howard's hollering.

When Howard decided the hole was deep enough, he asked Pamela to hand him the box. He placed it in the center of the hole, then had Stush pull him out. "OK, now if everyone is satisfied, we can shovel the dirt back in." Pamela started to cry and said she did not want to watch that part and went in the house.

"Stush, you shovel back the first half and I'll finish it up." Stush reluctantly picked up the shovel and halfheartedly tossed some soil at the box, tipping it over. He reached down with the blade of the shovel and tried to turn it upright but he had only the very end of the handle to hang on to and nearly fell in the hole. Howard yelled, "Quit shitting around and get on with it. It don't matter what side's up, ashes don't have no head or tail."

When the box was fully covered, Howard approached Stush, who was leaning forward looking into the hole. He reached back under his shirt tail, which was hanging out, drew his hunting knife; and, with a wide, powerful swing cut Stush's throat clear though to the backbone. Stush teetered at the edge of the hole with his arms waving in the air, then fell in. Howard caught the shovel as it was sliding into the hole. Stush's quivering body was lying on its side, with the head thrown back and the wound opened up like a second mouth, yawning before the big sleep. There was blood everywhere except on Howard, whose wide swing carried him out of the spray area. He took the shovel and holding it by the end of the handle swung it like a pendulum, hitting Stush on the back of the head. His head pitched forward, closing the gap in his neck. Howard stood up looking down at Stush: "There, you son-of-a-bitch, don't say I never done anything for you. You look better now with your neck back together—maybe you can git up now. Don't expect me to help you out of the hole, though." He scooped a shovelful of soil and threw it in his face. "OK, asshole, you wanted Verna and you wanted the property; well, you got em both, now and forever." He quickly covered the grave, washed the knife and shovel blade at the outside faucet and returned them to the barn. In the house, Pamela was doing dishes and listening to some twangy music on the radio. Howard retrieved the title to the house and put Stush's clothes in a bag for disposal later.

The next day Pamela asked, "Where's Stush?"

"He went to the Boar's Head after we buried Verna. He met a couple miners who said they were hiring again in Pennsylvania. They told him they were going up there first thing in the morning if he wanted to ride along. You were in bed when he came in last night. He told me to say *good-bye* to you if he didn't see you in the morning."

"That was nice of him," she said. "Mostly he wasn't nice to me, you know, even when he wanted me to do his thing for him, he was mean to me. I'm glad he's gone. Bye, Stush."

A week later, Shaflee was buying gas where Howard worked—said he hadn't seen Stush at the Boar's Head lately. He accepted Howard's story about Pennsylvania without question, and he suggested that Howard might like to take his place in their little group that helps out with some of the local problems. Howard had never been asked to be part of anything before. Shaflee told him they had talked about inviting him to join earlier, but Stush was against it. Shaflee told Howard he knew he had the same kind of civic pride the other members of their group had.

Howard's path through life was now defined. The Klan and the Boar's Head Tavern became his social outlets. His companions soon discovered he could carry out brutal acts some of the others were squeamish about. Pamela kept house for him and dutifully serviced his sexual needs. He never had a successful relationship with local girls. Occasionally he bought time with some of them that hung around the Boar's Head, but they complained about how rough he was. He had tried to be gentle with one of the whores he liked, but he was not able to perform. Humiliated, he became meaner than ever; and she ended up with a black eye and bruises. A couple of times he tried to be less rough with his sister, too; but, when the same thing happened, he stuck with what stimulated him most.

18

Shaflee took the lead in constructing the cross. He was the most experienced at working with his hands. Mostly he worked in the woods as a logger; between jobs, he cut and sold firewood, roofed houses, repaired porches and performed other handyman activities. He was frequently in between jobs. Although he was a hard worker, he liked to torment other people with practical jokes. Most were funny only to him; some ended up injuring other loggers. Like Burt, he was well over six feet tall, but Shaflee had a lean muscular frame, long arms and legs, and big calloused hands. A couple of front teeth were missing from his lower jaw and his lip was scarred from a cant hook that had kicked back and hit him in the mouth. He had been through two wives in two years; now he preferred the short-term investment in local whores. Shaflee lived alone in a shack the next ridge over from Burt and the preacher.

When the cross was finished, Howard called Sheriff Batley as Hogg had instructed.

"Me and Leroy will join you later out at Greyledge," he said. "A report just come in about a big accident out on the highway we gotta tend to first."

"What about the nigger?" Howard asked.

"I kind of favor swinging him from the magnolia tree— get Miss Charlotte to packing her bags more than anything. I'll see to it that no one responds to any hysterical phone calls tonight from out that way."

They slipped into their sheets. Howard grabbed his shotgun, a Mason jar of white lightning and they were on their way. When they turned on to the road where Lyle lived, Shaflee exclaimed, "What the fuck's going on? This street's usually crawling with niggers this time a night, ain't a fucking jigaboo in sight. Somebody's tipped 'em off."

"Who the hell knew 'cept us and Hogg?" Howard asked.

"I just bet Lyle'd like to tell us about it," Burt suggested. "Let's go ask him."

Burt banged on the door. When there was no answer, he tried it and found it locked. With a single kick, the door was ripped out of the jam and slapped flat to the floor. The four of them rummaged through the house hollering for Lyle employing all the popular racial epithets available. They knocked over lamps and chairs, turning the place into a mess. Then they left, unable to guess where he might be.

"Shit, that sort of spoils the evening, now, don't it," Burt complained.

"I'd hate to have it end right here," Howard said. "Why don't we just go out to Greyledge and burn our cross, make a little noise with our guns and yell at her some. Maybe she'll just pack off and leave us each 50 bucks richer."

"Hell yes, the evening's jes started," Shaflee agreed,

"but let's try some of that paint remover first."

Howard unscrewed the lid from the Mason jar and handed it to him. He took a big gulp and hollered, "Wow!" and with his mouth open, fanned it with his hand to put out the fire.

"Sheeeit," Burt said with disgust, "gimme that." His big gulp was followed by less theatrics than Shaflee exhibited, but tears were welling up in his eyes and his throat was so pinched he could barely speak.

"I usually just sip at it or take a little water with it," Howard said. "That's some of Eddy Elkhorn's; he claims it's 120 proof."

When they arrived at Greyledge, only a small night light was burning in the study. Charlotte had gone to bed early. She had an early class to teach and could no longer enjoy her reckless, late hours of summer. The two trucks pulled up in front of the house and parked on the concrete turnaround. "Ain't that nice now, looks like Miss Charlotte's gone to bed. We can get all set up and surprise her," Howard said.

They passed the jar around while they studied the layout. Then with a posthole digger they made a hole for the cross. After soaking the rag-covered cross with kerosene, they erected it in the hole and buried the base. Meanwhile, the jar continued to circulate and their spirits continued to rise.

As the flames climbed the cross, the four of them stood solemnly and watched, waiting quietly for her to become aware of their presence. They thought it would be more scary that way. After they had her attention, they would become loud and threatening.

Charlotte was not asleep yet when the eerie flickering light played across the wall of her room. Her first thought was that the house was on fire. She leaped out of bed, grabbed her robe and ran to the window, where she saw the cross and the white hooded figures looking up at her. In a rush of anger, she ran down to the study, loaded her shotgun, and headed for the front door. She flung it open and in full fury gave them five minutes to, "Get that thing down and get the hell out of here. You'll find a hose at the end of the porch and you damn well better use it."

Shaflee, who had seen her use a shotgun at skeet matches, paused. But, Burt said, "Women don't have the balls to shoot anyone." He walked up on the porch and said, "Miss Charlotte, you better give me that before you hurt yourself." As she pointed the gun threateningly at his chest, he reached out with drunken bravery to jerk it away from her, but she held on tight. "You better let go ma'am or your gonna get sorry hurt." Charlotte, with both hands still grasping the gun, did not see Burt's huge hand come up in a wide, full-arm swing. It caught her beside the head, lifted her off her feet, and drove her stumbling down the hallway into the study. She hit the floor on her back and was out like a light. The belt, holding her robe closed, was tied with a simple loop. When she hit the floor, her robe fell completely open. Burt whooped, "Holy fucking shit! Come look at this." All four of the hooded figures stood gawking at Charlotte's exposed body.

"I'm gonna have me some of that," Burt declared.

"Me, too," Howard and Shaflee said in unison.

Reverend Hainus said, "Oh, Lord, save us from the

temptations of this evil woman."

Burt took off his hood and sheet, dropped his bibbed overalls and tried to enter her but she was too dry and tight. After several attempts, he backed down to her crotch and licked it a couple times to moisten it, much to the delight of the others. Shaflee said, "Hey, Burt, how's that taste?"

"Nice and fresh. I can tell it ain't Jolene's pussy." As Burt shoved it in, Charlotte moaned and rolled her head from side to side. Burt triumphantly claimed she was enjoying it.

Howard said, "I think she's waking up. She'll be able to identify you without your hood."

In between grunts, Burt said, "Either hit her again or throw my sheet over her head."

Shaflee retrieved the sheet and told Burt and the others, "I don't want her hit in the face no more 'til I've had my turn. If I wanted to fuck hamburger, I'd buy a pound and go jerk off in it."

"One of you better hold her down then, she's startin' to buck some."

Howard held her shoulders to the floor while Burt finished his turn. By then Charlotte was screaming and struggling. Shaflee was on her as soon as Burt got off. It took both the preacher and Howard to hold her down. The rotation continued until it was the preacher's turn who, in struggling to resist evil, ended up last. Burt asked, "Well, you gonna take her, or ain't yuh?"

"Oh, Lord, forgive this poor sinner," and he pulled off his sheet and started to lower his pants. The others, amused with his moral struggle, relaxed their grip on Charlotte.

The sheet slipped off her head enough so she could direct a kick squarely into Burt's balls. While he howled, the others gaped in surprise. The preacher, with his pants around his ankles, was the only one between her and the kitchen. One shove and he fell over backwards. She made it to the kitchen and pushed the alarm button just as Howard grabbed her by the back of the neck and threw her to the floor.

Suddenly, she was terrified at what she had just done. They would kill Jude and they would kill her. She was still on the floor when the others came into the kitchen, Burt was limping and the preacher was holding up his pants so he could walk. None of them had their sheets on.

"So, you little fucking bitch, jes where the hell did you think you was going?" Burt asked.

"She was after that button," Howard said. "I don't know if she got to it or not."

"Tell us, sugar doll, did you summon the fucking cavalry?" Shaflee asked.

"Yes, you've got two minutes to get out of here."

"So, who the hell did she call?" Shaflee wanted to know.

"Maybe the sheriff," Howard suggested, and they all laughed.

Shaflee said, "They ain't nobody else in the house or they'd a showed up by now with all that screaming she's doing. She's bluffin'. Why don't we get that jar a shine, have us another round a that and another round a pussy— she's startin' ta look real good again spite a what Burt did to that one side a her face."

The preacher wondered if she didn't have, "Something around here better'n that linoleum cleaner."

Shaflee went back to the study; he returned with a bottle of Scotch and a bottle of bourbon. They each had a couple of drinks while Charlotte sat on the floor hugging her knees and silently sobbing. Shafflee asked the preacher if he was going to take his piece now or if they should start on seconds. The preacher had kept his eyes on her constantly from the time he had entered the kitchen. Although she had wrapped her robe back around herself, he thought she was still as desirable a woman as he had ever seen—he would just have to pray for forgiveness. "I'm ready," he said, "but, I think we ought to cover the front and back doors just in case that button does lead to somewhere." Burt agreed to take the front door if he could have the bourbon for company. He did not think his sore balls were up to anymore fucking tonight. He put his sheet and hood back on, picked up Charlotte's shotgun, and limped out to the porch with his bottle. Howard put his sheet back on, too, and said, "I'll take my turn with the rifle at the back door; but I'd like back at Miss Charlotte again when you're done."

The short buzz from the alarm barely penetrated Jude's sound sleep. He was not sure whether he heard it or dreamed it. After a few seconds of doubt, he decided to check to be sure. He raised the shade and looked up at the house. All the downstairs lights were on and a fiery glow formed a halo around the house. He pulled his pants on, grabbed his rifle and ran up to the house, buttoning his shirt as he went. A man with a rifle stood guard at the back door; other people seemed to be in the kitchen. He suppressed his first reaction, which was to rush the man at the back door;

instead, he worked his way around in the shadows to a kitchen window. He was horror-struck to see Charlotte on the floor, being held down by one man while another was on top of her. He almost went berserk, barely restraining himself from charging in with his gun blazing; but, another part of his brain took charge. He became calm and calculating. If an armed guard is posted at the back door, there would also be one at the front door. Whichever one he took out on the way in, the other one would drop him. He slipped around to the front of the house. The other guard was visible on the porch from the dying light of the burning cross.

Jude approached the two trucks in the driveway. With the leather punch on his Boy Scout knife and a rock for a hammer, he punched a hole in the gas tank of one, then crawled under the other and gave it the same treatment, while marveling at its disgusting odor. He wiped the gas off his hands on the grass and stood behind a large oak tree to watch the gas flow down the concrete. At the same time, he monitored the movements of the man on the porch, who was limping around in a small circle, occasionally looking in the open front door of the house. The next time he stopped to look in, Jude dashed out to the cross; and, with the muzzle of his rifle, hooked a piece of burning rag. He dropped it near the end of the stream of gasoline and dashed for cover behind the tree. There was a sudden WOOF as the stream of gas ignited and enveloped both trucks. The man on the porch pulled his head out of the doorway and yelled, "What the fuck!" He ran to the railing hollering for the others just as the first truck blew up, sending flames and truck parts in all directions. The blast knocked the man back against the front of the house. As he was regaining his footing, the second blast plastered him up against the house again. A second later, another man ran out on the porch, hollering obscenities and waving a shotgun.

Jude positioned his rifle against the tree trunk and said under his breath, "That's two." In another second there were three, and finally, the fourth appeared in the doorway holding his pants up with one hand and waving a pistol with the other. Four shots in less than four seconds sent all four of them sprawling. The last to be hit was the one in the doorway. He had let go of his pants and was trying to get a shot off at where he had seen the muzzle blast from Jude's gun; but he fired into the roof of the porch as the impact knocked him back into the hallway.

Within seconds, Jude was hovering over Charlotte. Before Shaflee had dismounted, he had grabbed her by the hair and slammed her head on the floor. She was still unconscious. Jude drew her robe back around her and began trying to revive her. After a few minutes, she opened her eyes and stared at him, "Jude? . . . How'd you get here? OH MY GOD! What happened?"

"It's OK, Charlotte."

"I heard shooting. You all right, Jude?"

"Yes, I'm fine now."

"Jude, there were four of them . . . Did you get all four?"

"Yes, I shot into the flock and all four came down."

As he fussed over her, he sensed a movement from the front of the house. Looking up he saw Shaflee crawl across the floor to his pistol. Before Jude could reach his gun, or jump out of the way, Shaflee emptied his gun at Jude. Two slugs hit him. He stumbled back, fell over Charlotte, and landed in a heap next to her.

Sheriff Batley and Deputy Bream entered the driveway to the mansion. They assumed that the fire they saw was the cross. "Looks like the party's still going strong, Leroy. Glad we didn't miss it completely."

Batley's joyful anticipation quickly evaporated. Most of the flame was from the burning tires of the demolished trucks—not much was left of the smoldering cross. "Jesus Christ, Leroy, look at those trucks. Something's fucked up here."

"Fuckin' worse than you think, Roy; look up there on the porch."

"Gaw . . . damn! They drunk or dead?"

"Look dead to me."

All of them on the porch were dead. Inside Shaflee, sat on the floor of the study with his back against Charlotte's desk—his pants still down. He tried to say something; but, only a gurgle came out, and a stream of blood that ran down his chest. He raised his left arm toward the kitchen, gurgled again then let his hand fall back to the floor.

The sheriff and his deputy went to the kitchen, where they found the bodies of Charlotte and Jude.

"Looks to me like it was a draw. Who the hell's that guy, Leroy? You ever see him before?"

"No. I don't even know which side he was on. Guess if he wasn't on Miss Charlotte's side, she sure gave a good single -handed account of herself."

"That bitch had a lot of fight in her but I ain't giving

her that much credit. He helped her all right. Must a been some kind of farm hand or something. Beats the hell out of me why he'd want to get mixed up in this."

"Why don't you ask him, Roy? The son-of-a-bitch is still alive."

The sheriff kicked Jude in the foot; when he let out a weak groan, Batley asked, "Who the hell are you? What's this got to do with you?"

Jude turned his head slightly and opened his eyes. When he saw two more hooded figures, he just closed them again, too weak to do anything about it or even care.

The sheriff kicked him in the foot again and yelled, "Say, boy, I just asked you a question."

About then Charlotte moved a little.

"Christ, Leroy, look who else is alive."

The sheriff lifted the bottom of her robe and said, "Come look at this, Leroy; they fuckin' gang banged her, drank her whiskey, and had one hell of a party. Then this asshole, whoever he is, come along and spoiled all the fun."

Charlotte started to regain her senses and called out, "Jude . . . Jude . . . you OK?"

Barely audible, he responded, "Yeah, I'm fine Charlotte . . . Think we ought to call the sheriff?"

"Probably. That's him in the big sheet with the cowboy boots sticking out from underneath . . . the one that was just looking under my robe. Yeah, I'd tell you to call him but you don't know enough dirty words to call him what he really is."

"Listen to that smart-ass bitch, Leroy? Damn near dead and still mouthing off."

"Yeah, I hear her; but I think this is a goddam shame. Shaflee and the boys sure made a mess out of this operation. I can't understand why Hogg wanted those dumb fuckups for this job, anyway."

"Me neither, I tried to talk him into using a different crew, but he said there weren't as many people as you'd think that are willing to bring trouble on Miss Charlotte. Lot of them talk a hard case but they ain't about to mess up a pretty lady. This bunch, on the other hand, is mean enough and dumb enough to do anything for a few bucks. What they have left us with, now, is a goddamn situation—you understand, Leroy?"

"What do you mean, Roy?"

"What I mean is, how the hell we gonna report this?" You know the Feds have been giving the Klan all the shit they can in recent years. They'll have a heyday with this one. Even people who usually support us aren't gonna understand four Klan members gang-raping a famous, white author—doesn't make any sense. Now on top of it, she's gone and recognized us. This ain't the same as hassling niggers. You heard that mouth of hers—she'll have a whole goddamn army of federal marshals down here pickin' at our bones."

"So what are we going to do?"

"First thing we've got to do is finish these two, then we've got to have a big ass fire to destroy the evidence. You shoot him and I'll shoot her. I want the pleasure of closing that goddamn mouth for good."

They fished around under their sheets and pulled out their revolvers. As they drew the hammers back and aimed at their heads, Jude reached out and found Charlotte's hand.

She said, "I love you, Nig." He squeezed her hand in response.

Leroy was not enthusiastic about this killing, but was not willing to let Batley know. "Roy," he said, stalling for time, "what if the State Police or feds get snoopy and start digging bullets out of charred bodies? You sure we want bullets from our guns in any a these bodies?"

"Maybe you got something there, Leroy. Go get Shaflee's gun."

When he returned, he announced, "Shaflee won't be needin' this no more," and handed it to the sheriff.

"I figured as much. He didn't look real good when we come in."

Batley went over to Charlotte and, while she looked straight at him, he put the muzzle between her eyes and pulled the trigger; it just went click. She turned her head and closed her eyes in the painful realization that it was not over yet; she'd have to go through this again.

Batley said, "Shit, Leroy, it's empty."

"There's a rifle next to this guy, you want to use it?"

"Naw, I got a better idea. Since we've gotta burn the house anyway we'll just leave them in it to cook."

"This one ain't goin' nowhere," Leroy said, kicking Jude's feet. "He's 'bout done."

"Yah, but this red-headed bitch, I don't see nothin' wrong with her, only she been hit on the head and near fucked to death. She could get up and go soon's our backs are turned . . . except of course for her broken leg. With that, he stomped his boot down, focusing 250 pounds of hate and meanness on one spot. Charlotte's leg snapped like a pretzel.

She let out a piercing scream and passed out.

"Leroy, check that red can out by the cross and see if there's anything left in it." Batley was helping himself to what was left of the Scotch when Leroy came back and announced that the can was still half-full.

"OK, now—I tell you what we're gonna do. We're gonna drag all those boys into the kitchen and have us a big wienie roast . . . and, we're gonna roast one pussy, too." While Leroy dragged bodies, Batley drank Scotch and splashed kerosene over the cabinets, floor and furniture. He had Leroy stack the four bodies, sheets and guns, then told him to take his sheet off, as he removed his own and tossed it on top. He soaked the pile with the last of the kerosene.

"Shouldn't you save some kerosene for them?" Leroy asked, pointing at Jude and Charlotte.

"Shit, Leroy they're still alive; you think I'm some kind a barbarian?" With that he took the Scotch bottle and, holding up Charlotte's head, poured in a couple of swallows, then took out his cigarette lighter and lit the kerosene in a couple of places. The blue and red flames danced along the surface of the counter and spread up the wooden cabinets. Once Batley was satisfied that the fire was going well, he said, "Leroy, I believe it is time to go." As they departed, he told Charlotte, "Hope you enjoy the wiener roast." She tried to respond but her mind was too filled with pain and with regret about what she had done to Jude to come up with anything.

Outside, the sheriff told Leroy to clean up what was left of the cross and anything else that might be traced to the Klan. Meanwhile, Batley paced back and forth on the porch, sipping at what was left of the Scotch.

Seconds after the sheriff and his deputy left the kitchen, the basement door opened and Lyle peeked in. Then Lyle and Salvi rushed into the kitchen. Charlotte was on her belly trying to drag an unconscious Jude toward the basement door.

"Lyle. Oh, God, Lyle, how did you know?"

"Salvi's daughter overheard them planning this at the Boar's Head. We got here too late to warn you but I remembered the tunnel."

Salvi's medical corps experience rushed back to him. Checking the wounded, he told Lyle, "This one can be saved, she's just busted up a little; that one don't look too good. Let's get her out of here first."

"No! If you can't save Jude, leave me, too."

"Pardon me, Miss Charlotte, we don't have no time for this dramatic shit. Lyle, hand me that magazine and find me some string." Within seconds he had the magazine folded and tied around her broken leg. He hoisted her up over Lyle's shoulder and Lyle staggered down the cellar stairs with her.

"Drop her in that old chair down there," Salvi called after him, then hurry back; we gotta get this guy out a here—smoke's getting thicker'n shit."

Salvi was packing towels over Jude's wounds when Lyle returned. Lyle headed for the study to search for Charlotte's purse, complaining between coughs, "She won't go out the tunnel without Jude, now she adds her goddamn purse to the list." While Lyle looked for it, Salvi called the fire department, then they closed off the kitchen from the rest of the house and carried Jude downstairs.

The basement had very little smoke. While the door was open, the fire upstairs thrived on fresh air it sucked through the tunnel and up from the basement. Charlotte was still fussing about Jude. Neither of them thought there was enough life left in him to bother with, but they did not have time to haggle with her over it.

"Salvi, how the hell we gonna carry them through the tunnel when its only high enough to crawl through on our hands and knees?"

"Those drapes covering that stuff in the corner—we'll have to crawl backwards and pull them on those drapes." Dragging them through the tunnel, then carrying them up the ladder out of the well pushed the two middle-aged men to their limits. If Jude had not been first in line to go up, it is not certain they would have had the strength to go back for him. Charlotte tried not to scream from the pain, aware that it could give away their position, but she just broke down and sobbed as they carried her up the ladder. When every-one was out of the well, Lyle and Salvi collapsed to the ground.

From behind the shrubbery surrounding the well, they could see Leroy's truck near the front of the house, and occasionally Batley and his deputy checking on the progress of the fire. The problem was how to move Jude and Charlotte to Salvi's truck. With the sheriff and his deputy still hanging around, they would have to carry both of them three quarters of a mile across the field to where they had hidden the truck. In their exhausted condition, they simply could not do it. Before they arrived at a solution, they heard the siren of the fire engine in the distance.

At the front of the house, Deputy Bream said, "Roy, you hear what I hear?"

"Yes, goddamnit, it's a fire engine. How the hell did they get a report so fast? We better get the hell out of here, it'd look a good sight better if we pulled in after they arrive." They scrambled into their truck and at the end of the drive turned up the valley and parked.

Leroy said, "Roy, you ever figure out who that guy was in the kitchen?"

"No, weren't much of a talker was he?"

"You remember what she said to him when you were about to shoot her in the head?"

"Yah, I wondered about that. She said, 'I love you, Nig.'"

"Roy, I think that was her short for, 'Nigger.'"

"You telling me, Leroy, that this white guy was her slave? Then, the guy in her book that Hogg was all worked-up about wasn't Lyle? haw! haw! haw! By God! That's one on Milo."

Lyle stood up to see if the truck had left the driveway, "Looks OK. "Miss Charlotte, you still got that station wagon?"

"It's in the carriage house if that hasn't burned yet."

"No, the fire is still at the kitchen end of the house."

"Shine your light in my purse so I can find the keys."

Lyle drove the station wagon across the lawn to the well; they cleared the driveway and headed down the main road just as the fire engine slowed to make the turn into Greyledge. Lyle stopped next to Salvi's truck and told Charlotte, "I don't believe you should be at the hospital in Grimble. If the sheriff discovers you're there, your life won't be worth a damn. I think Salvi should take you up to Charlottesville. I'll take Jude to Grimble, he'd never make it to Charlottesville." While she protested, Lyle and Salvi loaded her into the seat of Salvi's truck, and tried to make her as comfortable as possible, then departed for their separate destinations.

A sleepy-eyed attendant responded to the buzzer at the emergency entrance. Lyle told him, "I found this guy over near the park—looks like he's hurt or something—got him in the back of my wagon."

The attendant hollered, "Hey, Gilead, fetch the gurney."

When Jude was positioned on the gurney, one of the attendants asked Lyle to move his car out of the ambulance parking zone, then come in so they could take down his information about this guy. Lyle said,"OK," and drove away. Next he called the state police and reported a fire at Greyledge—set by Klan members to cover up a shooting. He also told them Sheriff Batley and Deputy Bream were Klan members and involved in this. Then he hung up.

Lyle parked Charlotte's car a couple of blocks from his house and walked home. Liz was still up. She had straightened the house as best she could and was sitting on the couch, worried sick about Lyle. She had tried to discourage him from going to Greyledge earlier but he went anyway. When he walked in now, she ran to him and buried her face in his chest. He held her. Neither of them said anything. Then, as he slowly recounted what happened, her relief over his safe return drained away. She began screaming at him over the risks he had taken to save *that white woman*, "After all the trouble she caused us, writing those dirty books."

"That *white woman*, as you call her, is the best friend the blacks have around here, and that includes the blacks themselves. You know goddamn well how many times she's risked her neck for Civil Rights causes and black education, and, what's more, she and Jude treated us right on that sharecrop deal, even after you and I stuck it to her. I don't intend to raise our daughter to be one of those niggers whining for their rights and taking no social responsibilities. We gotta set a decent standard for her."

"Decent!" she shrieked. "You're in love with that red-headed bitch." Lyle shook his head and left, closing the door quietly behind him. He went back to Charlotte's car and drove around for awhile feeling sorry for himself. Then, he felt sorry for Liz, who he knew was just upset. He went back to Greyledge.

Salvi was less secretive about entering Charlotte into the hospital. He told the people in the emergency room that he believed she had been raped and beaten and that they should notify the state police since the event took place over in Grimble County. Charlotte raised no objection to Salvi's story and nodded when they asked her if it were true. Once they had given Charlotte a shot to ease the pain, she was able to answer for herself. Salvi wrote his phone number on a piece of paper and told Charlotte to contact him if she needed help. The people in the emergency room tried to detain Salvi until the police arrived, but once he saw that Charlotte was able to talk, he felt it would be better for her to tell her own story.

19

A crowd had gathered at Greyledge. Cars were parked all over the lawn. In spite of the early morning hour, people had mysteriously become aware of the fire and had come to view the spectacle. Feelings ran high; some were glad to see the end of Greyledge—what it stood for in their lives and in the lives of their departed relatives; others were saddened by the loss of this historical monument. A rumor was circulating that Charlotte was still in there. No one received that news well. She was a celebrity; she put Grimble on the map; even the moralists enjoyed hating her too much to want to lose her—although some thought this is God's way of dealing with sinners.

The state police had come; an official-looking man in a suit was talking with them. Someone said he was an FBI agent. The sheriff and Deputy Bream stood apart, not having been invited to join this conversation with the other law enforcement officers.

Firemen were squirting water on the fire but the effort

fell far short of what was needed. One fireman, wearing a gas mask and fire-resistant clothing, returned from a quick pass through part of the house. "If she's in there, she's in the kitchen and I sure as shit ain't goin' in there." Then he wandered over to the sheriff and started to talk with him in an excited way, but quietly so others would not hear. One of the locals drifted nearer to eavesdrop but the sheriff shooed him off, "Get the hell out of here, Ed, this is an official conversation." The state police and plainclothesman saw this action and called the fireman over. At first he was reluctant to tell them what he told the sheriff; but, when he saw how interested the state police and FBI agent were, he began to feel important. "Well, sir," he said mostly to the FBI agent, "when I ran up on the front porch, I couldn't see real good with that mask on; I slipped on something and damn near fell on my ass. I thought it was water at first— from the hoses, you know—but it wasn't: it was a big pool of blood. There was another one in the hallway that looked like something or somebody was dragged through it. Then in that next room, you know the one with all the books and stuff, there was another big pool of blood on the rug and on the floor. A big trail of smeared blood led from there to the next room which must be the kitchen. I sure as hell wasn't about to open that door!"

"Get out of that suit." The plainclothesman shouted. "I'm going in there."

The fireman took it off and said, "You're crazy man, I wouldn't go in there again for nothin'. Any minute that fire's going to break through. It's so fucking hot in there the whole thing's going to go off like gasoline." Within seconds the plainclothesman was in the fire-resistant suit and on the porch. He checked the area with the fireman's flashlight, then made a quick pass through the hall and study before the heat and smoke drove him out.

"You see anything, Pearson?" one of the state police asked.

"Yes. I saw what the fireman saw, including a lot of blood on the porch. At least one, but probably several people were shot out there, then dragged into the kitchen. As you go in the front entrance, a hole in the doorjamb looks like a rifle ball smashed into it. It must have passed through a body first, though, and mushroomed before it hit the wood. Also, blood and pieces of meat are plastered to the paint around the hole. I don't think we'll get the chance to dig the slug out unless those clowns do a better job of putting that fire out than they have so far. I can piss harder than that."

The fireman said, "No fire hydrants out here, only water's what we brought with us."

Lyle, who had just walked up to eavesdrop, suggested, "Use the water from the swimming pool. If you need more, there's a pond a couple hundred feet down the slope."

Pearson exploded at the fireman, "You mean there's a whole goddamn swimming pool of water in the backyard and you're just pissing out what you carried in the truck! You guys aren't even trying to put that fire out. Who the fuck's in charge of this ragged-ass bunch?"

"Chief's over there, talking to the sheriff."

"Yeah, that figures. I suppose they're buddies?"

"Sort of."

Pearson, turned to the two state troopers and said,

"Come on, let's see if we can get some action around here," and led them over to where the chief and sheriff were standing.

One of the troopers said, "Sheriff Batley I'd like you to meet —"

Pearson ignored the introduction, and looking directly at the fire chief, said, "Chief, I want you to quit screwing around and put that fire out. Throw a hose from that pumper into the swimming pool and put some water on that fire—and do it now. Concentrate on the kitchen and then get going on the rest of the house, save as much as you can instead of just piddling around."

"And just who the fuck are you?"

"Cal Pearson, FBI, he said flashing his badge."

"Oh, wow, I'm impressed," the chief said sarcastically.

"Yes, you'll be even more impressed when I haul your ass in court for the deliberate loss of evidence at a crime scene."

The chief went off to do as he was told, but not with any sense of urgency. Meanwhile, the sheriff wanted to know what goddamn right any yankee FBI agent had to come down here and throw his weight around.

Pearson ignored his question and quietly asked him how he and his deputy got blood on their shoes.

"Where the hell do you think? We just came from an accident out on the highway."

"You help remove any injured people from the wrecked cars?"

"No, the ambulance attendants did that."

"Which of these vehicles is yours?" Pearson asked,

gesturing toward the accumulation on the front lawn.

Leroy pointed in the general direction of his beat-up truck and said, "We came in mine."

"How long after the fire engine arrived did the two of you pull in?"

"About five minutes," Batley replied.

"How'd you know about the fire?"

"We picked it up on our radio right after we left the accident."

"Your dispatcher called you and told you about it?"

"Yah, so what?"

"Let's go look at your truck, Leroy."

Pearson shined his flashlight into the cab. "Leroy, is that a two-way radio I'm looking at?"

"No, it's a regular car radio, 'cept it's been dead for about two years now."

Pearson then shined the light into the box of the pickup. Completely exposed to view, were two pieces of charred wood, each a couple of feet long, nailed together at right angles. Pieces of cloth, bound tightly around the wood where the two pieces joined, had prevented the wood from burning completely.

"Let me have the keys. I'd like to have the lab boys take a look at your vehicle. We can continue this conversation later. Right now I'm kind of interested in who's in the kitchen." Pearson turned to the state police officers and asked them to take the sheriff and his deputy into custody. "Also, you better impound that truck, and, as soon as you can, take their shoes and get them down to the lab."

"And what if we tell you to go fuck yourself," the sheriff said.

Without answering, Pearson turned to the state troopers and told them, "You said you wanted to cooperate with us on this one. You can start by relieving the sheriff and deputy of their guns and badges. I have to go make sure the firemen don't destroy what's left in the kitchen."

At the far end of the mansion, Lyle slipped into the carriage house. Flames were flickering over its roof; but, none had broken through to the inside, yet. When he emerged, he was pushing Charlotte's little red car. Once it was a safe distance from the house, he wandered back and mixed with the crowd, which was too absorbed in watching the flames to notice what was happening in the shadows.

When he was satisfied that no one was paying attention to his activities, he slipped down to the chicken coop, where he released the chickens. Then he went to the barn. Alfred could not see the activity up at the house, but he was aware something was wrong and was pacing around his stall in circles, whinnying. It was some time before Lyle could grasp his halter and lead him down to the back pasture.

Day was breaking by the time the fire was nearly out. The house was gutted; only the chimneys and portions of the walls were left standing—the roof, floors and furniture were reduced to smoldering rubble. Additional state police had arrived on the scene and several official-looking plainclothesmen were present. All of the activity was at the kitchen end of the house where Pearson was now very much in charge. He borrowed the fireman's suit again and went into the smoldering kitchen. It did not take him long to find the pile of bodies. Those on top were charred beyond recognition; but, of the two underneath, one was partially covered with the remnants of a sheet with a hood—each had a bullet hole in the chest. He could not tell if one of the bodies was the woman who was said to live in the house.

When he came out of the smoldering ruins, the two-way radio in his car was squawking. The voice at the other end said that a woman was brought into emergency at the University Hospital in Charlottesville, who claims she's from a place called *Greyledge* in Grimble County. "She says she was beaten and raped by four KKK members last night and that the sheriff and his deputy set fire to her house and broke her leg so she couldn't get away. What do you think of that at five o'clock in the morning?"

"I believe it. Did they say what her name is?"

"Yes, Henderson—Charlotte Henderson."

"OK, I'm headed up there."

Charlotte had requested a private room. She was alone sipping orange juice when Pearson arrived; the rest of her breakfast was still on her tray. Pearson introduced himself; and, with no polite expression of compassion, asked, "What can you tell me about last night?"

Charlotte was tired and confused. She did not know if Jude was alive or dead; but she had enough presence of mind not to involve Jude, Lyle or Salvi in this discussion. She decided to divulge only enough information to implicate the sheriff and his deputy as much as possible. She spoke softly and haltingly: "During the night—was it last night? It seems so long ago—four men in hoods and sheets burned a cross on my front lawn. From the porch with my shotgun, I ordered them to take their cross down and leave. One of them, a large man they called Burt, grabbed my gun and hit me. When I came to, he was on top of me sweating and stinking. He was inside me, ripping me apart . . . ." She turned her head away and was silent for a long time. Finally, she said, "They took turns . . . I must have drifted in and out of consciousness . . . I remember at one point thinking they were through, but then, they started talking about. . . about . . . another round. While they were in the middle of it, something happened outside that alarmed them. The one who was on top of me at the time grabbed my head and slammed it on the floor. I didn't come to again until the sheriff and his deputy arrived—also wearing hoods and sheets."

"How did you know who they were?"

"I'm familiar with the sheriff's voice, I've had previous dealings with him. Besides, they called each other by their first names, and, after I addressed him as sheriff, they made no attempt to conceal their identity. It was clear from the start they intended to kill me."

"What names did they use?"

"Mostly *Roy* and *Leroy*, a couple times Leroy called Batley *Sheriff.*"

"How do you know they planned to kill you?"

Charlotte related how the sheriff had aimed his gun at her, but, just before he fired, decided to use the gun of one of the earlier arrivals. She explained how, after attempting to fire the empty pistol at her head, they decided not to shoot her but to burn the place down with her in it, so as to destroy any evidence that this was a Klan-related activity. "They piled up the bodies of the men who raped me, soaked them with kerosene, and set fire to them."

The only reaction Pearson showed to any of Charlotte's nightmarish story was to wince slightly when she told how Batley had stomped on her leg and broke it. He waited quietly for her to gather enough strength to continue, but she was not able to. Finally, he prompted her by asking how she escaped from the burning house.

"I'm not sure. The pain was so great I drifted in and out. I remember two men came up from the basement right after the sheriff and his deputy left. They carried me down cellar and out through the tunnel."

"Tunnel?"

Charlotte told him about the tunnel and its Civil War origin.

"How many people know about the tunnel?"

"I don't know, I suppose several hundred thousand." Only after he looked baffled did she explain, "Anyone who read my first book would know about it."

Pearson's face suddenly relaxed. "Oh—now I know who you are—I read that book. So, Greyledge is the Plantation of Hope. Yes, I remember the tunnel, but I wouldn't know how to enter it from the outside."

"I don't expect you've had a chance to look around in the daylight. Anyone who has read *Plantation of Hope* and was looking for the well entrance would find it. Whoever rescued me must have had a pretty good idea where it was to find it in the dark, but I'm afraid I couldn't guess who that might be."

Pearson sensed that she was withholding information. He returned to his cold professional air, asking if she knew who killed the four men piled in the kitchen.

"I didn't see it happen. I may have been unconscious at the time."

"Did you know them?"

"The one they called *Howard* worked in a gas station in Grimble where I occasionally bought gas. A couple of the others I had seen around town. I think they're all patrons of the Boar's Head Tavern."

"Could you give me their names?" Just then a nurse came in and told Pearson he had to leave so Miss Charlotte could get some rest. She closed her eyes and gave him their first names. When nothing more was added, he suggested that she might remember more if he came back after she had rested. She nodded without opening her eyes.

As soon as he left, her thoughts turned to Jude. Why were Lyle and Salvi so sure he wasn't going to make it—so sure that they were willing to leave him to die in the fire? Hadn't he squeezed her hand just before they carried him out of the kitchen? Didn't they know how much she loved him? Didn't they know how strong he is—that he had saved her life—physically and emotionally? "He can't die. Not without me— we're going steady. " She cried softly to herself, and kept making up reasons why he must still be alive. Eventually, she lost track of time, drifting in and out, not knowing whether she was awake or dreaming—horrible dreams—about the fire and Jude dying with flames all around him, or sometimes he was carrying her to safety, but then dying. All the different versions ended with Jude dying; yet, when she was in her semi-awake state—with some control over her thoughts—she returned to telling herself that he couldn't die! He had to be alive!

The two attendants at the Grimble hospital quickly examined Jude and one said, "Holy shit, this guy ain't long for this world, call Dr. Neuman."

Dr. Neuman took one look at him and said, "Christ, we aren't equipped to deal with this. Call Charlottesville and tell them to get ready for an emergency chest operation. We'll give him some plasma while he's en route; tell them we'll get a blood type on him and call them back so they can have blood ready when he arrives."

By the time Jude arrived in Charlottesville, the hospital staff was assembled. They rushed him to the operating room and hooked him up to a tangle of wires and tubes. One of Shackley's bullets along with pieces of Jude's shirt were lodged in his lung. The operating team had to pry his ribs apart to get at the lung so they could remove the slug and clean out the wound. Three days later, Jude's gurney was wheeled onto an elevator. He was being moved from intensive care to a ward. When the elevator stopped at one of the floors, a red-headed woman wearing a cast on her leg maneuvered herself with crutches into the elevator. Jude's attendant interrupted his conversation with the linen lady long enough to ask the woman what floor she wanted. When she said she was headed for the lab, he pushed a button and returned his attention to the linen lady.

Jude was on his back; he could not see her in the corner of the elevator. But, when he heard her voice, he called, "Charlotte?" His voice was so weak Charlotte was not sure she heard someone call her name. She moved closer to where she could see him and the clipboard hanging from the gurney. Oh, my God, it is Jude! *John Doe; Ward B*—they don't know who he is. She wanted to touch him, to tell him she was there, to look into his eyes and tell him how much she loved him. The attendant's conversation with the linen lady was so loud that Jude did not hear her whisper, "Yes, Jude, it's Charlotte." The elevator stopped and Jude's gurney was pushed down the hall. I can't follow him and reveal that I know him. He has to remain John Doe. The sheriff will kill us both if he can.

When Charlotte returned from the lab, Pearson was waiting for her, still wanting to know who killed the four Klansmen and who helped her escape from the burning house. Now that she knew Jude was alive, she was even more determined not to give him that information.

"Does the sheriff know I'm alive?" she asked.

"Yes, we had to reveal that during the interrogation in an attempt to get him to admit to his involvement. Neither he nor his deputy were able to conceal their surprise that you were alive. You know, don't you, that they claim they didn't arrive at Greyledge until after the fire engines? So far, it's just your word against two law officers. The judge had to let him out on bail."

"Oh, that's terrific! And how long do you think I'll live once they find out where I am, or did you tell them that, too?"

"We'll do everything in our power to see that no harm comes to you."

"And what did you do today to protect me?"

Pearson gave her his best unsmiling, professional look

and said, "I've been talking with Washington about getting some people down here to guard you."

"George Washington?" she asked.

"I gather you're not impressed, Miss Henderson."

"I'm more impressed with the brazen ruthlessness of Batley and his boys. Apparently, I'm your whole case, and now you tell me that Batley and his deputy are free. I could have been dead today when you arrived. Do you know anything beyond what I've told you or am I really all you've got?"

"If we had one more witness to confirm that the sheriff and his deputy were at Greyledge before the fire, . . ."

"And, if I happen to remember a couple more names, Batley and his gang will put them away first."

"We would protect them," Agent Pearson assured her.

"Bat shit! You couldn't protect them or me with an army of agents. You lock those bastards up until the trial and prevent them from communicating with the outside, and I'll try to remember a few more details. Until the courts stop thinking that criminals should have more rights than victims, you'll never make any progress at cleaning up this kind of shit. More and more people will become lawless as they realize how helpless law enforcement and the justice system are. Justice will come only to those who take the law into their own hands."

Pearson was startled by her attack, and unprepared to argue with her. He told her it was unlikely that Batley's bail would be revoked, even if she swears that he killed the four men in the kitchen, broke her leg, and set the house on fire in an attempt to murder her.

Not long after Pearson left, a volunteer stopped by to see

if Charlotte needed anything. She made the rounds a couple of times a day with a cart from which the patients could buy magazines, books and games. Charlotte was pleased to see a copy of *Slaves Can't Read*. Already she was working on a plan to contact Jude. She bought it along with a copy of the *Charlottesville Herald*. There on the front page of the newspaper was her picture and a picture of what was left of Greyledge. When the woman left, Charlotte wrote inside the front cover, "To my new friend, John Doe—Best wishes for a speedy recovery—Charlotte Henderson." She was about to go looking for Ward B, where Jude's clipboard indicated he was being housed, when one of her doctors came in. "I've got your lab reports," he said enthusiastically—"all good."

"I didn't know we were worried about them."

"Really? Well, for one thing, you haven't contracted any venereal diseases as a result of your attack."

"I guess I'm still so overwhelmed at being alive I hadn't thought about that."

"The second piece of good news is that you didn't lose your baby."

"What!"

"You didn't know you were pregnant?"

"I'm not pregnant. I have an IUD."

"You may have had one, but it isn't there now. Haven't you been aware of missing a period—probably two?"

"I wasn't paying much attention. Sometimes, when I'm on a work binge, I become irregular."

"You OK about being pregnant?"

"I don't know. I don't know what my life is about anymore. These things that have happened will have to settle into place before I know how I feel about anything."

"Do you have people who can help you through this?"

"I think so. I don't know. I suppose people's attitudes change after you've been through something like this. Thanks for your concern, though."

As soon as he left, she reached for her crutches, put the book in the pocket of her robe and was about to leave when she decided to see just how much of the story was in the newspaper. It was all there: the burning of the cross, the assault, four bodies and the destruction of Greyledge. It even told that the *famous author* was recovering well at the University Hospital. Why didn't they provide my room number, for God's sake? The only thing that isn't in there is the stuff I didn't tell anyone. In despair she plunged herself face down on the bed and sobbed until she was too weak to cry anymore. An orderly came in with her lunch, set the tray down and left. Charlotte finally forced herself out of bed and hobbled into the bathroom to wash her face. Christ, you look terrible, Charlotte. One side of her face was still swollen and black and blue, and the back of her head had a couple of big lumps. Her left eye was barely open; and, now with all the crying, the other eye was swollen and red, too. Charlotte, she said to the pathetic face in the mirror, you have got to pull yourself together. You're on your own, kid. It's time to stop helping Batley finish you off.

She called Salvi, who seemed genuinely pleased to hear from her, but expressed concern about the newspaper article revealing where she is. His comment made it easier for her to ask him to pick her up after dark. Salvi agreed and said, "I noticed the visitor's parking lot the night I drove you to the hospital. Would you be able to meet me there?"

"Let me see if it's marked on the map of the hospital the nurse gave me yesterday when I was awarded my crutches. Yes, it shows the grounds as well as the floor plans. Salvi, would it be possible, too, for you to pick up a raincoat for me to put over these hospital clothes?"

"Sure, I'll have my wife pick one up. I'll deliver it to your ward in a sealed package so the nurse doesn't know what it is, then go back to the lot to wait for you."

Next, Charlotte located Ward B on her map and went looking for Jude. As she was about to walk by the ward's nurse station, the woman in charge asked if she could help her. Before Charlotte could speak, the nurse asked, "You're Miss Henderson aren't you? I'm so glad to see you. I heard you were staying with us. I bought a copy of your book, hoping that if I saw you, I could get you to autograph it for me."

Silvia was pleased when Charlotte wrote a personal note inside the cover. To keep the moment alive, the nurse said, "I was real lucky to get one, it was the last copy they had in the gift shop."

"When I bought one off the cart this morning, the woman told me they had ten left in the gift shop at the time she loaded up for her rounds. The newspaper article in the *Herald* this morning must have stimulated sales."

"Why on earth would you buy one?" Silvia asked, taking the bait.

Charlotte said casually, "I encountered a young man in

the elevator, he said my name—apparently he recognized me from a picture in one of my earlier books. He looked very sick. I was so touched, I bought him a copy of my recent book."

"That was real nice. What's his name?"

"All the clipboard said was John Doe."

"His recognizing you is the only encouraging thing I've heard about this patient—he doesn't even know his own name. He should still be in intensive care, but I suppose if you don't have a name, you aren't a paying patient. They brought him here from Grimble a few nights ago. The ambulance driver said some guy dropped him off at the hospital emergency entrance with a couple of bullet holes in him. The only reason they brought him here is because they didn't want any John Does dying on their doorstep—I shouldn't be running off like this—I'll see that he gets the book."

"Could I give it to him?"

"Oh, he shouldn't have any visitors . . . but, then, I guess you've had more response from him than anyone— maybe if you don't stay long."

Charlotte was not sure whether Jude was sleeping, or even alive—there were tubes stuck in his arm and up his nose, and his skin was pale especially against his dark beard. Charlotte felt queasy and her temples throbbed as she gently took his hand and whispered, "Jude."

Once he opened his eyes, he looked a lot better. "Charlotte? . . . Oh, God, Charlotte, . . . how come we're still alive? The last I remember is being surrounded by flames and you trying to pull me to the basement." His voice was weak and draggy from the sedatives.

"We have Lyle and Salvi to thank for saving our lives. They were waiting at the basement door for the sheriff and his deputy to leave. As soon as they were gone Lyle and Salvi carried us downstairs and dragged us out through the tunnel. The FBI and the state police are investigating the attack and the fire. They arrested the sheriff and his deputy, but they are now out on bail. I haven't told anyone about you, Lyle, or Salvi for fear Batley and his deputy will try to kill all four of us to keep us from testifying. Did you know, Lyle took you to Grimble General originally and Salvi brought me here?"

"No, I didn't know I was at Grimble. How did I get here?"

"Your nurse just told me you were moved from Grimble General up to Charlottesville the night Salvi checked me in here. Our being separated like that is why they haven't associated us with each other, nor have they connected you with Greyledge. If you can keep it that way, you'll be safe."

"What about you? You're the one could do them the most damage. I think you're in serious danger."

"I know. I'm going to sneak out tonight and go stay with Madge until they lock Batley up again, but I'm really frightened about leaving you."

"Do what you can to survive, Charlotte. Don't take any risks because of me. They don't give me much chance of making it anyway."

"Jude, don't talk that way. You have to make it, not only for me, but for our child."

"You going to have that IUD removed and climb in here,

so if I die with a hard-on, we'll have one last shot at parenthood?" In his draggy voice it hardly seemed like a joke, but at least some spirit was still alive in him.

"Jude, what I'm telling you is that I'm already pregnant. We're going to have a baby."

"Really? No kidding, Charlotte? Oh my God, I can't believe it."

"Yes, Jude, really. Apparently, I lost the IUD. I didn't know it was gone." He squeezed her hand as tears filled his eyes.

"Jude, that nurse is going to come and throw me out any minute. I have to quickly tell you some other things before that happens. As soon as you're strong enough to make it to a pay phone, I want you to call me so we can talk about what to do. Meanwhile, I don't think you should remember anything about your past. I wrote Madge's number inside the back cover of this book and put a twenty dollar bill in between the pages."

"Where did you get money? I thought everything went up in flames."

"Lyle and Salvi rescued my purse along with us. There was some cash in it, as well as my checkbook, credit cards and driver's license—I'm ready for the big escape."

"How come you bought this book for me? You know I've read it—even lived part of it."

"I wanted to make sure you remember me and the good times we had together. My picture is on the back cover. I want you to remember me that way and not as hideous as I am now."

"Charlotte, you're still beautiful—it's like having an

angel come to visit me."

"Jude, you can cut out that angel shit. We're both alive, and we're going to stay that way—I really need you. And, I love you more than you could ever imagine." She stopped talking. After a few seconds, she wiped her tears on the back of his hand, squeezed it and said, "I have to go now, so Nurse Silvia doesn't become suspicious. Once I'm out of the hospital, the FBI will probably be looking for me, and so will Batley. I'll help the FBI all I can later without exposing any of us to risk, but my help will be from a safer place than here. I love you Jude. Good-bye."

20

When Charlotte called Aunt Millie, she was relieved to hear from her. "Lyle come by tole me 'bout the fire an' you in the hospital; he don't know which hospital or nothin' else 'bout it. He don't know nothin' 'bout Jude neither. He OK?"

"I guess he's OK, he told me he was going on a vacation the day before the fire. Remember, though, if the police come asking around, you don't know anything about the sharecropper who sometimes stays overnight down there in one of the cabins. Also, don't worry about your job, you'll still get a check every two weeks."

"What I gonna do for that check? From the picture I saw in the newspaper, you ain't gonna need no cleanin' done."

"I'll call later and tell you what I want you to do."

"You mean when you git out a the hospital? Where you gonna stay? You can come here, but I don't know you gonna like staying here."

"That's awfully nice of you to offer, Aunt Millie, but I think I'll take a little trip."

"You ain't gonna go stay with that foul mouth woman in

Chicago?"

"Aunt Millie, if I don't tell you where I'm going, no one can worm it out of you. There's going to be a trial, and there are people who would like to make sure I don't testify—and some of those people are cops, so please don't tell anyone where you think I went."

After she hung up, Charlotte flopped back on the bed to rest. As she drifted off, the same dream clicked into place: someone beating and raping her on the floor while flames and smoke whipped all around them so she couldn't see clearly who it was. Sometimes she thought it was Burt or one of the others but sometimes it seemed to be John Paul or Sheriff Batley. She tried to scream but only a whimper came out. While it was happening, someone was shaking her shoulder and calling, "Charlotte, Charlotte." Finally, she realized it wasn't part of the dream; it was her mother-in-law hovering over her—she quickly closed her eyes again. "Come, come, Charlotte, you can't hide forever; news-papers all over the country know what an ugly mess you've made of your life. Earl thinks John Paul should divorce you now—Lord, you look terrible—you ought to take better care of yourself."

"Divorce me? At a time like this, when he must know how much I need his support and loving care?"

Theda could not tell if Charlotte was just being sarcastic or maneuvering to get something out of a divorce settlement. "Look, Charlotte, if you're worried about our trying to take Greyledge away from you, Earl and I don't see any problem with having John Paul sign his half over to you."

"Guess you noticed the roof leaks now."

"Charlotte, you never cease to amaze me. Here you are, all beat-up, your house burned down and you still insist on insulting me. I don't know where your mind is at this time, but we'll have the papers drawn up; if you don't contest the divorce, after a brief waiting period your marriage to John Paul will be over."

"It will be fascinating to see what he uses as grounds for divorcing me. Will it be because I abandoned him, failed to keep a proper home, or was a smart ass to his mother?"

"How about adultery with niggers, then selling the stories nationwide?"

"You think that's worse than sleeping with John Paul?"

"Bitch!" she said, and left.

A few minutes to eight Charlotte picked up the package Salvi had left for her at the nurse's desk and took the elevator down to the lobby. When the door opened, there not 20 feet away, was Pearson talking to a man who apparently was another FBI agent come to protect her. She quickly pushed the button to go up, but the door was painfully slow to respond. Just as Pearson gestured toward the elevators the door closed, but Charlotte was not certain if Pearson saw her. The elevator stopped on the third floor. An orderly entered and pushed the button for the lobby. When it stopped he held the door open so Charlotte could get off. The two agents were gone—probably up to my room she thought. She went down the empty hall to the side exit, opened the package and put on the raincoat. It was still a little distance to the parking lot. By the time she arrived, she was fatigued. When she could not see Salvi's pickup truck, a small panic grabbed her. Is this the wrong lot? Just then, a familiar voice said, "Miss Charlotte, don't be looking for my old truck. I got your station wagon from Lyle. It's that car in front of you."

She was embarrassed about standing in front of her own car and not recognizing it.

After Salvi helped her into the car and he was seated behind the wheel he asked, "Where do you want me to drive this car, Miss Charlotte?"

"I guess we should drop you off at your house. Then I'll head down the open highway."

"You going to be able to drive?"

"I think so. The accelerator and brake peddle are operated with the right foot. If I can find a place for my cast I should be all right."

Salvi drove out of the parking lot, then asked about Jude. When Charlotte told him, he said, "I sure hope he makes it. That cat is really something else, you know."

"Yes, I think he is." She was glad it was too dark for Salvi to see how quickly her eyes had turned misty.

"Do you have a full picture of what happened out there?" Salvi asked. "You maybe don't know what Jude did, do you?"

"No, I just have pieces of it, and they don't all fit together. I barely know how you and Lyle happened to be there."

"We'd of been there sooner, but it took Rosemarie's husband a while to find me and Lyle. After we heard about the meeting at the Boar's Head, we decided to warn you about it. We arrived too late, though, something was already going on. That's when we parked over in the field. We were walking toward the mansion when we saw Jude blow up the two trucks. He was so goddamn cool—he set the trucks on fire then just waited until the rats came streaming out to see what happened. He dropped all four in about two seconds—as slick an operation as ever I did see—even during the war. Soon's they was down he ran into the house, but one of 'em musta not been quite dead. All of the sudden there was five shots, then it was quiet. Me and Lyle ran toward the house. But, before we could get there, the sheriff and his deputy came roaring down the drive and we had to take cover. When we saw they was going to torch the place, Lyle suggested we go in through the tunnel—that's how we happened to be waiting at the cellar door when they left the kitchen."

"That fills in a lot for me."

"Yet, you know, Miss Charlotte, they're both riding around town in Sheriff's Department vehicles, and as far as I can tell, Batley's still running things."

"I suppose that's how it will be until he's convicted and sent to prison."

"You think that's ever gonna happen, Miss Charlotte?"

"Pearson says that all they have on those two is my word against theirs. He doubts that he can obtain a conviction unless I reveal the identity of the other participants in this event."

"What did you tell him?"

"I said I'd probably have trouble remembering who they were until Batley was locked up. But even then, I believe it should depend on how you, Lyle and Jude feel about it."

"Miss Charlotte, I think you've read us just right, at least Lyle and me. We'd like to see Batley get his, but we don't want to risk our families. At most, what do they have that bastard for? Attempting to conceal evidence and moving a body without a permit? Five years and he's out. Then he'll come looking for us."

"Could we add attempted murder and building a fire without a permit? Those ought to add five more years. . . . What are we doing, Salvi? Aren't we too young to be so cynical?"

"Ain't too sure about that, Miss Charlotte. Seems like around here the law is never on our side."

When they pulled into Salvi's driveway, Charlotte realized they were back in Grimble County. A shiver went through her at the thought of being on her own. She started to count out some dollars, "For the raincoat, gas, and a little extra for the time you've spent hauling me around." Salvi glanced at her wallet; it wasn't very fat.

"Miss Charlotte, I don't know where you're going next, but you shouldn't be going to the Grimble bank for money. Every time you cash a check it'll be returned to Hogg's bank stamped with the name of the place you're at."

"Salvi, I can't stick you with an unpaid bill."

"Oh, now, don't you be worried about old Salvi, he'll get by. If you'd like to relieve your mind of any obligation, though, take this two hundred dollars," he said, handing her a small roll of bills, "and write me a check for two hundred and fifty dollars. Just predate it before the fire."

She handed him the check and said, "Salvi, I just don't know where to begin to thank you. You've done so much for me, I'll always be in your debt."

Salvi stepped out of the car and waited while Charlotte

slid into the driver's seat. She dragged her cast over the hump in the floor, and pushed it out of the way with her right foot. Then, she checked to be sure she could operate the brake and accelerator peddles. When she was satisfied that she could drive, she reached out to Salvi through the open window. He buried her small, white hand in his and said, "Miss Charlotte, it has brought me great pleasure to help you. You're a very brave and beautiful lady. If you can stay alive long enough to stick it to Roy Batley, you'll repay me and most of the poor folk in Grimble County. You get into trouble out there on the underground railroad, you call me, you hear?—Good luck."

Charlotte was disappointed in her lack of stamina and how often she had to stop and rest. Several times along the way she called Madge to extend her estimated time of arrival. The car radio, even on the second day of her disappearance from the hospital, had no news that she was missing. When she pulled into the parking garage under Madge's apartment, she was spent and glad to be at her destination. The elevator operator had been told to expect Charlotte. Although he remembered her from a previous visit, she was glad he didn't feel familiar enough to comment on her beat-up condition. Madge, on the other hand, lacked any such constraint. "Holy shit, Charlotte! They really did a job on you. Well, at least they didn't burn your hair off."

"No, I missed out on that by about three minutes."

"Here, sit down. I'll pour you one, then, I'll get your luggage out of the car."

"Just orange juice, Madge, I need a little pick up."

"You want Scotch in it?"

"Yes, but I can't. Don't you hold back, though, one sober person in a room is already too many."

"Christ, at least your attitude is right, but clearly you need serious counselling." She put the orange juice in front of Charlotte and without sitting down, took a couple gulps of her Scotch. "I'll go for your luggage before we get too settled."

"Relax, Madge, that's it," she said, pointing to the paper bag she had tossed on a chair. "That and what I'm wearing are the only clothing I own and I just bought them."

"Oh God, Charlotte, I suppose that's true. I just find it hard to comprehend that it's all gone."

"Me, too, I keep thinking that pretty soon I'll go home and everything will be the same again." Her voice wavered as she talked, but she had promised herself not to burden Madge with her pain. But, when Madge saw her welling up, she went over and hugged her; that was all it took. They both wept without restraint.

Madge was the first to speak. "Good to get that over with, now maybe we can settle down to getting you healed. First of all, know that you can stay here as long as you like, even permanently if you wish. I don't plan to bring any more men into my life—at least not into my apartment, so there's plenty of room. We'll get you some new clothes tomorrow and you'll soon be feeling whole again."

"I wish it would be that easy, but I'm afraid I have a long way to go before I'm whole again."

"There's the *big wonderful whole*, like you had before the tragedy, and there's that step by step process back to a life you can live with."

"What I need, Madge, is somebody like you to talk me through the process or to at least tolerate me while I stumble through it."

"You know I'll do whatever I can. I would've done more for you when you went through the John Paul thing, but you wouldn't let me help you. You like to suffer alone. If Jude hadn't come along and saved you, you'd probably still be nursing the pain of John Paul. But speaking of Jude—he wasn't mentioned in the newspapers."

"Madge, there's a whole lot that isn't in the newspapers and a whole lot that even the police don't know about. That's why I'm here. I'm hiding out from the local cops, as well as the FBI."

"Why? What did you do?"

"It isn't what I did, it's what I know. The FBI wants me to tell all, and the sheriff wants to keep me from talking. I'm also protecting people who helped me—people Batley would want dead."

"Charlotte, are you telling me that this thing isn't over yet?"

Charlotte looked away without answering; her mind slipped off into her own thoughts.

"Hey, kid, where'd you go?"

"Madge, I'm pregnant," Charlotte blurted.

Madge was speechless. Finally, after a gulp of Scotch, she said, "Charlotte, I don't know what to say."

"Neither do I."

"You must know how you feel. You happy? Upset? How does Jude feel about it?"

"I just found out two days ago. I haven't had time to fit it in with all the uncertainties in my life—no, I guess it isn't a matter of not having time to consider it, it's a matter of not having a life to fit it into."

"What does the father think about all of this?"

"Madge, I don't even know if this baby is going to have a father."

"Charlotte, you're giving me disconnected pieces of pearls and shit. Do you expect me to string them together and make a necklace?"

"I'm sorry, Madge, that's what I've got in my bag. I can either tell you nothing, which would be in your own best interest, or I can tell you the whole story and give you the burden of having to keep it to yourself. If you don't, Jude's life will be at risk as well as the lives of two other people."

"If I'm going to help you through this, I have to know what we're dealing with. Besides, I can't stand not know-ing—anymore than I could not know if you and Jude were doing it— guess you were, huh?" she smirked. "So tell me about it—and you can start by explaining what you meant by not knowing if the baby was going to have a father."

"Madge, Jude was shot that night. He's in the hospital, they don't know if he's going to live."

"Oh my God, Charlotte—have you seen him?"

"Briefly, they have him on a ward as a John Doe. He hasn't been connected to the events at Greyledge. I sneaked in and saw him before I left—he looks terrible. He doesn't think he's going to live."

Madge stared at the drink in her hand, then slowly put it down. "Does he know about the baby?"

"I told him—he was pretty drugged up; I think he was

happy about it—even tried to joke about my failed IUD."

"Charlotte, Jude is going to make it; just be happy your baby's going to have a man like him for a father."

"Yes, I take comfort in that thought and use it to fight off thinking about the alternative of having a child out of wedlock in Grimble County."

"Shit, Charlotte, you aren't planning to live in Grimble County any more, are you?"

"I don't know where I'm supposed to live, or even if I'm going to live. If Jude and I survive this, we'll have to decide then. Madge, I'm fatigued. When that happens I get depressed. Let me rest a few minutes, then I'll start at the beginning and tell you all about it, as long as you promise not to tell anyone."

"I'll take the oath after you wake up. You know where your room is, can I help you to get there?"

"I'll just lie here on the couch while you go about your normal business, I don't want to sleep too soundly."

Charlotte slept for nearly an hour, even though Madge took several phone calls and rattled around in the kitchen. Then, Charlotte started to whimper and cry out like a hurt animal. Madge, frightened by the sounds, rushed to comfort her. But as soon as she touched her, Charlotte opened her eyes and bolted straight upright. When she saw Madge, she cried, "Oh, Madge, please help me. I can't handle this alone."

"It's OK, Charlotte, we're going to work this out. What was happening when you tried to scream and couldn't?"

"You knew?"

"Yes, I do that sometimes."

"I was being raped on the kitchen floor at Greyledge while the house was burning and Jude was lying on the floor dying. Sheriff Batley and his deputy were kicking him in the feet trying to get him to tell them who he was."

"That's horrible! Shit, kid, I cry out for a helluva lot less than that. How much of it really happened?"

"All of it, but the dream gets compressed and a lot of parts are left out."

"What could possibly have been left out? I read in the newspaper that you were assaulted, but what that meant wasn't spelled out."

"What you probably didn't read was that it was four drunken, filthy men. They were all wearing sheets and hoods."

"Oh, my God, Charlotte."

"Also, in this particular dream nobody pointed a gun at my head and pulled the trigger, only to be disappointed that the gun was empty. Nobody slammed my head on the floor to knock me senseless, and nobody jumped on my leg to break it, so I couldn't get out of the burning house. The dream is usually brief, I wake up before all of it happens. In the dream it's mostly visual and auditory—the odor of their whisky/tobacco breaths, and their sweaty, stinking bodies doesn't come through, and I don't feel the excruciating physical pain. Jude wasn't in the house when they were raping me. He hadn't been shot yet, and the house wasn't on fire—that came later."

"Oh, God, Charlotte, how could this happen to such a beautiful person? It's just incomprehensible that anything called *human* could carry out such acts."

The dinner was served and eaten. The drama went on into the evening as Charlotte tried to answer Madge's endless questions. Madge even wanted to know if Jude had been in the Army because of the way he handled himself so well in combat.

She sensed Charlotte's reticence and immediately wanted all the details. "Goddamnit, Charlotte, you were going to tell all, and now you're holding back."

"Jude's Army experience is his private matter. I expect he'll tell you about it some day, if he survives this."

"You can stop talking that *if* shit—Jude's going to make it! Can't we do something—get him a private room and better care or something?"

"Not without connecting him with me and Greyledge."

"Do you think Jude should testify, if there's a trial?"

"I don't know. Salvi cautioned me that the cops might decide to charge him with killing those four animals. I couldn't guess how a local jury would feel about a Yankee executing four of their fine citizens."

"You and Jude should start a new life in the North and forget the whole thing."

"I don't expect the Feds would settle for that, and I don't want to spend the rest of my life on the run. I also have to make a living. The FBI is probably looking for me now, but they didn't tell me not to leave town. How could they complain?"

"Probably didn't occur to them that this woman, who is all beat to shit, is going to hop in a car and drive over 800 miles, and speaking of that, I'll bet you're pretty tired. Shall we hang it up for the night?"

"Yes, I am tired, but it's getting so I'm afraid to sleep because of my dreams."

"Now that you've talked it all out, you'll sleep like a baby."

Madge arose early, but when she looked in the kitchen, Charlotte was already up and had a cup of coffee in front of her. "Hey, I like having the coffee ready when I get up, but this isn't like you. Couldn't you sleep?"

"Actually I slept well. I feel more secure here and didn't have any bad dreams until almost morning."

When Madge left for work, Charlotte had time to look around Madge's apartment. It was in great contrast to the cluttered museum she had lived in. Not that Madge was a great housekeeper, but it was the straight, clean lines of all the furniture and the absence of personal mementos that gave the place an elegant yet impersonal appearance—like an expensive hotel room. Madge's bedroom was quite different—a cluttered desk with a typewriter, her guitar, magazines and books, framed photographs of friends, an unfinished cup of coffee, and travel brochures. Charlotte surmised that Madge had a certain amount of business entertaining to do, sometimes without warning, and she was set up to always be ready—the bedroom was the real Madge—unrestrained and at home with herself.

Charlotte spent the day writing to Pearson, but her thoughts were continuously interrupted with her concern about Jude. Occasionally she dozed, only to be awakened by the horror of Greyledge flashing across her mind. In the late afternoon, Madge threw open the door and stood there with an armload of clothes and some shopping bags. "Madge!"

Charlotte exclaimed in surprise, "You really were serious about buying me new clothes. To be truthful, I haven't had anything new since . . . ." Charlotte stopped talking as she remembered the green dress she bought for the first evening she let Jude make love to her. Madge smiled, convinced that Charlotte was remembering the sexy underwear she had helped Jude buy her for Christmas.

After the pause, Madge announced with a flourish, "Extremes is looking for a new model—one with a cast and crutches for that *skier's look.* "

"Do applicants get extra points for a bashed head and black eye?"

"It couldn't hurt, they're looking for authenticity— how'd it go today?"

"Pretty well, I wrote a letter to the FBI guy; but I couldn't mail it. The cancellation mark would have Pearson looking in every corner of Chicago for me."

"Good thinking, Char," Madge said in the tone of an overacting detective. "I have to visit our store in Louisville in a couple days. I'll toss it into a box along the way— Hey, why don't you come with me? I just have to give our store manager a pep talk and some motherly advice, then we can go see the bright lights of Louisville."

"Are you sure you've got room for me and my crutches? I wouldn't be in your way?"

"Not at all, it only takes a little over five hours to drive down. When I'm through with business, I know a nice restaurant. We'll stay over and come back the next day."

"Let's do it," Charlotte responded, her mind quickly considering how close Louisville is to Fort Knox.

Anticipation of the trip helped Charlotte through the

next couple of days.

While Madge was in the store, Charlotte tried to read, but mostly she reflected on Jude's experience at Fort Knox.

It was not long before Madge reappeared. "Well," she announced to Charlotte, once she was settled back in the driver's seat, "In my usually tactful way, I fucked that up completely. It took me only three minutes to render him totally unreceptive to any of my suggestions.

They checked into their room, freshened up, then left for the restaurant. It was still early so they looked in all the store windows along the way, commenting on the displays as they traveled.

When it seemed right, Charlotte casually asked, "Hey, Madge, what time do you have to be back tomorrow?"

"No specific time, is there something you'd like to do?"

"Just a whim. Sometimes Jude talked about his experiences at Fort Knox. I know he would be pleased if I could visualize the things he's told me about."

"Sure we could do that, I've never been there. But, I think it's only a half to three-quarters of an hour southwest of here. We could have a leisurely breakfast while the rush-hour traffic subsides, then head down."

It was another fitful night for Charlotte. Tense over what she was planning to do at Fort Knox, she drifted in and out—she had nightmares when she slept and worried about Jude when she was awake.

From the next bed, Madge called, "Hey, kid, how'd you sleep last night?"

"Not bad," she lied.

"Uh huh—that's your normal sleep now, thrashing about and whimpering."

"Oh, Madge, I kept you awake—I'm sorry."

"No, I slept pretty well the first part of the night, but after I went to the bathroom, I had trouble falling back to sleep. I started thinking about that asshole store manager. That's when I noticed how you were sleeping. It's early but I guess we may as well get up."

They were on time to experience the wild traffic between Louisville and Fort Knox. At the main entrance to the military reservation, Charlotte asked where the M.P. Headquarters was. When they found it, she pointed to the visitor's parking place and said, "I thought we might be able to get a map here."

"Good idea, I'll see if I can get one."

"No, let me. My leg has to be moved around or it goes to sleep. You take a little nap while you wait for me."

Inside, Charlotte explained to a sergeant on duty that she was a writer and that she was seeking information on a double murder case she read about in the newspapers a couple years ago.

"You probably want to talk to Captain Ulman. I'll see if he's available."

He disappeared in a room several doors down the hall. "Captain," he said, "there's a woman out here asking about the Turcott/Roskov case—says she's a writer. You want to talk to her?"

"God, no."

"What should I tell her, sir?"

"Tell her to go away. Tell her the case is closed—she

good-looking?"

"Yes, but only on one side. The other side has a big bruise and a black eye; she's also on crutches with a leg in a cast."

"That's a shame," he said sarcastically. "Maybe I better talk to her."

The sergeant told Charlotte, "Captain Ulman will see you now, ma'am—third door on the right."

The door was open; she knocked and went in. Ulman ignored her for a while before looking up from his desk with an official gruff expression, "Good morning, ma'am, I'm Captain Ulman. What can I do for you?"

She gave him a disarming smile with the half of her face that was pliable—and said, "Good morning, Captain, I'm Charlotte Henderson, I'm working on . . ."

Before she could finish, he broke into a boyish grin and said, "Of course, I just finished *Slaves Can't Read*—wonderful book—here, have a chair, Miss Henderson," and he jumped up to slide it under her. "Now, what can I do for you?"

"Thank you, Sir," she said, with just a soft hint of the Old South. "I read about an episode that occurred here at Fort Knox a couple years ago—I'm working on another novel and thought I might be able to fictionalize this event into an interesting side plot. It involved a double murder. I saw only two newspaper articles on it and never did read about the outcome of the case. Do you know if they ever found out who did it or why?"

"I expect, Miss Henderson, you're talking about the Turcott/Roskov case. Other than what was published in the newspapers, nothing is available—the case is now closed."

"Does that mean it's been solved or did they close it without solving it?"

"I'm sorry, Miss Henderson, I've told you all I know—the case is closed."

"Well, perhaps you could tell me if Captain Stein and Lieutenant Cranston are still here at Fort Knox?"

Ulman went over to a file cabinet, looked at a folder for awhile. After doing the same thing with a second folder, he turned to Charlotte and told her that they had both resigned their commissions and returned to civilian life.

"What about Corporal Tandy?"

"Were all these people associated with this case?"

"Yes, according to the newspapers."

Ulman checked her folder and said, "*Private* Tandy completed her three-year enlistment and was discharged."

"I hate to be such a pest, but could I trouble you for just one more search?"

"It would be my pleasure, Miss Henderson. This in fact turns out to be interesting. However, I suspect you're getting more information about this case than the Army intended for the public to have."

Charlotte hoped he would not become too interested in it; but, having gone this far, she had to take the last step. "I'm also wondering about Private Jude Bartholomew—according to the papers, he was being questioned in connection with the two deaths."

For this file, Ulman had to go to another room. When he returned, he said, "There is no record of a Private Jude Bartholomew."

"Thank you for your time, Captain, I guess there isn't anything useful for me. I'm sorry I put you to all this trouble."

"No trouble at all—it's been a pleasure talking to you."

"Before I leave, and I promise not to bother you further, but just out of curiosity, what do you think happened here?"

"I don't believe the Army would like to have me speculating on a case like this, especially to an author who might, huh . . . end up embarrassing people in high places."

"Oh, I'm sorry. I didn't mean to put you on the spot. I was just curious and promise not to use any of this, even for fiction. I guess what you're saying is that this case was ordered closed by someone up high."

"Miss Henderson, this case was already closed when I arrived a little over a year ago. All I know about it is from rumor. I didn't know how much of that to believe until I looked in the files you inquired about. Now it looks like at least some of the rumors are true—possibly all of them. If I tell you what I heard, I would expect never to see any of it in print."

"I promise," she said as reassuringly as possible.

"Apparently two things happened. For one, Private Bartholomew went AWOL , before he left he wrote a letter to his company commander explaining how the M.P.s were attempting to railroad him for the murders. His C.O., a Captain Oris, believed him. Oris got pissed at the M.P.s and went over the heads of Stein and Cranston. After higher ranking officers evaluated the evidence on Bartholomew, it was clear the Army didn't have anything on him. To avoid a

Dishonorable Discharge, a former WAC Corporal, Patricia Tandy, told the whole story about the way they attempted to stick Bartholomew with murders. She was demoted for her part in it, but at the end of her tour of duty, given an Honorable Discharge. She implicated everyone involved and verified the things Bartholomew claimed in his letter. Oris assured them that if they attempted to court-martial Bartholomew, he would go public and they could kiss their careers good-bye. The M.P.s didn't want their bungling aired in an open trial. In view of what I am not finding in the records, I'd say they purged Bartholomew's file. I also heard that Turcott had a relative in Washington, an uncle or something, who brought a lot of heat down from above not to push the investigation."

"Why wouldn't his uncle want to know what happened?" Charlotte asked.

"Turcott had a history of getting into trouble and this relative was afraid the circumstances of his death could give him political problems. I gather from some of the people who were here when it happened that there were homosexual elements involved. One of them suggested, and I couldn't tell you if it's true or not, that this relative may have had a go at Turcott when he was a kid and feared that it would come out if there were a trial.

"Well, that's it, Miss Henderson, I don't know how you managed to get me to tell you all of this—guess I have no will power when it comes to pretty women."

"Especially if they're all beat up," she kidded.

"I read about the attack on you; that must have been a terrible experience."

"Yes . . . Thank you so much, Captain Ulman, it turned out to be a fascinating story after all. I'm sorry now that I promised not to use it, but I can see why you wouldn't wish to be given credit for bringing it public."

Madge had fallen asleep. She was startled when Charlotte opened the car door. "Hey, what the heck's going on? Oh, hi. Did you get a map?"

"Yes."

"You were gone long enough to take on the whole barracks."

"Madge!" Charlotte said quietly.

"Oh, shit, kid. I'm sorry, I didn't mean to remind you of that."

"It's OK, Madge, but let's skip our tour of the camp and head back to Chicago. I found out what I wanted to know, and I am kind of exhausted now."

"OK," Madge said, and they drove away.

After about ten minutes of silence, Madge said, "You mad at me?"

"Oh, God, no. I love you, Madge, I'm just resting and letting some of what I just learned settle into perspective."

"Something pretty big happened in there, huh?"

"Yes, really *big* . . . you know, Madge, Jude just has to live—there's hope now that our messed up lives can eventually be straightened out."

"All that happened in there? I suppose it's such a big fucking secret you can't tell me about it?"

"Actually, I think Jude wouldn't mind now—I want to tell you— God, I've got to tell somebody."

"Christ, it's about time."

"When Jude was here taking basic training, a double murder was committed. Jude was on guard duty that night in an adjacent area and was accused of the killings. Although they had no evidence against him, the M.P.s were going to railroad him for it, so he went AWOL. He hid out at that monastery we talked about when you visited us, but eventually, he decided it was too close to Fort Knox, and that he might be recognized by a visitor. When he showed up at Greyledge, he was hiking down the Appalachian Trail to a monastery in Georgia."

"OK, I think I've got it now," Madge interrupted. "Jude decided it would be better to serve on a plantation as the slave of a beautiful, depraved woman than to serve God."

"Madge, you already read *Slaves Can't Read*!" Charlotte said with delight.

"Charlotte, that is such a marvelous book! We've been so overwhelmed with the heavy stuff in your life we haven't had a chance to talk about the good things. I just love that slave called *Judd*—and such an imaginative name. How ever did you think of that? And you have the gall to call this stuff fiction! I can see why I couldn't get you or Jude away from the farm to work with me. Anyway, what did they tell you in there?"

Charlotte described her exchange with Captain Ulman.

"Wow! How did you get him to tell you all that stuff? It really makes the military look bad."

"I've always marveled at how willingly people tell me their secrets. I'm not sure why, unless it's an attempt to be on friendly terms with a public figure or a person they regard as famous."

"You must be right. Look how willingly I tell you my

innermost secrets, and how it takes a crowbar for me to pry anything out of you."

"C'mon, Madge, I tell you everything unless it would affect someone else. Then I don't feel it's mine to give away."

"You're such a sanctimonious liar, Charlotte. Look what I had to go through to get you to admit you were fucking Jude. You drove me right to the point of risking my own moral standards, and now on top of it, you publish the most intimate details of this affair with your slave for the whole nation to read."

"Madge, you don't think all of what you read in my book is based on real experiences, do you?"

"Charlotte, when I read about *fun at the pond* and *way down yonder in the cornfield,* I didn't get all warm and wet believing I was reading fairy tales."

"Madge, you're embarrassing me."

"Embarrassment is a small price to pay for the amount of pleasure you bring to the sexually deprived and the aspiring novices."

"You think I'm sort of like a missionary, then?"

"Oh, at least, Charlotte, but don't look for sainthood in this century.

"So, now that Jude is a free man, what do you think he'll do when he gets out of the hospital?"

After a thoughtful silence, Charlotte said, "Curious you should ask. Since talking with Ulman, I have been struggling with that. Don't liberated slaves usually leave the planta- tion? The farm is gone and I'm damaged goods. He must have seen it happening . . . he may not want me anymore—and now he's no longer a fugitive."

"Charlotte, I really didn't intend to raise that doubt in your mind. It never occurred to me that he would bolt. I just wondered whether he would want to continue farming, go on to school, or what."

"No, Madge, don't smooth it over. This is something I need to be prepared for. When I saw him lying there in the hospital, I couldn't help thinking how young he looked for me to be telling him he's the father of our baby. He may just decide on another life. After all, we aren't married and he's under no obligation to me."

"What do you mean! It's his baby as much as yours—and didn't you tell me he wanted one—that you were the one taking the preventative measures?"

"Yes, but since then, my whole world has disintegrated. One thing about it though, Theda stopped at the hospital just before I left to tell me that John Paul was divorcing me—I seem to have too much public exposure lately to be Earl's daughter-in-law. Besides, the plantation isn't worth much to them anymore. They're going to let me have it."

"Fucking generous of them."

"Madge—you won't believe what I did before I left the hospital." A spark of enthusiasm had crept into Charlotte's tone. "I called and had the power restored to the slave quarters. It went off when the house burned because the line was hooked into the main house. I also had a phone installed. Where do you suppose my mind was at that time?"

"You were looking forward to when Jude gets out of the hospital, so you can shack up with him."

Charlotte's anxiety about Jude continued to build until

in desperation she called Aunt Millie to see if she had picked up any news from the grapevine. Aunt Millie got all choked up. When she was finally able to talk, she said the police had put a chain across the driveway and some kind of sign. "Forgot my glasses, so ain't sure what it said. I walk down to the house—ain't much to look at. Don't see no sign a Jude. Somebody go through his stuff—don't be too neat 'bout it. I pick up little, then clean the refrigerator—some bad stuff in there, don't like bein' outa electricity. Look OK now. Don't know what happen to Jude. Don't look like he comin' back."

"Aunt Millie, do you think I should move back there?"

"You still Mistress of Greyledge—whatever left.

"Oh, Ah near forget, couple men come to my house, want to know where you at. Say they FBI. Next, they want know who live in cabin, and who that woman sometime stay there. I tell them I don't know nothin' 'bout that. He jus' work the farm, he ain't none my business. They act like they don't believe me, but they don't put me in jail."

Charlotte still had not heard from Jude. She could not stand it any longer. He could have died, she told herself; I wouldn't even have known about it. She decided to risk a call to Nurse Silvia. A different nurse was on duty in Ward B, but Charlotte asked anyway about a John Doe that was on that ward about three weeks ago.

"John Doe? Oh, yes, now I remember he wasn't with us long. He became delirious; they sent him back to intensive care. I haven't heard anything about him since—at least he didn't come back here."

In near panic, Charlotte dashed off a quick note to Madge,

gathered her stuff and headed for Charlottesville. She tried to drive straight through but fatigue forced her to stop at a motel, where she slept fitfully for a few hours. The next day she learned at the hospital information desk that John Doe from Ward A left the hospital two days ago. The woman at the desk suggested she ask the people on his ward if they knew what his plans were.

Neither of the women on duty in Ward A knew where he planned to go, but one of them said, "If you find him you might tell him we have his book. An attendant found it on the ward where Mr. Doe was before he came here."

Charlotte went back to her car and sat behind the wheel, fatigued and feeling down. At least he's alive, she told herself—but that didn't help—she needed him. She drove slowly out of the parking lot and turned toward Greyledge, her thoughts still on Jude. What would he do? When he left the monastery he had clothes, camping equipment and money. Now he has nothing. He could be picked up for vagrancy—or by Batley, if he hasn't been already.

As Charlotte drove down off the Blue Ridge, her concern about going back to Grimble County grew. If Jude is at the cabin, maybe I should just pick him up and the two of us go somewhere else. We have to be here for the trial, though—at least I do. By the time she reached Waynesboro, she had convinced herself that Jude would be at Greyledge and that she should buy a gun so they could protect themselves. She stopped at a sporting goods store in Waynesboro. The sporting goods store owner, had a jowly face covered with a two-day growth of stubble. He wore that knowing look Charlotte had seen so often when she entered gun shops where they didn't know her. She interpreted his expression to say, "The first thing that comes out of this woman's mouth is going to be dumber than shit. No matter what I tell her she'll only get confused and leave without buying anything anyway." Grudgingly, the man asked: "Help you ma'am?"

"Give me a few minutes first to look around if you would, please."

The few new guns he had weren't what she was looking for. As her eyes traveled the row of used rifles stacked along the wall behind the counter, the clerk wondered what the hell is this woman up to? "There," she said, "that semi-automatic Remington, fifth from the end. That is a 30-06 isn't it?"

"Sure is, ma'am, would you like to see it?" The smirk was gone as he waddled his pear-shaped body along the creaking floor to where she had pointed.

"Would you please draw the bolt back and hold it so I can look down the barrel. It's awkward to do that on crutches."

"If you're worried about the rifling, ma'am, that gun's like new—belonged to my cousin—only fired it a few times."

"How much are you asking for it?" Charlotte had a feeling the price was slippery and depended on the naivete´ of the customer.

When he gave her the price, she asked if she could look at his catalogue to see what she would have to pay for a new one. It turned out that a new one cost only a little more than the used one. They went back and forth a couple of times on the price and finally settled on one that Charlotte felt comfortable with. "Now then, if you'll throw in a box of cartridges, I believe we have a deal." He reluctantly put the box on the counter next to the rifle.

While he was writing out the sales slip he commented dryly that he hoped her leg was better by deer season.

"Oh, I'm sure it will be."

When Charlotte reached for her checkbook, though, he said, "sorry, ma'am, I can't take checks from strangers—been burned too many times. Maybe you could go to the bank in the morning. I'll hold the gun for you."

"I'm not a stranger around here. If you take a careful look at me I believe, you'll recall who I am."

He studied her carefully and slowly nodded his head.

"Ain't deer you hunt is it?"

She stared at him without expression and asked if he would mind carrying her purchases to the car for her. As she drove north toward Grimble, Charlotte reflected on the man's rude comment and began to question whether she had done the right thing to buy that rifle, but as she crossed the county line into Grimble, her doubts left her.

The chain across the drive was secured by a padlock at one end; the other end went around a tree and was attached to itself by a bolt. Charlotte removed the bolt with a wrench and a pair of pliers from her car—the chain was more symbolic than protective, but she reattached it anyway.

She ignored the burned-out hulk of the mansion as she swung around to the front of the cabin. Convinced by now that Jude would be inside, she threw open the door and rushed in. He was not there. His clothes were clean and folded neatly in his bureau and there was fresh food in the refrigerator—all Aunt Millie's work. "Jude hasn't been here," she said out loud, then lowered herself into a chair. As the last light of day withdrew, she lapsed into a troubled sleep. She dreamed that Jude had returned, but his image wasn't clear—only a misty outline and he stayed back in the shadows. She kept pleading with him to come back to her; but, he said, "I can't get back, Charlotte."

"You can, Jude. You can, if you really want to. Please come back, Jude. I love you. You know that, don't you? I need you—oh, God, how I need you."

He waved good-bye and disappeared in the mist that surrounded him.

Charlotte awoke shivering in a dark room. She tried to convince herself that it was just a dream. Jude is not gone. He'll be back. But, she didn't believe it. She wasn't able to revive any of the optimism she had when she burst into the cabin, full of expectation. The cabin door—left open—looked out on a pitch-black night. She fished around her chair for her crutches, chastising herself for being so careless. Before turning on the light, she drew the blinds and closed the door. For a few minutes, she just stood there—looking at the lonely room, trying to gather her wits.

When she realized she had not eaten since early morning, Charlotte forced herself to make a sandwich; but while she ate, her mind returned to the reasons why Jude was not coming back. He did not know the Army was no longer looking for him. Nor did he know that John Paul was divorcing her. He probably did not even remember that they were having a baby: he was so sick and drugged up at the time. But what he was sure to remember is that the sheriff and his deputies are still looking for him. Is he worried about being held accountable for killing those four men? Aside from all that he loves you, she tried to reassure herself. Does he? How will he feel about making love to you—after . . .? She thought about Jude's tender passion and how she hadn't even told him she loved him—not until they were about to be killed. Why did I hold back from him? I could have held him closer to me.

When she awakened, a light rain was falling. The rifle was on the bed beside her and the room was still filled with her loneliness and her memories. She raised the window blinds and looked out at the gray dawn. Just up the hill, the burned-out mansion dominated the view. She shuddered but decided to put on Jude's hat and raincoat and go see if anything was left of her life. Without digging around among the charred and fallen timbers, there would be no way of knowing if any small mementos survived the fire. After a few minutes she headed back to the cabin. As she was about to enter, her eyes caught a movement in the distance— something through the haze—too big for a man, or even a deer. She watched as it worked its way, up the lane. When it became more distinct, she realized it was a horse. Alfred? How did he get loose? Seconds later she realized someone was leading it . . . Jude? Oh, God, please let it be Jude. She hobbled toward him on her crutches, stopping from time to time to cup her hands to her mouth and call out his name. There was no response.

The rain was letting up. Charlotte called again. This time he stopped, and she could see him wave.